## Assassin!

Kate carefully sat on the edge of Millard's bed and aimed her pistol at his face. He looked very peaceful sleeping there. It seemed a shame to wake him, but she needed answers. She nudged him awake with the silencer.

He snorted. "What is it Fleming?" Millard said, groping for the mask.

She let him remove it and watched his eyes widen in shock. His hand snaked under the pillow. "Naughty," she said tapping him on the temple with the silencer. "Bring it out slowly, there's a good boy."

Millard withdrew a small snub-nosed pulser and she took it from him. It was a nice little weapon—short ranged and with a low firing rate, but easy to conceal. It would kill a person just as dead as her slug thrower.

"I'll keep this if you don't mind, Mr. Millard."

"You know who I am. Who are you?"

"Your executioner I'm afraid."

"I guessed that," the podgy man said bravely. "Sanderson send you?"

"That's what I want to talk to you about, Mr. Millard. Why was I sent to kill you?"

Also available from Impulse Books UK

## The Devan Chronicles

The God Decrees
The Power That Binds
The Warrior Within
Dragon Dawn
Destiny's Pawn*

## The Merkiaari Wars

Hard Duty
What Price Honour
Operation Oracle
Operation Breakout
Incursion!*
Countermeasures*
No Mercy*

## The Shifter Legacies

Way of the Wolf*
Wolf's Revenge
Wolf's Justice*

## The Rune Gate Cycle
Rune Gate
Chosen*

* Forthcoming from Impulse Books UK

These and other titles available from Impulse Books UK
http://www.impulsebooks.co.uk

# What Price Honour
by

Mark E. Cooper

Published by Impulse Books UK

Published by Impulse Books UK May 2007
http://www.impulsebooks.co.uk

**PUBLISHER'S NOTE**
The characters and events in this book are fictitious. Any similarity to real persons living or dead, business establishments, events, or locales is entirely coincidental and not intended by the author.

Books are available at quantity discounts. For more information please write to Impulse Books UK, 18 Lampits Hill Avenue, Corringham, Essex SS177NY, United Kingdom.

Cover Art: Mark Brooks
Cover Design: Samantha Wall

A CIP catalogue record for this book is available from the British Library.

ISBN: 978-1-905380-44-2

**impulse books uk**

Printed and bound in Great Britain
Impulse Books UK

# Acknowledgments

Special thanks go to Sylverre, Terri, Anne, Scott, Arlene, Sharon, Star, Rob, Erick, Lindi, and all the others hanging out at my favourite writing group. Last but not least, I want to thank Dave Milne for reading an early draft of this book.

Thanks everyone.

# 1 ~ Marine

Gunnery Sergeant Gina Fuentez slapped a hand to her cheek. With a muttered curse, she pulled it away to reveal a mosquito the size of a heavy cruiser splattered over her palm, still oozing the blood it had just hijacked... if it was a mosquito. Insects were about the only things on this cursed planet she did recognise, but the size and shape of this one was only vaguely familiar.

Earth was far away; familiar sights such as insects and trees on this world, gave only a skewed impression of a jungle on Earth. The sun was like, yet unlike Sol. It was almost, but not quite, the right size in the sky, and almost the right colour. The sickly orangey-yellow light of this sun filtered through the thick canopy of the jungle and heated the undergrowth almost beyond her Marines' endurance. The operative word here was almost. The Alliance Marines, of which she was a fifteen year veteran, were the best at what they did. A little heat and sweat wouldn't affect their performance one way or the other.

Gina glanced aside to check her people. All were well concealed and keeping low. Her squad consisted of ten of the best Marines she had ever met, and that included Major Stein back at base. They were her friends, her people, and the Corps was her home. She had no other home or family, but that didn't matter as long as she had the Corps.

She wiped the sweat from her face through her open visor, and then slapped it shut. Sweating was preferable to being bitten to death.

Her helmet systems reactivated the moment her silvered visor clicked shut, and she focused upon what the HUD (head up display) was telling her.

Not a hell of a lot.

She tongued a control and scrolled through the menu. She selected communications, and browsed the channels that were accessible to her. None of her squad was on the air—as it should be. She flicked from channel to channel hoping to get lucky and hear the rebels. Back at base, they often listened to the so-called Freedom Movement's propaganda. It was always good for a laugh, but today they were silent, which in itself was unusual.

She activated her comm. "Eagle One to all Eagles, status check."

"Eagle Two copies. No joy, repeat nothing in sight."

"Eagle Three copies, no joy."

"Eagle Four, no joy."

"Eagle Five…"

Gina acknowledged reports from all of her people. As had been the case previously, they had seen nothing. Every half hour she repeated the routine until Eagle Three suddenly broke it.

"Eagle One, Eagle Three. I have movement directly ahead. I make it two-point-three klicks and moving fast."

She didn't even think of checking her own sensors. If one of her people said there was something coming, then there was. "Eagle Three, Eagle One copies. Can you identify?"

"Negative. Repeat negative visual," Corporal Grace Wingate said. "It reads as Human in size," she added helpfully.

"Eagle One copies, keep your eye on it."

"Aye, aye. Eagle Three out."

Gina switched channels and contacted base. "Red One, Eagle One."

"Eagle One, Red One. Go," the quiet voice of Lieutenant Strong came back instantly.

"Am observing movement two klicks east of my position—advise over."

"Acknowledged, Eagle One. That's our boy. Take no chances—repeat no chances. Red One clear."

"Aye, aye, sir. Eagle One clear."

So, this was it. They had been briefed to expect a recovery operation but they hadn't been given a precise time, which in this case meant someone had been working undercover and needed extraction fast. She had no idea who this man was, but that didn't matter. Her job was to see to it that he reached base in one piece, and the bad guys didn't. She watched him on her sensors. He was moving damn fast, totally ignoring the danger of detection, which said to her he had already been detected—more, it meant he was being pursued.

Gina selected a channel. "All Eagles, this is our boy. Eagles Three, Four, and Five—hold position. I want the rest of you to pull in as he passes. Watch for pursuit and nail them."

"Eagle Three copies."

"...Four copies."

"Five copies."

Quiet acknowledgements came over the comm as she watched the man jump a fallen tree ahead of her. She blinked in astonishment as he flew through the air completely ignoring gravity. He landed hard and rolled to his feet, and that was when she saw the wound. One arm ended in a bloody and broken stump just below the elbow. To keep going with a wound like that, he had to be running on adrenalin alone. One last leap had him skidding to a halt, and rolling into her dugout. He was an Anglo, tall and broad shouldered with slim hips. He was wearing a mud-splashed brown coverall of civ design, with no devices or sensors on his person. How the *hell* had he known where she was?

"The name's Eric," he said without looking at her. He was staring hard at his back trail. "I suggest we get the hell out of here, Sergeant."

Gina blinked. He wasn't even breathing hard. "Your arm," she said reaching for her medikit.

Eric slapped his good hand onto hers in a blur of speed, but his grip was exceedingly gentle as if afraid of breaking her. "I'm fine, my bots took care of it." He studied the trees for a long moment and nodded. "Good, your people are moving back. Call the last three in and let's go before..." he snarled a curse. "Too late."

Gina's eyes focused upon the sensor data displayed on her HUD. A wall of light codes was approaching her position. Just as she was about to give the order to open fire, Grace opened up. The AAR (anti-armour railgun) thudded repeatedly, and was joined by the lesser stuttering of outgoing pulser fire from Eagles Four and Five.

*"All Eagles, Eagle One—fall back in pairs and give them covering fire!"* Gina screamed over the comm.

She couldn't see the enemy visually, but she added her weight to that of her people. A storm of pulser fire went out shredding foliage and anything hidden within it. Her magazine ran dry; she slapped another in place with economical motions barely halting her fire. When she ran dry again, she slapped another in place.

Pags and Pike pulled back leaving Grace to hold the line, and then set up covering fire for her. Grace gave the jungle another burst before diving beyond them and reciprocating in kind. The manoeuvre was perfectly executed.

Gina ducked as the rebels sought and found her position. She hugged the dirt as they saturated the air above her with lethal rain. Something tugged at her sleeve, and she hissed expecting pain, but to her surprise it didn't hurt. She glanced aside and found the sleeve of her uniform flapping free as if cut with a knife. It had been a near miss—a very near miss.

Grace was hosing the jungle on full auto as the enemy came into sight. Trees were turned to toothpicks and roman candles, as a railgun designed to take out armoured vehicles literally wiped the jungle ahead of her clean. Suddenly a thunderous explosion shook the air, and Grace vanished in an eye-searing ball of light.

*Heavy grenade launcher!*

Gina had no time to grieve for her oldest friend, nor for the AAR, which was her only heavy weapon. The rebels walked their fire along her position and away. Instantly, she propped herself on her elbows and switched to full auto in an effort to suppress the rebel's increased fire. Her people were still too far forward to concentrate their effort, but they were having an effect. The enemy was withering under the storm of pulser bolts, but her rifle was heating dangerously. She switched to semi-automatic, and picked her targets with care. The rebels were wearing armour, but a three round burst from an M18-AP pulser took care of it. With relief, Gina watched the enemy go to ground. Outgoing fire slowed to a trickle as her people changed to single shot. She was proud of their discipline, but as their fire died away, the enemy opened up all at once and it was her Marines' turn to hug the dirt.

She tongued a control in her helmet, and zoomed her optics trying to see where the grenade launcher was, but although these people were amateurs, they still knew to keep their ace well back. Her software package had located some of the rebels by backtracking pulser blasts—the locations were painted red on her HUD, but the grenade launcher was another matter entirely. The MkIV tactical helmet was proven technology, but grenades could not be tracked in flight, which meant the software had nothing to work with. She couldn't see the launcher, but she did see something else. Among the pulsers in enemy hands, there were old style slug throwers as well. She was glad the bastards had supply problems, but it didn't help her situation. A well handled slug thrower would kill her just as dead as a modern pulser. Her flapping sleeve testified to that.

Gina ducked as the enemy turned their attention back to her position. She tried to pull Eric down with her. He snarled something at her and pulled a pistol from inside his clothing. On one knee, entirely exposed to the enemy, he fired his own slug thrower and killed his target, and then again and again. His fire was unerring. Every shot found its target, and that target died.

*"Red One, Eagle One!"* Gina screamed over the din. Whatever the gun was, it was louder than her rifle.

"Eagle One, Red One. Go," snapped the reply.

*"We're under heavy fire!"* The grenade launcher dropped one nearby and the ground erupted. "Completely on the defensive. I'm pulling back—request air support."

"Negative, Eagle One. Ground cover is too extensive."

"Not anymore, sir. Grace cleared a large section before she bought it. Drop it in the centre and you'll nail most of them."

"Red One copies, it's on the way."

Gina opened fire again. "Eagle One clear."

*"I'm hit!"* a voice screamed from nearby.

"...God! Oh God..." bubbled another over the comm.

It was Pags.

Gina bit her lip, pushing the grief away, as Corporal *'Pags'* Paglino sobbed into his mike and died. Pags was... *had been* a good man. All of her people were. She had screwed up. Recovery operation or no recovery operation, she should have brought the heavy stuff.

"Eagle One, Eagle Nine."

"What is it, Frankowski?" Gina said and fired at what her HUD insisted was a rebel sniper in the trees. Her display flashed a good kill, and the red icon faded from her display.

"You saw Grace?"

*"Yeah!"* she shouted as the grenade launcher took out a tree nearby. It crashed to the ground barely a metre from her dugout. *"We're pulling back!"*

"No shit! Pags is dead, and Pike's hurt bad. I'm bringing him in."

Gina changed channels and gave her orders. "All Eagles, Eagle One: we're pulling back. *Marines, we are leaving!"*

She fired an unaimed burst into the trees and scrambled out of her hollow. Keeping low, she crawled into the undergrowth, but then cursed when she realised Eric hadn't followed her. She looked back over her shoulder, and watched him firing into the enemy like some goddamn mindless sentry gun on auto.

*"Let's go!"*

Eric nodded and threw his now empty weapon away.

She handed him her sidearm as they crawled over the edge of the riverbank. She looked back over the ledge and saw some of the enemy moving carefully into the clearing. She picked off those she could, and sighed in relief as Frankowski dragged Pike over the edge to safety.

Frankowski pulled out his medikit and pumped a dose of Phenazocine into Pike, before carefully cutting away the burned remains of his uniform. Pulser wounds were nasty and damn painful. The Phenazocine was a strong pain suppressor. It was stronger than Pike's bots could produce on such short notice. His face relaxed, and his breathing eased as the shot took effect.

"You're gonna be okay, buddy," Frankowski muttered as he applied a battlefield dressing to the hideous wound in his friend's side. The self-sealing sterile bandage adhered to the skin around the wound keeping infection away. "How's that?"

"I feel like shit..." Pike panted clutching at the loose soil. The pain in his side surged up one last time, but a couple of seconds later it was defeated by a mixture of drug and nanobot activity. "Gimme a weapon... where's my frigging rifle?"

Frankowski ignored the question to scramble back up the bank to add his fire to the defence. He glanced in Gina's direction. "He's hurt bad."

"He'll make it." Gina selected squad wide on her comm. "Save your ammo—single shot only."

She ignored Eric fumbling one-handed at her waist. He was going after the ammo for her pistol. She didn't have much, and in a quiet moment ordered the others to dump theirs for him to use. Eric thanked her calmly and began taking out the bad guys with unerring accuracy, even when they were under cover. She didn't know how he could keep going with only one arm. He said his bots were taking care of it, but still.

Nanobots were a fact of life for everyone, even more so in the military, but although they should keep him alive, fighting should be beyond him. Nanotech could do amazing things, but a body could only take so much. Using nanotech to boost a body's natural processes was dangerous in the extreme. She could tell Eric was boosted to the max by the look in his eyes. He was glaring into the jungle, unblinking, as if in a trance. His movements were so rapid they almost seemed to blur in her vision. She blinked trying to clear the sweat from her eyes. She couldn't be seeing what she thought she was. No one moved like that, boosted or not.

Dirt kicked up in front of Gina and she ducked. A moment later, she popped back up and fired an unaimed burst in the direction of the rebels. Eric's head turned like a laser turret tracking targets. He fired at a careless rebel while glaring at another section of trees on his other side. The rebel was blasted back, and Eric's pistol moved to the seemingly innocent trees. He fired again and moved on without pause. Glare to the left, fire to the right. Glare straight ahead, fire to the left. Glare, fire, glare, fire… Gina shivered. There was something not right about him.

"Eagle One, Falcon Leader."

"Falcon Leader, Eagle One. What've you got for me?" Gina replied before firing again.

"Three birds fully loaded. Where do you want it?"

"Dump it all on the clearing."

"Roger, Eagle One. Keep your heads down."

"Eagle One clear."

Gina looked around and found seven Marines and one civ hiding behind the bluff. If Eric was a civ she'd eat her rifle, but he looked like one. There wasn't much cover, but it was all they had. It would have to do.

"Everyone down," she shouted as the jungle erupted in death and fire.

The three FB-160 fighter-bombers screamed in low and deployed their munitions. The FB-160, unlike carrier based aerospace fighters like the SPAF-18 Nighthawk, was a ground-based fighter-bomber designed for COAS (close orbit air support) missions just like this. It was a perfect match for the mission of supporting a small squad of Marines under siege. Three flechette dispensing bombs, weighing thirty kilogrammes each, disengaged from each fighter and detonated as one at a preselected height above the clearing. The compression wave killed everyone in the clearing, and the razor sharp flechettes minced the remains finishing the job. The bombers however, weren't ready to leave just yet.

"Falcon Leader to all chicks. Second pass on my mark… mark."

The FB-160's banked sharply and climbed. At three thousand metres, the pilots pushed over into a dive and fired their Hornet-AG missiles… a full spread. The jungle erupted again as eighteen warheads ploughed into the ground and then detonated.

"Jesus *Christ!*" Frankowski shouted as he tried to bury himself into the riverbank. "Are they *nuts?*"

Gina could only cover her head as the world went mad. Flyboys were all crazy, but this was pushing it. Talk about overkill.

"Eagle One, Falcon Leader."

The explosions died away to be replaced by the crashing of falling trees and the crackle of burning undergrowth. Gina wiped mud and leaves from her visor and blinked at her surroundings. She could hardly believe what she saw. For almost a klick ahead of her, nothing stood above ground level. Fires were burning all over, and where huge majestic trees once stood, now all that remained were piles of broken kindling surrounding a deep crater.

The fighters screamed by overhead. "Eagle One, Falcon Leader," the call came again.

"Falcon Leader, Eagle One. You sure know how to trash a party," Gina said, crawling to the edge of the huge smoking crater.

"Navy training, Eagle One," the voice said with a chuckle before hardening again. "Falcon Leader clear."

"Always knew flyboys were nuts, but this is ridiculous," Westfield said in awe.

Gina nodded in complete agreement. "Sensors up," she ordered and rebooted her own software.

"No hostiles," Frankowski reported first and the others concurred.

Eric pointed off to his right. "I have one."

Gina didn't know how he knew that. He was a civ. More than that, he didn't have Marine armour or tactical helmet with its sensor package. There was a depth to his emerald green eyes, a kind of knowing weariness that puzzled her. He noticed her watching him, and his lips quirked into a crooked smile. He seemed to find her amusing, which was strange considering the situation they were in. Strange or not, there was something about Eric that said she would be wise to heed him.

"Frankowski, Westfield, go check it out. The rest of you cover them."

"Aye, aye," her people chorused and moved out.

Eric stood to follow.

"Not you."

He shrugged. "As you wish."

As she wished? Damn right it was. "Who are you? *What* are you?"

Eric smiled. "I think you already know, Sergeant, or perhaps you're only now beginning to guess."

She glanced at his stump. Now she had time, she noticed something odd. It excited her at the same time as it appalled her. The bone wasn't shattered or even split. Instead, it was bent and twisted at the end like metal. She knew why that was.

"A viper?" she whispered reverently.

Eric smiled again. "I think it's time you called in, don't you?"

"What rank?"

"Does it matter?"

"It does to me."

He straightened to attention. "I am Captain Eric Penleigh,

Special Assault Group, 501st infantry." He relaxed and laughed at her dumbfounded expression. "Don't bother to salute."

Gina nodded slowly. Of course he was 501st, all vipers were. To meet one was rare, especially when the Alliance consisted of more than two hundred member worlds, a total that didn't include those in the Border Zone like Thurston. Who knew how many Human settled worlds there were altogether? She certainly didn't. They had a great many worlds to cover.

"Don't make a fuss, Sergeant, and that *is* an order. I'm supposed to be Eric the terrorist while on this God-forsaken planet. If you want to tell your people something, tell them I'm an informer who needs protection."

"Aye, aye, sir." Gina almost saluted, but she managed to restrain herself in time.

"And watch the sirs," Eric added before walking away.

"Is there likely to be more of this?"

He looked back over his shoulder. "Probably." He went to join her people in their search.

Gina made her way to where Pike lay. She sat beside him and keyed his wristcomp to display a readout on his medical condition. It was in the red. She watched as his bots reported back that his condition was critical but stable. Reassured somewhat, she contacted base.

"Red One, Eagle One."

"It's about damn time," Major Stein said. "Report, Eagle One."

"Sorry for the delay, Gold One. Something came up." She wondered what had happened to Lieutenant Strong. "I have two dead and one seriously wounded." She patted Pike on the knee, and he smiled feebly back at her. "We have the package and—" she broke off at a warning beep in her headset. "Wait one." She changed channels. "What have we got?"

"We found a live one, Gunny," Frankowski said sounding surprised. "Our civ wants to take him in. I say we cap him for what he did to Gracey."

"Copy that." She wanted the bastard dead, but Eric was no civ. "Bring him in alive. I want to ask him where his bastard friends are."

"Aye, aye. Eagle Nine clear."

Gina quickly changed channel again. "Gold One, Eagle One."

"Eagle One, Gold One. Go," came Major Stein's quick reply.

"We have the package and one prisoner, sir. Request extraction co-ordinates."

"Gold One copies. Co-ordinates follow..."

Gina tapped the figures into her wristcomp and pressed save.

"Eagle One clear."

Frankowski prodded the rebel forward and made him sit before Gina in the mud. She gave Frankowski a meaningful look and he nodded almost imperceptibly. They had played this game with prisoners before. Gina casually pointed her rifle at the rebel and asked her question.

"I ain't talking to you *bastids*," the prisoner spat before she could say another word.

Gina grinned. Frankowski raised his pulser and pressed it against the man's right knee. The terrorist closed his eyes and sweated. Gina was impressed. He hadn't uttered a single word of protest.

"Gunny?"

Gina glanced at Eric. He was watching her intently. "Not yet… maybe later."

Frankowski nodded and lowered his weapon.

Gina knew that there was nothing left of Grace to recover, but maybe Pags? "Any sign of Pags?"

"He was near me," Pike panted.

Gina turned and surveyed the crater. Pike had been near the centre when he was hit. Nothing had survived. She said a silent prayer for her two friends, and then turned back to business. She had other friends that needed her. She downloaded the evac coordinates to their wristcomps, and then detailed off her people.

"Frankowski and Westfield can look after our friend here. Cole, you take point. Ridley and Gleeson, you two carry Pike in the centre. Hollings, you're rear guard—keep your eyes open for any more of this guy's friends."

PFC Liz Hollings nodded and raised her weapon eagerly. Pags had been her best friend and she wanted payback.

"And me?" Eric said.

Gina studied him for a long considering moment. Vipers were lethal to anything that moved, but her people didn't know what he was, and he wanted it kept that way.

"In the centre with Pike. You're wounded."

Eric nodded.

"Let's move Marines," she ordered and Cole set a fast pace into the jungle.

\* \* \*

**PRESIDENT'S OFFICE, PARLIAMENT BUILDING, THURSTON**

"We have their location Mister President," Major Patrick Stein said patiently.

He was quite pleased with the calm sound of his voice. In reality, he was boiling with anger. Rage would be closer to what he was feeling. Two of his people were dead, and one would be lucky if he was back on duty in a month. He didn't want to think what might have happened. The reality was bad enough.

His thoughts turned to Gina, more properly Gunnery Sergeant Fuentez, but she had been with him long enough to be counted a friend not just a subordinate. She had been quiet when her squad arrived back at base. Oh, she had said the proper things during debriefing, but he knew she was hurting. Losing people you cared for was always hard, but losing those under your command was harder. Gina felt responsible for their deaths, and as the one directly in command, she was responsible. He knew she'd done all she could, but it would be a while before she accepted it. Who would have believed the situation could go down the crapper so quickly?

Certainly not he.

Third battalion was exactly one thousand strong, of which no more than eight hundred and ten were line Marines. Eight hundred and eight now, he thought grimly. All Marines were rifleman first, and capable of fighting, but the odd one hundred and ninety were not truly meant for that. They were supply sergeants, cooks, and a hundred and one other things needed to keep a full battalion in the field for extended periods. He might need them all if this damn... if this *President* didn't make a decision soon.

"I just don't know," President Thurston said.

Stein clenched a fist. "With all due respect, Mister President, you petitioned the Alliance for help. You *do* still want membership... don't you?"

"Yes but—"

"Then I don't see the problem."

President Thurston sighed deeply and stood from his place behind the authentic wooden desk. He gazed out of his blast-proof window at the bustling city below. "Look out there Major and tell me what you see."

Stein stood and joined the man. "I see buildings and streets. People walking... what more is there?"

Thurston laughed. "What more he says. No, you're right, but what I see is a future for my people. Did you know that less than twenty years ago this city would have been no bigger than a half dozen shacks?"

"That's hard to believe, sir," he said respectfully.

"It's true, I promise you. My father lived in one. I did too for the first ten years of my life, but my father had a dream and managed to infect others with it."

Thurston stood silently gazing at what his father had wrought.

"Dreams, sir?" Stein prompted.

"Hmmm?"

"You said your father had a dream."

"Yes he did. Anyone who was anyone was a miner in those days. My father arranged a meeting with the others and they agreed to build a consortium. They signed their holdings over to the company and became equal partners. Ships rarely came here back then, much rarer than today." Thurston smiled. "I know what you're thinking, Major."

Stein tried to look innocent. "I'm not aware of thinking anything at the moment, sir."

Thurston grinned. "That's an amazing statement don't you think? What I meant was, shipping is still infrequent, but back then we would be lucky to see a ship every five years. Now we have dozens. Anyway, he went off-world and came back with the backing and machinery to mine the planet as it should be done."

"What has this to do with the terrorists, sir?"

"The money he generated paid for the city out there, Major. It pays most of my people's wages. Close to seventy-five percent of the population works for the company. The rest are in service industries, clothing, tools, food—things like that. More are starting up every year, but we are a long way from economic independence. Those terrorists, as you call them, are my employees."

Stein nodded. Now he was getting somewhere. "You are the elected representative of this world, sir. It's your duty to uphold its constitution."

"Don't tell me my *duty.*" Thurston snapped with eyes flashing. "Who do you think wrote the damn thing? My father built this colony and the company from nothing; without him this world wouldn't be what it is today, but for all of that he was still a dictator. The people elected me as their first president when my father died, and I wrote our constitution a week later. Do you really think I would betray that just to save *money?*

"I promised them a voice, and by God they will have one," Thurston ranted. "Those people you would have me kill, are not only employees of the one company keeping this world from barbarism, they are citizens. They have a right to a voice just as everyone else does."

"A voice yes," Stein said angrily. "But they have no right to go around blowing things up and killing my people."

Thurston's shoulders sagged. "I know."

Stein took a deep steadying breath and in a milder tone asked, "What are you going to do?"

"Call the election early," Thurston said squaring his shoulders. "Your terrorists don't want to join the Alliance? Fine. If they want to stand against me, that is their right. I will make joining the Alliance part of my campaign so that everyone will know where I stand. If I win, we join, if I lose…"

"If you lose?"

Thurston shrugged. "If I lose, you leave, and I hand over the government. I can go back to mining for a living."

Yeah right. He owned a tenth part of a company, which was sole owner of seventy percent of Thurston's resources, and the *only* company that could currently exploit them. He certainly wouldn't need to work, but perhaps he wanted to. Without the presidency, his life would have a void within it that he would need to fill.

"When?" Stein said.

"It has already begun." Thurston nodded out the window.

Stein turned to look and saw people rushing to view the public address screens scattered throughout the city. He hadn't taken much notice of them before now—he saw thousands like them on worlds throughout the Alliance, but this was the first time he had seen an entire city stop to watch.

Everyone was silent as Thurston's recording gave his people news of the coming election, and his reasons for calling it early. The recording ended with everyone staring in stunned silence. A moment later, they turned toward the parliament building and shouted in one voice.

"NOOOOO!"

"I think it's likely you will win, sir," Stein said wincing at the volume of the shout.

"Well, well. I don't know what to say… well, well, well," Thurston said touched.

* * *

# 2 ~ Night Ops

An old and well-used MPV (Multi-Purpose Vehicle) coasted along the quiet street with a turbine strong enough to rip trees out of the ground idling beneath its battered exterior. MPVs were often used for clearing stretches of jungle ready for construction. Although Thurston's capital was young, its streets were paved as befitted any major city, yet a kilometre outside of the city limits, it was almost impossible to tell that Humanity had ever laid claim to the planet. That being the case, most people still relied on MPVs to travel.

The vehicle looked not at all out of place as it slowed and stopped opposite the gate leading to the grounds of President Thurston's residence. Its windows were dark as if it had been used recently in the full bright of day, yet the addition of extra lighting seemed to deny that. The driver was a dark shadow within his air-conditioned cocoon as he watched the gates. When a guard began to take an interest in him, he accelerated away.

As soon as the MPV was out of sight, the guard relaxed and went back to his coffee.

"Well?" a second guard said.

"It was nothing, just some damn tourist."

"A tourist? You're dreaming. No one in his right mind would come here."

"We did."

"Exactly my point."

At that moment, the sound of a turbine split the air. It screamed like a banshee when the driver pushed the throttle through the stops and aimed at the gate. The guards pulled their weapons and ran out of the guardhouse. Both men crouched and fired repeatedly into the MPV's engine bay hoping to kill the turbine before impact.

They failed.

The reinforced gates gave way as the MPV struck them. Both guards dove aside and came up firing, but unbeknown to them they had no chance of disabling the vehicle. It had been fitted with heavy steel armour in strategic places. It was more like a tank than an MPV.

The driver didn't flinch as he smashed into the President's house, nor did he panic as the MPV ground to a stop embedded in an interior wall. Instead, he switched off the turbine and retrieved the detonator. He flicked open the red cover with a thumb and pressed the button concealed there.

Driver, MPV, and residence disappeared in an eye-searing ball of flame as two hundred kilogram's of industrial grade explosive detonated.

\* \* \*

Gina sat on her rack and field-stripped her rifle for the tenth time. The well-practised movements were automatic after all these years. The repetition of routine soothed her. There was nothing at all wrong with the weapon. If there had been, she would be screaming at the supply sergeant for a replacement component.

Grace had been with her in boot camp. Both of them had joined on the same day and had been fast friends ever since. Even her promotion over Grace hadn't dimmed their affection for one another—and now she was gone.

*At least it was quick. Not like Pags.*

She snarled something under her breath. Even she didn't know what it was. It was quick, so it was all right? To hell with that. It wasn't all right. It stank!

*Oh, what was the use?*

If she'd brought the launchers, Grace would still have died. That was what she told herself, but would she really? Toting a tripod mounted RPG (rocket propelled grenade) launcher through the jungle would have slowed them, but she would have known that and left earlier, so it didn't count. She would have set it up behind the riverbank, and given it to Frankowski and Westfield because they were the best at laying it on the target.

Eric arrives, the enemy arrives, she orders open fire...

Gina frowned. No, that wasn't how it happened. Grace had lit up the jungle with the AAR *before* the order was given, but that was okay because she was in the best position to see the enemy. Which in turn meant the enemy launcher had Grace zeroed even before Eric finished introducing himself. Grace was dead from the moment they set out on the mission.

No, she couldn't accept that.

How about this then? They could have taken an *automatic* RPG launcher. Again, it would have taken more time, but they had that. She would have set it up behind the riverbank—it really was the ideal place—and put Westfield on it because he was the best with the computer. Eric arrives, and the stupid launcher kills him because he isn't wearing Marine armour with its IFF transponder telling it not to shoot.

*Damn!*

The only thing that would have saved Grace was her giving up the AAR. She knew Grace wouldn't have given it up voluntarily. She had been the best with the weapon and had seniority. Taking it from her without grounds would have shown a lack of confidence in her that Grace would never have forgotten. If Gina had known then what would happen, she would have taken the weapon anyway and given it to... who? Whoever she gave it to would have died in Grace's place.

She could have used it herself and... Wrong!

Wrong, wrong, wrong.

She would have died and perhaps her entire squad with her. Grace was one person no matter how dear. There had been eight others that needed her—nine including Eric.

She sighed and finished the reassembly of her rifle. She slapped a full magazine into her weapon and raised it to sight through the window. Grace was dead, and there truly was nothing she could have done to prevent it—just as Stein said, but it hurt. Pags had been a friend, all those in her squad were, but she hadn't known him as long. She felt guilty that his death didn't hurt as much, but she was honest enough to realise it.

Gina lowered her weapon as Eric walked by the window. A knock sounded.

"Come," she said and stood to tidy her rack.

"Are you busy? I can come back later."

"It's all right, sir. I've just about finished. How's the new arm, sir?"

Eric wiggled his fingers in the air. "It will do for now."

She nodded. Eric was a viper and spares were hard to find. He wouldn't be a hundred percent combat capable until he returned to his base—wherever that was.

"Is there something I can do for you, sir?"

Eric frowned. "Yes and no. May I?"

"Sorry, take a seat." Eric sat in the only chair while Gina used her rack. "What can I do for you, sir?"

"You can stop with the, sirs for a start. I'm not a Marine."

She shrugged. "You're a viper."

vipers were accorded officer status among Alliance forces regardless of their actual rank. Eric was at the least a lieutenant of Marines, but in real terms, he outranked Stein. All those wearing the viper patch did of course. The snakehead patch that gave Eric's regiment its nickname became the symbol of the SAG (Special Assault Group) during the Merki War. Back then, all the 501st had worn it and that had not changed over the years since—the downsizing of the regiment after the war had never been reversed. Vipers were rare and special. The patch, showing a snake head with fangs bared ready to strike, was a warning to all.

"Rank is important to you isn't it?"

Gina shrugged. "No more than any other. I'm a Marine. I want to be the best I can be. Rank is just a way to keep score."

"There are other ways, but I'm not here to discuss such things. Have you heard the news yet?"

"I haven't been out much."

"President Thurston won the vote by a landslide this morning. No one was surprised—well, maybe Thurston himself. Anyway, the opposition have disappeared back into their holes."

She shrugged. "That's good."

"Not really. Before they left, they tried to blow him up. When that failed, they left a recording that amounts to a declaration of war."

"You're kidding," she said gaping in surprise. She hadn't heard a thing about it.

"Nope," Eric said with a grin at her surprise. "His residence was completely destroyed, but he and his family were out celebrating with friends. They're fine. What I came to see you about is a mission."

"You should be talking to Stein, not me."

"Already done. He says you're the best person for the job."

She frowned; Stein hadn't mentioned anything this morning. "Well then, I expect I'll be called for a briefing and… this is it?"

"Afraid so," Eric said with a smile.

It was highly irregular, but then she had never worked with a viper before. Maybe they were all unconventional.

"Well… go on then."

"I'll lead you and your squad into the Freedom Movement's

base."

She cocked her head. "To do what?"

"To take out the control centre and perimeter security. I worked inside for quite a while. You wouldn't believe the stuff they've got. No way they found it all here. Most came from off-world. Serious stuff."

"Such as?"

"Surface to air missile batteries for starters," Eric said with a nod at her surprise. "There's an extensive minefield both proximity and pressure activated. Laser turrets, but they weren't online when I was there. They might be now. The sentry guns are definitely operational. I saw a test firing. There are pulsers for ground troops by the hundreds, and men to use them. Slug throwers for everyone and a good many grenade launchers like the one you saw. They have plenty of combat body armour, but no mechs—powered armour costs too much, thank God. No tanks, hoppers, or aircraft of any kind, but they do have some old tracked vehicles they converted into mobile launchers. I haven't seen any railguns or handheld rockets, but that's about the only things they didn't have."

"Goddamnit!" Gina jumped to her feet and began to pace. "They could take out the entire battalion."

"That's the problem," Eric agreed. "Stein launched a drone detailing the situation and requesting reinforcement, but help won't reach here for weeks. It will be all over by then."

"So we take out the control centre for the missile batteries and mines," she said thinking ahead to the mission. "What about the mobile launchers?"

"I'm glad you asked. Did I ever tell you I'm a dab hand with explosives?"

She groaned. He was a viper; he was a dab hand at everything.

Eric gave her another grin. "Once we're done, we pull out and let the flyboys soften the place up ready for a battalion of Marines to come in and kick arse."

"That should do it."

"Let's hope so. President Thurston declared his intention to apply for Alliance membership. Over eighty percent of his citizens voted to support him. The rebels seem to think that reducing the number of voting citizens will even things up in their favour. Let's stop them shall we?"

"Absolutely."

That night saw them on their way. The noise of the C-120's thrusters drowned out any conversation Gina might have had with Eric, but that didn't matter. She could speak to him via comm, but it had all been said back at base. For this mission, Eric had been outfitted with the full Marine armour and sensor package. He was designated Eagle Two. His own sensors were superior of course, but he was still maintaining his cover. As far as the others were concerned, he was just a gifted amateur attached to the squad to lead them to the target.

It was night outside and they were racing at tree top level above the jungle toward the drop zone. Gina stared into the darkness mentally preparing herself for what was to come. Eric had briefed her regarding the layout of the rebel base before they left. The defences were formidable, but if all went well, she would open the way for the others before the night was out.

"Two minutes," the pilot said over the comm.

Gina opened a channel. "All units, comm check."

"Eagle Two, five by."

"Eagle Three, no probs."

"Eagle Four, reading you five by five."

"Eagle Five..."

She counted off her people trying to ignore the knowledge that she was two men short. She was three short if she didn't count Eric. He was a considerable asset, but she still missed her friends. Pike was recovering from surgery; he would probably rejoin them on the ship taking them off this rock.

Two minutes flew by in a flash.

She tensed as the pilot shut down the interior lights and activated the bay doors. As soon as the doors were fully open, the transport went into hover mode, and Gina pulled herself to her feet.

"By the numbers people," she yelled before throwing herself into the night.

Gina grunted as the speed brake on her harness brought her up short. Her panting breath was all she heard as she eased the clutch and lowered herself quickly through the trees. There was no way the transport could have landed here. The foliage was much too thick, but there was enough room for her people to descend without too much snagging. Once on the ground, she released her tether taking no notice as it shot back to the transport. All around her, Marines were dropping to the ground, but again she took no notice. Her eyes were surveying the jungle and the data that her sensors were displaying upon her HUD. Both reported no hostiles, but she had another resource.

"Eagle Two, Eagle One," she whispered.

"Eagle One, Eagle Two. Go," Eric replied softly.

"I have no hostiles. Do you concur?"

"I have no hostiles in range. Repeat no hostiles."

"Good," she said breathing easier. "Take point, Eagle Two."

"Copy."

She changed channels. "All units, Two has point. Keep your sensors on passive. Move out."

"Eagle One, Eagle Four," Westfield said.

"Eagle Four, Eagle One. Go," she said as she followed Eric at a crouching deliberate walk.

"We won't find nothing on passives, Gunny. I think I should go active."

"Negative, Eagle Four. Follow the plan."

"Eagle Four copies," Westfield said with a sigh.

She couldn't explain about Eric, or that his viper sensors were already trawling for rebel emissions. Even if she could, she knew Westfield would still want to go active. Moving through the jungle on passives felt like walking through a minefield with her eyes closed— not much fun, but announcing her presence to all and sundry wasn't her idea of fun either. She trusted Eric's abilities, and she trusted the plan they had worked out.

Gina had her night vision optics set on X2 to magnify what little there was to see. Trees, trees, and more trees. Her mikes were set on high gain, but all she heard was a gentle rustling as her Marines moved carefully through the undergrowth. Eric was utterly silent. She knew what he was, and she was still impressed. Her Marines were good. The little noise they made would not be heard, even her mikes barely picked it up, but Eric seemed to float through the jungle. He was like a shadow moving across the ground—utterly silent.

Eric crouched and waved everyone into cover.

Gina went to one knee amid the foliage and scanned her surroundings. Ignoring the dampness that seeped into her uniform from the mulch she knelt upon, she dialled up X4 on her optics and looked beyond Eric's position. Nothing. Her sensors reported the usual background heat sources, but nothing the size of a man. Animals often showed up on scans, but her sensors reported nothing Human ahead of them. Eric was a viper. If he thought there was something, then there was.

Dialling back to X1, she checked her back trail and found her people ready for action. Satisfied they were all under good cover, she turned back to speak with Eric, but he had moved. She swore under her breath until she located him stalking something up ahead. She didn't dare distract him. According to her sensors, he was stalking a target that her software insisted was a bear. Not that this God-forsaken planet had bears, and if it did they wouldn't be in the tropical zone, but that was what her software insisted it was. A bear, not a man. As she had come to expect in the Border Zone, the software had interpreted the sensor data into Earth terms. Its programmers could hardly be expected to know that she wasn't on Earth could they?

She snorted in disgust.

The core worlds provided the Alliance with downloads detailing the native wildlife to avoid this kind of thing, but border worlds rarely had the money for the in-depth studies required to compile them. The military had to make do, but that meant the sensor data was often interpreted incorrectly. Luckily, Humans were quite distinctive. The software rarely interpreted a Human profile as anything else. It seemed to have failed this time however.

Gina watched her sensors as Eric went to ground again. His target was not moving, which said to her it was unlikely to be an animal. Suddenly, Eric moved in a burst of speed that only a viper could produce. He pounced like some kind of big cat. He was a predator in that moment, and she shivered in excitement as he took his prey down.

"Eagle One, Eagle Two," Eric said under his breath.

"Eagle Two, Eagle One. Go."

"One hostile neutralised. You can bring them up."

"Copy one hostile neutralised. Is he a single?"

"Seems to be. I have no other targets in range."

"Is this standard procedure for the rebels?" she asked intently.

"No," Eric said sounding grim. "She had comm equipment, but she didn't have time to fire off a warning. I have no idea what she was doing out here. Unless they know we're coming."

Gina nodded. That's what she had been thinking. "We're moving up. Eagle One clear."

"Two clear."

Gina stood and waved the others forward before moving out. When she reached Eric, she hunkered down beside him, while the others took position in a circle around them looking outward in all directions. Eric was speedily searching the corpse, but he hadn't yet found anything of note. The rebel was a woman of approximately twenty-five years of age. Eric had killed her with a knife across the throat. Silent and efficient.

Gina approved.

"Anything?"

"Nothing much," Eric said. "She hasn't been out here long."

She looked the question at him.

"She brought her lunch with her, it's still hot."

Gina nodded and moved to the perimeter to keep watch. Why had the rebel been set to watch this approach? Why alone? Surely, it made more sense to watch in pairs.

"No way he's a civ, Gunny," Westfield whispered through his open visor. "Did you see how easy he made that kill? He a spook?"

Gina shrugged. "He's a concerned citizen who knows the target."

"Yeah right, he's a damn spook," he said this time with assurance.

Gina didn't disabuse him of the notion and a moment later Eric was again leading the way. Gina slapped her visor down and followed Westfield who was now in the number two slot. As before, they moved in single file. Silent and careful. If her data was accurate, they should reach the target in another hour.

The darkness was utterly complete, but the low light amplification of their optics brightened the night sufficiently for their needs. Although it would take a miracle for the rebels to locate their frequencies, conversation was kept to a minimum. Scrambled as they were, overhearing wouldn't get the rebels very far, but it would give away the fact someone was coming.

Gina found herself envying Eric. He exuded confidence and strength. Whether or not he felt that way within himself, she didn't know, but he certainly gave that impression. She had worked and trained for fifteen years as a Marine. She knew she was good at her job, but she also knew that she was a child compared to a viper. They were stronger, faster, and deadlier than any Human could ever hope to be. They healed faster. They could take horrendous damage and keep on going. They lived much longer—or rather, they would if they weren't killed in action. Viper losses during the Merki War had never been replaced.

Vipers frightened people. Unenlightened people said they were dangerous to the Alliance. She knew it was crap, but many believed it. Those from Bethany's World were the most vocal in opposing new construction, but none of the core worlds had fought the decision very hard. The Merkiaari were defeated they said, what need for vipers now? Short-sighted politicians made her want to puke. The Merkiaari might have been defeated, but that didn't mean they were gone forever. Who knew what they were up to?

Eric slowed his advance then went to his belly and crawled the last few metres.

Gina didn't need to give the order to her people. One moment they were moving in a crouch, the next they went to ground and hid themselves in the foliage. She crawled up beside Eric and followed his pointing finger to the target.

She nodded and opened a channel. "All units, target in sight, move up and spread out either side of my position."

As her people moved up, Gina surveyed what she could see of the rebel base. The trees gave way to a small open area about a hundred and fifty metres ahead. She could see a dimly lit compound with two tracked vehicles parked within it. Guards were pacing the perimeter at intervals, but they were of little concern. They weren't equipped with night vision optics and were essentially blind. The laser towers Eric mentioned were just visible in the gloom, but the turrets themselves were lost to the night. There was no way to be sure if they were operational. She couldn't see the missile batteries he had mentioned, but the snub barrels of Raytheon Auto-7 sentry guns were unmistakable. The Auto-7 was serious hardware by anyone's standard. They were computer controlled auto loading gatling guns, firing 7mm armour piercing rounds at a rate of 6000 per minute. When they fired, it was like the breath of God unleashed. Those guns would have to be dealt with before they did anything else.

"Automated," she said noting the sensor arrays. "Thermal?"

"And motion activated," Eric agreed. "But they had all kinds of trouble with the local wildlife tripping the alerts. They had to dial back their sensitivity to stop the things fragging everyone. I won't have a problem getting close to them."

"And the rest of us?"

Eric looked at her for a long moment in consideration. "You wouldn't get within a hundred metres."

She was hardly surprised. "That's what I figured. Is there any way you can tell if the lasers are active?"

"Not until they power up the coils. They're not powered right now, but that doesn't mean much."

"What model?"

"Not sure. They might be the old Northrop HK-2100."

Gina whistled silently. "Heavy stuff, but they always did take a minimum of two minutes to power up."

"I know, but they might be a newer model. I only glimpsed them for a second."

Gina pondered her options. She wasn't here to take the rebels captive, and she certainly wasn't here to take the base. Her primary mission was to deactivate the missile batteries, but if she could reduce the rest of the defences as well, so much the better.

"We'll use the launchers."

"No."

She tensed. "Are you pulling rank?"

Eric hesitated. "No."

"Then we use the launchers." She activated her comm. "Eagles Four and Nine, Eagle One. Get set up, but wait for the command."

"Four copies."

"Eagle Nine copies."

Frankowski and Westfield shuffled away to either side to set up the launchers. If all went well, they would take out the towers before the lasers could be powered up.

Gina shifted her attention to what she could see of the mine entrance—not a great deal in the dark. She switched to thermal imaging, but again there was nothing to see. Where was everybody? Where were all the rabid and rebellious terrorists? All she could find were a couple of civs playing soldier. Back in the monochrome world of light amplification, she studied the guards. She didn't think much of them. They were completely oblivious to her presence. They were walking the perimeter as if motion sensors had never been invented. How the idiots had ever been given such responsibility was beyond her. They were acting like a couple of goons on Zelda's show.

"Fools," she muttered.

Eric nodded. "Nothing but foolish children, Gina, but still dangerous. Anyone can set a fire that will burn down your house—even wilful children. The Alliance is full of them. You don't know how many times I have... never mind."

She would have liked to hear more, but she was interrupted by a warning beep from her comm. "Eagle Nine, Eagle One, go."

"Eagle Nine in position."

"Copy that. Wait orders."

"Copy."

Gina changed frequencies. "Eagle Six status?"

"Just about done, Gunny. I had to move further than planned. The damn trees were in my way."

"Copy that. On the command, I want two rounds apiece on the sentry guns—take them out first. The chances are good that the turrets contain AA lasers—the old Northrop HK-2100 model."

"That's handy," Westfield muttered.

Gina ignored the sarcasm. "I want the towers gone as soon as you finish with the guns. Copy?"

"Copy that. My pleasure to serve."

She grinned and changed channels to give Frankowski similar orders. Eric was watching the base intently while she spoke with her people. He had a vaguely puzzled look upon his face. Gina opened her visor and was instantly plunged into darkness. She didn't need her imaging systems to see Eric.

"What's wrong?"

Eric shook his head. "I don't know, something isn't right. It's too quiet."

That was a bonus to Gina's way of thinking. She had surprise on her side. "It's after midnight."

"That's the point. When I was here last, the rebels moved around mostly at night to avoid detection."

Gina frowned. There was nothing to cause concern, and that lack suddenly sparked it. It made her nervous. Trying to shake her unease, she concentrated on business.

"I've ordered the towers lit up after the guns. With luck they won't know what's hit them until too late."

Eric nodded. "I'll take out the guards. Be ready to lead your people after me. Do *not* deviate from my path, Gina, and that *is* an order."

"Aye, aye, sir," she said automatically and was glad the others hadn't heard her when Eric glared. He was supposed to be a civ. He really didn't like her calling him, sir.

Eric held up five fingers and began counting down.

Gina quickly slapped her visor closed and contacted her people. "...three, two, one, *now!*"

*Pooomf! Pooomf! Pooomf! Pooomf!*

The first four rounds were still in the air when another four were launched to join them. Explosions shattered the night. Gina's optics flared white as the flashes overloaded sensitive pickups. She switched to thermal imaging for a moment before giving it up as a bad job. She would have to rely on her MK1 eyeballs for now.

*Pooomf! Pooomf! Pooomf! Pooomf!*

The sentry guns were gone, turned to pillars of fire and flashes of light as their ammo cooked off. She winced as a particularly violent detonation shook the air. She ducked as something whirred overhead and struck the trees behind.

*It's bloody dangerous out here!*

Eric's pulser was tracking and firing. She watched him pick out one target after another with unfailing accuracy. It was like watching a sentry gun. He was machine-like in his precision. She had never believed the propaganda about the 501st. That they were consummate soldiers, yes. That vipers had saved Humanity at a time when nothing else could have—absolutely, but that they were inhuman robots incapable of real feelings... robots that killed without compunction or mercy? No. Seeing Eric like this shook her convictions, but then she remembered that this was Eric and not some machine. She knew him. At least she knew him enough to discount most of the stories.

*Pooomf! Pooomf! Pooomf! Pooomf!*

She watched the first tower fall, but she didn't have time to see it strike the ground. Eric had finished his methodical butchery and was getting ready to move into the minefield.

"Eagles Four and Nine, hold your positions," she ordered over the comm. "The rest of you follow me. Two has point."

Gina hastened to follow Eric as he meandered his way toward the objective. She was careful to follow his movements exactly. Only he knew the safe route through the minefield… if the rebels hadn't changed it. She breathed easier when they reached the perimeter fence without mishap. Eric cut the wire and was inside on his belly before Gina could blink. She followed and lay next to a makeshift APC. Both vehicles, though civilian in design, had been extensively modified through application of armour plating. She could see the twin snub barrels of what looked like an M306-AA pulser. That kind of weaponry was a serious threat to the regiment's transports and needed handling.

Gina quickly assessed her squad. They were prone and well hidden by cavorting shadows caused by the fires. "Eagles Six and Seven, take care of those pulsers."

"Copy."

"Copy."

While her people were taking care of the pulsers by application of CTX15 (remote detonated charges), Gina followed Eric as he ran across the compound toward the mineshaft.

"No guards?" Gina said as she peered into the mine entrance.

"Over confident," Eric said though he didn't sound sure.

Gina used her sensors to scan for the rebels, but the shaft seemed deserted. "Take us to the command centre."

Eric nodded and led the way inside. The tunnels were dark. Without her sensors, Gina would have been completely blind. Light amplification needed some light to work with and here there was none. She switched to thermal imaging and followed Eric carefully. She had to rely on his enhanced abilities now more than ever. Her own sensors were giving fuzzy readings and shadows where there should be none. There was something in the tunnel walls interfering with her equipment. She tried to refine the data her sensors displayed on her HUD, but after a moment, she gave it up as a bad job. Eric gave no sign that he was having the same difficulties; he crept by one side tunnel after another as if sure they were unoccupied. She hoped he was right.

Gina had her pulser ready, but she was still taken by surprise. She hit the dirt as the rebels opened up on her. Eric rolled to the left and used the tunnel wall to shield himself while she laid down covering fire. Eric aimed and took a rebel's leg off at the knee. The shrill screaming was an efficient way of distracting the man's comrades, and

Eric took full advantage. Almost as soon as the screaming began, the fight ended with his pulser bolts finding targets. Fire from the rebels ceased as the last man fell. The remaining rebel continued screaming in agony, but they took no notice. They were too busy charging into the empty command centre.

"What the hell is going on?" Gina said, and squinted around the brightly lit but empty control room.

"Don't know," Eric said absently as he sat at an empty board and used the controls to change the views on the security monitors. "The barracks and motor pool are both empty," he murmured. "They've abandoned the place."

"Abandoned it, or is it just empty at the moment?"

Eric turned toward her with a frown upon his face. "What?"

"Those guards you killed didn't abandon it did they? They fought as if this place was important."

Eric looked back at the monitors. "They've gone on a raid."

She nodded grimly. "Disable the mines and missile batteries."

Eric started trashing the consols. While he took care of that, Gina took a moment to contact her people.

"Eagles Four and Nine, Eagle One. It's all in the crapper here. Come in and meet me."

"Eagle Four copies."

"Nine copies."

"I'm done," Eric said looking up from a smoking consol.

Gina looked around at the destruction with approval. "Let's go, and don't forget your prisoner."

Eric ducked out the door to retrieve the still screaming rebel.

From the doorway, Gina glanced back at the destruction and decided the rebels might be able to repair the damage. She couldn't allow that. She slung her rifle and unclipped a brace of grenades from her webbing. She depressed the triggers and lobbed them underhand through the door.

"Fire in the hole," Gina shouted and sprinted down the tunnel. Both grenades went off and the tunnel roof collapsed behind her.

Outside in the compound, numerous bonfires lit the night. She took a second to reassure herself that all her people were unharmed before contacting base.

"Gold One, Eagle One."

"Eagle One, Gold One. Go," Major Stein said.

"The mission is a bust, sir. We neutralised the lasers, missile launchers, and pretty much the entire base."

"I hear a but coming, Gunny."

Gina grimaced. "Yes, sir, there's definitely a but. Apart from a few guards, the damn rebels are missing. Eric thinks they chose tonight for some kind of raid. I concur, sir."

"Copy that," Stein said grimly. "I think I know their target and there's not much time. I'm sending the transport to pick your team up."

"Understood. Eagle One clear."

"Gold One clear."

Gina turned her attention to Eric and his prisoner. Her Marines had fallen-in and set up a defensive perimeter around her and Eric. The prisoner stopped screaming as Hollings pumped a dose of Fentanyl into him. Although its effect was of a short duration, Fentanyl Citrate was the strongest narcotic they carried. The rebel was hardly likely to die from something as minor as the loss of a leg, but if he didn't cooperate, he would wish he had.

"What is the target?" Eric asked intently.

"*Fuck you!*" the wild-eyed man spat.

"Fuck me?" Eric said mildly. He reached out and crushed the man's stump viciously. "I don't think so."

"*AEiii!*" the rebel screamed and jerked trying to free himself, but Eric wouldn't allow it.

Gina swallowed but didn't look away. Westfield glanced over his shoulder at her, but she waved him back to his survey of the compound. They didn't need to be taken by surprise twice in one night. Looked at one way, the mission was a success. Her single squad had destroyed the rebel's entire base. Looked at another way, the mission was a bust. Destroying the base without killing the rebels was pointless; they would just set up somewhere else. Eric must be sick at the thought of all his work wasted. He had lived here undercover for weeks to learn what he needed to finish the rebels, but now all his work was threatened. No wonder he was pissed at being bad mouthed by this scum of a rebel.

The rebel screamed again. "God don't! No more… I'll talk!"

"Are you sure?" Eric said with another twist of the bloody stump. "I don't like lies."

"No lies I swear! They're hitting the parliament building!"

"When?"

"*Noon!* The President reconvenes parliament at noon!"

"Good boy."

Gina turned away and opened a channel. "Gold One, Eagle One."

"Eagle One, Red One. Gold One is out of contact."

"Copy, Red One. I have the target, Lieutenant. The rebels are hitting the parliament building at noon today."

"Copy noon today," Lieutenant Strong said. "Stein guessed the target, but we didn't know exactly when. Well done."

"Thanks, Lieutenant. Eagle One clear."

"Red One clear."

"They're sending the transport," Gina said over the all units channel. "Stein guessed the target would be the parliament building. If I know him, he'll be laying on a reception for them."

"We'll know soon enough," Eric said, turning to the west and watching the sky.

Gina tried to find what had caught his attention, but she couldn't see anything until she used her sensors at max range. A small blip appeared on her HUD marked with the regiment's IFF signalling its identity. It was a C-120—a Marine armoured transport and probably the same one that had brought them here.

"As soon as the transport lands, I want you all on board," she said to her squad.

"What about the prisoner?" Westfield asked.

Before Gina had a chance to answer, Eric did it for her with his pulser. One shot, and they no longer had a prisoner. She stared at the smoking hole where the prisoner's face had been, and then at Eric who was just then flicking the safety back on his weapon.

"What prisoner?" Eric said ignoring all the pulsers now aimed at him.

Over the noise of the transport's landing, Gina ordered her squad to lower their weapons. She glared at Eric, furious with his actions, but she didn't want to start an argument in front of her squad. She marched a short distance into the darkness knowing Eric would follow and then rounded on him.

"Don't ever do that again. *Not ever!* Marines don't work that way."

"No?" Eric said coldly. "Lucky I'm not a Marine then."

Gina stared at him for a long moment, and then turned away to order her people aboard the transport. Minutes later, they were speeding over the jungle toward the city and another fight.

"He's a spook," Westfield said privately to Gina. "What do you expect?"

Gina shrugged. She knew Eric wasn't a spook, and that made his actions worse to her mind. Vipers were special. In her opinion, Eric had just dishonoured his unit.

* * *

# 3 ~ Showdown

"I'm no hero," Eric said to Gina later that day while waiting for the order to open fire. "Get those notions out of your head. I do my duty to the Alliance with every breath I take. My decision was to execute a terrorist last night, and that too was my duty."

"Duty? Who decides when duty becomes murder?"

"I do as a captain in the 501$^{st}$."

Gina shifted position just a little. She wanted to keep an eye on the elevator doors behind her. Lieutenant Strong was with Stein, and had been for almost an hour. She wished he would hurry back from the briefing. If he didn't show up soon, she would have to start without him.

She glanced at Eric and then back outside at the plaza. "You must report *to* somebody, be held accountable *by* somebody."

"I report to my superiors as you do. General Burgton reports directly to the President." Eric took a breath and went on in a milder tone. "Don't judge me, Gina. You know nothing of what it takes to be a viper. We aren't robots that kill to order. We were designed to kill Merkiaari, and we do it well. That frightens people. These days I spend all my time pissing on fires—trying to stop those wilful children we spoke of burning the Alliance down. We have discretion, perhaps too much, but without it the Alliance couldn't have survived as long as it has. Besides, you have less right to judge me than others I could name."

"What do you mean by that?"

"Aren't you the one who nearly allowed the torture of a prisoner because he killed some of your people?"

"That was different," she said hotly.

"I don't see how. I'm nearly two hundred and thirty years old, Gina. You can't know what it's like seeing the Alliance stumbling from one avoidable bush war to another over and over again. I have penetrated terrorist cells so many times that the number blurs in my memory. No matter what I do, the same types of people go on repeating the same types of mistakes. I chose to stop that man permanently. If I hadn't, he would have been setting bombs and killing the innocent again in a year. They just never learn. So don't judge me until you have lived as long as I have and seen what I have."

Two hundred years of fighting terrorists? God, she'd had no idea. What must it be like seeing mistakes happen over and over, knowing they were going to happen, yet being unable to prevent them? It must be appalling.

"I'm sorry," she said.

"Forget about it. I would have reacted exactly the same way at your age, except I was fighting Merkiaari then."

"You fought in the war?"

"Of course," Eric said in surprise. "We were constructed for that purpose."

"I thought you might have… you know, been built after."

Eric shook his head. "No. We fought and there were eighty-nine of us left at the end. The Council allowed eleven more units to be constructed to bring our numbers up to a nice round politically correct one hundred, but those eleven were already part way into the construction process. It was a mercy they were allowed to be completed."

"Surely the Council wouldn't have left them half finished," Gina said, shocked at the thought. Surely no one would have denied those soldiers a normal life.

Eric's face twisted into a snarl. "You have more trust in the Council than I then. The councillor for Bethany's World campaigned hard to have us all scrapped, but public opinion was on our side. For a time, we really were heroes, but then fear replaced gratitude and here we are two hundred years later."

Eric had a bitter streak a klick wide, but it was hard to blame him. His regiment decimated and everyone afraid the vipers would turn on them; it was enough to make anyone sour. Gina wished she didn't know all this. She had been far happier in her ignorance.

"Look alive people," Major Stein's voice said over the comm and everyone stopped to listen. "The rebels are making their move. I have ten APCs approaching the plaza from the north with many civ vehicles as escort. Approximately a thousand rebels inbound. Satellite feeds indicate assorted pulsers and small arms as well as AA pulsers on the APCs.

"Alpha Company will concentrate on the APCs. I want them burning before they turn those pulsers on us. Bravo Company will concentrate its fire on the civ vehicles. Charlie Company will take targets of opportunity and defend the parliament building from any incursion. Good luck."

Gina selected squad wide on her comm. "All Eagles, Eagle One— you heard the Major—we take out the APCs, and that doesn't mean giving up our cover. Let them come to us. Frankowski, you hose them with the AAR. Try to bottle them up as they approach the fountain."

"Never liked that thing anyway," Frankowski said with glee.

Gina ignored that to sight into the plaza. She and her squad were just inside the main doors and should see some action. Other squads were with them, but the bulk of Alpha Company was on the first floor. It looked as if she would have to start without Strong after all. Boy, was he going to be pissed.

"Wait… wait…" she said as the vehicles entered the plaza. "Now! Let them have it!"

Gina added her fire to that of her squad, but it was a mere sideshow to the heavy thudding of the AAR. Frankowski targeted an MPV near the rear of the rebel formation and it blew up spectacularly well. The burning vehicle crashed back to earth blocking the route out of the plaza. She nodded with approval at his choice of target.

The rebels were taken by surprise by the first explosion, but as the APCs blew up one after another, they went to ground. They had lost a considerable edge with the destruction of the heavy pulsers in the APCs, but each of the surviving rebels took it upon himself to open up on the parliament building with an awesome barrage of pulser fire and grenades. Rocket propelled grenades struck the building launched from every side of the plaza. So many, that Gina feared her squad would be buried in the debris raining from the upper floors. Glass and chunks of plascrete crashed down on the street outside. She tried not to notice when uniformed corpses added themselves to the growing piles with meaty-sounding thuds.

The result of the rebel's initial attack was inconclusive with regard to the Alliance forces on the ground floor, but Charlie Company on the second floor took heavy casualties. Gina's squad was mostly unhurt. Frankowski and Hollings both had minor cuts and bruises caused by chips of plascrete, but the rest of her people were fine. Other squads were not so lucky. Marines were screaming for medics while others screamed in pain still firing their rifles wildly into the plaza. Sergeants and corporals shouted curses and orders to their squads, trying to restore order and discipline in a situation that threatened to get out of control. Dust and smoke hung thickly in the air. More windows blew in as pulser fire ripped the building's facade to shreds.

Gina's squad hunkered down as the rebels pumped overwhelming fire into the building in an effort to suppress the storm that had destroyed their vehicles, and was in the process of killing them. Fire from the Marines was reduced to a trickle, as plascrete walls and columns were pocked and hammered by slug throwers and plasma from the rebel pulsers. Frankowski killed the fountain he disliked so much, and in so doing deprived the rebels its use as cover. He left off when it was reduced to a smoking crater, but then he turned the AAR on the shop fronts where most of the enemy were attempting to hide.

"Hand me the launcher would you?" Gina said in a conversational tone of voice.

Eric handed her the shoulder rig and slid a box of ammunition closer before opening up with his pulser again. He was using single shot and making every round count. Bodies were piling up as he methodically moved along the line of rebels.

Outgoing fire from the Marines increased again until it was a hurricane compared to the rebels light drizzle. No word had been heard from the Major since Charlie Company was hit at the start of the action, but no one needed orders to kill the killers of Marines.

"You should have been a Marine sniper," Gina said absently as she loaded the launcher with a high explosive contact fused rocket.

"Been one," Eric murmured as he tracked and fired at his targets without pause. "Not a Marine, a sniper I mean."

"Oh?"

Eric fired again. "That's how I was recruited. The Colonel liked my moves and the next thing I knew I was going into surgery. When I came out I was no longer a man."

That was a strange way to put it. Many people said similar things, but she hadn't expected to hear it from him.

"You're still Human, Eric," she said and adjusted the launcher's targeting display.

"Sometimes," he agreed and killed another pair of men trying to set up a tripod mounted AAR behind the cover of a low wall.

Gina found what she was looking for—a group of rebels that seemed to be directing the fighting. They were doing a passable job, and she didn't like that. The rebels were amateurs, yet they had succeeded in keeping her head down and were advancing to a point where they would be ready to storm the building.

"Time to take care of business," she said and pressed the commit button on her display.

A high-pitched beeping told her the rocket was locked on. She depressed the trigger. The rocket flew straight on target and detonated in the centre of the command group. A crater was blasted into the plaza and a nearby building collapsed with a thunderous roar. Collateral damage was extremely heavy, she noted with approval. Rebels were dead on all sides, and those not wounded were attempting to retreat.

"Load me," she said and Eric did.

Gina targeted another group and fired. She didn't kill many, but the explosion added to the chaos she had generated by taking out the leaders. Eric loaded her again as rockets began launching from the upper floors. She had hoped, but not counted on it. Stein had wanted damage kept to a minimum, but there had been no word from him since the battle began. By using her rockets, she had likely opened herself to criticism, but better that than her people dead. She launched one more rocket then discarded the rig in favour of her pulser.

Gina tongued a control in her helmet and selected communications. "Eagle One to any surviving officer, come in."

"Eagle One, Red... Red One..." a halting voice came over the comm. "I'm hurt bad. Stein is down... don't know if he's alive."

"Orders, sir?" she said intently. "Orders, sir!"

"Orders?" Lieutenant Strong said vaguely. "Kill them all," he whispered. "...out and kill them all..."

"Red One? Lieutenant?"

"Eagle One, Blue One," Sergeant Denton said. There were screams and shouting in the background.

Gina ducked as one of the rebels targeted her. Eric glared and killed him before she could even take aim. "Blue One Eagle One, go."

"Stein is down, unconscious. Strong is dead. What are we doing?"

How the hell should she know?

"What about Captain Noble and the others?" she asked and fired a burst out the shattered windows.

"Dead."

"Lieutenant Goldman?"

"Dead too. They're all out of it, Gina. The rebels got lucky. They were on the way back to their units when Charlie Company got hit."

"Wake up Stein," Gina said and ducked as rebel fire hit her position again and showered her with plascrete fragments. Something was burning nearby, but she didn't have time to worry about it.

"I've tried. No go. You're senior to me, what are we doing?"

"We're following Strong's last order." She switched her comm to battalion wide before she could change her mind. "Alpha and Bravo Companies move in pursuit of the rebels by squads. Charlie Company will hold here and see to the wounded."

"Blue One copies."

"Green Two, moving out."

"Copy that, we're moving."

"…One copies."

"…Three, on our way."

"…Two, on our way…"

Gina listened only absently to the acknowledgements as they came in. She was too busy to answer or pay very much attention. She had no doubt her order would be followed. They were Marines.

Gina waved her people forward giving them covering fire until they could find good firing positions of their own. Eric was by her side as she ran in a crouch across the plaza toward a doorway. Using it as cover, Eric fired from one knee while she stood above him and took pot shots at what was left of the rebels.

She fired and took down a rebel attempting to retreat. She noted others pulling back in the same direction. Her thoughts raced as she realised they were getting away. She couldn't allow that. Her eyes narrowed as an idea came to her. Without hesitation, she ordered five squads forward, and another five down the side streets with the aim of squeezing the rebels between multiple fields of fire.

Gina was in her element; never had she felt so complete. The rebels were withering under a storm of plasma bolts as more and more Marines added their own fire to the weight already hammering them. One or two rockets went out but not many. Most were expended on the vehicles at the beginning of the action. The heavy thudding of multiple AARs blotted out the hiss-crack of plasma rifles. The occasional grenade exploded with men and pieces of men raining in all directions. Over it all, she could hear the battle chatter of nearly a full battalion, and she, a lowly gunnery sergeant, was directing it into battle.

She snatched a grenade free of her webbing and rolled it through an open door. She ducked back as the hiss-crack of a rebel pulser sought her life. A second later, the rebel's fire was silenced by the dull whump of her exploding grenade. She ducked forward and back, taking note of the building's interior and the bodies lying motionless upon the floor. When no one fired at her, she dove inside and up the stairs. The second floor seemed deserted, but…

She raised an eyebrow at Eric. "Anyone inside?"

"Two," he nodded at the first door. "One near the window... he must be a spotter—I'm picking up his comm traffic. The second is hiding behind the door—left side. Only the sound of breathing from him."

Gina nodded and aimed her rifle at the wall. "About there?"

"Just a bit to your right... that's it," he said as she made a correction.

She squeezed her trigger and held it down. The wall exploded into dust, and Eric charged through the hole. She quickly followed, but it was over before she could blink. The rebel by the window was dead. Only a red stain remained where the other one had stood by the door. She took a quick look out the window, and noted another attempted breakout by the rebels. She estimated their numbers and trotted back downstairs already calling ahead to Alpha Company's Second Platoon. Eric followed upon her heels a moment later.

Two hours later it was all over, and Gina found herself feeling depressed. A strange quiet had fallen over the city broken only by the wailing sound of the emergency services tackling the blazing buildings.

She made her way back surrounded by her squad, and entered the parliament building—what was left of it. Fire had damaged what had survived the rebel attack. It was in a bad way, but it was repairable. She pulled off her helmet to run a hand through her sweat-soaked hair. She reeked of blood and smoke. The stench clung to everything. She didn't want to consider some of the things she had seen burning in those now collapsed buildings. It would take days for the burned pork smell to fade.

She frowned at a scar running along the right side of her helmet. The nanocoat was completely burned away. She slid a finger along the groove trying to decide if the damage was repairable. Going by the depth of the burn, it wouldn't be. She would have to requisition a new one.

"Damn," she muttered. Setting up a new helmet's systems could be a royal pain in the butt.

"Stein's awake," Staff Sergeant 'Bulldog' Denton said as she entered the reception area. "He wants to see you."

Gina needed a shower and about two weeks sleep in her rack, but she had to make her report first. "Pete, see to our people. Food, water... whatever."

"No problem," Westfield said.

Gina nodded and followed Bulldog to the Major. "How bad is he?"

"He's got a concussion, but the Doc says he'll be fine in a few days."

"That's good."

"That civ friend of yours was with him a while ago," Denton said.

"Eric?"

"Yeah. He walked in bold as you please. The Major ordered everyone out while they chatted. What do you think of that?"

Gina shrugged. "Maybe he wanted another take on things."

Denton's eyebrows shot up in surprise. "From a *civ?*"

She shrugged again but was saved from any further explanations when she reached the door of the conference room.

"Stein's inside," Denton said and left her to it.

Gina ran a hand over her head again, but making a Marine's 'high and tight' crop presentable, especially after it had been crammed inside a sweaty helmet for hours, was impossible. She tucked her helmet under her arm, knocked once, and entered to find a number of people attending the Major.

Eric was standing to one side of the room watching the proceedings. He was wearing a viper's black BDU (battle dress uniform) complete with rank insignia of a captain in the 501st infantry. He nodded to her, but did not speak. Stein was half reclining on a couch, while Doctor Pearce, still wearing his bloodied combat armour and sidearm, worked on him. One look at Lieutenant Pearce's face relieved Gina of some part of her worry. He was concerned for his patient, but it was nothing more than that. Stein must be on the mend.

Gina came to attention and saluted. "You wanted to see me, sir?"

Stein waved Pearce aside so that he might see her better. "Yes, Gunny. You were aware, were you not, of my orders concerning the rebel attack?"

"Specifically, sir?" she asked in puzzlement.

"Specifically the orders pertaining to collateral damage."

She stiffened. "Yes, sir. We were to keep collateral damage to a minimum, sir."

"And did you?"

"No, sir."

"Why not?"

"No excuses, sir."

Stein smiled. "Relax, Gunny, I didn't call you in here to ream you out. I want to hear what you did and why."

Gina glanced at Eric, but he gave nothing away. She didn't believe his innocent expression for one minute. He had been telling tales—

she would bet her pulser on it.

"I took command and attacked the rebels with everything at my disposal, sir."

Stein laughed but winced and raised a hand to his bandaged head. "I'm aware that you attacked, Gunny. How did you deploy your forces?"

"I ordered Charlie Company to hold here and defend the parliament building, while Alpha and Bravo advanced by squads into the plaza. Once the rebels had been softened up with rocket and pulser fire, I sent five squads from each company down the side roads in an effort to flank the enemy and bring them under multiple fields of fire."

Stein nodded slowly. "I see. And did that work?"

"Yes, sir," Gina said with just a trace of pride in her words. "The rebels failed to take note of the manoeuvre, and were utterly destroyed some little time later."

"Prisoners?"

"No one surrendered, sir." She glanced at Eric again. He had a small smile on his face.

She hadn't lied. The rebels hadn't surrendered, but then, she hadn't given them time to offer. Lieutenant Strong had ordered her to kill them, and that's exactly what she had done—down to the last man and woman.

"I'll be writing a commendation in your permanent file, Gunny," Stein was saying. "You cared for my people when I was unable to. That holds great weight with me. I'm promoting you to lieutenant for your outstanding contribution to our mission here."

Gina gasped. A battlefield commission? Such things were almost unheard of these days.

Stein smiled briefly. "Well, have you nothing to say?"

"Thank you," she gasped. "I mean thank you, sir, but I don't deserve—"

"Cut the crap," Stein said with a mock glare. "You deserve it. You know it and I know it. In just a month or so, headquarters will also know it. I have no doubt they will concur with my decision, but until then you have the grade, but not the pay I'm afraid."

"The Alliance always was stingy," Eric said with a straight face. "Congratulations."

"Thank you, sir." Gina shook his hand. She turned back to Stein. "The money means nothing. That you believe my actions deserve this means a lot to me, sir. More than you can know," she said in a choked voice.

Stein looked pleased. "Your actions deserve this and more. By rights, you should receive the Alliance Star for bravery as well, but I thought the rank would mean more to you than another ribbon on your chest."

"I have more than enough ribbons. The rank does mean more to me."

"I knew it would," Stein said with a small smile. "Dismissed, Lieutenant."

Gina braced and saluted before turning to leave. She could hardly wait to tell her squad the news.

\* \* \*

# 4 ～ Assassin

Kate Richmond stepped off the stolen shuttle and scanned the area. She found nothing but steaming jungle in the dark. The screeches and cawing of strange beasties didn't help, but her electronics told her all she needed to know.

She was undetected.

Tigris was a border world with few things to recommend it. It was hot and humid jungle for the most part, and uninhabited by Humans except in carefully selected areas. Tigris was a heavy grav world, though 1.12g was hardly excessive. People could afford to be choosy with so many Earth-type worlds available. That being the case, Tigris was an essentially untouched resource.

Why then was she here?

"That's a damn good question."

She mopped sweat from her face and continued her sweep.

The briefing had been very sketchy about the reasoning behind the mission. That made her uneasy. She knew who her target was, she knew what he looked like—Intel had managed to scrape up an old picture of him. It was out of date but she would manage. What she didn't know was why he must die. In her experience, when they failed to tell you why, someone high up was playing games. That meant the mission was blacker than black, probably off the books altogether. Someone on Bethany, a member of one of the ruling families it had to be, was using his contacts to protect his interests or hurt a rival. She had seen it before on other missions. All they cared about was their stupid power games, and if she died, so what? Tools got broken all the time—just buy a new one. She scowled.

The ten ruling families of Bethany had ultimate power back home. That meant they owned her and all she held dear. Not that there was much. Her brother, Paul, was all the family she had, and she wasn't even sure he was alive. Paul was the reason she was here. Her own sources had come up empty, and she had been forced to go to her handler for help. He had promised to look into her brother's disappearance in return for a couple of favours. Kate had agreed knowing he was padding his retirement fund at her expense, but Paul meant more to her than her own safety. She had promised to look after him; it was her fault he was missing. If she had done better by him, taught him better, or been there more, he would still be safe. So here she was, AWOL technically, though no one would ever know. She had completed her official mission on Thurston in record time simply to give herself this opportunity. There would be no evidence of her little detour, she had seen to that.

Kate continued her scan of the vicinity noting a huge range of bio-forms. So many in fact, her software was having difficulty identifying them all. That wasn't surprising. Tigris' main industry, hell its only industry, was medicines. It was a strange fact that no matter how clever the Alliance became at synthesising new drugs and treatments, nature was better. Find a cure for a particular disease, and another cropped up to take its place. Medicines were always highly sought after. Unlike Earth, planets like Tigris had abundant sources of green things, which might hold the secret to cure the latest plague.

Still, she wasn't here for medicine.

Satisfied with her sweep, she closed down her sensor suite and re-boarded the shuttle to fetch her kit. She glanced at her wristcomp, it was midnight and time she was gone. Taking a last look around, she locked the hatch before heading west into the jungle with her rifle in hand ready for trouble. Her destination was a little over three klicks away. Ostensibly a small harvesting operation, it was in fact the headquarters of a man styling himself General Millard.

Kate stopped at irregular intervals to check her back trail. She knelt amidst the undergrowth and carefully scanned the jungle all around her position. She ignored the fetid smell that arose, and the damp that seeped through her leggings where her knee crushed rotting vegetation. All was quiet. Her back trail was invisible even to her, which was good. Her sensors informed her of multiple targets all round her with flashing red icons detailing range and vectors, but she ignored most of them as the animals she was sure they were. She could be wrong of course, but that just made the whole thing more interesting. Although her sensor package was a small handheld unit, it was state of the art tech. Small and lightweight; it had the power and sensitivity of rigs three times its size.

She moved out again keeping an eye on a large target that her sensors said lay ahead of her. She didn't like the look of it. It was too big to be a man, but who knew what nasty critters were hiding out here? She detoured wide and kept a wary eye on her sensors, but the thing was uninterested in moving. She breathed easier once she had left it behind.

A trickle of sweat ran down her spine. Her sneaksuit was stuck to her in uncomfortable places. She ignored the discomfort and kept to the same methodical crouching walk. She always wore the same thing on a job like this. A black one-piece coverall with non-metallic zippers, combat boots laced halfway up her shins, and cutaway gloves to provide some protection for her hands without fouling her fingers for intricate tasks. The sneaksuit's hood covered her face, its nanocoat protected her against airborne agents—nerve gasses and the like. The legs of the sneaksuit were bound tightly over her boots with tape to prevent insects and other critters getting in and having their way with her. There were a lot of venomous nasties living on Alliance worlds—none of which had any business munching on Humans, but they didn't care about that and would happily have a go if you let them. Making the acquaintance of one of them while moving through the jungle wasn't her idea of a good time.

Kate crouched and took another reading. According to her electronics, she was within a klick of the target. She memorised the layout her sensors reported to her, and shut her stuff down for the final time. She had no reason to believe Millard could detect her approach; her sneaksuit's infrared masking capabilities should preclude that, but why risk it?

Kate crept slowly closer to her objective. She ducked under low hanging foliage, and climbed gingerly over fallen and rotten tree trunks, always careful to prevent noise. At what she guessed to be fifty metres from the target, she went to ground and crawled into a dense patch of undergrowth to watch the goings on in the brightly lit compound. There were three buildings laid out in a rough horseshoe with the central space used for a vehicle park. She recognised the harvesters for what they were, but it was to the half dozen tracked APCs that her eyes were drawn. They weren't bodged together junk that some amateur mechanic had built from spare parts. They were straight out of an Alliance weapons factory. Those heavily armed vehicles had no place in the hands of civs. They were more suited to a Marine armoured detachment and looked brand new.

"What the hell is this?" she hissed under her breath.

Her brief hadn't mentioned anything on the scale of APCs. What else was she likely to find? She lay still and tried to sense the trap. With her electronics shut down it was all she could do, but she had a knack for this kind of thing bred from constant use and a lot of training before that. She was good and knew it. She settled down for the long haul, determined not to move until she had learned the puzzle this place represented.

She was pleased to note the absence of sentry guns, automatic or otherwise. Spy eyes and other surveillance gear could be secreted all over the compound of course, but somehow she thought not. The setup was too amateur—too sloppy for that to be likely. As far as she could see, the operation was unprotected by alarms or guards. She was itching to go active on her sensors to make certain, but she restrained herself. She was all too likely to give herself away. She would watch and make a decision based on a visual inspection.

An hour into her vigil, she made a judgement call. Millard *was* just an amateur as she had guessed, but he was an amateur with powerful toys. He was obviously being financed from off-world, but he didn't appear to have more than a token force stationed here.

Her mission would go ahead as planned.

Kate watched the night progress hoping Millard's people wouldn't work through 'till dawn. As zero three hundred approached, things settled down. Lights were extinguished and the camp cleared of people—except, she noted, two guards standing at the door to the central building. She raised her rifle and sighted on the leftmost guard. He was one hundred metres away. A hundred metres was nothing to a rifle like hers. Heavy tactical rifles (HTR) like her Steyr 7.62mm TacSix, had enough juice to accelerate a steel-jacketed tungsten dart to kill at ranges well over a klick away, but there was a problem. If she fired, the other guard might have time to sound the alarm. She moved to view the second guard and found a woman this time. It was obvious how inexperienced she was by the way she held her weapon pointed upward. That was no way to treat a pulser's sensitive barrel. In this humidity, moisture would collect inside and could well screw up the induction coils.

Kate decided to drop the man first. With luck, the woman's inexperience would slow her reactions. She should hesitate long enough for the second shot to take her out with none the wiser. Kate slowed her breathing and settled the target reticule onto the man. She pressed a thumb against the safety and flicked it to off. The whine of the rifle's capacitors charging was almost silent. She smiled as her target said something to his girlfriend. She couldn't miss.

*Zzzzzing!*

The hyper-velocity round hit the guard squarely between the eyes. His head mushroomed outward with the force, splashing his brains over the wall behind him. The other guard opened her mouth to scream as blood and brains ran down her face.

*Zzzzzing!*

Kate smiled grimly as another head exploded, and the body slumped bonelessly to the ground. She waited for a minute, but there was no sudden outcry. Another minute and she was certain her shots had gone unheard. Leaving the rifle hidden where it was, she scrambled across the open ground expecting to hear shouts of discovery at any moment. She threw herself onto her stomach beside the harvesters, and listened intently. Nothing but the sound of the jungle came to her. Panting with adrenaline rush, she moved alongside huge tracks taller than she was. They were good cover, but she moved beyond them and was in the open all too soon.

The guard's bodies remained undiscovered in twin lakes of blood.

The night was silent except for the distant sound of the jungle like background music to some holodrama. Kate's attention skipped from building to building, from window to window, but all was quiet. No one stirred, and the camp remained dark. No shouts of horror and disgust came to her. Hoping to remain undiscovered for a while longer, she dragged the bodies away from the door, and hid them in the deep shadows between the harvesters.

Kate stepped up to the door of the central building and listened with an ear pressed to the wood. Silence greeted her. She eased her pistol out of its holster and worked the latch on the door with her other hand. Inside, she found more darkness. Her eyes adjusted quickly and she began to make out a room sparsely furnished in the style of someone's residence. Instead of a harvester's shack, which this building most certainly had been before Millard's arrival, it was a palatial residence—by Tigris standards. One wall held electronic equipment for Millard's embryonic army, comm and vid mostly, but there was also an entertainment centre with a good selection of films. She took a moment to peruse the titles.

*Zelda and the Spaceways, Zelda Force Recon, Zelda and the Chaos Engine... Hmmm, a Zelda fan was he?*

That didn't really surprise her after seeing Millard's security arrangements. She crept through a door and found a long hallway with numerous doors leading further into the building. She was beginning to wonder if anyone was home. The first door on the left opened silently to her touch, but the room beyond was unoccupied.

The next opened—

Someone crashed onto her shoulders.

Kate rammed herself backward and slammed her attacker against the wall, fighting to keep her pistol out of his grasp. Rather than allow him to have it, she dropped it and kicked it away. With that done, she counter-attacked in earnest. Her left elbow pistoned back. The explosive grunt behind her said she was on target. Once and then twice, she slammed it back to break his grip on her. She spun in a crouch to face him just in time to take a kick to her thigh. She went to one knee as her leg went numb, and a fist to the jaw rocked her head back against the wall.

"That hurt," she growled licking blood from her split lip. She pulled her knife from the sheath at her waist, and held it low before her. She was hoping he would move within reach. Her throbbing jaw made her want to gut him.

"I meant it to," the shadowy figure said and came forward.

Kate swiped the knife at him, making him leap back, and that gave her time to regain her feet. Miracle of miracles, her leg supported her. She punched the knife forward and followed it with a high kick aimed at his head. He dodged both the knife and the kick, but he didn't see her other fist coming.

"*Ughh,*" he grunted as his nose was smeared across his cheek.

"You Millard?" She feinted with the knife. "Well are you?"

His eyes widened in sudden fear at the name. "No," he gurgled, snorting and spitting blood.

She didn't believe him. Although he wasn't a perfect match for his picture, he was the right age and build. If he wasn't Millard himself, he must be a relative—the likeness was that good. Flicking the knife at his eyes to distract him, she went into a whirling dervish of kicks and punches designed more to confuse than kill. He blocked some with skill, but many more went home. He grunted repeatedly at the power she brought to bear. He lashed out and her head rang, but her blood was up and she butted him right on his broken nose.

He went down.

Kate dropped to her knees with both hands on the knife, and slammed it down to the hilt in his guts before he could move. His eyes popped wide in pain and shock as she worked the knife in his belly. He clutched at her arm like a drowning man clinging to a rope, but his grip was already weakening.

She leaned close and stared into his eyes. "Why am I here to kill you, Millard? Why?"

The man gave her a bloody grin. "I ain't Millard..." he sighed and went still.

*Damn!*

Now Kate believed him. She retrieved her pistol from where she had kicked it, and paused to listen for any disturbance. Nothing. She checked the other rooms, not expecting to find her target, but she didn't have another plan. The noise of her fight would surely have woken the dead let alone Millard. If he had been here, he would be long gone by now... but maybe not!

She stepped into a bedroom and found a pudgy man sleeping soundly with a mask over his eyes. This idiot couldn't be Millard could he? He couldn't be Millard the revolutionary leader... could he?

He was.

Kate carefully sat on the edge of Millard's bed and aimed her pistol at his face. He looked very peaceful sleeping there. It seemed a shame to wake him, but she wanted answers. Information was always desirable, especially when she might learn something to pay off her handler that much faster. Knowing the identity of his paymaster seemed a good starting point. She nudged Millard awake with the silencer.

"What is it, Fleming?" Millard said, groping for the mask.

Kate let him remove it. His eyes widened in shock, and he slid a hand under the pillow. "Naughty," she said tapping him on the temple with the silencer. "Bring it out slowly, there's a good boy."

Millard withdrew a small snub-nosed pulser, and Kate took it from him. It was a nice little weapon—short ranged and with a low firing rate, but easy to conceal. It would kill a person just as dead as her slug thrower.

"I'll keep this if you don't mind, Mister Millard."

Millard's lips trembled. "You know who I am. Who are you?"

"Your executioner I'm afraid."

"I guessed that," the pudgy man said bravely. "Sanderson send you?"

"That's what I want to talk to you about, Mister Millard. Why was I sent to kill you?"

Millard's eyes narrowed in sudden calculation. "You don't know?"

"Would I be asking if I did?"

"I am... I *was* building an army to fight President Sanderson..."

"I know that," Kate interrupted. "What I want to know is who cares enough about a piss pot planet like Tigris to have me sent here?"

"Why should I tell you? You're going to kill me anyway."

"True," she said with a smile. "But I don't like being used—especially not for something like this. I'll make you a deal. After I kill you I'll kill the man who sent me here. How's that?"

"How can I refuse?" Millard said with lips trembling. "Sanderson—"

She shook her head. "No, no, no. I won't be fooled into finishing your little war for you."

"Sanderson has a deal with a corporation on Bethany I tell you. He—"

"Bethany?" What chance this? He couldn't know she was from Bethany. "You're sure?"

"Everyone knows. Sanderson is skimming from the harvest. He's been doing it for years. The harvesters are desperate!"

"Hush." She prodded him with the gun. "So he's skimming, so what?"

"So he's working with the Whitby Corporation. He supplies them with what they want, and Whitby supplies him with guns and men to keep the harvesters in line. You saw the APCs outside? We stole them from the spaceport before he could take possession. They're brand new, diverted straight here from an Alliance weapons factory. God knows what they sent instead. Some General is probably spitting mad about that."

Whitby... her handler's paymaster was a Whitby? Damn them! They were behind everything that was wrong with Bethany. They had destroyed her father's life, leaving her alone and unprepared to care for her brother, and now here she was helping them! Sanderson had called on Whitby's help to put Millard's rebellion down, and there was nothing she could do about it... or was there? Her eyes narrowed as a plan began to form.

Millard was still babbling. "...all his ships. Whitby keeps Sanderson in power. It must be Whitby who sent you. Was it Whitby?"

*Pfft!*

"I don't know, Mister Millard," she said to the corpse. "But I think I'll finish this little war for you after all."

Kate stood and quietly left the building.

\* \* \*

# 5 ~ Undercover

Back at the shuttle, Kate changed out of her sneaksuit and back into civilian clothes trying not to think about Whitby, but it was no good. Whitby was one of the ten ruling families of Bethany. Nothing of importance happened there without the Ten's say so, which seemed to add credence to Millard's accusation. The Alliance might be ruled by the will of the Council, but Bethany was ruled by the will of the Ten.

The Alliance constitution held sway throughout the Human sector of the galaxy, but it still left a great deal to be decided by each planet's home government. The Alliance Council had ever been reluctant to interfere too boldly in a member world's domestic affairs. As long as the constitution wasn't bent out of shape too badly, the Ten had almost ultimate power within the Bethany system. Kate would bet her life savings that abuses of the constitution were never reported. They answered to no one but themselves back home, but out here at the arse end of nowhere their interests were vulnerable. Perhaps she could give them a bloody nose without getting caught. Her thoughts turned to Paul and her determination hardened.

Her brother was younger than she was by seven years. Tall and dark haired as she was, they even had the same eyes. Blue like ice and cold as a glacier her mother said of them in admiration. Her father's eyes were grey and her mother's blue. The combination of the two was striking. About eight years ago, her father fell afoul of the Baxters (one of the Ten) and lost the business that his father, and his father before him, had built up. Paul had promised he would get their money back.

Together with some friends, he had set out to do it, but something went wrong and he never returned. A week later, the bodies of his friends were found dumped near one of the city's auto-recyclers. They would have become fertiliser if not for an unscheduled shutdown for some minor repair or other. The official explanation was that Paul had teamed up with a group of con-artists, and tried to rip off someone from the Baxter family. Paul was never found. It was assumed his body had already found its way into the recycler before the shutdown. Kate had never believed the story. Yes Paul had been seventeen and full of bravado, and yes he had said he would get their money back, but he was good, and kind, and honest, and…

*He isn't a criminal and he isn't dead dammit!*

Kate took a deep breath and continued dressing. The bright orange top left her midriff bare, and the tight criss-cross straps restricted her breathing. It was uncomfortable as hell. The lime green trousers she pulled on, hung too loose on her hips. They felt in danger of pooling at her feet at any moment. The slashed open styling on her arms and legs, especially on the thighs, made her want to cringe, but it was the height of fashion in the core. Fashionable or not, her father would faint if he could see her now. She wished she dared wear something plain, but she needed the disguise the clashing colours offered her.

She checked her appearance in the mirror one more time and shook her head. Zelda's marketing department had a lot to answer for.

Once dressed, Kate broke her rifle down to its component parts, and stowed them out of sight in her kit bag before moving forward to programme the computer. She gave commands for an auto takeoff and flight toward the spaceport. While the computer did that, she spent her time in the head polishing her disguise. Hair was first. Applying a handful of Goop Original, she greased her hair flat then applied a comb to make it spiky all over. Turning this way and that she admired the results in the mirror. She looked truly awful.

"Perfect," she said and applied the setting agent that came as an aerosol with the Goop.

Heavy lipstick and eye shadow came next. Reading the instructions on the side of the applicator, she found the appropriate code and chose a red that was almost fluorescent for the lipstick, and dark purple that was almost black for her eyes. She dialled in the numbers and went to work. By the time she was finished, she looked fifteen years younger and just like a dippy teenaged tourist.

"That should do it." Kate smirked at the image in the mirror. "Hello Cherry, long time no see."

Cherry was a cover she had used before. Although of course some details like her last name had changed many times, she always looked like a rich man's rebellious daughter. The clothes and makeup made Kate seem years younger, and nothing like Kate Richmond—spy and assassin. Cherry was a real person to her. Kate could slip in and out of her Cherry persona easily whenever the need arose. She had others, many others in fact, but Cherry suited a surprising number of situations. People liked her, wanted to help her, or bed her, or simply dance with her. Some had even wanted to take her home to meet the parents! Kate snorted at the remembrance and shook her head. The illusion of naïve youth and money was very attractive to some.

Kate sat in the pilot's chair to watch as the jungle grudgingly gave way first to tamed forests, and finally to cultivated farmland. The shuttle made a small course correction, and a road flashed by beneath her. Roads meant civilisation. She was nearly there. She keyed the microphone and began to play her part.

"Can anyone hear me? *Please* say you can hear me… mayday, mayday. How do I land this thing?"

"This is Tigris port control. Identify yourself."

"Oh thank *God.* My name's Cherry and I'm on a shuttle. There's no *pilot!*"

"State your designation," snapped the flight controller.

"Touchy, touchy," Kate murmured to herself before keying the microphone live again. "Cherry, I just told you."

"Not your name, your shuttle. What is your registry?"

"I don't *knoooow!*"

"Calm down and start at the beginning. What happened to your pilot?"

Kate launched into her prepared story. "…said he knew this great place we could go, but when we landed, we were in the middle of the jungle! He grabbed me, but I stamped on his foot and got away. He chased me into the trees, so I hid until I could sneak back to the shuttle. I locked the hatch and pushed the button that said auto, but now I can't *laaaand.*"

"Ah, hmmm… everything will be fine now, ma'am. Shuttles are very safe, but I need you to do something for me. Can you do that?"

"I'll try," Kate said in a small voice.

"Good, that's good. Now what I need you to do is…"

Kate almost shouted in triumph as the controller's attitude changed. He was treating her like a not very bright child now. That could only help her when she landed. She reached for the transponder control and waited.

"…you to look above your head. Can you see all the knobs and switches?"

"I see them."

"That's good. Now, near the centre of the panel there's a row of knobs. Don't touch them, but at the end of the row is a switch that says transponder. Have you got it?"

"Yeah. It says disable at the top, autonomous in the middle, and enable at the bottom." Kate rolled her eyes and waited for the command she knew was coming.

"Very good. It should be pointing to the word autonomous, but I want you to flick that switch all the way down to enable."

"Now?"

"Yes, do it now for me."

*Hallelujah!*

"I did it. There's a blinking light on the panel—"

"Don't worry about that. It just means I'm flying the shuttle now. You stay strapped in, and I'll have you on the ground in no time."

"Thank you," Kate said in a meek voice and threw the microphone down. "The things I have to do for this job."

Kate kept a wary eye on her instruments, ready to intercede should that be necessary, but the controller seemed competent enough. Her disguise was important, but not more important than her life. She kept a close eye. The shuttle came in slower than she would have flown it, but that didn't concern her, what did was her reception committee. There was bound to be one. As the shuttle landed, she took a sniff from the aerosol that she'd used on her hair. It was astringent and made her eyes water. Through the cockpit window, she could see that powerful floodlights lit the taxiway and shuttle parking bays, making the night flee and welcoming her to civilisation. While she cried alone in the cockpit, the shuttle automatically taxied toward a small group of people waiting for her outside the brightly lit terminal building.

"There you go. You can move around now," the flight controller said.

"I don't know what I would have done if you hadn't been there. Will I see you outside?"

"Ah… about that. I'm on duty so I can't come down there, but I've sent a friend of mine. His name's Robert; you'll like him."

"Oh, okay," she said.

Kate was peering out the cockpit window looking for anyone in uniform. She didn't care whether the flight controller came to meet her or not. All she cared about was the lack of security personnel in her reception committee. It looked as if they had bought her story.

"Before you go, I need your name. I had to log your mayday call, and my supervisor will want to ask you a few questions."

Kate frowned, suspicious of his motives, but then she shrugged. "It's Cherry Jackson. What kind of questions? Does he need to ask them tonight?"

"Nothing to worry about, just routine. I know you must be tired. I'm sure he won't mind waiting until tomorrow. Look, I've got to go. Good luck, and let Robert take care of you. He's a nice guy."

"Thanks."

Kate's eyes were red and puffy by the time she opened the hatch and barrelled into the arms of one of the waiting men.

"Thank you, thank you, *thank you.*" She forced more tears to come and cried on his shoulder while trying to watch his friends' reactions.

"Hey Robert, you've caught a wild one this time," one man called and the others laughed.

For the most part, Kate found amusement at their companion's situation when she studied their reactions. To them, he had his arms full of a hysterical teenager, and a goddamn *tourist* at that! Tourists were universally despised as rich know-nothings in the Border Worlds. No one had time to spare on them, especially not when they were busy with their own survival. If she had been one of their own people, their reaction would have been one of concern, but as she wasn't, they were amused and angry at the same time.

That was fine by her.

"You're all right now," Robert said casting around for help from his friends. Said friends simply grinned and backed away with their hands raised to ward him off. They were more than happy to leave him to it.

"I want her arrested for stealing my shuttle," a distant voice shouted.

Kate stiffened and pushed away. She wanted her hands free in case of trouble. Everyone turned toward the man storming across the taxiway.

"What an arsehole…" one of Robert's friends said. He was a maintenance engineer going by his clothes.

Another man nodded. "I told Jennings not to leave it unsecured."

"…does he think he is, strutting around like he owns the place?"

Kate relaxed just a little. Jennings was obviously an outsider. They seemed solid in their disapproval of him. She slipped her hand into her pocket and grasped Millard's dinky pulser, but she doubted she would need to use it.

"Now, now Jennings. I told you about leaving it like you do. It was bound to happen."

"That makes no difference. She stole it."

"I *never,*" Kate gasped using Cherry's outraged voice. "*You take that back!*"

"It's all right... Cherry," Robert said stumbling on her alias as if about to laugh. "We'll handle this."

While Robert was reassuring her, the others had closed ranks against Jennings. Kate listened in genuine admiration as they battered him into submission.

"...accessory after the fact."

"But—" Jennings began.

"And it's your fault she was abducted in the first place."

"My fault? How is it—"

"We told you about it before. You can't leave your shuttle unsecured like that, it's begging for trouble. Lucky for you miss Cherry doesn't want to press charges."

"Charges?" Jennings said faintly and visibly wilting under the storm.

"Charges," Robert agreed firmly. "Your shuttle is back safe and sound, and the thief is marooned in the jungle. I suggest you be satisfied and let the poor girl go home. She's had a bit of a shock."

"In the jungle you say?" Jennings said and at Kate's nod, his face lightened. A calculating look replaced his earlier outrage at the theft. "Well I suppose... and it does appear unharmed and all. It would be churlish of me to hold this young... err *lady* responsible. Let's leave it at that."

Kate released her pulser as Jennings went to inspect his shuttle. Her allies wandered off when they realised the crisis was over, and left her in Robert's hands.

"Well, can I drive you somewhere?"

Kate thought fast. "I need a hotel. I didn't have time to find one before..." she looked down shyly. "You know."

"Hey, it's okay," Robert said softly to console her. "It wasn't your fault, and the bastard is history."

"What do you mean?"

"You marooned him. The jungle is wild. He'll never make it back here on foot."

"Oh," she said in a small voice.

"Don't beat yourself up about it. He deserved it."

"I suppose so."

"This yours?" Jennings said descending from the shuttle and locking the hatch. He was carrying her kit bag.

Kate nodded and reached for it, but Robert was becoming a pest.

He got a hand to it first.

"I'll carry it for you, Cherry. It's heavy, what's in it?" Robert asked hefting the bag experimentally.

"Just girl stuff."

"Girl stuff?" He grinned. "Like what?"

"Clothes and stuff," Kate said with a disinterested shrug.

"Ah."

Robert escorted her toward a row of battered ground cars. All of them were covered in dust and had seen hard use. If Kate had been alone, she might well have stolen one of them. A ground car would be useful later. There were a few ground effect vehicles at one end of the row—a truck with its own crane attached to its cargo bay, and two executive saloons that had seen better days, but most of the vehicles ran on tyres with deep treads. Wheeled transport was more common in the Border Worlds; hover vehicles had problems with uneven ground.

"This yours?" Kate asked admiring the dirty and beat up exterior of the truck they approached. The cargo bay was full of odd pieces of junk and tools that had been haphazardly thrown inside, but the cockpit looked clean and well cared for.

"Yeah," he said blushing in embarrassment as they climbed in.

Transport like this could be very useful. It wouldn't stand out on a world where the lack of decent roads made four-wheel drive a necessity, and its battered appearance automatically labelled the owner a harvester—a useful mistake for people to make.

"I know she doesn't look like much, but she's really something where it counts."

Kate raised a sceptical eyebrow. "Oh?"

"Yeah," he said with a mischievous grin and started the turbine.

*Weruuuuummm!*

Kate winced as the turbine started in a thunder of noise. The power under the hood was unexpected. These things were notoriously easy to tune, but he had more than tuned this one.

"What the hell did you do?"

"The turbine is straight out of a auto-harvester," he said with a another cheeky grin. "Twelve hundred horsepower on max boost."

Kate whistled silently and gave him the admiring look he craved. "Where did you get it?"

"I have lots of friends, Cherry. We do each other favours." He backed out of his parking space and then floored it.

They accelerated along the road like a shuttle boosting to orbit. He was grinning like a kid, obviously trying to impress her. He must have decided that she wasn't as young as she first appeared, and that he might have a chance with her. He was *dead* wrong there, but she wouldn't hurt his feelings by letting him know that. The only thing in her pants he would get was her pulser in his face. She didn't react to his reckless driving. She had seen worse; hell, she had *done* worse.

"So, you here on vacation?" Robert said.

Kate shrugged. "Sort of. Daddy wants me to take over the publicity side of things for him next year, so I said he had to let me have this year to myself. He wanted me to stay in the core, but I said to hell with that." She grinned and Robert returned it. "I was on my way to Arcadia via Thurston, but I heard there's fighting there. So I came here instead."

"Why here?"

"Why not?" she said with a shrug.

"Well, there's been some trouble here too. Nothing really serious," he hastened to add seeing the worry blossom on her face. "Don't worry about it. I'm sure it will blow over by tomorrow. So, what do you think of Tigris, nothing but trees and more trees huh?"

That was a trick question if ever Kate had heard one. "I like trees," she said enthusiastically.

"Really?" Robert said, raising an eyebrow in surprise.

"Yeah. It's so great being able to walk on the surface for as long as you want. It's like having a huge agridome all to myself. You're lucky living here." Kate shook her head in awe. "All this space and air for free, and you don't have to watch how long you're out in it."

"Where you from?"

"Didn't I say? Garnet."

"Garnet… no wonder you like trees," Robert said with a snort of laughter.

Kate tried to look hurt. "What's wrong with Garnet? Ever been there, ever seen the sunset over the Cheji Mountains? It's beautiful. So what if we haven't got lots of stupid jungle. We've got trees… lots of them. And we've got crystal forests—they're so huge they go on forever, and they're really useful too."

"I'm sorry," Robert said contritely. "I didn't mean to belittle your home. I'm sure it's beautiful. Maybe I could visit sometime."

Kate wasn't going to let him off that easy. "*Hmph.*"

"I apologise, Cherry. I mean that. I was born on Tigris and I love it, but I'm not used to visitors saying they like it."

Kate frowned and unbent a little. "Why, what's wrong with it?"

Robert smiled pleased at the confusion he heard in her voice. "Nothing by my way of thinking, but you know what people are." He shrugged. "The tourist types say things like how quaint it all is, or how terribly brave we must be living on the frontier, how scary and dangerous the animals are… my god they say, you have real live animals walking about without supervision where people might run into them. They treat us like backward savages. They actually get a thrill out of mixing with us," he finished in disgust.

"I'm not like that. It's exciting being here, but not because I think you're all savages. Its exciting being on my own away from home, that's all."

Robert nodded. "I would love to travel like you're doing."

"It is fun," she agreed. "But Garnet will always be home."

"I understand perfectly. I feel the same way about Tigris."

The crashing of abused suspension over ruts and potholes gave way to the comforting purr that Kate always associated with civilisation. The plascrete road that Humanity always inflicted upon its worlds, hummed and purred with the speed of the tyres racing over it. At this rate they should reach the city of Rhagnall in no time. She was glad of it.

Kate tensed when Robert suddenly slowed down. There was some kind of checkpoint up ahead. She eased her hand into her pocket and retrieved her new pulser. She kept it low beside the seat, and waited to see what would happen. Robert hadn't noticed the weapon. He didn't appear concerned when a man in uniform stepped onto the road in front of the barrier and waved him down.

Robert opened his window and leaned out. "Hey, Johnny. What's happening, man?"

The soldier, Johnny, came forward, stuck his head through the open window beside Robert, and peered around the interior. His eyes brightened when he noticed Kate. He smiled and she forced herself to reciprocate. Her pulser was aimed to take him in the upper chest—maybe the neck. The door would be no hindrance to her shot, it would simply burn through. She couldn't do better without pulling Robert down or revealing that she was armed.

"How's it going, Roberto?" Johnny said looking Kate up and down and enjoying the view.

Kate felt like blasting him just for that, but she held off. Johnny's friends wouldn't take kindly to her burning his face off. They were bound to get upset about it, and then she would have to kill them too. No, it was better to keep her cover uncompromised. Anyway, Cherry always aroused this kind of interest. It was part of what made her a good disguise. No one expected violence from her.

"Good, and you?" Robert said.

"Not so hot. We had another bunch of riots in the city. Not good man, not good at all."

"Yeah, I heard about it on the news. How is it now?"

"Quiet."

"Well that's good," Robert said.

Kate didn't agree and neither did Johnny by the look of his face. Things tended to go quiet just before the storm.

"This is Cherry," Robert went on. "She's on vacation here."

"Nice to meet you, Cherry. Are you staying long?"

"Not long," Kate said wondering if he was asking officially. "Just the week."

Johnny nodded. "We aren't supposed to let anyone through, Roberto, but seeing as it's you…" he gestured to one of his men to raise the barrier. "You be careful tonight. If you see anyone on the streets, for God's sake don't stop. There's a curfew, so no one should be out, but just in case there is—don't stop. Okay?"

"Okay man," Robert said easily. "Can I drop your name if a patrol stops me?"

"No problem," Johnny said and stepped back.

"Thanks," Robert said and drove on. "A friend of mine."

"Yeah?" Kate kept her eyes on the soldiers in the mirror. "Known him long?"

"Johnny and me go back. He's not like the others—he believes in what he's doing."

That was interesting. "How do you mean?"

"Sanderson has been buying troops from all over the place." His face twisted into a snarl, "Mercenaries can't be trusted. Johnny can be. He was born here just like me."

Kate privately agreed. A man with no stake in a place could not be relied upon to defend it. Tigris would be far better off building its armed forces from locals. They at least had something to lose if they did a bad job.

The city was dark and quiet as they drove through the streets. Street lighting had been turned off in an effort to discourage people from leaving their homes. It had worked. The city felt abandoned. Robert was silent as they drove along. He was concentrating upon his driving as if he feared to fail some kind of competency test. The only light, other than Robert's headlights, came from the public address screens. Every one of them showed the same thing—a screenful of text warning people to remain calm and off the streets. The glow emanating from them seemed somehow sad. Each one a lonely island in the unremitting darkness the city had become.

They were stopped twice.

The first time was another roadblock consisting of two APCs blocking the main route through the city. Kate realised why they had chosen the location the moment she saw them. The road they were on would lead them right by Tigris' centre of government—the Assembly Building. Not a good place to allow rebellious persons to approach, and not somewhere she was interested in seeing anyway. By all accounts, it was a spectacularly ugly building.

Robert slowed and stopped when the officer in charge of the roadblock waved him down. Kate counted more than twenty soldiers wearing battle dress and body armour. Each man carried an M18-AP pulser—the standard rifle for the majority of forces deployed throughout the Human sector. They knew what to do with them too. She could tell by their reactions that they had been in similar situations before. She watched the soldiers spread out to cover them from all sides. Mercs they might be, but they were seasoned mercs. The officer—she assumed he must be an officer though he had no visible rank insignia on his uniform, was wearing a pulser on his hip. The snap holster containing the weapon was ominously unsecured. She watched him warily. He placed a hand casually on the weapon and strolled toward them. By his attitude, he thought he was something special.

The merc knocked on the window with a knuckle and Robert lowered it.

"Identification," the merc snapped with his hand out.

Kate relaxed a little when she noted the merc wasn't carrying a simcode reader. Not that it would have done him any good where she was concerned. Like billions of others from the core, her simcode implant was an integral part of her spinal cord, but unlike them, hers was a little bit special. It was programmable—a thing not possible without very sophisticated equipment that only governments supposedly possessed. The Border Worlds didn't support the use of the simcode implant. It was one of the things that made living outside the core so attractive to certain kinds of people. Tigris maintained only a basic system of identicard to keep track of its citizens. Visitors were issued with temporary cards up at the station.

Robert handed the merc his identicard. "We just came from the port. This is Cherry."

"Last name," the merc snapped again.

"I ermmm…" Robert said and broke off in embarrassment when he realised he didn't know the answer.

"Jackson," Kate said and quickly retrieved her forged card. "Here."

Robert took the card and handed it on.

"Destination," the merc said after scrutinising the card long enough to make her fidget.

The merc peered into the truck and double-checked her picture.

Kate smiled, trying to appear innocent, but his eyes remained cold. He had a killer's eyes. She had seen the same in the mirror enough times to recognise it in him. Cherry of course had puppy eyes—eyes that said let's be friends. He didn't want to be friends and was unaffected by her innocent look. He checked the card a third time.

Kate's palms began to sweat.

"We're heading for the Mayflower," Robert said unaware of the merc's suspicion. "You can let us pass can't you? It's only three blocks down."

"By order of the President, no one may pass. No one." The officer handed the cards back to Robert. "Turn back."

"Oh come on, you can—"

"You heard the man, Robert," Kate said watching the merc's eyes. "There must be another route we can take."

"Yeah but—"

The merc's eyes were hard. "The city is under martial law. Turn around or be arrested. I won't tell you again."

Robert opened his mouth to protest, but Kate clamped a hand onto his knee in warning. "No need to threaten us, sir. We're going... *aren't we?*"

Robert winced at the pressure she exerted on his knee. "Yeah... I guess we can take another route—sure we can."

"Then do so," the merc said and stepped back.

"Arsehole," Robert hissed under his breath. He slammed the truck into reverse and accelerated hard with a squeal of rubber. "They make me want to puke." He braked with another squeal of abused tyres. "I would love to kick his arse up between his ears." He turned onto a side road, and accelerated hard enough to leave tyre smoke in his wake. "Bastards..."

Kate said nothing, though privately she agreed completely.

They were stopped one final time almost at the entrance to the hotel. This time Robert managed to exert his charms upon the officer in charge. She was a local woman name Charlene, and it turned out that Robert was a friend of a friend. He dropped Johnny's name without hesitation.

"Johnny's so charming," Charlene gushed. "I just love the way—"

Kate stared at the blushing soldier in something akin to horror. Charlene was fifty if she was a day. She was wearing battle dress and was carrying an M18-AP rifle in addition to the pistol on her hip, yet she was blushing like a damn schoolgirl over a man half her age. There should be a law or something. She was a soldier for God's sake!

The barrier lifted and Robert was waved on. "What's wrong?"

Kate was still scowling. "Nothing."

"Something is," Robert said glancing at her then back to the road. "You look like you swallowed a bug."

"I'm just feeling a little tired. It's been a long day, Robert, and a lot's happened. Is the hotel far?"

"We're nearly there." He pulled into a parking area outside a tall building proudly displaying the name *Tigris Mayflower* in glaring blue neon over the lobby doors. "It's the best place in the city."

Kate climbed out of the truck carrying her kit bag. The Mayflower Hotel was a tall chrome and steel building that would be better suited to a corporate headquarters if not for the balconies. They appeared to have been tacked on at some later time, and didn't match the building's architecture at all. The parking lot was a simple plascrete area surrounded by gardens on two sides, the road on the third, and the hotel on the fourth. There was a duplicate of the building, minus the balconies, seemingly unused on the other side of the road.

"They were built by McPherson," Robert said watching her study the towers.

"McPherson?"

"McPherson and Dermott used to make drive coils, but they went bust years ago. The towers are all that's left."

Kate hefted her kit and walked toward the lobby. The night was quiet, but the hotel was anything but. When they entered, they found the lobby bustling with people coming and going. From the sound of muffled music, she decided there was a party going on somewhere. Men and women were walking arm in arm toward the elevators, while others walked behind her and through the double doors on her left. The music's volume increased then dropped away as the doors closed.

"What's the occasion?"

"Don't need one to have fun," Robert said with a grin and draped an arm around her shoulders.

Robert escorted Kate to reception where she asked for a room. The receptionist, a slim balding man, asked her how long she planned on staying. She said a week, though she had no intention of staying that long. As soon as she completed her self-imposed mission, she planned to leave on the same ship that had brought her to Tigris. She had killed Millard as down payment for the information she needed to find Paul, but although it had been necessary, it didn't sit well with her now that she knew Whitby was ultimately behind it. To redress the balance, she was going to end Millard's war for him. The receptionist named a figure. It was daylight robbery, but she had expected nothing less. A place like this probably saw no more than one or two new guests a week. It was already obvious from the pounding music that the hotel made its profit from something other than renting rooms.

"I'll take it," she said.

"Payment all in advance, food is extra." The receptionist tapped a finger against the screen in the desk. "It's the law."

Kate dropped her kit bag to the floor and Robert retrieved his arm so that she could sign the register's screen. Kate was careful to use her alias. She pulled her credit wand from her pocket, and slid it into the receptacle in the desk as the receptionist keyed a figure into his consol. Kate took note of the amount before pressing the transfer button. He hadn't tried to con her.

"Thank you for using the Tigris Mayflower," he said in a bored voice before handing her a pass card. "Have a nice night." He glanced at Robert and smirked at her.

Kate ignored him.

"Thanks for everything," she said turning to Robert and taking her kit from him. She had to tug it free of his hand, but he did release it no matter how reluctantly.

"It was nothing. I'll escort you up—"

"No, that's okay," Kate said firmly and his face darkened. "Please Robert, don't be like that. I really like you, but I'm so tired. I haven't slept since I arrived in-system…" she checked her wristcomp. "That was almost thirty hours ago. No wonder I'm so testy! Can you forgive me? Maybe we could have dinner tomorrow… no, I'll be asleep. What about lunch the following day?"

Robert's face lightened. "There's nothing to forgive, Cherry. I should have realised after what you've been through. Can *you* forgive *me?*"

Kate smiled coyly and nodded.

"Lunch here on Wednesday then?" Robert said.

She nodded and smiled again. "I'll look forward to it," she said and headed for the elevators. She let Cherry's smile drop from her features the instant the doors closed and blocked her view of Robert.

The first thing Kate did upon entering her room was check for places she might be observed. The bedroom had its own balcony, but it was unlikely to provide anyone with access. Similarly, the sitting room had a balcony and was secure from intrusion, but unlike the bedroom, there was the other tower on this side that could be used as a platform to observe and listen in. Pulling the drapes closed would stop the one, and switching on the holocentre would limit the other. She did both in the sitting room before closing the drapes in the bedroom.

After taking a long awaited shower, Kate sat cross-legged on the floor in her skivvies listening to the news broadcast. Now that she had time, she took the opportunity to strip and clean her weapons, before turning her attention to her new toy.

Millard's pulser was a nice little weapon, short ranged and compact with a sixteen round magazine. He had chosen well. Pulsers, or more properly pulsed plasma particle weapons, were the most commonly used handheld energy weapon in the Alliance. Although this one was more compact than most, they all work on the same principle. Whether you called your weapon a plasma rifle, a plasma pistol, a pulser, a PPG, or a PPC, they all worked the same way.

An energy cell is used to reduce a round of ammunition into positively charged ions called plasma, which is expelled as a bright flash of light using a solid-state laser with a ruby core. Pulsing the laser gives the best stimulus. They were often called *pulser* or *plasma* pistols for whichever part of the process the manufacturer felt to be the most important. The induction coil in the barrel was there to excite the charge adding a little *oomph*.

The coil of such weapons was the component most responsible for the pyrotechnics accompanied by firing. Removing the coil to eliminate the display would turn a good pulser into a useless piece of junk that resembled a PPG or PPC. Construction is similar, but particle projection guns and particle projection cannons were almost worthless as handheld weapons. They were naval ordinance almost exclusively. On any scale less than ship to ship actions, pulsers had superiority over other energy weapons due to their physical size and the damage they could inflict. In space, where almost unlimited energy could be used to add destructive punch, particle projection cannons held sway, with grazers and lasers following a close second.

Kate studied her new toy turning it this way and that. It appeared well cared for, but she stripped it down and reassembled it for her own peace of mind. She left her hands to the task they knew so well, and watched the news on the holo.

"...Garnet. Shares in mining and steel industries received a major boost today, as President Dyachenko announced a new contract to increase production of the new *Washington* class heavy cruisers. President Dyachenko stated that the Fleet's newest heavy cruiser had proven itself superior to the older *Excalibur* class in exercises designed to test its potential, and having done so, it would go into full scale production with immediate effect. This decision by the Council was not unexpected and came on the heels of..."

"Yeah, yeah, yeah. It's old news," Kate muttered as she reassembled the pulser.

That was one problem the Alliance had failed to solve. Member worlds were separated by vast distances, and news travelled slowly.

The President had announced the Council's decision to increase production months ago, yet here on Tigris it was being aired as if it were only yesterday.

"President Sanderson..." the announcer was saying.

Kate stopped what she was doing to listen to the report.

"...failed to address the harvesters' concerns yesterday when he announced a further increase in export tariffs. The news has sent shock-waves through Tigris. Rioting on the streets in towns and cities all over the continent has caused much loss of life. The decreeing of martial law, and the suppression of the riots by Tigris armed forces has, thus far, been successful in calming the situation. The use of non-lethal force has proven effective in reducing the bloodshed, and with President Sanderson's plea for restraint from both sides calming the situation still further, a return to normality is once again in sight."

Kate snorted. There was nothing normal about Tigris. Arriving at a border world was always like stepping back in time, but Tigris evoked it stronger than others she had visited. Admittedly, she never had time for tours when on a job, so her experience was limited to those areas surrounding her target, but *rioting*? That would never have happened in the core.

She turned her attention back to the pulser and listened only absently to the announcer's voice.

"...hospitalised during the outbreak of violence were reported to be off the critical list mere hours after the confrontation took place. Our earlier announcement of deaths among the rioters has now been confirmed, but the report stating figures reaching into the thousands has been proven erroneous. Med Admin stated an increase in admission figures on the order of a few hundred, with deaths confined to a few dozen only..."

Kate frowned; the city could be under martial law for weeks. She couldn't afford to have her movements curtailed. She relaxed slightly when she heard that most of the restrictions were being rescinded now that the actual fighting had ceased. President Sanderson had apparently retired to his mountain retreat where he was recovering from the stress of ordering the army to open fire on their own people.

"Stress... *rigggght*," Kate drawled. She listened to the rest of the news broadcast, but there was nothing further about Sanderson. She finished assembling her new toy and reloaded it.

Why wasn't Tigris a member of the Alliance? All Human worlds had an open invitation to join, but as far as she knew, Tigris had never petitioned for entry. It might be a piss-pot world compared with some, but it had the potential to be much more. Already its produce was sought after, evidenced by the huge export industry it had. Was

Sanderson holding the planet back for fear of its over-exploitation, as some border worlds insisted would happen, or was it something more personal? A fear of competition perhaps, or worry over a light being shone into his term of office. Whatever the reason was, the people of Tigris had no one to speak for them on the Council. Whatever Sanderson wanted done was done. His word was law.

"How long has he been in office?" she mused, and frowned when she realised that for all she knew, Sanderson could have a life presidency.

The Alliance presidency used a term of five years. On every Alliance planet, a councillor was either elected or appointed by his world's government to serve on the Council for three years. One councillor per world meant two hundred and thirty-four councillors—though Kate had heard Thurston had applied to join only recently. So then, two hundred and thirty-five men and women led the Alliance, with President Dyachenko at its head, but here in the Border Zone a single man ruled it all.

Kate yawned and stretched. It was definitely time to try out her bed. She turned off the holo and climbed under cool sheets. Her silencer-equipped pistol came with her under the covers, and her new pulser went under the pillow. Why change what works? She frowned uneasily into the darkness. It hadn't worked for Millard. She snorted at her sudden apprehension—she wasn't *that* superstitious.

Kate pushed her hand under the pillow and fell asleep with the pulser in her fist.

* * *

# 6 ~ Sergeant Checkpoint

Kate stared at herself in the mirror.

"My God, this is starting to look natural," she muttered and applied a last dab of colour to her left eyelid.

She dropped Millard's pulser into a pocket and checked her reflection one last time to make sure it didn't show—it wouldn't do to have someone pointing at her. Before leaving her room, she stabbed the button next to the door to illuminate the do not disturb sign, in case a cleanbot came by while she was out. It would be best if the HTR remained undiscovered under the bed.

Down in the lobby, she chose the doors that were so popular the night before, and walked straight into chaos. As expected it was a club, and also as expected there were plenty of people for her to choose from. Men and women were dancing in an arm waving frenzy to the heavy whomp-whomp beat of the music. Lasers strobed through the darkness, and holo screens flashed images of worlds and patterns that made no sense, but seemed to vaguely match the music.

She made her way around the outskirts of the revellers refusing to be dragged in amongst them. Twice she had to become physical, as men on a high of testosterone and designer drugs, grabbed her and wouldn't take no for an answer. No one heard the screams, or if they did, they didn't care. Both men would recover—sprained thumbs were nothing. She doubted the chemical cocktail running through their veins would let them feel pain for longer than a second or two.

She made her way toward the crowded bar.

Kate had to use her elbows, and many apologetic smiles to burrow between people, but finally she succeeded. Joining those propping up the bar, she ordered a drink from one of a half dozen harried looking barkeeps.

"A *what?*" the barkeep yelled over the noise in surprise.

"A glass of ice water," she yelled back.

"That's what I thought you said." The woman had a puzzled look on her face as she went to fetch it.

Kate wasn't thirsty, but it was always good to have something in your hands in these situations. A pulser would draw too much attention; a glass of something non-alcoholic would have to do. She stood propped against the bar on one elbow trying to look as if she belonged, and defended her territory from predatory drinkers. Her eyes tracked targets as they approached and receded from her, but none of them appealed. She was hoping for a merc. Everyone was dressed like civs, but she should be able to pick one out fairly easily. Soldiers had a certain presence that she would recognise. They walked different—more confidently, and they seemed to own a room without trying or even noticing the effect they had on others not like themselves. She tried not to show her distaste for the revelry going on around her. Men and women were entwined together at tables and booths around the room. Some were shouting to be heard, some were laughing, but the greater percentage by far were kissing and fondling each other.

*In public!*

She couldn't believe how far some people would go in a public place. Some of them were so close to performing the act itself that the difference was hard to determine. Bare flesh and stroking hands met her eyes as she watched for a target she could use. She didn't avert her eyes from the goings on, even though she dearly wished to. Instead, she steeled herself to accept what she saw. She could handle it if she had to, and she did have to. She used her coldest mask to cover how uncomfortable she was, and continued surveying the room. A few men did begin to approach her, but they sheared off abruptly as she looked their way. They sensed perhaps that she was a predator and not their prey.

Nothing like this place would be tolerated on Bethany; the mere suggestion that it could be would have people staring at her in disgust. She was very aware that a good Bethanite, man or woman, would never have come in here in the first place. Had one come in by mistake, she would have gasped in shock and run for the spaceport. No proper Bethanite would do what she was doing. That of course was the point of her being here and not one of them. No proper Bethanite *could* do what she did every day. Her work had changed her far more than she would have thought possible. Watching the sex show going on around her proved it more than anything else she could think of.

"Jackson isn't it?" a man said loudly from behind her.

Kate started and cursed under her breath for not paying better attention. The owner of the voice was familiar, and she cursed again. She wanted a merc, but not this one.

"That's right. Do I know you?" she yelled, as she turned toward him. It was the merc from the checkpoint—the one Robert wanted to kick into next week. "Oh it's you. Run out of travellers to hassle, Sergeant Checkpoint?"

He smiled his cold-eyed smile. "Funny. It's Sheldrake... *Captain* Sheldrake to be precise. Where's your boyfriend?"

"Robert? He was only good for one... ride," she said with a wicked grin. "He was just my driver."

"I know," Sheldrake said in amusement. "I checked."

Kate's thoughts raced. "Is that so?" She tilted her head coyly and ran her tongue over her lips. "Find me of interest do you—" Someone bumped into her spilling her drink on the bar. She glanced in annoyance at the heavily muscled boy, and he gave her a cheeky grin.

"Can I get you another?" he said, nodding at the spill and stepping between her and Sheldrake. "Why make do with an old man like him when you can have me?"

Kate looked him up and down dismissively. Nothing of substance there, she decided. "Flit, beefcake. It's thrilling I want, not killing."

He scowled and faded back into the crowd.

Sheldrake was smiling at something he found amusing. He nodded at the barkeep and pointed to his glass. "I asked around about you. It's funny, but no one remembers you up at the station. You just appeared out of nowhere on the shuttle coming down here." The barkeep filled his glass with an amber coloured liquid and moved on. "It's part of my job you know, looking for suspicious persons."

Her eyes narrowed. What was the bastard after? Kate casually eased her hand closer to her pocket. "Is that what you're doing here, you're job?"

Sheldrake saluted her with his glass and took a healthy swallow. "I'm off duty."

Kate didn't believe that for a second. If he really had checked up on her, then he probably knew that Cherry Jackson was an alias. Her false identicard was a good one, but nothing was foolproof. Cherry was booked as having arrived on a civilian liner—*Rising Sun*, but a more thorough investigation would reveal that no one had seen her on that ship. Bribes had been paid to ensure the ship's passenger list contained her name for both her arrival at Tigris, and her departure from it, but a little digging would prove she had never seen the inside of that ship.

She leaned forward until her lips were within kissing distance of Sheldrake's. He didn't pull away. Her hand was firmly around the grip of her pulser. The safety was off and it was aimed at his crotch. If she fired, she would have maybe three or four seconds to lose herself in the panic her shot would cause. Not enough time, but there might not be another option.

"Who else knows of your interest in me?" she said purring the words seductively and letting Cherry have control. She traced a finger over the stubble of his jaw. "Hmmm?"

Sheldrake's smile was forced and his eyes were wide. His pupil's were dilated, but it wasn't the darkened state of the club that caused it. Unlike most of the club, the bar was brightly lit. He had knocked back two large glasses of something alcoholic while with her. Who knew how much he had drunk before that? She was pleased. It made her job that much easier.

Sheldrake's smile strengthened suddenly. With a sinking feeling, Kate turned to find a couple of Sheldrake's friends moving toward her. Both were in uniform, and she doubted they were paying a social call. An ocean of open space suddenly appeared around her as the people propping up the bar hastily got out of ground zero. She released her pulser and reached for her glass. She used the movement to create a little more space between herself and Sheldrake. Not that it would do her any good now, but it made her feel a little more in control of the situation.

"Captain," one merc said upon reaching them. He didn't reach for the pulser on his hip, but it was obvious he wanted to. The other one kept to one side and watched her intently. "This the one?"

Sheldrake nodded. "Yes, sir."

"This girl?" The merc looked at Kate in disbelief. He eyed Sheldrake's empty glass on the bar. "You're positive?"

"Affirmative, sir. She's the one." Sheldrake sounded annoyed at having his word questioned.

"Who the hell are you?" Kate said to the newcomer.

"Major Fairhead's the name. I have some questions for you."

She reluctantly lowered her empty glass to the bar just as one of the barkeeps came by.

"Another?"

Before Kate could answer, Fairhead did it for her. "She won't be having another."

"We don't want any trouble here. Take it outside," the barkeep said.

Fairhead glared and the barkeep backed a step. "Mind your business. I suggest you flit before I take an official interest in you."

The barkeep didn't need telling twice. She flit.

"Well, it was nice meeting you," Kate said taking a step away from the bar.

"You're not going anywhere." Fairhead nodded to his silent companion. "Cover her."

The merc pulled his pistol and aimed it at Kate's chest. The space around them suddenly doubled in size, as her fellow drinkers scattered out of the way. The rest of the club didn't notice. The music pounded, the dancers gyrated, and the lovers still fondled each other to their own internal rhythms unaware that a life was in the balance. She doubted they would have cared if they had known.

Kate didn't quite raise her hands, but she held them away from her sides to prove them empty. "What's going on?"

"You'll find out soon enough," Fairhead said. "Are you carrying?"

"Carrying?"

"I won't ask you again."

Kate saw the decision forming in his eyes. She glanced down to her left and turned that hip toward him. "Left pocket," she said finally dropping Cherry from her voice. "Safety is off."

The warning made him hesitate for a fraction of a second before his hand went into her pants. When he felt the weapon, he pause to look into her eyes. She smiled sweetly at him when he withdrew the pulser and held it up.

"A toy for a child. It doesn't surprise me in the least."

Fool. Kate felt the sneer forming on her lips, but managed to compose herself before Fairhead noticed. Millard's pulser was a fine weapon. Easily good enough to kill these idiots, and it was easy to conceal. The huge pistols the mercs carried might look impressive and have a longer range, but she believed in using the right tool for the right job. If she wanted longer range, she would use a rifle not a pistol.

"Follow me," Fairhead said and turned to leave.

Did she have a choice? One look at the merc gesturing at her with his pistol made it plain she didn't.

Fairhead led Kate out of the club, but instead of escorting her outside and into a vehicle as she had assumed he would, he turned deeper into the hotel. Their destination was the manager's office. Kate entered first, closely followed by Fairhead. Sheldrake and the pistol wielding merc remained outside. The office was empty but for one man sitting behind a desk. He had thinning hair and a skeletally thin face. Kate guessed his age to be in excess of a century. His fever-bright eyes studied her intensely as she walked, making her very uncomfortable. Those eyes burned with something she was tempted to call madness, but he did nothing else to lend credence to her judgement. He didn't speak, and after a moment he returned his attention to the inhaler he was loading. Kate stood before the desk quietly watching as he dosed himself. The fancy gold inhaler he used proclaimed him as a wealthy man, but to her he was still just another doper.

The doper looked up and smiled. "Please take a seat, Miss Richmond."

"Who?" Kate said with a suddenly dry mouth. "My name is Cherry Jackson. I've never heard of—"

"Please credit me with some intelligence. You are Katherine Richmond, late of Bethany's World—a spy and an assassin for hire. I had the Major bring you to me so that I might ask you some questions. My name is Maximilian Skinner… have you heard of me?"

Kate shook her head.

"A pity."

"Why?"

Skinner shrugged. "If you had known of me, you wouldn't have tried lying. My time here is limited. Please do me the courtesy of answering my questions truthfully."

Kate glanced at Fairhead. He was standing to one side covering her with her own pulser. "What do you want to know?"

Skinner nodded in satisfaction. "You were hired to do a job. Is it complete?"

Hired to do a job? No one hired her, she wasn't for rent. "What do you know of why I'm here?" she said trying to hedge until she had more information.

Skinner sighed. "I thought we had an understanding you and I. It seems I was mistaken."

"I understood you well enough, but my… *clients* demand absolute secrecy."

"*I* am your client," Skinner roared completely out of the blue. "I represent President Sanderson you fool. I would have thought that was obvious by now." He gestured at the Major's presence as proof.

Whatever Skinner had doped himself with, it had obviously made him unpredictable. Kate was betting on some kind of mood enhancer, which was bad. The drug would amplify whatever emotions he was feeling, and he was obviously feeling annoyed with her evasions. How much had he taken? She had only see him trigger the inhaler once, so maybe he wouldn't get completely out of control. She could hope.

Kate figuratively crossed her fingers. "But I can't know that for sure. You are not my contact... I don't know you."

Skinner brightened. The change had taken something like a microsecond and Kate shivered at this fresh evidence of his mental state.

"That's very true. I commend you on your discretion, but I must insist you tell me what I want to know."

"Perhaps..." she licked her lips. "Perhaps if you named the target and my contact?"

"Oh very well," Skinner said testily. "If that will get this over with the quicker. Your contact's name is Gerald Whitby, and the target is a man styling himself as General Millard. Satisfied?"

Kate nodded. Gerald Whitby, the head of Whitby Corp. and current holder of the Whitby seat on Bethany's ruling council. She was more than satisfied; she was elated. Her handler would be much more amenable when she told him she knew who was paying him. Maybe she could even get him to give her a discount on the data she needed.

"Very satisfied. Millard is dead, Mister Skinner. I executed him late last night while he slept. Do you want the details?"

Skinner sat back and nodded in satisfaction. "In your opinion, could those he led mount an effective attack on President Sanderson?"

Kate snorted. "Not a chance. They're a bunch of amateurs. They couldn't mount a raid on my piggy-bank let alone something the size of the Assembly Building."

Skinner beamed. "Excellent. What else have you to report?"

Kate scrambled for an answer, and her thoughts flashed to the APCs outside Millard's house. "I saw three brand new APCs but not much else... lost any?"

Skinner glanced at Fairhead.

He nodded and lowered the pulser. "They were stolen not long ago from the port."

"From under his very nose," Skinner said with a glare at Fairhead. "They cost us a lot of money, and Millard took them just like that. He had to have inside help of course. I did send my people to round up the obvious suspects, but none of them talked."

"You knew Millard had them?" Kate said in surprise.

"I knew. I wanted to be sure you did."

Kate nodded, a test then. "You wanted to be sure I'd been to his base."

Skinner nodded and stood. "Well, I think that's about everything."

Kate got ready to lunge for her pulser.

"Not quite," Fairhead said. "If the job is done, why is she still here?"

Skinner raised an eyebrow. "Well?"

Kate shrugged. "My ship doesn't leave until tomorrow. I thought I would take the opportunity to have a little fun."

"Hmmm. Major?"

Fairhead weighed the pulser in his hand and frowned, but after a moment he shrugged. "I see no problem with that. I'll make sure she doesn't leave the hotel, and I'll have a couple of my men escort her to the port when the time comes."

"Excellent again," Skinner said and pulled on the coat he retrieved from the back of his chair. "I have a meeting with the President in an hour, so I'll say my goodbyes."

Kate watched him leave and turned back to Fairhead. "So that's it?"

"That's it."

She eyed the pulser in his hand. "Not going to kill me are you?"

"I'm a soldier not an assassin," Fairhead said looking at her in disgust. "Unlike some, I do not murder unarmed men and women."

"No?" She bet he would like to make an exception in her case. She could see it in his face. "You don't like me much do you?"

"Is it that obvious?"

She ignored his sarcasm. "You don't like Skinner either."

"What's your point?"

"No point. Just wondering why you didn't take out Millard yourself if you knew where he was. You must have known. How else did you know to use the APCs as a test?"

"Of course I knew," Fairhead said angrily. "What do you think my men and I do all day—sit around with our thumbs up our arses?"

Kate didn't get the chance to answer that.

"I didn't want Millard killed; he was serving a useful purpose out there in the jungle. Shit girl, I could have taken out his entire base with a single barrage any time I wanted. Know why I didn't?" He didn't wait for her to answer. "Because I wasn't ready, that's why. Millard was my hothead magnet. Get it?"

Kate nodded. "You were using him to draw out the troublemakers."

"And now Millard's dead and his followers have scattered into hiding. I told that idiot Sanderson to let Millard rally the malcontents behind him—I knew where to find him, but no, he had to go behind my back and get his partner involved. Bloody Whitby. He's so used to knocking off rivals that his first thought was assassination. So he sent you to take care of business."

Kate smiled grimly. "You'll just have to start again. Wait for another leader to arise."

Fairhead glared. "Exactly. That will take months, the riots will get worse, and even more innocent people will die."

"I shouldn't think that would worry you. You'll still get paid. In fact, killing Millard has probably increased the term of your contract."

Fairhead's face reddened and he raised the pulser. "You think because I run a mercenary company I would condone the murder of innocents? You, an assassin, a common murderer, have the utter gall to judge me? Let me tell you something: I spent fifteen years of my life in the army moving from post to post—wherever the Alliance sent me. I've seen people die in every way imaginable, and for every stupid reason under the suns. Dying in a riot, because a stupid man raised tariffs so high that his people would rather sit idle and starve than bother harvesting, has got to be one of the stupidest."

"So leave."

Fairhead sighed and his shoulders slumped. "My contract with Sanderson is airtight. I wish it weren't. If I break the code, the Guild will pillory my company. My men and I would lose everything."

He was right. The Mercenary Guild was well known for lacking a sense of humour. The guild, and the merc companies it served, survived only as long as they obeyed the rules. The guild enforced those rules rigidly. The Alliance tolerated their existence, even welcomed it in some instances, but it wouldn't take much for the Council to review the situation and pull the plug. Broken contracts, war crimes... anything might be enough to set that review process in motion.

Kate nodded thoughtfully. "You're screwed. I'd fire your lawyers if I was you."

Fairhead hung his head for a moment then he shook it and began to laugh. Kate watched his shoulders heaving with the force of his hilarity, and shook her head a little. He had obviously been here way too long. Finally he calmed enough to explain.

"I fired them years ago." He looked at the pulser in his hand then tossed it to Kate. "You wanted some fun you said. Better get to it."

Relief flooded through Kate—enough to make her go weak at the knees. Until that moment, she hadn't dared to believe that he wouldn't kill her. Being armed again left her almost gasping. She quickly flicked on the safety, and dropped the weapon back into her pocket before opening the door to leave. Fairhead had one thing more to say. She paused on the threshold to listen.

"Have your fun, but don't try to leave the hotel. My men will have orders to kill you should you try. I'll have Captain Sheldrake drive you to the port in time to catch your flight up to the station. Understood?"

Kate nodded and left.

Kate's meeting with Skinner focused her attention like nothing else could have. It had the effect of making her even more determined to punish the Whitbys and one in particular. Gerald Whitby, the head of his family and the one ultimately responsible for her father's suicide. Fairhead's threats didn't concern her. She was confident she could find her way out of the hotel when the time came, and she had a way off the planet already arranged, so that was no problem. Tyco had been well paid to wait for her. His little in-system runner would get her to the ship. No, she had no concerns about Fairhead. Her problem was that she was no closer to a location for the President's retreat than she had been. There was no personal information about Sanderson on Tigris' Infonet. None at all, which was a neat trick considering how nosy people were, and how easy Infonet seemed to fill up with such trivia. No doubt he had his security people sanitise it and keep it that way. All she knew was the most basic of information about him. She knew what he looked like, that he had remarried after the death of his first wife, and that he had one grown daughter from that time. She knew more about the members of his cabinet than she did about him.

So, it was back to the club to sniff out a lead.

"Everything all right?" The barkeep yelled over the music. She filled Kate's glass with water and dropped some ice into it. "Didn't expect to see you back so soon. We get soldiers in here a lot, but they don't usually bring their guns with them."

Kate made a face. "Scared me a bit, but everything's fine now."

"Glad to hear it. What did they want?"

"Wanted to check my papers. They said the station had a warrant out for me, but it turned out to be someone else. I wouldn't want to be in her shoes. Soldier Boy was really pissed off when he realised I wasn't the right girl. If I was her, I'd flit quick."

The barkeep nodded in agreement.

Kate noticed a sudden parting in the crowd. Two women entered the club with their arms around each other. They kissed briefly and parted ways. One went off toward the restrooms while the other aimed for the bar. Kate watched as the dancers moved out of the woman's path. It was fascinating to watch. They didn't even stop dancing or fondling each other. They simply drifted out of her way and back again after she went by. Who was this girl to receive that reaction? She had obviously been drinking, though she might not be drunk. She was weaving on her feet a little and was obviously different in some way. Men were tracking her with their eyes, but far from being lecherous, they were full of loathing.

Why?

Kate was hetero of course, but even she could appreciate the woman's beauty. The girl was tall and slender. What she could see of the woman's body looked firm and decently muscled. A woman any man would go for. Why then was she disliked? It was a puzzle, and an interesting one.

"Gimme a drink," the girl said in a hard but sober sounding voice.

The barkeep continued polishing non-existent dust from her bar. "You've had enough. Go home."

"I've as much right to drink here as… as *she* does!"

"She's drinking ice water."

"Really?" the girl said in surprise and turned to look. "That's a first."

"I'm Cherry—" Kate began to say.

"I just *bet* you are," the girl said snorting laughter.

Kate ground her teeth and kept a smile fixed to her face. "And your name is…?"

"Bobbi Lemmington."

The barkeep rolled her eyes at something. Was there something Kate was missing? The barkeep was definitely amused about something.

"Nice to meet you. Am I supposed to know that name?"

"Everyone knows my *father*," Bobbi spat.

"Oh?"

"You really don't know who I am?"

Kate clamped her mouth shut and counted to three under her breath. "I really don't," she said with a grin more like a grimace of pain.

"Good."

Kate's eyes blazed and she clenched a fist out of sight. She turned to the barkeep. "Who is Lemmington?"

The barkeep glanced at Bobbi and then shrugged. "The President's minister of finance."

Jackpot! The minister of finance must know all there is to know about Sanderson and his dealings. He had probably visited the President at his retreat. What chance he had taken his daughter with him? My God, she had hit the mother load. Bobbi Lemmington was her ticket to Sanderson.

"Give me that bottle there, would you?" Kate said.

"This?" the barkeep said pointing to a bottle of faintly green coloured liquid. "It's expensive. The best we have."

"I know. Yantai from Alizon's Chayton valley."

"You *do* know," the barkeep said in surprise and carefully lifted the bottle down.

Kate didn't say anything further. She knew Cherry looked like a dizzy tourist. She was meant to. It was good that people fell for it. She pulled out her credit wand and paid for the bottle. The price was astronomical, she noted gleefully. It was a good thing that her wand came with her forged ID. It was ironic that Whitby's money was paying for this little extra mission.

She put her wand away and turned to Bobbi. "Would you like to come up for a drink?"

The barkeep's eyes widened. Her speculation slowly turned to the mistaken realisation that Cherry was trying to pick up Bobbi. Cherry was hetero just as Kate was, but it served a purpose for the barkeep to assume otherwise.

Kate smiled. "Would you like that?"

Bobbi stared into her eyes and nodded silently.

"Come along then," Kate said and gave the barkeep a challenging look. The woman smiled in amusement and shook her head.

\* \* \*

# 7 ~ Retribution

Once safely up in Kate's room, she let Bobbi wander around the suite while she went to fetch some glasses from the mini-bar. The girl checked out the holocentre and suddenly the entire suite filled with music. Kate found herself tapping a toe and humming in time with it, while she carefully poured two large glasses of Yantai. The girl had good taste in music.

The thing to do with Yantai was to take your time. Pour very slowly, and the sediment at the bottom would stay put allowing the full flavour and strength of the liquor to come through. Poured quickly, it would be sour and undrinkable. She poured very slowly, and then held the glass up to the light. The emerald green colour of the Yantai was pure and free of cloudiness. Perfect. A glass this size would make a Marine try to hump his rifle—not that hard to do actually. She grinned at the image that popped into her head. Two glasses of it, and he would be incapable of anything but snoring.

"Dance with me," Bobbi said coming up behind Kate and draping her arms over her shoulders.

Kate turned holding the drinks. "Drink first, dance later."

Bobbi pouted but she took the offered glass. She took a long swallow and her eyes bugged. She coughed and gasped. "What the hell is it?"

"Yantai." Kate raised her glass and pretended to drink.

"*This* is Yantai? I've had it before, but it didn't have a kick like this." Bobbi took another swallow. "Yum."

Kate raised an amused eyebrow. "You've had it before?"

"Hmmm," Bobbi said whirling around the room. She stopped and swayed a little. "Yours is better." She finished the glass and tossed it over her shoulder where it bounced and rolled under the table. "Let's dance."

"I have to finish my drink. You go ahead and I'll watch."

Bobbi grinned mischievously and began a sensuous dance full of suggestive movements and casual caresses. She turned away and began undressing, making the movements a game. She turned back with her top gaping open and revealing small pert breasts and froze.

Kate smiled.

"What... I don't understand," Bobbi said staring at the pulser in Kate's fist.

Kate gestured with the gun. "Sit and drink this."

"I don't want any more..."

"Take it!"

Bobbi jumped a little and took the glass. She stepped back, not taking her eyes off the pulser, and fumbled for the couch behind her. She sat and took a small sip of Yantai. She coughed and Kate waved away the fumes. The girl smelled like a damn brewery.

"You won't kill me... will you?" Bobbi said trembling with fear.

Kate didn't answer the obvious. The girl wasn't stupid. If she said she would let her go, Bobbi would know she was lying. She sat on the table and prodded the girl between the breasts with the gun.

"Sit back," she said and Bobbi complied. "Drink your Yantai. You said you liked it."

Tears spilled over Bobbi's cheeks as she drank.

"Good girl. Throw the glass—*carefully!*" Bobbi lowered the glass. "Throw it *behind* you, there's a good girl." The glass landed and shattered into a million fragments. "Now then Bobbi Lemmington the finance minister's daughter, I have some questions for you."

"Please... please don't hurt me... I'll do anything. I'll be good," Bobbi said reaching tentatively toward Kate.

"You will tell me everything you know about Sanderson. Where the mountain retreat is, what it's like, how it is guarded. Everything."

"You're going to kill him. Kill Sanderson?"

"That's not your concern."

"I'll help, I will," Bobbi said suddenly excited. "Everyone hates him. With him gone, people will like me again."

Kate shook her head. They wouldn't forget her father's place in Sanderson's schemes that easily. The best thing for her would be to book passage to another world where no one knew her, but that was Bobbi's problem and none of hers.

"I don't need help. What I need is information, and you're going to give it to me. Understand?"

"Yes," Bobbi whispered in fright and began to detail what she knew of the set up at the retreat.

Ten minutes later, Bobbi was flagging as the Yantai had its way with her, but Kate had what she needed. She watched the drowsy woman for a time debating the pros and cons of the situation, but finally she fetched her other pistol. The slug thrower was better for this. Quieter.

Bobbi struggled to rouse herself just as Kate returned. "Can we, you know… can we still do it?" she said ignoring the pistol pointed at her.

Kate goggled at the stupidity of the woman. "I don't swing that way."

"Pity, I do like you…" Bobbi began and fell back unconscious.

Kate sighed and put up her gun. It was a risk, but Bobbi was too stupid to kill. She carried the unconscious girl into the bedroom, and dumped her on the bed before turning to leave.

"Oh hell," she growled and turned back.

She stripped Bobbi out of her clothes and tucked her in properly so that she would have a good sleep. Some people were like puppies. They needed someone to look after them. Bobbi was the biggest puppy she had ever seen. After folding the girl's clothes neatly on a nearby chair, she retrieved her kit and left, illuminating the do not disturb sign as she did so.

The dining room was her destination. She couldn't chance going out the front after her meeting with Fairhead. She had no doubt he meant what he said, but she was hoping he would underestimate her. She was counting on it actually. She rode the elevator down to the ground floor. The receptionist was busy with new guests checking in, and didn't see her walk by.

The dining room was dark with chairs stacked upon the tables. Kate looked around briefly and located the service way. She hurried across the room and ducked through the doors. A short corridor led into the kitchens, which were also dark. At first she couldn't find what she was looking for, but a little scouting revealed another door leading to the stores tucked away behind a huge industrial sized autochef. A service elevator led from the stores deep into the bowels of the hotel. She rode it down three levels to the sub basement and took the opportunity to change into her sneaksuit.

The darkness of the basement was relieved here and there by maintenance lighting, and winking lights on the unfathomable controls of humming machinery. She guessed that most of this junk supplied the hotel with clean water and heating. She recognised some of it as air conditioning units by the ducting attached to it.

The light was at such a low level, she decided to pull on her goggles. Setting them at low power, she explored her surroundings. When Robert first brought her to the Mayflower, he had explained that the two towers, one of which had been converted into the Mayflower Hotel, had been owned by McPherson and Dermot—a now defunct drive coil manufacturer. It had been nothing but trivia at the time, but now it gave her a possible escape route. Both towers were identical in design on the outside (except for those horrendous balconies) and would have similar support needs. She was betting that both towers were linked together by maintenance tunnels.

Kate looked up at the ducting and pipes overhead and grinned. "Damn, I'm good."

She traced the pipes from one of the machines, which registered brightly on thermal imaging. She guessed it was the source for some of the hotel's hot water. She trotted along following a huge pipe that glowed hotly on her display, until she reached a T junction and two huge valves. One pipe was hot, the other cold—the valve was shut. She followed the cold pipe into the darkness.

As she had hoped, the pipe she followed was joined by many other ducts and pipes that eventually led her into a tunnel. If not for the occasional lamp embedded in the floor or wall, she would have been in complete darkness. Her goggles were excellent tech, but they did need something to work with. The pipes were cold and the ambient temperature low. Thermal was useless, and low light amplification nearly so. Nearly was good enough. With her goggles set at maximum amplification, she emerged into a basement similar to the Mayflower's sub basement. The machines were silent, the only sound was her echoing footfalls raising miniature dust storms. No one had been in here for years.

Kate quickly located the elevator, but cursed when she realised it had been shut down. The entire building was on power down. She would need another way up. Scouting around the basement, she found the emergency stairs, but the door was locked. Typical. She supposed some lucky guy had received a bonus for realising the stairway was a security risk for the hotel, but she couldn't work up much enthusiasm for his lucky break. She dropped her kit bag and rummaged through its contents until she found what she needed. Inserting the compad's probe into the card reader, she quickly broke its code and unlocked the door.

She trotted up the stairs the now open door revealed.

The reception area was dusty and abandoned. A dead potted

plant was the only witness to her emergence from the stairwell. She quickly crossed the empty space to the main doors and crouched to check outside. No one was in sight. She could see an occasional vehicle coming or going on the road, and the hotel was clearly visible on the other side, but she couldn't see any of Fairhead's...

Her eyes narrowed. "There you are."

Parked in the hotel's lot were a pair of hoverjeeps. They were sitting hull down on their skirts, but she knew they could be quickly powered up for a chase. She didn't plan on giving them one and had no intention of going near the hotel. She broke the glass in the door and slipped out into the night.

Finding a vehicle was easy. A woman alone at night, and looking like Cherry did, attracted the wrong sort quite easily. She had only been walking along a side street for a couple of minutes when a car pulled up. It was wheeled, which might be important, and quite new, which wasn't. It didn't have four wheel drive, and that was annoying, but the guy leering out the window at her clinched it. She didn't like him. She quickly lowered the zip on her sneaksuit.

"Hi," Kate said leaning down to give him a nice view down her top. "Can I have a lift?"

He grinned. "Sure you can, sweetness. Where you heading?"

She let her tongue peep out between her lips and smiled coyly. "Wherever you are."

"Hop in."

Kate rounded the car, zipping herself up again in the process, and climbed in beside him. She threw her kit bag on the backseat using the movement to cover her retrieval of her pulser. She pushed it between her knees and clamped it there out of sight. She watched the buildings going by for a few minutes to make sure they weren't heading back toward the hotel. The Assembly Building went by on the left, and she relaxed a little more. They were heading the right way.

The driver eyed her and smiled. "What's your name?"

"Does it matter?"

"Runaway huh?"

Kate shrugged.

"How old are you?"

"How old do I look?"

He inspected her like a piece of merchandise. "Sixteen, maybe seventeen."

Kate smiled, but her skin was crawling. He was some kind of pimp, not that he would name himself as one. He probably called himself a Human resources consultant or something similar. It didn't matter what he called it. She knew what he was, and what he was after.

"I'm old enough to know what I want and how to get it."

He leered at her. "Yeah? Got any money?"

"Why?"

"Want to make some? I know some people."

She was sure he did. "Yeah? What kind of people?"

"People who won't ask questions, people who pay well. You interested?"

She was sure now. He was a procurer… probably a kiddie fiddler himself. He had that look. She glanced outside to find the street deserted, and night coming on fast. She still had an hour or two before curfew, but she didn't plan on cutting it too fine. She wanted out of the city as soon as possible.

Kate summoned a smile. "Pull over."

"Why?"

"I want to show you something," she said, playing with her zipper. "Pull over."

He grinned and pulled over to the curb. He turned toward her in time to see her raise the pulser. "Don't—"

She shot him in the face.

"Damn kiddie fiddler," Kate said with loathing. There was nothing worse in her book. "I should have burned your balls off, but lucky for you I have places to be." She checked outside, and then looked back at the still smoking corpse. "It's the trunk for you."

Minutes later, Kate was on the road heading for the Coyne Mountains with a dead kiddie fiddler in the back, and humming along to a popular tune blaring from her car's speakers.

Sanderson glared at his daughter over the breakfast table.

"Where have you been?"

"Oh daddy, can't I have any fun? I went to a party," Bobbi said.

"What party? Where? You've been gone two days and nights. The security people said you gave them the slip again. I can't have that, Bobbi. I know it's hard, but I have enemies."

"Yes, daddy," Bobbi sighed.

"There's a good girl. Will you promise not to escape again?"

"All right," Bobbi said with a put upon sigh, and sat down to breakfast with him. "Where's Lynn?" she asked stirring the food around the plate. She didn't feel like eating now.

"I've asked you, and asked you, and *asked you* not to call your mother—"

"*Step* mother," Bobbi said hotly.

"She's your mother now. You know she doesn't like being called

Lynn."

"All right. Where is Gwen-do-*lynn* then?"

Sanderson glared, but gave up the attempt to discipline her. "She's not feeling well. She won't be joining us today."

*Oh dear, what a shame!*

"Oh."

Bobbi stirred her food around the plate and thought about Cherry. It had been a shock awakening naked in a strange bed with no idea how she'd gotten there. She was sure she had dreamed it all at first, but then she realised she could never have dreamed up someone like Cherry. She didn't remember very much about that night, but what she did remember scared her to death. Cherry had asked lots of questions at gunpoint, and Bobbi had answered, but she couldn't quite remember what the answers had been. She prayed she hadn't told Cherry the truth about Millard and that it was she and not him leading the fight against her father. She had realised early on that people needed someone to lead them, but that they would never take orders from her. So she had searched for a front man. Millard was that man. He was nothing more than that. Why would he go behind her back and hire an assassin? It was too soon for that. Sure they had discussed it, but they needed more of their own people in high places before taking that step. What was that idiot playing at? Cherry could have killed her and ruined everything!

Bobbi stirred her food, frowning thoughtfully. She had been quietly working toward her father's removal from office for some time now. Someone had to do it. Why not the person who knew his evil the best? She knew every dirty little secret he had, but the one that had hurt her the most was her mother's murder. She could have forgiven him almost anything, but not that. Her father had killed her mother, killed her because she threatened to leave him and take Bobbi with her. It made her strong in her hate.

Was Millard playing his own game now? Maybe. Did he think he could overthrow her father without her support? If he did he was a fool... scratch that, he was a fool and she knew it, but he had always been her fool to use. Maybe his ambitions had grown. Did he think he could actually pull it off without her, maybe even run for election afterwards? It had long been her intention to do something similar. If her plan succeeded, she would have the popular support to win a fair election. With Cherry out there somewhere, she needed to make some adjustments. Was there anything she could do to make Cherry's job easier?

"Are you driving to the capital today?" Bobbi asked.

"I'll fly. Things are still unsettled. By air is safer. Why?"

Bobbi shrugged. "I was going to fly out to the lake."

"There's a perfectly good pool here."

"It's not the same," she snapped. "Mother used to—"

"I know she used to take you up there," Sanderson said not looking up from the roll he was buttering. "But it's dangerous on your own."

"I could take one of your men."

"Three."

"Two," she replied quickly.

"Done." Sanderson grinned. "But no skinny dipping. They're only men after all."

"But that's the best part," Bobbi said laying it on, but she was pleased. She had no doubt Cherry would thank her for making him go by car.

"Bathing suit or you don't go. I'll drop you on the way."

"But..."

"Yes?"

"Nothing," Bobbi said hiding her anger at being thwarted. It would do no good. It never did. "When are you leaving?"

"An hour or so."

"Fine, I'll get my stuff," she said leaving the table.

"What about my kiss?"

Bobbi stopped by the door and walked back to him. Leaning toward him, she kissed him. "Love you, daddy."

"I love you too, sweetheart," Sanderson said pleased. "My darling girl all grown up." He patted her behind. "Off you go then."

Bobbi smiled tightly and left to get her swimsuit and a towel. *Damn him!*

\* \* \*


Damn him! A day and night stuck in a bloody tree, and nothing. Not one glimpse of the bastard.

Kate shifted a little trying to ease the ache in her hipbones. Laying face down on a knobbly branch was damn painful after a single hour; after twenty-four, her body was screaming for relief. She endured with the use of discipline learned early in her training, and meditation she had learned later during hurry up and wait missions like this.

*Accept the pain. It is nothing. Be one with it. Take it into the centre of your being and you will control it, and not it you.*

It did work... usually, but she had never needed to do it for this long a time. She had a fierce headache and her eyes were burning with tiredness. She shook her head at the double image that had begun plaguing her last night. She squeezed her eyes shut then opened them and wiped away the stinging tears with gloveless fingers.

That was better.

Kate settled down again. "Oh thank God," she whispered as the door opened and a security detachment exited.

A man she recognised as Sanderson followed the detachment. She took a breath and flicked off the safety. The shot was long—right on the limit of her rifle's killing range. It was exactly eleven hundred metres as the dart flies.

*Zzzzzing!*

The dart flew.

\* \* \*

The dart flew toward its target, but the range was long. As it slowed to subsonic speed, it began to tumble. When it struck, it did horrendous damage as it buzsawed through Sanderson.

Bobbi screamed in shock as her father's chest blew apart and his body fell. It was horrible and shocking, and her scream seemed to echo in the air. People were running and shouting, some at her, while others screamed into their comm units to get a doctor.

No doctor was good enough to fix the hole in her father's chest. If he'd ever had a heart, he didn't now. Bobbi stared into the trees and felt Cherry watching her. Was she the next target, had Millard betrayed her? She was trembling so badly that Cherry could probably see it. She couldn't run and she couldn't hide; it was much too late for that. She did the only thing left. She forced herself to smile and mouthed the words silently.

"Thank you."

\* \* \*

Kate cursed her foolishness. Why hadn't she killed the little bitch?

Bobbi wasn't the finance minister's daughter. She was Sanderson's mistress or something. The news broadcast said Sanderson was in seclusion from his government, from everyone in fact. That being the case, Bobbi should not be here. First Whitby uses her to clear the way for his dealings with Sanderson, and now this little bitch had pulled the same stunt! What was it about Bobbi that had gulled her? Was it the lost puppy look she had given her when they first met? It didn't matter.

She sighted on Bobbi and took a steadying breath…

Bobbi looked up and right at her. Right at her and said thank you. Kate could read lips well enough to see the exaggerated words on Bobbi's. It was definitely thank you.

Her finger tightened…

She flicked the safety on. "You're welcome kid."

Kate looked down at the ground far below, and groaned. She would have to be gone quickly now. Aching as she was, a long hike back to her car was not appealing. She took one last look at Bobbi through her range finder this time, and smiled before scrambling down.

* * *

# Part II

# 8 ~ Testing

Gina stepped out of the transport tube and into Alliance HQ proper. She didn't class the landing pad and travel tube as part of HQ of course. As soon as she crossed the yellow line, she felt herself and her duffel lighten under Luna's one-sixth gravity. Taking no notice of the strange looks she received, she braced to attention and saluted a huge depiction of the Alliance flag on the wall opposite. She had nothing but contempt for those who took for granted the flag and what it stood for. It was shocking, but many of HQ's personnel were civs. There were plenty of men and women walking by in uniform, but the majority by far were civs in their ridiculous fashions that tried to blind the eye. If she ran this place, everyone would be in uniform—no exceptions.

She looked around expecting to be challenged, but security was very lax. She was standing in the hub of the Alliance military, and no one cared to find out if she belonged here! All orders flowed from here, and all reports flowed back. What better place was there for a spy to snoop around? Her eyes locked on a civ across the way. He was lounging against the wall looking directly at her. He was a broad shouldered black man, a little on the short side for her taste, but he had a presence that caught and held the eye. What he was supposed to be doing she couldn't fathom. Didn't he have anything better to do than stare at her?

Gina shook her head at her preoccupation and started walking. It wasn't hard to find her way. Just a short distance along the concourse, she found a terminal with a notice beside it telling her to insert her orders for directions. This she did and received a detailed display of the entire base with a red line indicating the route she should take. She memorised the route and keyed no when asked if she wanted a printout. Hefting her duffel, she made her way to the training centre.

Gina managed to squeeze into an overfull elevator car. She had to hug her duffel tight to her chest to let the doors close. Someone behind her had dragon breath and she tried not to breathe. The car dropped six levels before the doors opened to allow her to stagger out onto the station's platform. There were many like it servicing bases and manufactories all over Luna, most of which were subsurface like HQ itself. Others, automated defences and tracking facilities for the most part, remained above ground uncaring of the intense solar radiation that bathed the surface.

Gina made her way along the busy platform hoping to find a spare seat, but before she could do so, a rush of wind announced the imminent arrival of the train. She stopped and waited with the other expectant looking pedestrians.

The train slammed into the station chasing its own wavefront of displaced air down the tunnel. It was a sleek looking bullet-shaped power car towing a dozen passenger cars full of people in its wake. It was moving so fast, she wondered if it would stop or blow on through the station. She checked her wristcomp, but she had plenty of time. If not this train, then the next would see her to her destination with time to spare.

She needn't have worried. The automated train sensed the braking zone, and with a deep thrumming noise reversed its maglev propulsion system. With a rapidity that still surprised her after all these years, the train slowed to a halt. As luck would have it, a door opened right in front of her. Two quick steps was all she needed to claim her LZ—the very last empty seat in the car. By the time she had settled her duffel between her feet, the car was filled to capacity with disgruntled-looking people standing along the aisles. The train pulled smoothly out of the station.

"First time, Lieutenant?"

Gina turned to find herself sitting next to a man in Fleet uniform—a lieutenant commander. Protocol would normally have her bracing to attention and saluting him, but not on an overcrowded train like this. Common sense did have its place. HQ was full of officers of all ranks and branches of the service. If they went around saluting each other all the time, they would never get any work done.

"Sorry, sir?" Gina said belatedly realising she had been woolgathering.

"I said is this your first time here?"

"On Luna, yes, sir. I've been to Earth a couple of times though—just to say I've been there… if you know what I mean?"

He nodded. "Everyone should visit at least once. Just spent some R and R there myself as a matter of fact. Place called Grand Canyon. Ever heard of it?"

"North America?"

"Right. Beautiful place, but the canyon isn't the biggest I've ever seen. Ever been to Garnet?"

"Twice, not sightseeing though."

He understood. Both times had been training missions. Stein had led the aggressor force of which her squad had been a small part. She remembered Garnet from the point of view of her discomfort. The air was breathable, but prolonged exposure was unhealthy. The soil and air were laced with heavy elements that made the use of environment suits and canned air essential. The natives could risk more exposure—they were descended from generations of people that had slowly adapted to the environment, but even they retreated to their domes after a few hours.

"My ship was stationed there a couple of years ago. There are some serious mountains and canyons to see. They have these crystal spires taller than the tallest buildings in Chicago… that's a city on Earth."

"I know," Gina said and smiled at his condescending tone.

"Oh, sorry."

She shrugged the apology away. There were so many worlds and cities that Chicago could have been literally anywhere in the Human sector.

"So, what are you doing here?"

"Redeployment," he said with a grimace. "I'm on the beach for the next two years, filing reports and making coffee for the admiral. Apparently it will be good for me." He rolled his eyes and Gina grinned. "I guess I do need some admin under my belt. Don't want to be a commander all my life."

Gina nodded. Fleet took the well-rounded education of its officers seriously. If he wanted his own ship, he would have to 'do his time' in administration. If it had to be done, what better place than here at the hub of the Alliance?

The train slowed abruptly as it approached a station. She checked its name automatically, but she knew there were two more stops before hers. Her chatty companion however, rose to his feet.

"This is mine," he said. "Maybe I'll see you around."

Gina doubted it. "Nice to have met you, sir."

He nodded and worked his way to the door and onto the platform. As the train pulled away, she realised she hadn't even asked his name. She shrugged. It wasn't as if a grunt like her would ever move in the same circles as a future Fleet Captain.

When her stop arrived, Gina quickly exited the train and made her way along the platform. It was busy with people coming and going. She wove her way between civilians and military alike, wondering where they were all going. Didn't they have work? She wasn't used to such large crowds. It reminded her of what she had found on Earth, and she didn't like it. Grace would have loved it though. She had always preferred big cities over provincial ones like Thurston.

Gina shied away from thoughts of her dead friend and unerringly chose the right exit from the station. Perhaps ten minutes of walking saw her turning a last corner toward her destination. She stopped in surprise. Here, finally were guards, and what guards! vipers. There was no mistaking those black uniforms. What were vipers doing guarding a mere hatch?

She stepped up to the guard on the left and offered him her orders. He inserted the card into his reader without comment, and used it to scan her simcode for a match. While he verified her identity, she amused herself by trying to examine the pistol on his hip. Both vipers wore heavy plasma pistols with a modified grip. Without being obvious, she tried to see the palms of their right hands. She wasn't very successful, but thought she caught a glimpse of the gold contacts in one man's palm. Vipers were all right handed so that special weaponry could receive targeting information through the weapon's data bus in their hands.

"You're early, Lieutenant, but that's okay." He handed back her orders and palmed the sensor on the wall. The hatch slid open. "Good luck, sir."

"Thank you, Sergeant…?" she said waiting for a name, but both men just looked at her in silence. "Thanks."

Gina stepped through the hatch. It slid shut and locked behind her.

The corridor was straight without hatches or other corridors to adjoin it. It was silent and empty. She marched at a brisk pace, but was tempted to lope along in the low gravity. It was something of a treat moving about like this. She felt like a little girl at a play centre. She resisted the impulse with images going through her mind of security watching and laughing at her antics… not that there appeared to be any. Ships always maintained one standard gravity of course, and most Human inhabited worlds were close to that of Earth for obvious reasons. Rarely were heavy grav worlds settled, though two did come to mind. Surprisingly, low grav worlds were also shunned. The lowest she had ever heard of was Alizon at 0.85g, but it was such a lovely world that she didn't blame the colonists for settling there.

She reached the end of the corridor and found another pair of vipers barring her progress. She approved of the security measure—HQ could do with more security in her opinion, but this was a little over the top surely? vipers were too rare for hatch guarding. The viper, a woman this time, handed her orders back after verifying them and opened the hatch.

Gina stepped through and it locked behind her. She glanced around at the waiting area. It was populated with red plastic chairs standing in neat and precise rows—all of them vacant, and a reception desk held down by another viper—an officer this time.

Gina crossed to the desk and came to attention. "Lieutenant Fuentez, reporting as ordered, ma'am." She offered her orders one last time.

"Lieutenant Hymas, Lieutenant. No need for that." Hymas waved away the card. "You wouldn't be here if you weren't supposed to be."

"Yes, ma'am. Sorry, ma'am," Gina said replacing her card in her top pocket and securing the flap.

"I note your campaign ribbons, Lieutenant. You've seen action on most of the Border Worlds."

"Yes, ma'am, but more are colonised each year... or so it seems to me."

Hymas tilted her head and looked thoughtful. "Do you agree with Alliance policy regarding those worlds?"

That wasn't a frivolous question. Hymas was looking at Gina intently—evaluating her. "I do not make policy, ma'am. I *enforce* it."

A small smile flickered into being on Hymas' face. "A nice safe answer, Fuentez, but I want your opinion."

"My opinion, ma'am? My opinion is that the bigger we are, the safer we are. Those worlds provide a buffer between the core worlds and the Merkiaari."

Hymas nodded without revealing her opinion of that. "Losses would be heavy."

Gina nodded once, firmly. "But not as heavy as allowing a Merki incursion into the core of the Alliance. I'm not suggesting we abandon them, ma'am. We would fight as hard for the Border Worlds as for... *Thorfinni* let's say, but the Border Worlds are less densely populated. They're an ideal battleground."

"Well reasoned," Hymas said and keyed her terminal to life.

"Walk to your left and enter the first door on the right."

Gina braced to attention and saluted before moving to the room she had been ordered to enter. Inside, she found a small room with one chair, a table with a standard terminal, a locker, and a rack. She opened the locker and stowed her gear. On the table beside the terminal was a set of instructions to follow. The first part told her the room was hers for the duration of the test; the last part ordered her to activate the terminal and answer the questions.

She sat before the terminal and switched on. The usual questions appeared. Name, rank, and serial number all went into the machine, and the screen cleared to display the questionnaire. She scanned the questions and frowned. They didn't appear to have any relevance to weapons testing. Maybe she and Stein had it wrong. Maybe they were testing *her* for some reason. She didn't like being kept in the dark, but she obeyed orders and began answering the questions.

Orders were orders—period.

\* \* \*

Private First Class Kate Richmond, 2nd Airborne Rangers, was not a happy woman. Correction, she was steaming mad. Why did she have to choose that shuttle? Hundreds arrived and departed from Earth every day, yet she had chosen one that happened to be carrying Captains Hiller and Whitby.

*Whitby!*

It was beyond galling having a Whitby ordering her around, and Hiller seemed cut of the same cloth. Both captains seem to assume it was the duty of a lowly PFC to wait on them, and tag along behind them, like some kind of personal pet. She couldn't tell them her real rank. She certainly couldn't tell them that she was an undercover operative of ISS. The uniform she wore, though hers, hadn't been worn for five years or more. She had last worn it to her ISS recruitment briefing, and not one day since. No, she couldn't tell them why she was here. She had to take whatever they dished out, but damn it was hard.

Kate surreptitiously checked her wrist comp and scowled at what it revealed. Her orders were specific. She was to report to the training centre on her arrival at Alliance HQ no later than zero-seven-hundred on the 26th. It was zero-nine-hundred now, and neither captain appeared in any way interested in reporting in.

"Captains, with respect, I must insist that we report in."

"Insist?" Captain Whitby said, turning to confront her. "Since when does a private insist on anything? If you think that being off

Bethany gives you leave to take liberties with me, think again. I am a Whitby, and you had better remember it."

Whitby's face was within centimetres of Kate's during the harangue. It was all she could do to prevent herself from killing him. One blow to the larynx and there would be no more high and mighty Captain Whitby. Did he know about the loss of his family's operation on Tigris yet? She hoped they all choked on that bit of news.

"Don't ever presume to disapprove of me or my actions," Whitby was saying oblivious to her thoughts and growing anger. "Now come along. I want to have a late breakfast before going over to the training centre."

The pompous arse! She had killed people for less cause than he had just given her. She gritted her teeth and swallowed her anger. How she wished she had her gear with her. But then, if she had brought it along, all hell would have broken loose. Weapons were frowned upon within the confines of Alliance HQ.

Kate followed along behind Hiller who had remained silent throughout the exchange. She wasn't surprised by his lack of support. Although his family ranked among the Ten, it was of lesser importance than the Whitbys. Whitby was a name well known on Bethany for power and prestige. Money most definitely talked, and the Whitbys had plenty. The Whitby name was preeminent among the families originally settling Bethany. There were very few people, if any, willing to cross them and that included the Hillers. Still, Kate was considering just that as they moved through the crowded concourse toward one of the finer eating establishments on Luna.

Whitby and his ilk made her want to puke. He had the money, so he had the rank; it was as simple as that. That he couldn't find his arse with both hands never entered into the equation. God help Bethany and the Alliance if he was ever in command during a Merki incursion. She knew his type well. There were many like him on Bethany. Know-nothings—powerful know-nothings who acted as they pleased believing themselves to be the lords of creation. Although few Alliance worlds truly had an aristocracy any longer, Bethany was by far the worst of those that did.

As a lowlife commoner, Kate had a surprising amount of freedom thanks to ISS and the military before that. She was happy with her life mostly, and did not want to change it by falling foul of these arrogant fools. They of course had more pressing worries to concern them than a lippy PFC. She shuddered; not for her the worry of political backstabbing or the sucking up necessary to get ahead at the rarefied heights of Bethany's government. She had no responsibilities except to herself and the mission.

That's how it would stay until she found Paul again.

Her last mission on Tigris had gone a fair way toward helping her with that. Her contact had been pleased with her handling of Millard, and had not connected her with Sanderson's assassination. He had kept his end of the deal by finding some information that pointed off-world as a probable location for her brother. That didn't surprise her; she had searched everywhere on Bethany for him without success. No, she had known that if he lived he must be off-world; but where exactly? Without solid leads she could search for her entire lifetime and never find him. That's why the data her contact had turned up was so exciting. It pointed to some kind of deal between her brother and the Baxters. Unbelievable at first glance—it was the Baxters who had ruined her father—but maybe this deal with them was Paul's way to take back all they had stolen.

Kate's gaze swept the concourse and locked onto a man like a laser turret onto a Merki ship. She was always surveying her surroundings, it was a good habit in her line of work, but this time she caught sight of someone who should not have been there. The broad shouldered black man was hanging around again. She first saw him upon her arrival, hanging around the embarkation lounge, but had thought nothing of it then. He had been just one of many people waiting for friends to arrive. Now though, his presence set alarms ringing. He had shown up too many times on this ill-advised tour of Alliance HQ for it to be a coincidence.

The man stared directly into her eyes, making her bristle and check her stride, and shook his head. He looked meaningfully at his wristcomp, and she flushed in anger. He knew she should be elsewhere and was chiding her for her lateness. How did he know who she was, and how dared he look at her like that? If she hadn't been in the midst of a crowd, he wouldn't look so condescending. He nodded up the concourse and she flicked a glance that way. The toads were continuing on their tour oblivious to the fact she had stopped.

*Good enough.*

Kate hefted her kit and lost herself in the crowd before the toads saw her. She knew the route to the training centre. She had been there before when her old captain recruited her. Captain Newell hadn't been too bad for an officer. He had seen the killer in her and nurtured it by pushing her to try for her marksman's certificate, which had inevitably led to other training. She had enjoyed learning so many ways to practice her craft.

Kate didn't need a weapon to do her job, but she much preferred the HTR to any other weapon. The Heavy Tactical Rifle was a precision railgun with a range close to a klick and a half. What she liked about it was its untraceability and the terror it inflicted on those near the target. Unlike every plasma weapon ever produced, railguns and other projectile weapons did not give away their presence with a glaring display of released energy. Being tracked by the simple expedient of following an energy pulse by eye, wasn't something she ever wanted to deal with. Those who thought projectile weapons outdated and crude were fools—dead fools quite often.

She turned down an empty corridor and used the low gravity to make up some time. At least she was on the right level. Loping along, she soon reached the hatch at the end, but she skidded to a halt well short of it when she saw the black uniformed sergeants guarding it.

Her mouth went dry and her heart raced at the sight of the cyborgs. Her trigger finger twitched. She fought her fear not realising that the snarl on her face had been seen. Cyborgs were not Human, they were machines that looked like people, they were dangerous and should be dismantled, they let Bethany's people die during the Merki War. It didn't matter that vipers liberated her world in the end, it didn't matter that without them the Alliance would likely have been scorched beyond recovery, it didn't matter—

Kate took a deep steadying breath and expelled it. Another, and calm began to return. Her childhood lessons on Bethany whispered in her mind of terror and destruction, but she throttled the fear with the simple expedient of overwhelming it with anger. Anger was good; she was intimately familiar with anger. It overwhelmed her fear. She was no child to feel threatened by the bogeyman!

"Orders," one of the cyborgs growled with his right hand upon his pulser.

Kate approached warily. Her body was loose, prepared to kill if the need arose. If the cyborgs attacked, as everyone on Bethany said was certain sure, she would sell her life dearly. She didn't like the knowledge that she was at this thing's mercy. People were at her mercy, not the other way around. It upset her view of the universe knowing these things existed and that they were infinitely more deadly than she.

The cyborg inserted Kate's card into its reader and quickly scanned her simcode. He scowled at the result the reader displayed. "You're late, Private."

"And?" Kate said with eyes tracking from one cyborg to the other.

"And you had better get in there."

The cyborg flicked the card toward her making her grab for it. She caught it against her chest. The hatch slid open and she edged sideways through it keeping the machines in sight every second. The hatch slid shut and locked, but she didn't take chances. She backed for a hundred metres before loping down the corridor. When the second hatch came into sight with its guards, she was ready and more in control of herself.

"You're late," the female looking thing said handing her card back.

Kate didn't answer.

The thing looked at Kate strangely for a moment before its eyes flicked to her uniform. Kate saw recognition flash into its eyes when it saw the ranger patch on her shoulder and linked it to Bethany. The thing's face turned to stone, and its right hand slapped the hatch's sensor... hard.

The hatch slid open, and again Kate backed through. She waited for it to close and lock before turning her attention upon the waiting room. She knew this place of old, but never had she seen the corridors adjoining it so full of people.

Soldiers in battle dress were entering and exiting the rooms seemingly at random. Battle dress was pretty much standard within the Alliance. It was composed of camouflage tunic and trousers with the lower legs bloused and tucked into boot tops as per regulations. Kate felt over dressed in her Class-A uniform (full dress uniform including medals) and couldn't wait to get into her own battle dress so that she might blend in more readily. She was feeling exposed, not good for any ISS agent, and certainly not good for Kate Richmond.

"Planning on standing there all day?"

Kate's eyes flew to the officer sitting behind the desk. She paled when she realised the lieutenant was another of the machines. How many were running loose in this place?

"Is this how you report to a superior officer, Private?"

Kate had no choice, but it was galling. She saluted and walked the last few steps to stand at attention before the desk. "PFC Richmond, reporting as ordered."

"You're late. Sightseeing were you?"

Kate clenched a fist. "Not willingly."

"I know about the two cretins you were with, Richmond. They have no call on you. You, *and* both of them, had orders to report here at oh-seven-hundred. You should have informed them of the fact and then reported here."

Kate clamped her lips shut. How dare this thing, this *machine*, berate her? She was not in the wrong... well all right, she was, but only a little bit! She released her pent breath and acknowledged the rebuke with a nod. Though annoying, it was just.

"I should have, but they outrank me."

The lieutenant pursed her lips then said, "For the record, and for the duration of your testing, you have no superiors not wearing viper uniform. Understood?"

Kate blinked in confusion. "No. I see many who outrank me here."

"Wrong. All are of equal rank while undergoing the testing. You will respect all those here, but orders will come only from those authorised to give them, namely viper personnel."

"Yes, ma'am," she said doubtfully.

"My name is Lieutenant Hymas, and these are the rules. Regardless of your prejudices, you *will* address me with respect—by rank or by the use of, sir or ma'am. Any other form of derogatory address to any viper will see you out of here *and* the service." Hymas' eyes flashed. "I *guarantee* it."

"I *am* from Bethany's World, ma'am, but I'm somewhat different to most living there."

"I know," Hymas said tapping her computer's display meaningfully. "It's lucky for you in a way. In my opinion it will be a miracle if any from Bethany pass this testing. Other worlds are more tolerant of differences. That could be important later."

"How so, ma'am?"

"I can't say, and you are late. Your room is already taken. I have just assigned one of the spares to you. Walk to your left and enter room three-seventeen. You have some catching up to do. I suggest you get on with it."

Kate saluted in haste and struggled through the crowded corridor to her room. Inside was utilitarian, but clean. She rather liked the beige colour of her table and chair. Firstly, she stowed her kit and changed into battle dress. Feeling better, she switched on her terminal and read the instructions. Moments later she was typing like a demon intent on proving to that damn... *woman* that she could ace any damn test a cyborg could think up.

\* \* \*

"What do you think of her, Marion?" Master Sergeant Stone said buttoning his uniform and discarding the garish civ clothing he had worn on his tour of the concourse.

"I think she's a bigoted snot. A damn dangerous one," Lieutenant Hymas said, watching the retreating figure of PFC Richmond.

"Psychotic?"

"Beyond a doubt. She has a killer's eyes. She's not viper material, Ken. No one from Bethany is."

"I don't know about that. I thought she was going to kill those two Captains. They were leading her around like a damn tourist, and she was getting madder than hell. Her eyes were like laser turrets when she saw me for the third time. Damn glad she didn't have her gear with her... not that she needs it."

"She's unenhanced, Ken. You have nothing to worry about—not yet at least. If I had my way she would be packed off to the psychs right now."

"But you don't," Colonel Flowers said as he rounded the corner. "The General was specific and so are our requirements. She fits the profile, as do all the others here. We test the most likely candidates first, then the second best, then the third and so on until we have what we need."

"Begging your pardon, Colonel," Stone said. "But you know that method is as likely as any other to give us washouts. I've seen it and so have the both of you."

Flowers nodded. "True, but it's as good a way as any. Even if we had green recruits that fit the profile, which we don't, they would take too long to train. You both know what's required to survive enhancement. Finding recruits that can survive the process is hard enough. Finding some with the discipline and the mental strength to live with the results has proven almost impossible."

Stone nodded reluctantly. "Marian thinks our little secret agent is a psycho."

Flowers frowned and turned to Hymas. "A hunch or your expert medical opinion?"

"A little of both. She hates any kind of command authority, and tolerates it only to stay in the job. She will always find a way to avoid responsibilities, usually by picking a fight and getting busted. Her record is full of disciplinary offences. She's been demoted five times from staff sergeant, three from corporal and get this: *eight* times recommended for promotion to master sergeant, all denied. They picked her for the ISS after she nearly killed her commanding officer with her bare hands. What does that say to you?"

Flowers smiled crookedly. "It says we have another Ken Stone on our hands."

Stone spluttered. "That's not fair, I didn't kill you did I? Besides, I was only a kid back then. Two hundred and thirty years mellows a guy."

"We don't have two hundred and thirty years, Ken. We barely have five if the General is right."

"Always is," Stone said gloomily. "That's a damn annoying habit he's got there."

Hymas glared in frustration. "Enhancing that girl, assuming she passes her psych eval, which I doubt she can, is a *mistake!* She's too damn dangerous."

"vipers are dangerous," Flowers said coldly. "We're meant to be dangerous. You know how the process changes us. Some mellow while others become more aggressive, and it's a tossup which."

"If Richmond gets any more aggressive than she is now, we'll need a damn sight more than ten units to stop her."

"Make sure it doesn't happen."

"I'll try—" Hymas began to say.

"Don't try, *do it,*" Flowers snapped before stalking away.

Hymas stared at her Colonel's back in hurt.

Stone could read her thoughts clearly, and the pain on her face. "Don't mind him, Marian. He took the failure of Robbins hard. He doesn't want a repeat performance that's all."

"We all liked Robbins. Why does he feel it more than the rest of us?"

His jaw dropped. He couldn't believe she had said that. "Might be something to do with him being the one to take Robbins down."

"Yeah, might be," Hymas said not hearing his sarcasm.

\* \* \*

# 9 ~ Harsh Measures

In reality, Gina was lying in a simulator couch, but to her the fight she was engaged in was brutally real.

"…will take care of green sector."

"Copy," Gina said automatically as she studied the map displayed by her HUD.

Like all simulations, this one left her with a vague sense of unreality not easy to pin down. It was just a feeling—a kind of sixth sense that whispered in the back of her mind that all this was illusion. Sight, sound, smell, and touch were all handled by the sim. If she had occasion to eat, she was sure that taste would be also. The feeling of unreality wasn't a physical thing—how could it be when the sim was entirely virtual? Nor was it due to the knowledge that her two companions were dead these many weeks on Thurston. Grace and Dan had been plucked from her memory and used to bring the simulation to life. Although she knew it was a sim and that her companions were dead, still they affected her as if they lived. She knew the sim made it happen, knew she had no choice but to feel this way, but it made no difference. She acted as if they lived, and the computer constructs did too. When she had a moment to really think, something she wasn't given much time to do incidentally, she was angry at the violation bringing forth her friends represented, but it also gave her an opportunity to see them one last time.

"Eagle Two, Eagle One," she said over her comm.

"Eagle Two, what's up?" Grace said.

Gina smiled at hearing the well remembered voice. "We have a little job to do, Grace."

"Bring 'em on."

"We have Merki troopers in our sector." She tapped a control on her wristcomp to highlight green sector on all their HUD maps. "We flush them out."

"How many?" Pags asked.

"Only three."

"Three?" Grace said. "You're sure?"

She was about to nod but hesitated. She had only been taking these tests for a week, but already she knew Stone could be sneaky. "That's what the intelligence suggests, but we take nothing for granted. We clear our streets and await orders."

"Copy," Pags said.

"Copy that, I'll take point," Grace said.

"Not this time Grace," Gina said quietly. "I'll take it."

"But—"

"That's an order, Eagle Two."

"Copy," Grace said reluctantly.

It was uncanny how closely the constructs' reactions mirrored the real Dan and Grace. It was only Gina's knowledge that they were in the simulator room that told her they weren't real people.

Gina moved out using her sensors to sweep ahead and to the sides. The first trooper opened fire the instant her sensors picked him up. She was diving to the left even as the searing bolt of plasma came her way. It missed by bare millimetres. So close was it, the nanocoat of her armour reacted as if taking a hit. It took mere nanoseconds for her armour to stiffen and for its surface to become reflective. The heat of the plasma branded her neck and stung like crazy.

Grace opened up on the shop front with the AAR and Pags finished the job by hosing the place on full auto. Gina got off a couple of shots from where she lay prone just as the simulated world flashed red indicating a good kill.

"Are you okay?" Pags said through his open visor. He pulled Gina to her feet. "Speak to me."

"I'm okay, stop fussing," she said and winced as she tentatively touched her burned neck.

"Okay. It's just… okay."

Gina shivered at the real sounding emotion in the construct's voice. He sounded so real, so *alive*. "Let's finish our business. As before, I'll take point."

They didn't argue with her. This time they tried disapproving silence.

\* \* \*

"No, no, no." Stone glared at the monitors showing Fuentez throwing away her chance. "*Dammit!*"

The technician glanced at him and then back to her controls. She didn't like him, but that was okay. He was used to it.

Stone knew Fuentez was good at the job; Eric's download of the Thurston op proved that. Her permanent file was replete with commendations, acts of courage under fire, comments on her coolness during the chaos of battle... she had medals galore. Her fitness to command was not in question. She was everything a good officer should be, but she was letting her inner demons take over. He knew her as he knew himself. She had lost friends; worse she felt responsible for the loss. He had lost *thousands* of friends, and *was* responsible for countless other deaths, but you had to go on. Vipers couldn't allow sentiment to get in the way of the job. The job was all a viper really had. After two hundred and more years of strife, they were all a little crazy, but one thing above all they lived for—the Alliance. Fuentez was throwing away her chance to make an impact on the Alliance's future, and there was nothing he could do about it... or was there?

He frowned as Fuentez took out the first target, two more and the sim was over. He nodded as the decision crystallised into action. First, she needed to be slowed down so he had time to do something. He began furiously typing in his commands all the while wishing they were home. He could do a lot more with viper equipment, and it was faster too. This junk didn't have a port to accept commands from his weapon's bus. The keyboard would have to do.

He typed fast.

\* \* \*

"Move out," Gina said to her electronic henchman.

Grace moved left, Pags right, while Gina moved up the middle of the street. Pags nodded abruptly and Gina dove for cover just as a sniper took a pot shot at her. The pain was shockingly real.

Grace returned fire and the world flashed red confirming the kill.

Back on her feet, Gina staunched the blood pouring from her shoulder grimacing at the pain all the while. The wound was bad. The high velocity slug had gone straight through her shoulder. She struggled out of her armour, tore her uniform clear of the wound, and coated it using the canister of synthskin Grace held out to her. The synthetic sealant mimicked skin to prevent blood loss, and would aid her bots in their job of repairing the damage.

"Here, gimme," Grace said taking the canister and spraying the exit wound in her back. "You damn fool, what was that stunt?"

"I know what I'm doing," she grunted trying not to shout with the pain as she pulled her armour back on.

"Do you? You could have fooled me."

Gina hefted her rifle and winced as her shoulder shifted. "We have a job to do. I don't have time for lectures."

She pointed at Grace and indicated a house-by-house sweep for the last one. Pags came across the road with his weapon swinging left and right. Grace kicked in the door, and Gina shoulder rolled inside to fire into the shadows. In the real world, she flinched in her couch as the recoil hammered her wounded shoulder painfully. She grunted, but fired again. The world flashed red confirming the third and final kill, but something was wrong. She did not awaken.

\* \* \*

"Do it now," Stone said to his assistant in the simulator room.

The technician opened her mouth to protest the illegal order, but one look at his face had her gulping and keying in the hastily programmed sequence.

\* \* \*

Grace came into the house walking sideways keeping her back to the wall. "Upstairs," she whispered over the comm. "I thought I heard something."

Gina frowned and rose to her feet. Something wasn't right about this. "Take point, Eagle Two. Pags, you bring up the rear and cover me."

"Eagle Three copies."

Gina shook her head and frowned. Something definitely wasn't right, but what was it? There was something bugging her, *nagging* her. This was just a sim.

*What sim?*

"Copy, proceeding on mission," Grace said responding just a little late for her.

What mission? She wanted to rub her temples. She couldn't think straight. This was all wrong. She wasn't supposed to be here, she was supposed to be… she was supposed to be… she started to panic as she realised she couldn't remember what they were doing. Grace was oblivious to her agitation. She ascended the stairs leading the way for her squad as she had always done. She climbed one step at a time, moving silently with her AAR pointed at the balcony and into the trees.

*Trees... what the hell...*

The buzzing in Gina's head was getting worse. What the hell was wrong? She glanced back looking for the source of the noise, but she didn't find it. Pags moved up behind her with his weapon scanning the other way.

"Eagle One, Eagle Two," Grace whispered.

"Eagle One. Go," she said shaking her head at her preoccupation.

"I have motion ahead, less than a klick and moving fast. Might be the package."

*Package? What...*

"Take no chances, Grace. I have nothing on my sensors."

Gina looked around and could hardly make out the stairs she was climbing. She wiped her visor but it didn't help. She felt weird, something was wrong with the sim.

*What sim?*

\* \* \*

"She's hyperventilating. We have to stop," the frightened technician protested. She reached for the abort control, but Stone's hand clamped her wrist like a vice.

"No," he said coldly. "Go to full sensory."

When she failed to comply, he pushed her aside and keyed the command himself. He watched with satisfaction as the readings slowly returned to normal.

Normal for combat.

The matrix took a firm hold, and Fuentez was back on Thurston.

\* \* \*

Gina breathed a deep sigh of relief as her confusion sloughed off. She remembered the package Grace was talking about. That's right. Stein had ordered her to meet someone and escort him back to base.

"I can't see a damn thing through these trees," she said in frustration. She dialled X2 on her optics and smiled in satisfaction. "I have him Eagle Two. That's our boy. Hold here and I'll go get him."

"Eagle One, Eagle Three."

She aborted her move and keyed her comm. "Eagle Three, Eagle One. Go."

"I should go," Pags said.

"Negative," she said in sudden agitation. "You can cover me."

"That's not procedure, Gunny," Pags said in surprise. "I should go."

*He's right; he should go, but...*

"No, I'll go," Gina said starting to move out.

"Eagle One, Eagle Two."

"Eagle Two, Eagle One. Go," she said aborting her move a second time.

"Pags is right, Gina. What the hell's the matter with you? He should go."

"I said I'll go *damn you!* I want you to pull back into cover. That's an order."

"Two copies."

"Eagle Three copies."

Grace and Pags pulled back and went to ground. Gina moved ahead as carefully as she could. The package was not far ahead. He appeared to be wounded. On her belly, she crawled the last few metres.

The wounded man rolled onto his side to look at her. "The name's Eric. I suggest you pull your people out before... too late!"

A terrific explosion shook the jungle, and Grace disappeared in eye searing boil of light. The jungle was ablaze with falling trees crashing down all around and soil raining back to earth.

*Heavy grenade launcher!*

"Oh God... oh God..." Pags gurgled over his comm before he gasped his last breath and died.

The buzzing in Gina's head was back louder than ever. Images flashed before her eyes, one after another. Grace and Pags smiling, laughing, arguing. Grace chasing Pags as he ran off with her boot... something snapped, and Gina suddenly knew where she was, and who had put her here.

*Noooo!*

"I'm not doing this again," she screamed. "You hear me, Stone? Do you hear me out there? I'm not doing this damn you!"

Eric opened fire not even noticing her shouting or her agitation. Of course he didn't, he was just another construct and wasn't programmed to notice. She ducked as the enemy sought and found her position.

"All right, all right you bastards."

Gina made use of every scrap of cover and moved forward hoping to find the grenade launcher. She found it. The crew served launcher had been set up behind the bulk of a fallen tree. She smiled grimly. A moment later, she weighed her grenades in her hand but shook her head and added a third. Best be sure. She depressed the triggers and threw them behind the log.

*Crump! Crump! Crump!*

Launcher and men blew apart and earth showered down.

"That was for Grace," she said softly.

Standing by Eric's side, she opened fire on the now retreating rebel infantry. She mowed them down on full auto slapping a seemingly inexhaustible supply of magazines into her weapon as it ran dry. Minutes later, she stood looking at what was left of the enemy. Pieces of meat, that's all they were now. The jungle was burning and many of the trees had been blown apart, but there were plenty more where they came from.

Gina found a relatively intact body and looked into his staring eyes. "For Grace and Dan," she growled. "For Grace and Dan," she said again wiping away the tears.

Slowly, the scene before her faded to black.

"Snap out of it Fuentez."

Gina opened her eyes and glared at Stone. Her right hand blurred upward like a knife blade to strike his larynx, but he blocked the blow with ease. He was a viper.

"You're awake," Stone said with a wry smile. "Sit up and vacate the couch. We have a schedule to keep."

"Screw your schedule. Where do you get off doing that to me?" She leapt to her feet and landed in a fighting crouch with her face inches from Stone's.

"How do you feel about your friends' deaths now?"

"How do you think I…" she began but faltered. She felt different somehow—easier within her own mind.

"Now you know why. In the sim you held the others back time and again. You used yourself as bait in the street scenario, and sent the others back to cover in the jungle. Would you do the same again now?"

"I might," Gina said angrily, but she knew she wouldn't. Not unless there were no other options.

"You're lying, Fuentez, but that's okay. We have what we need from you."

"Did I pass?" She carefully probed the memory of her friends. It didn't hurt. There was sadness and loss, but it didn't hurt as it once had.

Stone looked at her strangely. "There is no pass or fail."

"But it's a test."

"Yes."

"Well…" she said uncertainly. "You pass or fail tests."

"Not mine you don't," Stone said with a put upon sigh. "I want your reactions, not some number out of ten. Go back to your room. Someone will come to see you in an hour or so. Be ready."

Gina saluted instinctively. "Yes, sir." She about faced and made to leave the simulator room, but she stopped short in embarrassment when she realised she was still in her skivvies. She dressed quickly before leaving the simulator room with her face flaming.

* * *

Stone watched Fuentez leave and smiled. Eric would be pleased he had found a way to snap her out of her funk, but bearing in mind the method he had used, it was best he not mention it.

He turned back to the techy. "Well that went well didn't it?"

"Er… yes?" she said fearfully.

"Best not tell anyone how we did it though."

"Er… no?" She whispered and paled as his look sharpened. "I mean *no*, sir. Of course not, sir."

He pursed his lips. "Get the next one set up."

"Yes, sir," she said and hurried out to the waiting area.

Stone shook his head. "Damn techy."

Maybe it would be wiser to have one of the others in here with him from now on. They were more reliable and less squeamish. He grinned. Marian was taking an interest in Richmond, he would ask her to join him during the session.

* * *

# 10 ~ Breaking Rules

Stone went through his special scenario one last time. It was perfect, just as he knew it would be; he had checked it ten times. There was no way he could get caught.

"This is highly illegal," Hymas said uneasily. "You do know that don't you?"

"Interesting things always are, Marion, you know that," he said with a boyish grin.

Hymas sighed and shook her head at him, but that was all right. Sometimes it felt like they had known each other forever, which wasn't far from the truth when you realised his years as a viper far exceeded the thirty years previous to that. The boy he had been died the moment the surgery began, and days later a viper had emerged like a butterfly from its cocoon. All vipers went through a transformation, and not just physically. The mental adjustment was extreme. Like Robbins, some were unable to handle the trauma and had to be scrapped for the good of the regiment.

"I'm about done here. Are you going to squeal on me?"

Hymas thought about that and Stone began to sweat. The Colonel wouldn't like him downloading his log into the simulator. It was never done away from home, especially not to an unenhanced subject. It was more than illegal in the Alliance. It ranked closely to misuse use of hypno, which was punishable by mind wipe. Only at home did a viper download for another viper's use, even then, it was used only when recon data was needed. Training new units would break the unwritten rule time and again, but by the General's order, it was to be done only at home under strictly controlled circumstances. It had taken some creative talking to get the components necessary to build even a makeshift interface, but he had done it with none the wiser. He patted his creation affectionately. It might look ugly as sin, but it worked great.

*If the General ever finds out… but he won't.*

His little toy would be nothing but scrap a few hours from now. The simulator would automatically erase the data at the end of a single session, and the matrix would be reformatted for good measure. He frowned and double checked that all traces would be erased, but everything was fine. There was absolutely no way he could get caught. None whatsoever—he was sure… he bit his lip and reprogrammed the simulator to format *three* times. Just in case.

"I won't squeal, as you so quaintly put it, Ken," Hymas said finally. "You do know your retro crap went out fifty years ago, don't you?"

"I'm no retro," he protested with a grin. "I've always talked this way."

"Yeah, yeah. You old timers are always pining for the old days."

Stone snorted. "You're older than me by two years—at least!"

"It's not polite to mention a lady's age," Hymas said primly but she was grinning.

"So, you think I'm right on this?"

Hymas sobered. "It might be the only way to fix the problem. Assuming it can be fixed. I won't sanction this for the others, Ken, but for that one, yes."

"I know you're not happy, but it's the only way I can think of to give the Colonel what he asked for."

"You know what I think her chances are, but as I said, I'll go along this once."

"Okay, bring her in."

"What about the techy?" Hymas said moving to the hatch and deferring to him in his own area of expertise.

"Nah, she would only make a fuss. Probably go running to one of the others."

"You're probably right," Hymas agreed and stepped out. "Richmond, you're first."

Stone smiled. Not probably. After the last time, it was a certainty.

\* \* \*

"Richmond, you're first."

Kate nodded and entered the simulator room trying not to show her unease at being in the presence of two cyb… vipers.

"Up you go. You know the drill," Stone said.

Kate stripped out of her uniform looking straight at the wall. Her face was heating, she could feel it, but she refused to make a fuss about undressing in front of Stone. She turned, still not looking at him, and climbed onto the couch. Lieutenant Hymas came forward to attach the sensors and electrodes to her head and body, while Stone attached the rest to her arms and legs. While all this was going on, Kate concentrated on images of home and the regiment, sometimes she imagined herself sneaking through the jungle on Tigris, anything to help herself ignore the two cyborgs in the room and what they were doing to her.

"Now then, Private," Stone said as he attached the final electrode. "This is the final sim in your program. Those that went before tested your skills in various combat situations. I'm sure you already know that you did well, but this sim is different. You won't like it, I *guarantee* it. With luck you might survive long enough to look around, but it's more likely you'll fail within minutes. It will take more than skills learned as a ranger to do well in this one. If you can look beyond your own wants and feelings, you may have a chance—a *small* chance of passing into the final stage."

"Get on with it," Kate said harshly, but Hymas' face darkened and she hurriedly added courtesy. "*Please.*"

She was feeling a little cold lying there in only a t-shirt and panties. She was not impressed with Stone's warnings and wanted to get it over with.

The vipers crossed the room and sat at their consols to monitor the session. Stone initiated the simulator's control mechanisms, and Kate twitched as it calibrated itself to match her reflexes. She grimaced at the feeling of losing control; she had always hated that about sims. Slowly she began to lose feeling throughout her extremities. She blacked out as the couch lifted and swung into the chamber.

Kate knew something was not right the instant she awoke. She knew this place; she was back on Bethany's World, standing outside of Hangar F at Callista air base, which was home to the 2$^{nd}$ Airborne Rangers—her old home.

She flinched and ducked at the sound of an explosion nearby. She looked around quickly and ran for cover. With her back pressed against the wall of the hangar, she peeked around the corner looking for the cause of the explosion. In the distance she saw boiling black smoke rising from a crashed Alliance fighter, and figures in familiar uniform fighting not far from the still burning craft. Her right hand flashed down to her hip and pulled her pistol. Before she could register surprise—she was left handed and always had been—targeting information appeared before her eyes.

She struggled to understand what had happened while flashing icons and numerals detailing range and vectors competed for her attention. She waved a hand in front of her face, but it had no effect on the illusion. The holographic display appeared to hover at arms' length from her, but she knew that no one else would see it. This thing, this data was for her alone. The shock on her face would have been comical if not for the horror that followed it a moment later. She looked down at her clothes; she was wearing viper battle dress. Not for them the standard camouflage of Alliance forces. She had been brought up to believe this uniform was another of the elitist notions embodied within the cyborgs, but at least she could discount that. Her sneaksuit was black, it was her favourite colour.

This had to be Stone's work; he wanted her to fail. He knew what this uniform and the cyborgs that wore them meant to all those born on Bethany. Kate growled angrily, already seeing the smirk on his face when she failed his damn tests. She would show him a Richmond could take anything he threw at her.

*The bastard, bastard, BASTARD!*

Peering around the corner, she watched as Bethany's forces were overwhelmed—another affront by Stone—and the enemy advanced. She looked at the pistol in her hand doubtfully and wished for something more substantial. With her rifle she could have taken this group out with little trouble. With a shrug she lifted the weapon and sighted on the lead figure. He was too far for...

Targeting information flashed before her eyes once again, or within them she should say. That realisation made her queasy. She pushed thoughts of cybernetics out of her head to deal with the current problem. Thinking about the distance caused a numeral to strobe in the upper left quadrant of her display. A moment later, the enemy suddenly rushed toward her. She stumbled back in surprise as an icon marked X2 blinked on and off before her eyes then parked itself to one side of her display.

"Damn me," Kate said in wonder. That was handy. She targeted the figure again... *Merkiaari!*

Kate stared in horrified shock. There was no doubt. There couldn't possibly *be* any doubt. Everyone was taught Alliance history, and that included the dark times of the Merki War. There wasn't a man or woman living who wouldn't recognise these monstrous creatures for what they were—they were etched forever upon the Alliance's collective psyche as Humanity's deadliest enemy.

Merkiaari were bipedal like Humans, but they were much bigger and stronger. They averaged over eight feet in height, and had powerful clawed hands and feet. The females were even bigger than the males. Both sexes had large tusk-like fangs, and shaggy hair covered faces and bodies. They all wore the same thing—grey one-piece uniforms, and armour that was proof against most small arms fire, but not the heavy stuff or plasma. The Alliance didn't have anything better even now. Armour that was proof against plasma was too heavy to be man portable.

A targeting diamond appeared on her display, briefly hovered over her chosen target, and began rotating. Flicking her attention to the top right of her display, she selected max power and fired one shot for effect. The pistol bucked in her hand; the recoil was surprising, but her viper reflexes were ready. The trooper went down with a hole the size of her fist blasted through its chest.

"Ha! Got the bastard."

The pistol packed a hell of a punch and she was glad of it. She ducked back out of sight and ran to find a new firing position. Inside the hangar, she sprinted for the far wall and nearly killed herself as her viper body accelerated to almost forty klicks an hour. She aborted her sudden dash just in time and made it to the wall safely. She wasn't even breathing hard, but a fraction later on the brakes and she would have smeared herself over the cinder block wall.

Her display warned her of targets approaching. She quickly moved to find an observation point. A window overlooking the wreckage of the Alliance fighter proved to be the best vantage. She reduced magnification to X1.5 and targeted a big Merki female through the window. She didn't break the glass like an amateur. She allowed the super hot plasma to burn through.

"I love this gun," Kate howled in glee when the huge monster fell.

The Merki platoon swung toward her position in one precise move and opened fire. Plascrete exploded and rained down on her, but her dive saved her from serious injury. Her display brought up a wire frame silhouette of her body. It was flashing yellow battle damage to her right knee. The percentage indicated the wound was superficial.

"How the hell do I get rid of this damn display?" she growled irritably.

As quick as thought, the outline of her body receded and parked on the lower left of her display. It had minimised itself like a window on a computer terminal. It was still active but out of the way.

Kate crawled through the rubble ignoring the blood she left behind, and climbed the stairs to the ground crew's locker area before the Merki troopers saw her. It was close, but she ducked through the door as the first bug ugly male stepped through the hole in the hangar's wall. The locker room was a tactically unsound location—the partition wall was flimsy as hell, and the door was the same. Defence however was not why she had chosen to come up here, the window at the back of the room was. She opened it outward as far as it would go and looked outside. Scanning the open space between her hangar and the next one along, she found no hostiles. Her range finder said the ground was 19.14 metres from her present location. She had no idea if she could jump such a distance, but the grunting guttural language of the Merkiaari approaching said she had to go now.

She holstered her pistol and jumped.

\* \* \*

"Good girl," Stone said in approval of Richmond's courage.

He watched her fall and strike the ground with enough force to kill an unenhanced Human. As a viper, he had survived it, but he hadn't enjoyed the experience.

"She's hurt," Hymas noted. "The knee is weakening."

"Yeah I know. I set it up that way."

"You did? Why?"

He shrugged. "Because I want her to have the experience of my fight on Bethany as close to real as I can make it. Her decisions are her own, but I can stack the deck enough to limit her options. That way I can make her do what I did that day, while still leaving the actual choice to her."

"That's hard, Ken," Hymas said sounding as if she sympathised with Richmond.

"Of course it is. I'm a hard charging fighting machine. Emphasis on the machine there." He waggled his eyebrows to make his friend grin. "The decision was a hard one to make, but I made it. If she can bring herself to do the same thing for the same or similar reasons, I think we might have a winner."

Hymas grunted noncommittally. She watched the girl limp around the hangar in pursuit of heavier firepower. "Will she find what she's looking for?"

He grinned. "That would be telling."

\* \* \*

The pain in Kate's knee was indescribable. Sweat was beading on her brow and she couldn't hold back a grunt as she put weight on it. She limped around the side of the building and pushed herself into a mild trot. Agony flared with every footfall, and her damage indicator insisted on telling her the obvious. Yellow was flashing around her right knee, but it had darkened toward orange. When it reached red it would indicate critical damage, but she was sure to be well aware of that by then.

She had thought viper units were tougher than this. She grunted as the pain flared higher. Her nanobots should take care of the damage in time she supposed; already the blood had stopped flowing, but she couldn't stop to rest it for the time it would take to heal completely. She managed to put several buildings between herself and the enemy in short order, but she kept her sensors on maximum and swept a full three-hundred and sixty degrees around her position. Luckily, her viper sensors displayed information in a fashion she was familiar with. Anyone who had piloted mech armour would have recognised their output instantly.

Kate watched the red icons representing individual Merki troopers leave the hangar. They separated into teams of three to cover more area in their search for vermin. That's how they thought of Humans. Non-Merkiaari were vermin to be exterminated, or some said, enslaved. No one knew for sure. Those listed as missing had never been found, but that didn't mean anything. Billions had died in the war, and many of the bodies were never identified.

Kate reached her objective and without hesitation blew the door off its hinges. She quickly ducked inside before the Merkiaari could locate her. Limping hurriedly down the empty corridor, she turned right at the second junction and keyed open the hatch she found there. She breathed easier when she stepped into the dimly lit storage facility nicknamed the morgue. Lights flickered on as she entered and revealed hundreds of mechs standing in neat rows waiting for their masters, the rangers, to come for them. No rangers would be coming, she knew. Those few who had died on the runway had been left to delay pursuit of the base personnel as they evacuated toward the city. Millions of people in that city would die later today, or had already died two hundred years ago.

"I'm here *now*, that's all that matters," she growled and quickly activated the crane.

To suit up, she had to remove the torso of the armour. She chose the first unit and a moment later she was clambering inside. She activated the controls and brought the armour's computer online. Keying in the close and capture sequence, she raised her arms to accept the torso section and arms. Fully encased in the mech, she activated the motor systems and stepped out of the cradle to turn deeper into the morgue.

Walking by the dead sentinels of mech armour she came to the vault. As she keyed in her serial number, she had time to wonder if Stone had screwed up. Would her code work in a simulation that was constructed from a two hundred year old download? The vault door sighed as the compression seals let go and the huge door swung open. She stepped inside.

"Now this is what *I'm* talking about."

On the rack in front of her was an H3B-AC, or Heavy Tri-Barrel Auto Cannon. It was a thing of beauty. She reached forward into the H3B's docking port and turned her left fist clockwise. The weapon icons in the mech's HUD had been dark, but now one blinked to life and flashed red as the armour ran a diagnostic. She watched it turn from a blinking red to a pure and solid green.

"Oooh yeah, gonna pay motherfuckers." She frowned, and wondered why she was talking retro. "Stone, must be."

Thoughts of Stone's sense of humour made her smile, but then she sobered a moment later when she remembered he was a cyborg. He was a machine, not a real person. He had no soul; she had to remember that. She reached out with her right hand for an AAR and locked her fist into it. She didn't strictly need the rail gun. The Merkiaari hadn't brought armoured vehicles with them in the first wave of attacks on Bethany, but she didn't worry about that. A rail gun was a handy thing to have against any target. The AAR turned green in her display and she decided it was time to take care of business.

Back outside the armoury, her sensors detected two Merki fire teams at three o'clock, another two at six with a further three passing seven and probably heading for nine. It was obvious they had detected her and were moving to encircle her. Deciding to take care of those at three first, she moved out toward the maintenance sheds using as much cover as she could find.

The heavy thudding of a gauss rifle staggered her. She took a step back, and then three more, as a Merki fire team found her and hammered her torso. She glanced at her mech's damage control sensors, but they were still dark. That was at it should be. Ranger armour should sneer at slugs from a mere gauss rifle. She would have been splattered to hell and gone without the armour.

"Lucky I chose the morgue and not the barracks then wasn't it?"

Kate doubted it was luck. The entire sim was a set up. Stone had used an illegal download to drop her in at the deep end—unless his superiors had ordered this? Surely not, but...

Yes, there was that wasn't there?

As those thoughts went through her mind, her body was reacting. She turned toward the maintenance sheds and activated the H3B. The whine of its motor spinning up was nothing compared to the ripping sound of hyper velocity rounds sawing the sheds in half at knee level. She contented herself with a single sweep; she was husbanding her ammo, but she was more than satisfied when something in the now collapsing sheds exploded with a thunderous roar.

*CRUMP, CRUMP, CRUMP!*

The sheds disappeared in a ball of fire a hundred metres high at least. She must have taken out the spare fuel pods for the fighters.

*Oops!*

Her sensors indicated more troopers coming at the double. She swung to her right and hosed the barracks with the AAR. Thin plascrete walls blew apart and the roof collapsed with a crash that shook the ground. The opening was only partially blocked, but again that didn't matter. The temporary barricade was enough to slow the group at six o'clock, and give her time with those at three.

She throttled the mech to a lumbering run, and slammed into the Merkiaari as they appeared from around the officer's mess. A single burst from the AAR took out the first one, but the second was a female. She was enormous and towered over the mech. The monster grappled with the AAR and tried to tear it loose. Kate tried to lift the creature, and the mech's servos whined in protest. Her own viper strength made the difference, and the Merki trooper was lifted off her feet.

The warnings on her mech's display spoke of a second Merki trooper attacking the emergency hatch in her back. The steady beeping of overload warnings decided the matter. She swung her H3B toward the female, which was busy trying to gnaw through her armour. Kate rammed the barrels in the Merki's mouth and fired. She heard the clanking rattle of the barrels gouging soft flesh and shattering fangs even inside the mech, but once the motor finally reached thirty thousand rpm, the auto cannon fired a burst through the shrieking creature's head.

No more problem, Kate thought happily, and dropped the twitching carcass to the ground.

The last one was a male and he was not co-operating. When she turned, he turned with her and continued attacking her back. Her sensors said the others were coming into range now, but the pest on her back wasn't letting go. She turned and located the troopers running toward her. She fired the H3B, but the attack on her rear hatch caused her to stagger. She killed the officer's mess, but that was all.

\* \* \*

"Dammit girl," Stone swore. "You know what you have to do. *Do* it already."

"She's thinking like a ranger. It's the armour."

"I know," he said with a sigh. He had really thought Richmond would come through, but now…

He sighed again and watched the show.

\* \* \*

In desperation, Kate kicked backward and shattered the Merki's leg at the knee. Her own knee screamed at the impact, but she didn't care. She was frothing mad. She pointed the AAR at the writhing figure on the ground and fired. The trooper blew apart and so did the plascrete below it and the soil below that. She released the stud and stepped back from the smoking crater.

The proximity alarm heralding the approach of more hostiles, snapped her back to reality. She activated the H3B even as she turned. A hundred rounds a second spat from the whirring barrels destroying everything in their path. Walls were shredded, windows shattered, plascrete was pockmarked, roofs collapsed, fires took hold… and Merkiaari were sliced in two. Silence descended as the H3B ran dry. The only sound was the crackle of the flames and the whirring of the auto cannon's motor as it spat nonexistent ammunition.

"Oooh yeah, that did the trick all right."

Kate released the stud and disengaged the now useless cannon. She dropped it and turned to the north. She knew her comrades were fighting for their lives in the city. The Merki landers would be coming down in their thousands now, firing into the tall buildings in a planned manoeuvre designed to kill Humans quickly at the same time as blocking the Alliance tanks and APCs.

She throttled up and ran to help.

When Kate arrived, the city was burning, but it wasn't yet the complete disaster it would later be. Refugees were everywhere, but panic had yet to set in. Bewilderment was the expression on most of the soot-covered faces, horror on others.

As Kate made her way in amongst the buildings, her mikes picked up the sound of a Merki troopship overhead. Her sensors reported another wave of ships coming in. She cursed as the first Interceptors roared by. She had missed her chance. With the AAR raised skyward, she waited and fired at another group of enemy ships passing overhead. She hit one of the Interceptors, but failed to knock it down. The second blew apart most satisfactorily. Burning wreckage rained down upon the street. The drive section smashed through a shopping arcade, and added to the destruction being heaped upon the city.

Kate blocked out the shrieks of people hiding inside, and moved on looking for ground targets instead.

She found another target not ten minutes later. A platoon of Merki troopers was performing a sweep through a housing district. Two troopers went into a building to flush out any vermin hiding inside, while the bulk of the platoon waited outside to ambush them. Kate kept her distance. She used the AAR to knock down the building and bury them all under tons of plascrete and steel.

Her next target was a troopship near a chemical manufactory. She had no chance of destroying such a ship. It was much too big, but she might inconvenience those within it. She waited for it to begin its landing cycle before blowing away the pressure lines feeding one of the chemical storage tanks. The explosion was like the end of the world. Kate gaped as a wall of fire rolled over the ship and descended upon her. Without a second thought, she engaged maximum thrust and jumped as hard as she could. Her jump jets were not designed for flight, but with luck…

Kate landed and looked back to see the ship explode. The chemicals in the storage tank must have reacted with the air in some manner. She had certainly not expected the results she achieved, but it had worked. The troopship's fuel pods exploded as she watched. She ignored the burning fuel raining down on her, and walked through it looking for more Merkiaari to kill.

Sometime later, Kate's chrono said it was 18:10, but she hadn't detected the launching of the drone. Thinking she had missed it, she asked her mech's computer to confirm the launch.

"NEGATIVE. NO LAUNCH DETECTED."

That was wrong. Her lessons all agreed that the drone jumped at 17:52, it was 18:13 now.

"Computer, confirm any launch with a destination outside the planet's atmosphere."

"WORKING… NO LAUNCHES DETECTED."

She was supposed to launch it; it had to be that. Damn Stone for this. He hadn't told her the aim of her mission here, but now she knew. She throttled up and ran for the centre of the city.

\* \* \*

"About time," Stone said angrily. "You would have thought someone from Bethany would have known the importance of that launch.

Without it, the entire planet would have been scoured clean!"

"I told you, Ken, she's thinking like a ranger in that mech of hers. She knows now though. When are you going to stick it to her?"

"Now?"

Hymas nodded and he keyed in the final blow.

* * *

"For God's sake, you have to help me," a man shouted grabbing at the running people. His clothes were ripped and bloody. Blood trickled down the side of his face, and he wiped it away with a shaking hand. "You don't understand," he screamed, as everyone he tried to stop pushed him away. "They're killing the children. Somebody, help me!"

Kate skidded to a stop and turned toward the crying man.

"Please, oh please. You're a soldier; you have to help me. A soldier has to help, yes... you will help," the man said with certainty.

Kate scanned the area, but there were no targets nearby. She activated her external speakers. "Who are you? What's this about killing kids?"

"I'm the principal of... but that doesn't matter. The aliens are killing the children. You have to help me," he screamed up at her armour where she towered over him.

*Kids... oh no.*

Kate's thoughts whirled. Just as she was about to demand directions, a viper ran toward her. He was a captain. She had never seen this one before, but he obviously thought he knew her.

"Stone?" the viper said in amazement. "What the *hell* do you think you're doing in that crap?" he said looking over her fire-blackened mech. "You were supposed to launch the drone, not stand there flapping your gums. Christ... you haven't launched it," he said in sudden realisation. "They are going to take out the launch centre you idiot!"

"Sir," she said hesitantly. She was off stride and worried about the kids. "Sir, this man says they're killing the kids."

The viper squeezed his eyes shut in grief, but when he looked at her again, he had eyes of flint. "If we don't launch the drone before they take out the launch centre, we lose Bethany and all who live here will die. I can't... I *cannot* abandon this world to save a few kids. I can't..." he finished sickly.

"Please, you must help," the principal said begging the captain and clutching at his arm. "It's not a few. My entire school is being butchered. Thousands, *thousands.* For the love of God man, you have to help."

"I can't help you, *we* can't help you," he said and looked back up at Kate where she loomed over him in the mech. "Get out of that stinking armour. We have to launch the drone before it's too late."

Kate watched the viper accelerate toward the centre of the city. He was almost flying he was running so fast. She would never keep up. She hesitated one more time, but then she deactivated the mech and popped the emergency hatch to climb out. When she saw the damage it had taken at the back, she was amazed she had survived. Power leads and hydraulic lines were exposed and fluid was leaking out. The thing was fit only for scrap.

"The school is this way," the principal said running to the corner. "It's not far."

Kate glanced at him and then down the road where the viper had gone. She ran toward the city centre.

"You bastard! You're not a man… you're not even Human! You're a cyborg, a disgusting soulless freak! I hope you die screaming in agony! I hope you rot in hell…"

Tears were running freely over Kate's cheeks. It must have been the pain in her knee. Her thoughts were on her brother and what he would have said. Leaving the children to die—he would have been disgusted. She knew he would have saved them if he had been here. She left the principal's curses behind as she attained her maximum speed. Her knee was screaming in agony and her damage control display was indicating major damage. She shouldn't have kicked that Merki trooper, but if she hadn't she would be dead now. Tears of pain and rage blurred her vision.

She ran on.

* * *

"I never knew," Hymas said quietly. "I was on Alizon then. The Merkiaari sent two ships, but they never gained the upper hand."

Stone shrugged. "Yeah well, shit happens."

"Did the kids survive?"

"Of course not," Stone snapped looking away from the compassion he saw in her eyes. He didn't deserve compassion, not for what he had done. "Sorry, Marian, but I don't want to… oh hell, you might as well hear it. The Merki squad killed the teachers when they shielded the kids with their bodies, then they killed the kids. The principal survived and denounced the entire regiment as cowards and murderers."

"I know that part. I didn't know the Colonel and you were

involved."

"He was a captain then," he whispered, seeing the past come to life as his processor resurrected it from his permanent memory. "Bethany's World has always hated us, but it was much worse after I killed their kids."

"You didn't—"

"I don't want to hear it okay?" He glared at his friend. "Just leave it will you? It's old news, *very* old news."

Hymas nodded and turned back to the consol.

* * *

Kate found the viper captain lying in pieces outside the launch centre and took cover. His legs were both severed above the knee, and his left arm was shattered. Unbelievably he was still alive, but he was too far gone in shock to talk to her. She crawled by him without stopping.

Slugs chewed up the ground near her ear and she rolled left. Her right hand was tracking toward the target before she knew to aim. The diamond spun in her display, she fired twice and ran forward having no doubt the trooper was dead. She ran through the double door skidding on the shiny floors of the reception area. Broken doors and computer terminals greeted her. The enemy was already inside somewhere.

With her heart thudding fit to burst out of her chest, Kate dashed up the stairs as fast as her viper body could go. She didn't dare chance the elevators. Her diagnostic display told her the knee was going to give out any second, but she raced for the twentieth floor regardless. On the nineteenth floor, her display was pulsing red, and the pain was making her cringe at every footfall, but she struggled up the final flight only to duck back as a Merki trooper appeared. Kate fired from the hip not needing her targeting reticule this close. The monster was blasted back and out of sight.

Kate advanced cautiously, but yelled in shock when another trooper appeared out of nowhere. She wasn't sure afterwards who was the more surprised, but the Merki female did get her shot off first. The nanocoat of Kate's armour reacted to the attack instantly. Its surface became diamond hard and shiny as a mirror over her ribs, as it tried to nullify the sudden influx of energy. Kate fell trying to twist out of the beam before it penetrated. She hit the floor and fired twice into the snarling face. The headless monster collapsed and wrung a scream of anguish from Kate as it landed across both legs. Her damage display stopped flashing warnings about her leg and went dark—the knee was crushed beyond repair.

Ignoring the pain, Kate shoved the corpse off with her good leg, and skidded back to lean against the wall. Her head rolled to the side in an effort to survey the control room. It was wrecked; she had failed her mission. But what of the drone itself? Surely there was a manual launch sequence. The more she thought about it, the more certain she was that there would be a backup.

She dragged herself into the stairwell and up the stairs bumping her shattered leg with every move. She hardly knew where she was now, but up seemed the right way. Sweat rolled off her and her teeth chattered. Despite all her bots could do, she was going into shock. Finally, she fell through the door and onto the roof. The drones were still in their cradles awaiting the launch order.

Kate dragged herself to the first one and opened the panel in its side. "Oh God, what do I…" she panted in time with the throbbing agony her leg had become. She looked at the controls in confusion. She didn't know how to operate a foldspace drone, or even key in a message.

The shot from the doorway nearly ended her life right there. The Merki trooper she had shot in the stairwell was in the doorway clinging to the wall. He fired again, and Kate shrieked as her left hand was smashed to a pulp by a huge slug. Hugging the spurting stump to her chest, she screamed in agony and fired her pistol at fall auto. She held the trigger down until there was nothing left of the trooper, or the door, or the top of the stairwell. Her vision blurred and darkened as the ammo indicator beeped empty.

*Peep, peep, peep, peep…*

The annoying beeping roused Kate a moment or so later. Her hand had been deleted from her diagnostic display. It matched her leg now. An absurd chuckle tried to force its way out of her. Her bots had dealt with the injury by sealing it off to prevent blood loss, and a neural block would shortly be in place for the pain. A readout on her display was insisting she report to medical immediately. She was apparently combat ineffective and needed maintenance.

Kate laughed tiredly. "No shit."

She struggled up to the control panel next to the launch rail. The buttons seemed simple enough on this part at least. One said launch, another said abort and beside them was the usual palm scanner for clearance. Did she even have clearance? She flattened the launch button, and laid her right palm on the plate.

*WHOOSH!*

The first drone was ejected from the rails and the others slid forward one space.

Kate watched the drone begin to fall back to earth. She had time to wonder if it was broken before the rocket motors detected the descent and fired. The drone shot into the sky and disappeared. She looked wearily around, but the sim didn't end.

"Sonofabitch…" she mumbled. Kate opened the hatch on the second drone to study its controls. "How do I make you go to HQ, damn you?" She began pressing buttons at random. "Aha!"

A menu appeared in the tiny display. She read the options and pressed six. As she read the help file, her thoughts turned to the Captain. Was he still alive? If he was, she might meet him when she woke up, and they could talk about this day.

"It's been a doozy and no mistake."

She cursed Stone for his damn retro sayings. What the hell was a doozy?

She finished reading the file and punched in a code for Alliance HQ. The screen cleared and she typed a message.

*Full scale invasion of Bethany's World underway this day. Alliance forces routed, population being exterminated. Request Fleet intervention with heavy ground support. Recommend full battalion of vipers be in first wave.*

*PFC Richmond, SDN-559-210-229, reporting.*

Kate closed the panel and dragged herself to the consol. She smashed the launch button flat, and placed her palm on the scanner.

*WHOOSH!*

* * *

"You did it," Stone said. Behind him, the simulator was busy lobotomising itself to protect its programmer.

Richmond groaned at the imagined agony in the stump of her hand, but then she looked and saw it was whole again. She was still clutching it protectively to her chest, but of course it was whole. As reality reasserted itself, she relaxed and worked her fingers against phantom pain.

"Welcome back."

Richmond's eyes narrowed. "You…" she croaked. "You bastard… what have you done?"

Stone raised an eyebrow in surprise and glanced at Marion. "Do you know what she's talking about?"

Marion shook her head.

Richmond sat up and swung her legs over the edge of the couch. The wires running to the sensors tangled, and she angrily ripped them off not caring if she damaged them.

* * *

Kate ripped the wires from her body and reached for her uniform. She stuffed herself into it, ignoring Stone and the smirk she was sure she would find on his face if she looked. She couldn't get the sim out of her mind. Lies, all lies. Once dressed, she made to leave but stopped when Stone called out to her.

"When you've had time to think, come and see me. We'll talk."

Kate turned to face him wanting to be angry, but confusion was her greatest emotion. Confusion, and a bone deep weariness. All she thought she knew about her world and its history was a lie. All she had been taught was based on lies. Her life, her entire goddamn *life* was a lie. She couldn't think beyond that, couldn't get beyond it to what was important now. The Ten must know. They at least must have known the truth... they probably knew it all along. Why? Why teach lies and half-truths to Bethany's children?

"Richmond?" Hymas said in concern.

"Why?" she said. "Why did you do that to us... to me?"

Stone shook his head. "We did nothing to you."

"But you were there. You let them lie to us. Why did you let them lie to us?"

Hymas made to answer, but then she shook her head. Kate turned away and slowly made her way out of the simulator room. Outside the hatch she found dozens of concerned recruits awaiting their turn to enter the sims. She must have looked ready to pass out, because one man, Cragg it said on his uniform, stood and offered her his seat.

Kate shook her head. "I'm fine... I'll be all right."

"You don't look so hot. Are you sure?"

Kate nodded and turned along the corridor that eventually led back to her room. She looked back once to find Cragg still watching her. "Be careful of Stone. Be careful in there. They lie to you." She looked down and hunched her shoulders. "Everybody lies."

"I don't understand," Cragg called but she didn't stop.

"All lies."

* * *

# 11 ~ Decision Time

Kate lay on her bunk staring at the overhead going over the sim in her mind. No matter how she looked at it, she knew it was real and not fiction. She had been exposed to too many sims in her time not to know the difference, and deluding herself was not something she was prepared to do. Stone's sim hadn't truly been one at all, not in the accepted sense of the word anyway. It had been no imitation, but the real thing. She had relived an historical event of epic proportions; the Merkiaari invasion of her homeworld. Stone had actually been there when it happened, he had fought for his life and been terribly wounded trying to send word back to the Alliance. She had lived it herself from his point of view. There could be no ambiguity, no weaselling out of it. For centuries The Ten had lied—and still were—on a massive scale. Every school taught every child on Bethany a false history of that time, and no one knew it but the government.

Why? How? Did it even matter now?

Kate rolled onto her side hugging herself to stop her hands shaking. You betcha it mattered. It mattered a goddamn lot! The how though, wasn't as important as the why. At least to her way of thinking. No, she didn't need to know the specifics of how it was done, but she would like to know why. Perhaps then she could stop thinking about it and move on.

There was still Paul and her own mission here to consider. She had planned to send her latest report after the sim, but it didn't seem so important anymore. The report was hours late, but she doubted it would make a difference. She had sent her contact plenty of stuff to be going on with. Mostly information about the other people being tested; things like names and backgrounds she had been able to weasel out at mealtimes. Nothing vital or even that interesting really. Her contact wanted more hard data, of which there was precious little. He wanted most of all to know the reasons behind the testing of so many veteran soldiers from such diverse backgrounds. Until today she hadn't a clue, but it seemed obvious to her now. Stone was looking for viper candidates, and the only reason for that she could think of terrified her.

"Another Merki incursion?" They couldn't keep something that huge a secret, surely? Kate bit her lip hard, thinking about the massive hoax perpetuated on her own people for more than two centuries.

What was going on? She didn't know, but what Stone had done to her was illegal. Why had he done that, and what was she going to do about it? She could have told one of the other cyborgs, but Hymas was right there at the session and hadn't seem disturbed one bit by it. She certainly hadn't tried to stop him. Maybe the session had been sanctioned by his superiors. Kate sighed. There really was no one she could tell and be believed anyway. She had no evidence, and besides, she wasn't sure now that she wanted to turn him in. He had shown her the truth with his download.

The comm chimed, announcing a visitor. She reached over and pressed the admit key. When she saw who her visitor was she nimbly swung her legs off the bunk and stood to attention. Stone stared at her for a moment and then let his eyes wander around the room. His hand reached out and the hatch closed. When he locked it, Kate tensed, but he did nothing more than stare at her, waiting. She remained at attention, her thoughts frantic as she tried to think of something to say.

Stone grunted. "I said we would talk, but you didn't come see me."

Kate swallowed. "I've been thinking about stuff... things. I have questions, but—"

"I bet you have, I just bet you have at that. Okay, Richmond, sit down. No need to be formal. I said we'll talk and we will, about a great many things."

Kate relaxed a little and sat on her bunk. Stone pulled the chair toward him and sat facing her. He swung a compad forward and back, letting it pivot between his thumb and finger down by his side. Kate dragged her eyes away from it and up to meet his eyes. She found it hard to maintain her composure with that too-knowing stare upon her. She shifted, realising that this was the first time they had been alone since she got here.

"Why did you do it?" Kate blurted when she could tolerate his silence no longer. "You went to a lot of trouble."

"You have no idea how much, Richmond, but I think you'll be worth it. The Colonel doesn't know if you're wondering."

Kate frowned. That was only one of the things she had been wondering about. Stone's caginess didn't sit well with her; it didn't suit him. She had come to know him better than she wanted to admit over her weeks here, and the sim had reinforced her view. What he had done to her in that simulation took a certain kind of dedication and disregard for consequences. Stone was as hard as his name and twice as cold. She had known a few people like him in her time, all psychos, but she doubted any of them could compete against him in ruthlessness. He was the kind of man that did whatever it took to get the job done. A bit like her actually.

"If you're not here to answer my questions, why *are* you here?"

"I came to make sure you make the right decision when the time comes, and to tell you that I know."

Kate frowned. "Know? Know what?"

"Richmond," Stone sighed. "Did you really think you could get away with a hack into the comm system without me finding out? I'm insulted you even tried."

Kate licked suddenly dry lips. He couldn't have detected her intrusions into the system. He couldn't have! "I don't know what you mean—"

Stone cut her off with a raised hand. "Don't take me for one of your marks, Richmond. You can't manipulate me with a coy smile and soft words. Besides, I'm not trying to burn you. I'm trying to help you. It wasn't anything you did that gave you away if that makes you feel better. Your contact was blown before you even set foot on this rock."

Kate leaned forward, resting her weight on elbows and knees. She didn't doubt him, not with him right there looking at her with those knowing eyes. Her contact had messed up. It didn't really surprise her. She stared at the floor trying to think of a way out, but there wasn't one. If she did somehow get out of the room, where would she go? She was deep inside a moon with no atmosphere and no ship waiting even if she could reach the surface, which she couldn't. Stone was a viper; she had no chance of overpowering him. The idea was laughable. She had seen what a viper could do in the sims. She had *been* one in simulation long enough to know she had no chance at all.

"What are you going to do with me?"

"It's not a matter of what I'm going to do, Richmond. It's more about what you want and what you're prepared to do to get it."

"I don't understand. Aren't you going to arrest and question me?"

Stone sighed. "Haven't you been listening? I already know all the answers, and I don't care. Your contact is going to meet with a little accident later today. None of the data you transmitted has left Luna. Believe me, it never will."

"I do believe you. Not that any of it was worth anything."

"I know that too. We only let you keep transmitting so we could map your cell."

"I don't know any names, and I wouldn't talk if I did."

"Again, I don't care. I didn't ask for any." Stone handed the compad to her. "It makes interesting reading."

Kate activated the compad and read the first of many pages. It was a dossier on her, and it was accurate down to her favourite colour and the name of her first boyfriend. She browsed the rest of the report. It had everything about her. Everything. Names of her instructors at school, her test scores, dates of major events in her life. It even had the date she was recruited from the Rangers into ISS. The only thing it didn't have was details of her missions for them. Where did he get all this, how did he get it? Did he have contacts on Bethany? He must have, and high ranked ones too.

"Why give me this?"

"So you'll have what you need to make the right choice."

"Yeah? What choice?"

Stone looked away, uncertainty etched on his features for the first time. "A hard one, Richmond, the hardest you'll ever make. You don't have to make it right this minute, but soon."

Kate nodded. So, she had guessed right. There was a Merki incursion on the way and the vipers were being mobilised to meet the threat. "Oh, you really are recruiting us then."

Stone snorted. "You guessed."

"When are the Merkiaari coming?"

Stone stared, and then shook his head. "Is that what you think this is about?"

"Well isn't it?"

"No. They have nothing to do with this, but we *are* recruiting up to strength. I'll let the Colonel tell you more. He wouldn't like me jumping the gun this way. I strongly suggest you accept the offer."

"Do I really have a choice?"

"There are always choices, Richmond. Sometimes they're all bad."

For a moment Kate shared Stone's pain as they remembered

Bethany's murdered children. "And this time?"

Stone smiled, banishing the nightmare thoughts. "This time, your choices will change your life, hopefully for the better." The hatch slid aside and he stepped through. "Oh, I nearly forgot; read the section about your family before you reject our offer out of hand. You'll regret it if you don't, and don't forget to remove your handiwork from your comp when you're done. I'll know when it's gone."

The hatch slid shut, hiding his smug grin.

"Shit," Kate whispered and frowned. Why was she still talking like a foulmouthed retro? "Damn! I was going to ask him about that..."

She sighed and lay back on her bunk to read the section about her family. It described in brutal detail how Gerald Whitby had used his influence with the Baxters to ruin her father. It didn't say why, and Kate had long ago given up trying to find that out. None of it was important until she found the section on her brother. It listed his vital stats, much like it had hers, and she only skimmed them. Then she saw the shattering revelations on the last page. Paul was alive and well, living and working off-world. He was alive! She had hoped and prayed for it, but all her searching, all her shady deals had turned up nothing. He had ceased to exist. How could Stone find her brother in mere weeks? He couldn't have searched harder than she had these last few years. A lucky hit on his first try? No way, she didn't believe in luck.

Kate read further and found part of the answer. It was a mission overview detailing an op that took place not long ago on Thurston. She whistled, realising how close she had come to being tangled in a viper operation staged against the Freedom Movement. Paul had been there, they had missed each other by a week. No more than that! There were photographs of him exiting a shuttle and meeting someone. She read the results of the operation, not caring about the Freedom Movements annihilation, interested only in her brother. Thankfully he had not been part of the fighting and had left well before it got messy. The ship was owned and operated by...

"Noooo," she hissed. "Whitby you bastard, you took my father from me. I'm not letting you have my brother too!"

Kate leapt off the bunk and nearly smashed the compad against the hatch in her rage. She had to do something, but what could she do? Paul was god knows where, and she was stuck on Luna. Even if she weren't, Gerald Whitby was one of The Ten. He was a member of Bethany's ruling council. What the hell was Paul thinking linking himself to that family? It might have been the Baxters that ruined their father and ultimately killed him, but Whitby was the puppet master.

Kate's thoughts raced. She finally had a lead on her brother's whereabouts; she couldn't quit now and let the trail go cold. If she couldn't trace a single ship and all its passengers she would eat her damn computer. Paul was as good as found. It would still take some digging to ferret him out, but she would find him. There was no doubt in her mind any longer. She would find him and soon.

Kate sat at her comp. Stone had given her what amounted to an ultimatum, and she didn't dare disobey. She would remove her shunt and other hacks from the comm system as ordered, but first she had to warn her contact that his cover was blown. Maybe he could beat the odds and escape, though she doubted it.

"You're three hours late!" her contact snarled.

Kate smiled. "Yeah, sorry about that, I had this thing. Listen—"

"No you listen. I need your report right goddamn now! I think they may be on to me."

Her smile slipped and she nodded. "Yeah, I think you're right. You better disappear."

"That's what I said. Now send the damn report and let me get out of here!"

"Ah, about that… there's no report and I resign."

His face darkened. "You can't resign, no one leaves ISS."

"I can, I just did. I quit."

"Kate, be reasonable. Just send your data and we'll talk about this later. I know you want to find your brother. I'll help. You know you'll never find him on your own."

Kate smiled coldly. "I have a better offer," she said and broke the connection. A few more commands and her comp reset itself to its default configuration leaving no evidence of her tampering.

\* \* \*

Colonel Dan Flowers studied the faces of two hundred and twenty young men and women. The youngsters were silent and sitting at attention waiting for him to speak, while Stone, Marion, and the other vipers he had brought with him stood silently along the walls looking on.

His eyes sought out Richmond, and found her sitting quietly in the second row. She looked pale and distracted. Of all the recruits, she was one of those that concerned him the most. Stone and Marion had worked their miracle to keep her in the program as he had asked, but something deeper seemed to be going on in Richmond's head than a Bethanite's fear of cybernetics. She was withdrawn and moody with the other recruits, but wouldn't talk about it. Neither would Stone.

Marion was a qualified Psych Tech as well as an MD, but she wouldn't break confidence. All he could do was hope that she was keeping a professional eye on the situation, and that she would intervene if and when the time came.

Flowers stood at parade rest before his audience. "My name is Flowers, Colonel currently commanding 1st Recruit Training Battalion, 501st Infantry... you lot in other words. You will be seeing a lot of me over the coming month." That caused a stir. His name was not unknown in the Alliance. He raised a hand to silence the murmuring recruits. "Pipe down people. We have time to answer a few questions." He pointed to a woman in the third row. "You are?"

The woman stood at attention and replied. "Sir, Lieutenant Fuentez. Alliance Marines, sir... I mean I used to be."

"Ask your question, *Recruit* Fuentez."

"Sir, I heard the Council ordered a hold put on new construction of vipers after the war, sir."

"You heard right, but policy does change. After the war, we were allowed to recruit back up to a nice and even one hundred units. A lucky thing for the Alliance. We can train you and more like you."

No one was really comfortable with nano enhanced cyborgs. One of the first major uses of nano technology was that of nano-bots injected into the blood stream to protect from disease. In the military, the idea was enhanced with the bots being tasked specifically to heal battlefield injuries. During the war, ever more applications were discovered until the first viper unit was created. Using nanotech to enhance bone structure and musculature, a stronger faster soldier was produced that eventually led the Alliance to victory after victory.

The downside was that vipers scared people. They were designed specifically to maim and kill Merkiaari in milliseconds. No one was easy around a loaded gun with a hair trigger. It was the same with vipers. They were feared and respected—but mostly feared. Only another viper was truly content to be near one. Everyone else shunned them. If asked, most would say it was only good sense to fear them.

Cyborgs and neural implant technology were feared partly because of what happened when Douglas Walden and his hackers began their reign of terror in the mid 3300s. The so-called Hacker Rebellion saw the end of widespread use of implant technology. Before that time, nearly everyone was fitted with neural interfaces that allowed them to access AI controlled networks spanning systems all over the Human sector of space. Walden and his fanatics changed all that when they tried to free what they called the oppressed mentalities that Humanity had enslaved.

Millions of people died horribly—turned to mindless zombies

when Walden unleashed his viruses and worms upon the networks. Economies of entire planets went into free fall, defence nets and power grids had to be shut down for months to prevent damage to critical systems. What Walden failed to consider, or perhaps didn't care about, was that those same AIs he wanted to free couldn't function separated from the network. They *were* the network. Thousands of AIs were destroyed by those same hackers—men and women that had sworn to free them.

Almost four hundred years later, there were no more AIs and a ban was in force to prevent construction of more. There were no solar system spanning networks, very few neural networks or interfaces of any kind existed anywhere in the Alliance, and all because of one man—Douglas Walden. His name was universally despised. He was known throughout the Alliance as one of the most evil and hated men in history. Being called a hacker by someone was the worst insult imaginable.

As for the vipers, an army of cyborgs controlled by hackers was a nightmare scenario that no one wanted to contemplate.

Flowers nodded to another recruit. "You have a question, son?"

"Sir, Lieutenant Cragg, Alizon Rangers. My question is: why are they increasing the number now, sir?"

Flowers pursed his lips. "The answer to that question is classified, Recruit. You are not to discuss it with anyone outside of this room. The simplest answer is that we have discovered another alien species."

That caused quite a stir. Everyone started talking at once, all trying to ask for details.

"Simmer down people. You are soldiers, act like it." He glared around the room. "We haven't been attacked, and I have no reason to expect we will be, but we're not taking chances. I've seen some of the data. I believe we may have found allies rather than enemies. In any case, I have been tasked with recruiting and training you lot, while Colonel Stanbridge will look for another group to test." He paused for more questions but there were none. "Attention to orders: All those here present will immediately embark a shuttle to *ASN Washington*.

"You will be issued new uniforms on the shuttle. Put them on immediately. You are forbidden to wear anything else until I say otherwise. Your old uniform will be disposed of, and any personal items will be locked in my safe until we reach base. Don't think this trip is a vacation, people," he warned when he noticed shoulders relaxing throughout the room. "You will be taught the anatomy of a viper, including the construction process on the way. While aboard *Washington,* you are forbidden to enter any unauthorised compartment. In fact, you are authorised only three areas. One, your sleeping area. Two, the refectory that I will show you. Three, the toilet facility.

"You will *not* fraternise with crew members. Any recruit seen discussing viper business, or anything else for that matter, with a crew member will be dismissed and mind wiped. Any infraction of the orders I have just made clear to you from this point on, will lead to instant dismissal and mind wipe. Embarrassing me, or any other viper unit, will result in instant dismissal and mind wipe. All understood?"

Silence.

He scowled. "My hearing must be defective. Is all UNDERSTOOD?"

Two hundred and twenty voices said as one, "Sir, yessir."

He glanced at Stone. "Carry on, Sergeant."

Stone braced. "Sir." Turning to the recruits he gave his orders. "Listen up. From this point on you are viper recruits. Any one of you can prove himself worthy to be an officer, and the reverse is also true. The first fifty men, starting from the man on my left closest to the hatch, stand and follow your sergeant." Stone watched as fifty men and woman followed his instructions. He went through all the rest until the last group. "Sir, we seem to have seventy men here."

"Why, I do believe you're right, Master Sergeant. I'll take the last twenty personally."

"Yes, sir," Stone said. "The next fifty follow me. You are now Fourth Platoon."

Flowers studied his twenty recruits, among them was Richmond and Fuentez. "You know the drill by now. Follow me Fifth Platoon."

\* \* \*

Gina marched automatically in step with her new comrades. Her situation was hard to take in. It had taken a police action on a border world not yet officially part of the Alliance to gain her stripes, and another on Thurston to gain her commission. Being a recruit again felt unreal, as if the last fifteen years had been a dream. All her achievements had been wiped away by two little words spoken quietly yesterday in her room.

"I volunteer."

The Colonel had nodded solemnly and shook her hand before leaving her to ponder all he had told her. He had been almost brutal with his descriptions of the surgery and the consequences of it, but that had not been the hardest thing for her to take in. She had already been aware of some of the details through her association with Eric, but not all them. For one thing, she hadn't been aware that all viper units were sterile—a consequence of the process used to create them. By volunteering to join those elite soldiers, she was giving up the possibility of a family and children in the future. She was agreeing to leave her Humanity behind. She understood Eric so much better now.

She made her way to the shuttle and pondered what they had and hadn't been told. The news of another sentient race was astounding. Everyone knew Humanity's old enemies, the Merkiaari, were still out there, and because of that the drive to go out specifically looking for new races had waned. It sounded as if the Council was being cagey this time. A good thing. Mishandling first contact could send Humanity into war with another alien race. How many times could the Alliance win against a superior force before going down into defeat?

Once aboard the shuttle, Gina pulled on her new uniform. The only insignia on it was her name on the pocket over her right breast, and the viper patch on her left shoulder. The battledress uniform was the same as every other she had ever worn except in colour, but this one made her feel different. No rank now, but that wasn't it. It was the mental baggage that came with the black uniform and the viper patch that caused it.

She had made an irrevocable decision when she hadn't backed out at the briefing. The rumours of what happened when you became a viper were rife throughout the Alliance. Some said vipers were nothing but robots and were not Human. Others said they were cyborgs and too powerful a threat to the Alliance. There were many other rumours, but one thing they all agreed on was that vipers were not completely Human any longer. By not backing out she had chosen to give up part of her Humanity. She had seen Eric in action, and she had watched the Colonel and his sergeants throughout the testing. She couldn't distinguish any external differences between them and any other person, except the weapon's data bus in their right palms.

Until they moved.

They seemed to glide along, as if they might take to the air at any moment. She knew the illusion was caused by the strength they embodied, but the grace was surprising. Images of clanking, clumsy robots were very far from the reality.

She handed her Marine Lieutenant's uniform to the sergeant that came to collect it with a pang of loss. She was a Marine no longer, not really. The saying: *Once a Marine always a Marine*, came easily while still in the Corps, but from the outside looking in, there was a world of difference. The Corps was all her family… *had been* all her family. She glanced around at her new one and hoped she had made the right choice. Being a Marine was more than wearing the uniform. It was doing one's duty no matter what, being ever faithful to what the Corps and the Alliance stood for. Wearing black didn't change who she was, and she was determined her transformation into a viper unit would not change her either.

She strapped into her seat, knowing what would happen if she didn't. The shuttle was much too small to have an internal gravity field. She was used to living and working in micro-gee environments and did not concern herself when the shuttle accelerated hard just a few moments later. One or two of the others were caught off guard, and she didn't think much of their chances at promotion. They had been given plenty of time to change, but she noticed with amusement that some of the recruits were shy about undressing with men in view. They were probably from Bethany's World. It was surprising to see viper recruits from there, especially when Bethany's government had voted against their creation during the Merki War, but she supposed there had to be some normal people living there.

The Alliance had only been a dream back then. Earth, though highly respected as Humanity's homeworld, had been only one of many separate voices. It had taken a war to make the dream of the Alliance come to life. Worlds had banded together to resist the aliens, but they failed to hold the enemy at bay until Earth finally stepped to the fore with its forces. The Alliance was born and the Merki advance was slowed but not stopped. Ten years of harsh fighting culminated in the creation of the first vipers, and they slowly reclaimed the lost worlds. The war lasted almost twenty years—twenty years, and an estimated sixteen billion people died before it was done. It could have been many more—the Merkiaari were very thorough. They left little evidence of their genocide behind them. No one knew the exact figures.

The Alliance did succeed in pushing the aliens out of its systems, but at a high cost. Gina thought they should have pushed on and annihilated the Merkiaari down to the last male, but she understood why they hadn't. Eighty percent of the new Alliance had needed massive reconstruction, and resources were at an all time low. It took almost fifty years to bring those worlds back to their pre-war condition. During that time, the Alliance Council became a way of life. Headquarters of the combined military remained in Sol system on Luna. Earth, as Humanity's homeworld, became the capital and therefore the centre of the Human sphere of influence—though of course it wasn't central in purely spatial terms.

Peace and the rule of law reigned within the Alliance, but those yearning for a frontier type life had an outlet. These became known as the Border Worlds. They offered a hard and violent life to their citizens, but their sparse populations preferred it that way. They were left alone for the most part, but the Alliance did offer membership to them if they could reach a consensus among their people to join. Some of the Border Worlds had turned to piracy to supplement their lack of trade. Fleet was kept gainfully employed suppressing such outbreaks.

Gina studied the faces and postures of those around her. Most seemed cheerful and nodded to her before continuing their conversations. Her eyes locked on one woman who was silent and brooding. The woman's eyes sharpened when she noticed Gina's regard, and her hand twitched as if reaching for a weapon. The woman was a killer, pure and simple.

Gina forced her eyes to move on and the chill in her spine eased.

She couldn't see outside. The shuttle was a military vessel and not a cruise ship, but she still knew the moment they arrived. Gravity returned as the shuttle crossed the threshold in the bay, and moments later a slight bump heralded touchdown. Various clanking noises announced the ship was secure and she unbuckled her harness.

Colonel Flowers stood in the centre aisle and surveyed the recruits. "Listen up! You will follow your sergeants to quarters. You will not deviate from the course he sets. You will not lag behind gawking. You will not talk. You will not do anything other than march to your assigned quarters. Understood?"

"Sir, yessir!" Gina yelled with the others. It was like being back in boot camp.

"Carry on, Sergeant."

Stone straightened. "Yes, sir. Each platoon will march in good order behind their sergeants—which means no pushing and shoving for you new people. Fifth platoon, you're first."

*Obviously.*

Fifth platoon was the last to board after all. Gina had been a sergeant herself, she knew the game, but Flowers seemed to be taking the security arrangements to extremes. *Washington* was Fleet for goodness sakes. Surely everyone on board her was reliable.

Gina marched behind Flowers into the bay. The place was deserted. There would usually be crewmen working to refuel the shuttle, not that it needed refuelling, but navy types always took the opportunity to do so. No captain of a ship, whether that ship be a battle group carrier or a lowly shuttle, would miss the opportunity to top off his bunkers. In this case that seemed to be exactly what was happening. She kept her scrutiny of the bay to herself and followed Flowers through a hatch deeper into the ship. She had never been on board a *Washington* class ship before, let alone that class' namesake, and she wanted to look around, but the Colonel had ordered otherwise. She took him at his word when he declared mind wipe as the punishment for infractions.

Mind wipe was only used on violent criminals such as murderers and rapists. It had come about when bleeding heart liberals had managed to have the death penalty taken off the books. Hypno had been around for a while, but was used for entertainment only. It didn't take long for the courts to see a use for it, and a new punishment for murder was introduced—personality death. Later the punishment was used on convicted rapists and then on all violent crime. It was amazing the difference it had made. Crime was cut to barely sixty percent of its previous levels in the core, and it had declined every year since hypno's introduction. Whatever you called it, mind wipe or personality death, it was worse than true death and therefore a fitting punishment. How Flowers could justify it here she didn't know; she wasn't willing to find out.

"This is your toilet facility," Flowers indicated a hatch on the other side of a section seal.

Gina paid it no mind, saving her attention for Flowers as he walked on.

"This is your refectory and day area. All platoons will share this space, and the toilet facility. The first compartment on the right is fifth platoon's sleeping area. The next is for fourth and so on. Once everyone arrives, the blast door will be sealed.

"These areas are where you will live for the next three weeks. The rest of *Washington* is off limits. Anyone seen outside this section will be dismissed and suffer mind wipe. Anyone seen talking to a crew member will be dismissed and suffer mind wipe. Understood?"

"Sir, yessir!" Gina said along with her platoon mates.

"Good. Get settled in, and we'll start work at zero six hundred tomorrow—dismissed."

Flowers walked away and entered another compartment this time on the left. Gina couldn't see inside, but she assumed it was his cabin. She moved away from the chattering recruits and entered the area set aside for their barracks.

To her surprise, her name was already stencilled on a locker next to a rack. She opened it to see a full set of toiletries, a viper class-A and class-B uniform, and a box of compads with the viper patch displayed prominently on their cases—manuals. In the bottom was her kit bag. She opened it and found everything she had brought with her minus her old uniform. She found every one of her old ribbons and medals in a neat wooden presentation box. They had even unpicked the stitching and removed her unit patches from her old dress uniform to place them here. They were certainly thorough, she thought, fingering the patches.

Gina smoothed one of them flat in the palm of her hand. "Seventh Marines."

As easy as that, she was no longer a Marine.

Storing everything back as she found it, she sat on her rack and began going through her manuals. They detailed the complete process of building a viper unit. She was surprised to see all the models listed and not just the newest version. She frowned for a moment, and then nodded in understanding. In the field, it might be necessary to make good a unit's battle damage. It seemed unlikely she would need to repair a Mk1, or that she would have the biomech components necessary to do so, but better safe than sorry she supposed.

"What are you reading, Fuentez?"

Gina looked up and found one of the recruits. The name on his chest was M. Cragg. She remembered him. He was the lieutenant... ex-lieutenant now, who had asked the second question in the briefing. She showed him the case of the manual she was reading.

"Hmmm. Viper sub-systems: Internal sensors. Not the sort of light reading I would expect at bed time."

"That depends on your definition of light reading," she said.

Cragg laughed and sat on the rack opposite. He offered his hand. "I'm Martin, and you are?"

She shook his hand firmly. "Gina."

"Pleased to meet you. The others are all sitting around chatting, don't you want to join them?"

"Not really. I'm happy enough reading these, but don't let me stop you."

"Are you trying to get rid of me?"

"Yes. My chance to become an officer in the 501st is important to me. If I can start learning now, it won't be so hard for me later."

Cragg frowned. "You're right."

He stood and walked along the aisle until he found his own rack. He retrieved his manuals and came back to sit opposite her.

Gina watched him find the same manual she was reading, and begin to work through it.

Cragg looked up and saw her staring at him. He grinned and gestured for her to get back to work. They both laughed and settled down to read.

\* \* \*

# 12 ~ Ghosts

Kate couldn't believe she was here on the way to becoming a viper unit. What had that bastard Stone done to her? It had to be something in his download. The sim had changed her somehow. Before she went in, she had been her old self and hardly able to tolerate the cyborgs near her, but when she came out, she had agreed to become one. And what about Hiller, he was here. How did Stone persuade a rich son of Bethany to give it all up and become a despised cyborg?

"Recruit Richmond?"

Kate blinked and blushed when she found all eyes turned her way. "Sir?"

Colonel Flowers tilted his head to regard her, as if wondering what kind of noise she would make when stepped on. "Am I boring you, Recruit?"

Kate reddened still further and tried to sit at attention. "No, sir."

"Oh good. Then perhaps you will be kind enough to recap what I just said?"

Kate glanced down at the compads on her desk. Only one was active. It was displaying the inner workings of a viper unit. Specifically, it was displaying a viper unit's sensor and electronic warfare suit.

"Sir, you were describing a viper's EW and sensor suite, sir."

Kate knew she had blown it when the rest of the recruits winced and shook their heads. Flowers on the other hand just pursed his lips and looked disappointed.

"We covered that section a half hour ago, Recruit."

"Sorry, sir."

"I know it's a lot to take in, Recruit, but when we go dirtside, there won't be time for any more lessons like this. There won't be time for very much at all before you're all prepped for surgery. Sorry doesn't begin to cut it, Recruit."

Kate looked down to hide her embarrassment.

"As I was saying," Flowers went on in a brisker tone. "You all have a lot to learn. Aside from mastering a viper unit's systems, which will take months, there's the artillery course, the sabotage and subversion courses, various special weapons courses... the list goes on. Master Sergeant Stone will be cooking up all kinds of nasty simulations to test you throughout the learning process. My point is, ladies and gentlemen, and this goes double for you Richmond, you do not have time to waste."

"Question, sir?" Fuentez said and Flowers nodded to her. "I have no objections to learning whatever you want, but... artillery? We're infantry."

There were nods and murmurs from among the recruits.

"Don't you like Arty, Fuentez?"

Fuentez grinned. "Only when it's on my side, sir."

The recruits laughed and Flowers smiled. "Fuentez is right in what she says. Vipers are infantry, but things have changed just a bit since the war."

Kate grinned.

Flowers went on. "Back then, we were deployed with other Alliance forces. Mostly in the first wave, sometimes ahead of the first wave, but we always had backup. Now we mostly work undercover on solo ops, but the General believes in being prepared for all contingencies. Even outright war. That means, you will learn whatever we decide to teach you. How many of you know how to pilot a shuttle?"

Kate raised her hand, as did a dozen or so others. Fuentez wasn't one of them.

Flowers nodded. "By the end of your training, all of you will be able to steal a shuttle and use it. All of you will know how to load, aim, and fire a range of artillery pieces. And your fire will be *dead* accurate. Vipers live a very long time, people. You will spend a lot of that time learning everything there is to know about the art of destruction." He glanced at his wristcomp. "Dismissed!"

The recruits stood to attention.

Kate relaxed after the Colonel left, and the recruits milled around discussing what they had learned today. All week long, the Colonel had held lectures from zero six hundred to twelve hundred hours. The afternoon was theirs, and the evening was given over to tactical problems, based on their supposed understanding of the day's lessons. She had done well so far, but then she should. She had the advantage of Stone's download to draw on.

She frowned. Why hadn't she blown the whistle on Stone? And that was another thing, why was she still thinking in retro?

Moving away with a scowl on her face, Kate tracked down Hiller. He was lying on his rack with a compad propped on his chest, displaying one of the viper manuals they had all been issued. He didn't notice her come in until she snatched the compad out of his hands.

"We have to talk," she said sitting on the rack next to his.

Hiller sighed and swung his legs down to sit opposite her. "I should have spoken up to him, but I was beholden to him."

Kate blinked. "Huh?"

"The Whitbys own me," Hiller said in humiliation. "That's why I stayed silent that day."

Kate's original intention was to ask about Stone, but this was more interesting.

"You're a Hiller, one of the *families*."

Hiller's lips twisted into a snarl. "I'm the son of a family—a family with no money left! Hiller survives only as long as I do what the Whitbys say. They own me. They own all that Hiller was, and they own my vote on Bethany's council."

Kate blinked stupidly at him. Hiller was destitute? That news would rock Bethany to its foundations were it ever to become known. Hiller was one of the *families*. One of the original settlers of Bethany's World. How could it happen? Whitby owned the Hiller vote?

*My God, how many others?*

"Whitby failed the testing?"

Hiller snorted. "Of course he did. He's nothing but the pompous windbag he appears to be. He bought his commission the same way he buys everyone and everything he wants."

"But the Hiller name is everywhere back home. I've seen it."

Hiller nodded. "His father ruined mine and gave us the scraps from his table. Our name still appears on our old holdings, but Hiller actually owns nothing. My sister and I are all that Hiller really has. She went into medicine and turned away from me. She hasn't even kept the name. Whitby props me up so that my voting rights remain in force."

Kate grinned. "Wait until they hear about your new job."

Hiller smiled wearily. "When they hear about this, the name will finally be erased. Not that I care anymore, but I would like to think the Whitbys would be hurt by the loss of the vote."

"But you don't think they will be?"

"No chance. They've blackmailed their way into holding most of the votes on Bethany. One vote less will be an embarrassment, but nothing more than that."

That was something Kate needed to think about in-depth, but later. "I came to ask you whether Stone... whether he *did* anything to you to make you become a viper?"

Hiller frowned. "Stone? No, nothing. I haven't spoken to him at all. The reason—the *only* reason that I'm here is my wish to get away from Bethany and Whitby."

Kate believed him, but what did that mean regarding her own reasons for being here? She was confused about the entire thing. She knew the power and excitement the viper systems imparted from her time in the sim, but that wasn't the reason... was it? She hoped not. She was a Bethany Ranger in her heart still, a killer, a sniper, and she liked what she was. Would becoming a cyborg change what she was inside? Not the biomech and cybernetics, but her soul? Bethany taught that cyborgs were soulless, but she had witnessed Colonel Flowers' anguish in the sim. He had been a captain then, but the pain in his eyes at hearing about the children was real. She would stake... yes, even that. She would stake her very *soul* on it.

"I have to see Stone," Kate mumbled and made to leave.

"Richmond?"

She turned back. "Yes?"

"Are you... are you scared? I am. I'm terrified of becoming a machine. Everyone knows—"

Kate shook her head quickly. "Everyone on *Bethany* knows. We've had almost two hundred years of lies forced down our throats."

"Lies? But our history—"

"Happened," she broke in. "It happened, but not the way they say. I can't tell you how I know, but Burgton's vipers fought hard for us when the Merkiaari came."

"You're sure? Really sure that it will be all right?"

"It will be all right," Kate said and left.

She was unable to find Stone at first. Was he hiding from her? She shook her head; he wouldn't hide, but where the hell was he? He could usually be found sitting in the refectory at this time of the day, but when she checked, he was nowhere to be found.

"You seen Stone?" Kate said to one of the recruits passing by.

"Nope," the recruit said and walked on.

After walking aimlessly in the hope of finding him, she finally found someone who might know. She braced to attention and saluted.

"This recruit needs to find Sergeant Stone, ma'am. Might you know where he is?"

Lieutenant Hymas turned from her conversation with another recruit and frowned at the interruption. "Dismissed, Takeri," she said to the dark complexioned woman.

"Ma'am," Takeri said saluting before leaving.

Takeri was from Earth. Kate had spoken with her a few times about their customs and the strange way she had at looking at things.

"Stone is resting in his quarters."

Kate frowned; she hadn't thought to check his quarters. The day was only half over. What the hell was there to do on this tub that could require him to rest?

Hymas' eyes narrowed. "What's this about, recruit?"

Kate hesitated. "I would rather not say, ma'am."

"You would rather not say," Hymas said soto-voiced. She stared at Kate for a long moment before stepping to the wall and pressing the button there. "Computer: page Sergeant Stone."

A voice barked from the comm. "Stone!"

"Recruit Richmond wants to see you, Ken... yes I think so," Hymas said and glanced at Kate before continuing.

Kate strained to hear what Stone was saying, but all she heard was a few words. Out of context they gave her nothing of what he was asking the Lieutenant.

"Fine. Do you want me to... right. See you later." Hymas turned and regarded Kate thoughtfully. "Sergeant Stone has invited you to visit him. That was nice of him wasn't it?"

"Yes, ma'am," Kate said giving the expected answer. "In his quarters, ma'am?"

Hymas nodded. "Now would be a good time, Recruit."

"Thank you, ma'am," she said, and ducked by Hymas before her superior could ask her any questions.

When Kate reached Stone's quarters, she pressed the call button. A moment later the hatch slid aside and she entered the dim cabin.

"Sergeant?"

"Step in won't you?"

Something was up; she could feel it. Kate stepped fully inside, and the hatch slid shut darkening the cabin still further. Gradually her eyes adjusted and she began to make out shapes. A terminal to one side was dark and the chair before it was empty. The rack was unoccupied and scrupulously neat. It was as regulation as anyone could want. Turning to her left, she found Stone sitting on a couch watching her. That couch surely wasn't regulation. Fleet must be going soft. Maybe such comforts were within its regulations, but she doubted it. Kate preferred austerity to comfort. Comfort could betray you into wanting more of the same.

Kate was very aware that Stone had her on his sensors from the moment she stepped inside. Hell, he could pick up everyone aboard the ship if he wanted to. She had used those sensors in the sim. She knew how good they were. He had her targeted, she was certain, but he didn't have a weapon on him. He didn't need one.

Kate fidgeted uneasily. "I want to... I mean I need to..."

"Know what I did to you?" Stone finished.

"Yes, Sergeant."

"Come here."

It was the last thing Kate wanted to do with him in this strange mood, but she had always fought her fear. She stepped toward him, and stopped a pace from his still reclining figure. Close up, he still looked the same. She laughed silently. What had she expected to see, an unshaven ogre?

Stone watched her unblinking. "I did nothing to you except show you the truth."

Kate felt her face heat with anger. "Whose truth, *yours?*"

"Mine, the Colonel's, the Regiment's..." he shrugged. "Yours too now."

"I want to know why I agreed to be enhanced. I want to know why I keep saying things that sound retro when I never have before. I want to... *understand.*"

Stone laughed, but the sound was bitter. "Understanding, who doesn't want that? I could have used some on Bethany... we all could. Do you know how many ghosts walk beside me and the Colonel and the others?" He shook his head. "Of course you don't. How could you? I am two hundred and twenty nine years old—two hundred and thirty in a week. Two hundred years of killing. You think you're a killer now? Wait a few centuries and you'll know different." He stared bleakly into the distance at nothing. "I see them all. My fine and strong platoon of vipers, my first one, going into the fire, and only two of us coming back broken and bloody. My second, and only I came back, my third and three of us survived, my fourth..." he closed his eyes, but when he opened them again they were hard. "I bet you remember every kill, not so?"

"It is so," Kate agreed.

"vipers can't forget, Richmond. They never told us that when they made us. Nothing I can drink, or smoke, or inject can ever give me peace. Our bots won't allow it. Senility was a curse for millennia, now it's rare, but even that won't save me. We remember *everything*, forever and ever and ever... until the end of time for all we know. Ghosts... but ghosts of comrades are still comrades. My victims now, they're worse."

"You don't have victims, Sergeant. You're a killer like me, but you fight in the open. I take them down in the dark from behind. I like it, and I'm good at it."

Stone smiled grimly. "I knew that about you the moment I laid eyes on you. If looks could kill, Hiller and Whitby would have been stabbed to death that day on the concourse. Stabbed in the back, *repeatedly.*" He laughed. "I have victims, believe me I do. A school full of kids is one instance, but there are others. They come to me you know, those children. Not often, but more of late—since the download."

Kate nodded, thankful for the turn the conversation had taken. "That download is what I came to talk about. It changed me; *you* changed me."

"Not so. The download let you see the truth. The truth is what changed you. Not that I believe you've changed very much. You're seeing things more clearly now. Maybe this is the first time you've ever seen clearly. You know Bethany was built on lies, built by liars. You know—"

"I know what you want me to know," Kate said. "That sim could be a lie."

"You know it wasn't. You were me. You did what I did, saw what I did..." Stone broke off staring over her shoulder at nothing. "And what I didn't do."

"I went in hating cyborgs, and came out wanting to be one. How can you say you haven't done something to me, to my mind?"

"I say it because it's true. You want to know how I knew what to do?"

"You're damn right I do."

"Remember your first day of testing, the questionnaire?"

Kate nodded but frowned. There had been a lot of questions on that thing. Some had seemed irrelevant; others had been obvious in their aims to weasel out her secrets. She had sneered at the so obvious attempt to get inside her head. She answered the questions on military matters with truth, and the prying ones with creative fantasy designed to pass the psych eval.

"You told me how, Richmond. Or rather you told the psychs, and they told me."

"I was careful," Kate protested.

"Psych evals can't be fooled. If they could, they would be useless. Why do you think there were so many different questions that seemed to ask the same thing, but with different words?"

"What did they find?"

"Your brother. Your weakness was clear to the psychs. They checked into your background thoroughly to find the source. They found it. I had exactly what I needed to hit you harder than you had ever been hit before. I knew that if you could overcome that weakness by ignoring the children, knowing that doing so would sentence them to death, you would be what we needed. We are the same. I am you, you are me. The download proved it."

"I'm me!"

"You are you," Stone agreed with a sharp nod. "But you think like me. Kill thousands of children, save the world. Simple decision wasn't it?" he said bitterly.

"Anyone with sense would have made the same choice," Kate protested.

"Not anyone. Some would have, and we'll be trying to recruit all we can find, but most would have ignored the drone to save the kids hoping that someone else would launch it. You saw the Colonel in pieces outside. That happened. You lost a leg and a hand, so did I. You kept going, so did I. You're already a viper in your head, Richmond. The uniform just warns people."

Was he right? Was that why she had felt right as a viper in the sim? She had played her part as if born one. She had known it was a sim all the way through, yet she had been at home with her abilities, and had enjoyed using them.

"I want... *need* to talk about my brother. He's why I joined ISS in the first place."

Stone nodded. "That was my guess from the moment I read the psych eval. It gave you the freedom to search for him. How did it go, do the mission in a day instead of two and use the time saved for your own mission?"

"Something like that."

"Thought so. Didn't work though, did it?"

Kate shook her head.

"I can tell you why if you want to hear it?"

"I need to."

"Your own people were actively working to stop you," at her confused frown he went on, "I don't mean Bethanites. I mean ISS. Your data came from contacts you made through your missions for them. They were all ISS assets before you came along, Richmond."

"I *knew* that," she said derisively. "As you say, that's how I met them in the first place. Why would they give me false info?"

"Because they were ordered to do that. Look Richmond, you seem to think that ISS are the good guys in this. They aren't, not by a long way. You *did* read the report I gave you?"

She flushed. "Of course I did."

"If you read between the lines it's obvious that ISS knew all along where your brother was keeping himself, and that he worked for your government among others. They were shielding him from you for reasons they must feel are good ones."

"Yeah? He isn't like me at all, Stone. He's not a spook, or a fighter of any kind. What good is he to them? And besides, I wanted to know he was alright, not hurt him!"

"He's a merc, Richmond. He works for the highest bidder."

"He's not a merc."

Stone sighed. "You won't see it because to you he's still your brother. Why do you think he was there on Thurston meeting with the leader of the Freedom Movement? I'll tell you. He was delivering an arms shipment to them."

"So he delivered a cargo. Doesn't mean he knew what the cargo was. He's just a crewman on a ship."

"You don't seriously believe that, Richmond. Who sends a mere crewman to meet with a buyer like that? Come on, think it through."

Kate shook her head.

"You have to let him go. You have a new life now, and so does he."

"Whitby won't have my brother. You don't know what they did to us. I can't leave it."

"You'll have to."

"I can't!"

"Listen to me, Recruit. You will let this go, because if you don't and you go off on your own, the General will brand you a rogue and have you scrapped. Is that clear enough for you?"

Kate shivered. "But he's my brother. I thought you would help me."

"I give you my word that I will help you see your brother again, but first you have to get the enhancement out of the way. We have to get this done by official means."

"How?"

"I don't know, but I'll figure it out. I always do."

Kate looked Stone in the eyes and nodded slowly. He had already gone out of his way to recruit her, and he hadn't informed his superiors about her hacks into the comm system back at HQ... at least she didn't think he had. They wouldn't have recruited her if they had known about that. He had gone above and beyond to shield her already. She trusted him when he said he would find a way.

"So," she said, slumping into the couch with a sigh. "Why do I keep saying things in retro?"

Stone grinned. "It will wear off. I'm old. You just picked up my idioms."

"How long?"

"Don't know. A year or two… maybe."

"You're shitting me," Kate yelled and spluttered over his laughter.

"I ain't shitting yer bitch-girl. Don't worry about it. One day you won't even notice."

She shook her head at the familiar sound of more retro spilling from his mouth. It shouldn't have been familiar, but it was god help her. "That's what worries me."

Kate climbed back to her feet.

"One more thing before you go, *Recruit*," Stone said all business now. "If you mention one word about the download, I'll—"

"You'll what?" Kate said with a grin that wilted the moment he told her.

"I'll kill you," he said, his eyes glittering malevolently.

Kate snapped to attention and saluted. "Understood, sir."

\* \* \*

# 13 ~ Snakeholme

SNAKEHOLME (NGC 1513-4962)

Officially, the system had a number not a name, but for nearly two hundred years NGC 1513-4962 has been the home system of the 501st infantry regiment; more precisely, the fourth planet of that system including its two moons. The world came to be known variously as Base, Home, or more popularly Snakeholme. The larger moon came to be called Gabriel, or light of God, named for the spectacular display its reflected light caused upon Snakeholme's ring system. The smaller moon was called Uriel by General George Burgton, named for the station that was constructed upon its surface. In *Paradise Lost,* Milton described the archangel Uriel as: *the sharpest sighted spirit of all in heaven.* Burgton thought the name appropriate to the station's purpose of keeping watch upon his system's approaches.

Milton's work is still a particular favourite of his.

Snakeholme's catalogue number still exists in the Alliance database, but the interesting thing is what does not appear there. Six planets huddle around the warmth of Snakeholme's sun, but according to the Alliance database, there are none. General Burgton wanted it that way. If General Burgton wanted a thing, that thing happened one way or another. Call it a whim, or call it foresight of things to come, but a few years after the war ended he said: *it would be really nice if people left us alone here.*

He said it to a certain Daniel Flowers as they breathed the invigorating, but slightly chill, evening air from the porch of his residence. They were admiring the glory overhead that was

Snakeholme's sky at night. Snakeholme's ring system was the remnants of its third satellite, smashed by Gabriel millennia ago. It was spectacularly beautiful as it shone silver in the moon's reflected light.

No one came here. No one knew there was a *here* to come to. Rather, only vipers came here. That was how the General, and hence the entire 501st, wanted it.

Gina stood upon the parade ground staring at the beauty, nay, the sheer *grandeur* of her new home. The snow capped mountains and tree covered slopes a few klicks to the north were breathtaking. Petruso Base was built on the smaller northernmost continent of Snakeholme to take advantage of the climate. Although the weather was sometimes a little unpredictable, it couldn't be called extreme. It was perhaps a little breezier than she was used to, a tiny bit more chill in the mornings and evenings, but by no stretch of the imagination could it be called a hardship. The winds were caused by the proximity of both the mountains to the north, and the ocean to the west, but of course it was the 1.29 gravity that shouldered most of the blame.

Gina covered her ears and watched as another heavily armed transport took off and headed west. Dozens like it flew to and from the base every day. She watched until she lost it to distance, and wondered where it was going. It was probably destined for one of the island chains that the regiment used for training ops. The Colonel hadn't been kidding when he said there was a lot to learn. As soon as the first enhanced recruits had come online, the flights had begun and they hadn't stopped since.

Gina faced into the blustery wind, and tried to relax tight shoulders, but it was hard. She was scheduled for surgery later today and she was tense. In one way, she was looking forward to her enhancement. She longed to join the others on those speeding transports, and put what she had learned in the classroom into practice. Seeing the others receive their enhancements, and later board those transports without her, was hard. But worse than that, was watching people she had come to know leave the barracks, and return days later, changed. The changes weren't just physical, and that scared her. She didn't like being left behind, but the thought of her own enhancement was scary.

"What do you think?" Richmond asked.

"*Yip!*" Gina jumped almost a metre straight up in surprise despite the gravity, but her reflexes were good. She landed facing Richmond in a fighting crouch.

"Whoa," Richmond cried capping her right hand with her left to make a T. "Time out, time out. I didn't mean anything by it."

Gina scowled. "Sorry, I'm a bit jumpy."

"I noticed," Richmond said dryly.

"It's my turn onto the table. They just told me."

Richmond's grin wilted. "Oh… you worried?"

Gina snorted. "Me? Not me… yeah, scared shitless."

Richmond shook her head. "No you're not. That's not fear you're feeling, it's excitement."

"You think so?"

"I know so, Gina my girl," Richmond said, and clapped her on the shoulder. "No, you're not scared. It's the waiting, the anticipation of knowing what's coming and being unable to prepare yourself any more than you already have. It happened to me too, but here I am—a whole new woman."

"That's what I'm afraid of," Gina muttered.

She was more nervous now that she knew what to expect, than she had been on the ship that brought her to Snakeholme. For one thing, Richmond had come out of enhancement only a few days ago, and it was obvious how different she was now. Richmond had been the hardest-eyed killer Gina had ever met before she went under the lasers. Now she was the most outgoing joker among the recruits. What had happened to the self-centred bitch they all knew and loved?

"Kate…" Gina hesitated. "Are you still… you know, *you?*"

Richmond smiled crookedly. "What a peculiar thing to say. Of course I'm me. Who do you think lives in here?" she said thumping her chest.

"It's just that you seem so different. Back at HQ you were… I mean before you went into enhancement you were…" Gina sighed. "Look, don't take this wrong, but I thought you were a cold-hearted bitch."

"Yeah I know. A cold-eyed kill anything sniper bitch, that's me. Hey, I'm still in here. It's just… how can I tell you?" Richmond frowned. "Okay, it's like this: On Bethany, the Families run everything. That means if you're not one of them, you are *owned* by one of them. Clear so far?"

"I guess," Gina said wondering where this was going.

"The name Richmond is nothing on Bethany. *Literally nothing.* If you're not one of the Ten, then you're less than dirt to those people. The only way out is the military, but even then you find yourself commanded by know-nothing arseholes who belong to one of the Families." Richmond's face blanked of all emotion, and Gina shivered. The cold-eyed killer was back. "I hated them all," Richmond said in a deadly voice. "I still do, but I've outfoxed them. I've outrun their reach, Gina. A viper you are, and a viper you will always be. The

Colonel said that, and he's right. They have no hold on me any longer. I'm *free!* And not only that, I'm going to outlive them all."

Gina laughed.

"Does that help?" Richmond said.

"Yeah, I think it does."

"Well… *good!*" Richmond draped an arm around Gina's shoulders as they slowly wandered the parade ground. "What do you think of Snakeholme and the rest?"

"It surprised the hell out of me."

And it did. The world was a beautiful place, but what was surprising was the number of people to be found here. Already the recruits had learned of the General's skulduggery, and approved of it. The 501st had saved the Alliance. The survivors of the Merki War deserved a place of their own, especially when public opinion turned against them. No one but 501st were allowed here.

*NO ONE.*

Petruso Base was mostly empty of people, and had been since the regiment was annihilated during the Merki War. The facilities, including supplies and equipment, were all intact though—ready and waiting for more recruits. Colonel Stanbridge was even now looking at the next possible group to be tested and once the orders went out for them to report in, another round of testing at HQ would begin.

"The city was a surprise," she said. "Nice layout, but where did all the people come from?"

"I found out some of it by pumping Stone."

"Pumping—"

"Not that kind." Richmond blushed. "Though I tell you, Gina, I wouldn't mind if he asked."

"He won't. Not until our training is done at least. Sex in the ranks is one thing, but you know what they'd say if it went on between a drill sergeant and someone subordinate to him."

"Yeah, you're right. But I'll tell you something, the 501st is different in a lot of ways."

Gina nodded. It was more focused on the job and less on ceremony for one thing. She would prefer a little more ceremony actually. Unit cohesion always benefited from it. It always made her feel a part of something greater than herself.

"It's not that different. We're still Alliance forces, still under orders from HQ, and I hope still expected to follow the regs."

"Oh sure," Richmond said easily. "Stone and the others are sticklers for the regs. No question. I'm kind of glad, you know? I've always been that way myself."

"Me too. So now I know what kind of pumping you were doing

to Stone, what gives?"

"As best as I can understand it, the General wasn't pleased with the way the families of his vipers were being treated back during the war, so he offered them a place here safely tucked away from the Merki advance. When most of the 501$^{st}$ died in action, their families simply stayed on. Their descendants run the station for us, and they maintain the outpost on Uriel. Hell… they own and run everything but the base itself. Without them we couldn't survive here. The farms, industries, clubs, *breweries*, shops, power plants, *breweries*… everything we need is right here."

Gina nodded in agreement. They had everything but Fleet to take them to war, and ammunition to use during it—except they had ships didn't they? *Washington* hadn't brought them all the way here, instead, it had handed them off to another ship for the final leg of the trip to Snakeholme—a destroyer crewed by vipers. She had to wonder how many more ships General Burgton had managed to purloin and how.

"We haven't got a weapons factory by any chance have we?" she said in an off-hand way.

"Not that I know of, but we've got plenty to train with. I've seen the supply bunkers, and they're full."

"That's what I'm afraid of," she muttered.

"What?"

"Nothing."

"Come on," Richmond said. "You meant something by that, and I want to know what."

"All right. Doesn't it seem odd to you that the base is stocked well enough to fight a war when there hasn't been anyone to use the stuff?"

"We're here…"

Gina waved that away. "Yeah now, but that stuff has been stockpiled for years. I didn't see much unloading, did you?"

"No but—"

"And what about all the security? What was all that crap about on *Washington*? She's Fleet for Chrissakes, yet we buttoned ourselves up like we were in hostile territory. And what about *Hammer*… a destroyer crewed by vipers? Don't you think that's a little odd?"

"I don't get it," Richmond said with a frown. "My CO sent me to HQ. We were tested right there! We were ferried by Fleet, so the Admiralty must know, which means the Department of Defence itself must know too. It seems kosher to me."

"Kosher?" Gina frowned. "What has food got to do with it?"

"It means okay… sort of." Richmond reddened. "Hell, I mean everything seems fine to me. The General is one of the good guys.

He's a *hero*."

To hell with it. Richmond was right. What could possibly make a man like the General turn on the Alliance? "You're right. I'm just jittery about the op. You got any advice for me?"

"Yeah, wear clean panties."

Gina bent double with laughter. It was so unexpected after all her worrying about silly conspiracies. She felt the knot of tension dissolving. "When do they switch on all your goodies?"

Richmond shrugged. "Not until they have enough of us to build another squad. Doesn't make sense going over the same ground two hundred times when they can teach us by squads."

"Good thinking. You'll make lieutenant in no time if you keep on like that."

Richmond looked uncomfortable at the idea. "I don't know. I've always made sure I'm never in a position where I have to order someone. I prefer solo ops, always have."

"Too late now," Gina said with a smirk.

"Why?"

"Vipers are treated as officers when working with other forces. So you see, Kate, you're already an officer as far as your friends in the rangers are concerned. Just imagine what Whitby and his cronies will think when they hear."

"Yeaaaah…" Richmond said with a grin. "Hell, maybe I should go for major. It would serve Whitby right. I would just love to order him to carry my kit around HQ."

"Why not go for colonel?"

"Nah, no fun, but majors do see action now and then."

Gina nodded. "Good point. You be major, I'll be captain, and we'll throw Cragg the Lt's slot. Okay?"

"Fine by me," Richmond said with a sloppy looking grin.

Gina checked her wristcomp. "We better head back. My time's almost up."

"You're *time* is only just beginning," Richmond said seriously before grinning again. They turned around, and with the blustery wind now at their backs, they made their way toward the Tech Centre. "We ought to get ourselves some hang gliders. This wind would see us up there all day if we wanted."

"Ever done any?"

"*Have I!* I was Airborne before ISS took me on. I still have my jumpmaster's wings in my kit. Of course I've done some gliding. If it's in the air, I've done it."

"Sorry," Gina said and grinned at the indignant look on Richmond's face. "I was only asking. What about mountain climbing?"

"Not yet, but I'm willing to learn."

"Me too."

They entered the Tech Centre together.

The Tech Centre housed medical as well as the workrooms containing the equipment necessary to make viper biomech components. They had been given a tour of all the facilities when they first landed. They were extensive. The biomech vats, the nan-assemblers, and bodymod processors were a little scary. The recruits had been silent and apprehensive as the Colonel explained the uses of each machine. The operating theatres seemed mundane in comparison. The recruits knew they would be fed into those silent machines at some point in the enhancement process, and from their expressions, no one looked forward to it.

"I'll hang with you until you go in, okay?"

"Suuure," Gina drawled. "Glad of the company."

They made their way through empty and echoing corridors imagining the voices and bustle that must have filled this place during the Merki War. It was spooky imagining black clad vipers walking here performing various tasks. They were all gone now, only echoes filled this place.

They entered the medical section and were finally greeted by activity. Medical was probably little different from its Merki War days. Recruits wearing black viper battle dress were sitting nervously along the wall on the red plastic chairs that seemed to breed throughout Alliance space. Men and women wandered from one room to another with compads in their hands. They typed as they walked, but no collisions occurred. Viper sensors allowed them to move without looking. They all wore surgical gowns over their uniforms, but there was no doubt they were all vipers. Gina recognised Lieutenant Hymas, but that wasn't how she knew. They had a... call it a presence. Richmond had it, Hymas had it—vipers had a quality that made a person notice them in a crowd. She remembered her first step onto the concourse of HQ. Her eyes had wandered and suddenly locked onto a man. It had been Sergeant Stone, but she hadn't known that then. All she had known was that he stood out, and it wasn't his obsidian black skin either. It was power barely contained.

"Recruit Fuentez reporting, sir," Gina said as one of the gowned men approached her.

"Yes I know. Captain Patel, Fuentez. You're just in time."

"I'm early, sir, aren't I?"

"Yes, yes, but we're a few units ahead of schedule. Follow me and we'll get started."

"Yes, sir." She smiled nervously at Richmond. "Gotta go."

"You'll be fine. Think about those mountains and how we'll run up them."

"Yeah," Gina said and followed the now impatient Patel down the corridor and into a treatment room.

"Now then recruit. The first part of the process is to deactivate your med system, which means removing all trace of your existing bots."

"Sir, may I ask questions?"

Patel frowned at the interruption. "Seeing as you're already asking them, I don't see why not."

"Thank you, sir. Why destroy my bots? They've looked after me all this time without trouble."

"Why do you think?"

"I don't know, sir." If she knew she wouldn't be asking.

"Your IMS consists of various types of nanobots—highly specialised nan-assemblers and nan-disassemblers mostly. I always like to think of them as your own little regiment of soldiers. You have the officers, those that make decisions. You have the scouts, always on the lookout for trouble and reporting back to the officers. Then you have the soldiers consisting of nano-d on the frontline ready to eliminate the enemy—disease and various toxins in this case. And finally you have the engineers, consisting of nano-a, ready and waiting to repair any damage. The system is designed to maintain you as you are now—hopefully in perfect health. It's a good system."

Patel told her to hold up her right arm. Gina did so, and Patel punched in a request for a status update on her wristcomp. Her IMS reported back and Patel nodded. He keyed in a shutdown sequence and her wristcomp went offline for the first time since it was issued. He removed it from her arm revealing pale skin underneath and discarded the device to one side. Gina felt its loss acutely. It had been with her since she joined the Corps fifteen and more years ago.

Patel rummaged in a drawer for something he needed and continued his explanation. "The problems start when you realise just what enhancement truly is, Recruit; it's the restructuring of the body into something else. Enhancement is a process completely at odds with your med system's purpose. The second stage of the enhancement process prepares your skeletal and muscular structure for its transformation. If we left your old IMS in place, your bots would continually try to undo all our work, in effect maintaining you in your present form."

Patel found the syringe he was looking for, and placed it on a metal tray sitting on a wheeled stainless steel trolley to one side of the room. The syringe was huge, much bigger than usual. Gina watched him add a few more things to the tray, and nodded when he looked at her and raised an eyebrow.

"I understand. Thank you, sir. Are first stage bots combat ready?"

Patel shook his head. "No. As the name implies, they're first stage and of limited duration. They're programmed to expire when the job is done. Anything else?"

There were a great many questions she wanted to ask, but by Patel's tone, she knew not to ask them. "No thank you, sir. That's about all."

"Good. Lay down on the couch."

"Should I disrobe?"

"Not at this stage," Patel said and fetched a stand with all kinds of monitoring equipment on it.

He rolled the equipment next to the couch that Gina was reclining on, and attached the sensors to her body. A steady beeping began and the monitors lit to display data regarding her bodily functions. She could read the screens, but the fluctuating lines and numbers might as well be Sanskrit. She could not understand them. Patel dragged the trolley closer and filled the huge syringe with a clear liquid.

"Roll up your right sleeve," Patel ordered and Gina obeyed. "Now this solution is full of stage one nanobots designed to clear your system to its natural birth state. It will take two hours at most. The monitors will tell me when they're finished."

Patel tied a band around Gina's upper arm to bring up a vein, and then used the syringe to inject the solution into her bloodstream.

"You may feel some small disorientation, but don't be concerned. Dizzy spells and temperature fluctuations are both normal for this process."

"Yes, sir."

Gina imagined her old bots going to war with the new ones inside her.

"Try to relax. Have a nap if you can. If not, we have a few novels here." He picked up some compads and shuffled through them. "Do you like Zelda and the Spaceways? No? How about a detective story?"

"I'll try to sleep, sir, if that's all right."

"Certainly, certainly. I'll come by in an hour to check on your progress."

Gina closed her eyes and pretended to sleep. She listened for the door and heard it finally, but Patel was like all the enhanced. He was very quiet on his feet. The door slid shut and she opened her eyes to watch the monitors.

Fifteen minutes later, Gina was sweating as if back in the jungle on Thurston. Her joints ached and her head also. Patel had not mentioned pain as a side effect of the process, but she had suffered worse and determinedly put it from her mind. Her teeth were chattering a few minutes later, as if the air conditioning had been turned up full. Her head was a blinding mass of pain, and she had a stomach ache. She couldn't open her eyes without groaning as the room spun around. She tried to lie still, estimating the first hour was close to being up, but she had to do something about the pain in her guts. She pulled her legs up to her chest and hugged them tight, fighting not to throw up.

Ten minutes later the monitors were beeping frantically, but all she could do was pant. Sweat was rolling off her in rivers and her mouth was parched. She had been through worse—hadn't she? Desert fighting was rare, but Marines were trained for any eventuality. She looked up at the blazing sun, but blinked in puzzlement to see Patel's concerned face looking down at her. He was saying something, but he swam in her vision, and she was unable to respond. There were people running by in the background, and others prodding her. She wished they would leave her alone.

Gina watched the ceiling flowing by. She watched the lights receding and wondered where she was going. Was it time for second stage already? Patel was asking her if she was allergic? Allergic to what? He had only pumped nanobots into her. No one was allergic to bots. He must mean something else... what...

Alarms screamed, and everything went black.

* * *

# 14 ~ Simulations

Kate heard the news about Gina in a glum silence. She sat on her rack in the barracks listening to the others speculating on the reasons behind Gina's reaction to the enhancement process. Why did it have to be her? Why couldn't it have been that arsehole Callendri? If anyone deserved this, it was Mr. Wonderful Roberto Callendri.

"What are her chances?" Kate asked and everyone turned toward Cragg.

Cragg shook his head. "Not good, Kate. They don't know what's causing it. They say she quit breathing a couple of times. I don't know... I think she's a goner."

"We don't know that for sure," Takeri said. "She's strong."

"Yeah," they all agreed that she was.

Kate nodded along with the others, but if Gina had this reaction to the purge of her old bots, how was she likely to react to the other stages? Enhancement was an invasive procedure—very invasive. Biomech and cybernetic components had to be implanted, grown, and sometimes a combination of the two. A viper unit consisted of a unique combination of a Human body modified with plasteel, optical data feeds, servos, mylar musculature, and computer circuitry.

Kate sighed. "We have a sim in an hour." She resolutely pushed thoughts of her friend aside. "Better get squared away for inspection."

The others moved off and began stowing their gear and tidying their racks.

A short while later, Sergeant Rutledge came in and the recruits stood to attention at the base of their racks. He made a show of checking their appearance and opened a couple of lockers at random, but like Roscoe and the other veterans, he was more interested in their performance during the training than in a tidy locker.

Everyone passed inspection.

"First Squad will follow me to the simulators, the rest of you will wait for Sergeant Roscoe."

Kate marched with her squadmates outside, and then double-timed it across the parade ground and into the Complex. The Complex was a single story building that sprawled over a large area opposite the Tech Centre. The parade ground was between the two. She and the rest of the recruits had been here before to watch holo footage of the regiment in action. Vipers, most of them long dead now, routinely downloaded data into the regiment's archive after every mission. Those long dead heroes would never be forgotten as long as one viper lived. It was a form of immortality that appealed to all of them.

Today would be a little different from their earlier visits; in that they would live the memories not simply view them. They would fight the battles fought so long ago, and perhaps win those that had ended in defeat. Kate was aware that she had done this before, and that the others hadn't. They were nervous, but she dared not reassure them. No one must know of her time as Stone. She was determined they wouldn't find out from her.

They entered the simulator room. It was the biggest one she had ever seen. There were enough simulators here for the entire platoon to participate let alone a single squad. Usually these places held one or perhaps two rigs not forty-plus.

"Richmond," Rutledge said pointing to a rig and she stepped beside it to wait. "Takeri, Cragg…" Rutledge detailed each of her squad mates to their rigs in the first row. "Remember your sim assignments. It will save me having to do this again."

Rutledge stepped behind the programming deck and activated the rigs. Kate moved aside as her simulator tank opened with a shushing sound of compression seals releasing, and the couch lifted out to settle neatly to the floor.

"You know the drill, leave the wiring to me. I have a few helpers coming for that."

Kate stripped and climbed onto the couch eagerly. Others were less happy, but minutes later, everyone was ready. Rutledge began with her, but half way through his work, he looked up to find Stone and Hymas entering the room.

"The matrix is ready," Rutledge said to them. "Start connecting the others would you?"

Stone and Hymas nodded and began connecting the other recruits to their rigs.

Kate relaxed and wondered where she would be in a few minutes. Would the sim take her to Bethany again? Or would she go to Thorfinni and participate in a larger action? With the entire squad involved, Rutledge may well go for the latter, but there were many other options available. Stone was an excellent programmer. Hell, with him involved, she might find herself on Earth fighting a fictitious battle. He was that good.

"Right, Richmond, I have one last connection to make and you're done."

"Weapon's bus?"

"Close," Rutledge said and smiled briefly. "Your weapon's data bus *could* be used in a pinch, but it's not really the best choice for this. Your primary node has a much higher DPR."

"DPR?"

"Data Pass Rate," Rutledge explained. "Turn over for me."

Kate rolled onto her stomach careful not to dislodge any of the sensors. Her primary node was located at the base of her spine. It tapped directly into the optical network running through her entire body and had been used during the final stage of enhancement. Final stage was uploading all the viper software she needed to operate her enhancements. Out of the corner of her eye, she watched Rutledge gently polishing a jack plug that matched the socket in her spine. There was a large central pin surrounded by two rings of much smaller and more delicate looking pins. He studied it critically for a second or three then bent to ease it into her. She twitched and hissed at the feel of his hand on her butt.

"Don't move," Rutledge said sharply. "If I mess this up, you will not like it."

"Sorry, cold hands," she said trying not to feel the pins sliding into her.

"Cold hands are the least of your worries, Richmond. If I screw up your node, it will take surgery to fix."

Kate froze. She'd had enough surgery to last her a lifetime—a viper lifetime.

"It feels weird."

"You don't say," Rutledge said dryly. "We were told that we couldn't possibly be feeling what we reported. The R&D people insisted that the node doesn't have touch receptors."

"What about the link to our nervous system?" Kate said

visualising the schematics they had all studied.

"That's what we said, but they said it's an entirely different sub-system, and could not be the cause of the *phantom* feelings we were feeling."

"Techies," she snorted in disgust.

Kate knew the moment the connection was made. An icon burst into life on her otherwise blank display, and a text message blinked before her eyes, or rather, that's what it seemed like.

### Connection Achieved

"That's got it, Sarge."

Kate's display was purely internal. It only appeared to hover before her eyes. This kind of thing still had the power to make her uncomfortable, but her reaction was mild compared with how she once would have reacted.

Rutledge taped the wiring to her thigh to prevent accidents. "Okay Richmond, you can turn back."

Kate carefully turned over. "I've never seen simulators like this, and I don't mean the extra connections."

"They're a little different to others you've used," Rutledge admitted. "We can do a lot more with a direct connection."

"Example?"

"I could download recon data directly to you for instance, or use a download to create a sim so real you become me for the duration of the sim, or any degree between the two."

Stone's sim at HQ was based on his download, so she'd known it was possible to do that here, but she hadn't been enhanced back then. Maybe this sim would be even more real.

"What about this time?"

Rutledge grinned. "That would be telling. We don't need your node to run this sim, but it does make it easier for us to monitor your responses. The hardware was wired this way back before the war."

"Looks brand new," Kate said and it did. Everything gleamed as if just unpacked from the factory.

Rutledge shrugged. "My training was a long time ago, Richmond. We haven't needed to use this stuff for centuries. No wear and tear. Don't worry, we've kept them upgraded. You'll not find better anywhere in the Alliance."

"Where did we get them?"

Rutledge winked and said one word before walking away to connect another of her squadmates. "Flotsam."

Kate gaped then smiled sheepishly as she realised he was pulling her leg. Flotsam indeed. Flotsam was supposedly a world in the Border Zone where anything could be bought for the right price—anything at all. It was a myth. A place where Zelda supposedly came from, and made her piratical living making fools of Fleet captains and quite often the Marine Corps as well. It wasn't a real place. She frowned. Rutledge hadn't laughed… nah! Everyone knew it was a fictional world. It had been created specifically as the setting for Zelda's holodrama series.

A short while later, Lieutenant Hymas left the room. Stone and Rutledge sat behind the consols to run the computers.

"Listen up," Rutledge said raising his voice. "You will all be running the same sim here today, so be aware that your performance will be graded and compared not only against the ideal of a perfect mission, but also against your squadmates performances." He grinned. "I thought that might get your attention."

It certainly had! Kate had joked with Fuentez that a major's slot in the regiment would suit her preferences, but maybe it shouldn't have been a joke. Years of being led by incompetents had made her think of all officers that way. She had made dodging promotion at every turn an art form while in the rangers, and it had never been an issue with ISS. She saw things a little differently now. No viper, no matter his rank, could be called incompetent at anything. She had always taken the easy way out, performing her missions and following orders, never trying to change things. To be fair on herself, changing the system on Bethany was beyond any single individual, but that didn't mean she should add to the problem. That was exactly what she had been doing by ducking the responsibility that came with higher rank, but no more. Her new friends deserved the best leadership, and she was, in her own mind at least, one of the best recruits here.

Now was the time to prove it.

"Let's see if you can make use of what you've learned so far and survive longer than five minutes," Rutledge said and with that the couches all lifted and swung into the chambers.

Kate lay still, or tried to. The computers calibrated themselves to her reflexes causing her to twitch uncontrollably just as they always did. She hated that about sims and probably always would. Slowly her world disappeared as the simulator's matrix imposed itself upon her senses.

The world went black, but then blinked to life less than a second later.

"Sit down, George," General Blackthorn said.

*George?*

"Thank you, sir," Kate said and sat not knowing what else she was supposed to do. Who was George? She was it seemed.

"You know Admiral Kinley of course," Blackthorn said indicating the woman to his right sitting in the only other chair.

*I'm aboard ship, I'm sure of it.*

"Certainly, sir," Kate said automatically though she had never seen this woman before in her life. "How are you, Liz?" She tried not to show surprise at what was coming out of her mouth. Whoever George was, he had obviously known the admiral a long time.

"Better for seeing that black uniform. How have you been keeping?"

"Fine. As well as any of us can expect these days... the war." She shrugged. "I'm still breathing."

"A captain now, how the hell did that happen?"

Kate actually felt her face stiffen. It was weird. She was still herself, but she was wearing another's face, or rather that's what it felt like. "Tony is dead," she said in a voice as cold as space itself.

"Oh God..." Liz trailed off. "I hadn't heard. You were promoted to..."

She nodded once. "Fill his slot."

*Tony?* Kate concentrated and was almost able to bring the young and smiling face into focus, but then it was gone. This sim was the strangest she had ever encountered.

"Well," Blackthorn said as the silence threatened to draw on indefinitely. "I called you in here because we have a problem. Specifically, Fleet has a problem with Garnet."

"A Merkiaari type problem?" Kate said already expecting Blackthorn's nod. "What do you need?"

"You," Liz said. "I need you to volunteer for a solo op."

"You've got it."

"We knew you would say that, George, but listen first okay?"

Kate nodded.

"Garnet was taken two months ago."

"Garnet?" she said and guessed what the mission was. It was one she was particularly well suited for.

"Doesn't sound very impressive does it?" Liz said with a smile.

It didn't, but Kate knew it was. Oh, not from an ascetic point of view. Planets colonised purely for the metals below ground could hardly expect to look like Bethany or Alizon, but from a strategic point of view, it was an impressive gain for the Merkiaari. Using Garnet for a staging point, they could strike at any number of core worlds in a short period of time. Garnet's occupation could not be allowed to stand.

"I know where it is, Admiral. I reiterate, what do you need?"

"I want you to go in ahead of the fleet and take out the Merki high command."

Whoa, she was right. This mission, and one just like it in the Thorfinni system, was famous throughout the Alliance. Kate suddenly knew beyond a doubt just whom she was playing. She was the General!

"...the Marines in," Blackthorn was saying. "If you agree, you'll transfer to *Prince Rupert* within the hour. She will proceed independently of the fleet into the system. You'll go in under cover of darkness, and make your way to the capital, which is, according to the reports received from the resistance, where the Merkiaari have their HQ."

"We're in contact with the resistance?" she asked not knowing the answer this time.

"Sporadically," Blackthorn nodded. "We have a few satellite relays in the system—heavily stealthed of course, but every message sent means another one found and destroyed. They're not inexhaustible, so we have to use them sparingly. The resistance will be notified to watch for you. They will provide you with any last minute intelligence."

"Ships?" Kate asked trying to get a feel for the situation. To her, the Garnet mission was long dead history and that was no way to proceed. She needed to live it to succeed in her mission, or so she felt.

"We have a frigate lying well outside the zone listening for transmissions. *Thunderer* stayed behind when the system picket was blown away. The enemy have two squadrons of the line in the system with escorts, and we're expecting more at almost any time."

"You're waiting for them to assemble?"

Liz nodded but she was surprised at Kate's quick grasp of the situation. "You should have gone navy, George. Home Fleet *and* my Second Fleet will go in as soon as the rest of the enemy arrives."

Home Fleet, meaning Earth's only naval protection, would arrive late, but it wouldn't affect the outcome. Second Fleet, led by Admiral Elizabeth Kinley, had been savaged, but it had managed to survive while taking a heavy toll on the Merki dreadnoughts. Home fleet eventually arrived and blew the rest of them into space dust before moving on to the system's only habitable planet.

Almost three quarters of a million men were dropped on Garnet in the biggest land battle the Alliance had ever put together. The Merkiaari were annihilated when their entire high command was assassinated by a lone viper—a captain named George Burgton. Almost ten Merki divisions reeled in confusion at the loss of their commanders, and then began to die as they were struck from the air and the land without let up for a month. The result was Garnet back in Human hands with ninety percent of its population dead.

That was all ancient history, but from the perspective of the sim, it was the future and still to play for. What mattered now was doing as well or better than Burgton had. Kate had a few ideas.

"I volunteer," Kate said playing along with the sim.

Blackburn nodded. "Your gear is aboard *Prince Rupert* waiting for you." He stood and Kate shook his hand. It felt real. "Good luck, Captain."

"Luck has nothing to do with it, sir," she said with massive confidence.

Kate turned toward the hatch after shaking the Admiral's hand, but before she reached it, everything went dark and she found herself strapped into an acceleration couch. She was piloting a one man unarmed space plane. It was of a type popular among flying enthusiasts in the Alliance, for its quick responses and its ability to reach orbit. It had limited range and no weapons, but she needed neither of those things. All she needed was a way to get from orbit to Garnet's surface. The little plane was ideal. According to her instruments, she was coasting without power, and would enter Garnet's atmosphere in just a few minutes. She was no longer wearing the class-B uniform she had met Blackthorn in, instead she was wearing viper battle dress, and at her hip was a V2 pulser... no it was a V1.

V1's had a shorter range and were the forerunners of the V2, but they were also contemporary with the Merki War she was about to re-fight. She found her rifle clipped to the bulkhead behind her. It also had some minor differences to the most current model. Smaller magazine, she noted, and it had a larger power cell. It was heavier too, though not significantly so. She was happy enough to have it even though this model predated the addition of the grenade launcher that was currently standard viper issue. On the co-pilot's seat by her side was a pack; inside she found rations and water for three days, and a black case. She grinned. The case held an HTR or she had never seen one. She stroked it and her lips formed themselves into a small smile before she tied her pack closed.

"One minute to atmosphere," the computer's voice said, sounding remarkably like Sergeant Rutledge.

Kate turned back to her controls and turned off the autopilot just as she hit atmosphere. The plane skipped and bounced once before cutting into the air. Wing tips began to glow and the plane shook violently as friction and turbulence had their way, but she was unconcerned. She had flown this type of plane in all kinds of conditions. They were tough, easily able to withstand buffeting much worse than this.

She let her hands guide the plane by feel, while she took a moment to send a coded thought to her processor. It took a second and third attempt before the command was accepted, and she growled angrily under her breath. She had done well in the classroom. The Colonel's demonstrations and lessons had been easy to understand, but putting what she had learned into practice was proving harder. No doubt that was part of the reasoning behind all the sims scheduled for the weeks and months ahead. Sergeants Roscoe, Rutledge, and Stone were great believers in practice.

Her processor finally cooperated and accepted her commands. A map of a city appeared before her eyes. Corigin City was small as cities go, but then Garnet was hardly what she would call a core world even though it was damn important to the Alliance. The Council didn't agree with her. Garnet had been named a core world ever since its colonisation. Its location alone was enough to make it so, but the mining operations on Garnet's surface and throughout the system's extensive asteroid belts, could only add to its importance. Garnet's pre-war population was already low—barely twenty million. Post war, there had been a little over a million half starved and crazed people left alive.

Corigin City was the capital, but there were only seven decent sized cities on the entire planet. A significant percentage of the population spent their lives living and working on site at the factory and mining complexes that Garnet was famed for.

Kate concentrated and ordered her current location added to the map. She didn't expect the result she received.

**"UNABLE TO COMPLY. LOCATION IS OUTSIDE CURRENT TARGET AREA."**

The voice in her head always sounded like that idiot Whitby to her. As soon as she graduated, she was going to change it. She continued on her current glide path and considered a new command. She settled upon displaying the entire continent, including her current position marked in green, and all known Merkiaari positions in red.

That worked.

She studied the map and discovered a great many splashes of colour glaring balefully at her. Every city was solid red, and there were a good many areas outside the city limits as well. Her course was completely wrong. She quickly corrected the matter by turning twenty degrees starboard.

Kate was well into the atmosphere now, and was concentrating on her little craft's sensor display. The single passive array was enough to detect electronic emissions from Merki vehicles and targeting systems, but was not powerful enough, hopefully, to betray her presence.

At two thousand metres, she found what she was looking for and manoeuvred for a landing. She dove steeply, spilling air and wasting altitude like a spend thrift, until she was on her desired approach. She hadn't powered up the thrusters once and was pleased. Trees sped by below, but she took no notice as she concentrated on the clearing coming up. She shoved the stick forward recklessly, only clearing the last trees by bare millimetres. Skimming the ground, she braced herself and wrenched the stick hard back. The little plane stalled and slammed to the ground in a spectacularly inept looking landing, but the semi-crash had an important purpose. As she had planned, the little craft, broken and battered now, stopped abruptly and did not strike the trees that edged the clearing on this side.

Thumping the harness release on her chest, Kate sprang from her couch. Snatching up her rifle and pack on the way to the hatch, she took one last look around, and leapt through the broken aperture and into the trees. The instant she left the safety of the plane, an alert starting flashing on her display. It was warning her of heavy concentrations of lead and cadmium in the soil and atmosphere. There was nothing she could do except get inside as quickly as possible. As soon as she had some cover, she went to ground listening and scanning the area intently.

Nothing.

She didn't move. It was unlikely she had been seen ghosting in, but unlikely wasn't impossible.

Kate's sensors reported all quiet, and she finally believed what they were telling her. She stood and moved southeast through the trees making for her rendezvous with the resistance. She heard the firefight long before she reached her objective. The shattering sound of pulser fire, and the dull thump of grenades exploding, had her diving into cover and calling up a long range scan. It was a risk, but she felt it a necessary one. She would rather risk detection than walk blindly into a battle.

What her sensors revealed had her cursing.

A trio of combat sleds was attacking the resistance cell at the rendezvous point. The resistance had sensibly chosen to take cover in the available buildings, and were using them as platforms to snipe at the Merki gunners. She approved of the plan, but she didn't think much of their marksmanship. The Merkiaari were dominating the fight. They would win. They had the heavier weapons and could simply standoff and pound the buildings into rubble.

Kate moved up and chose a vantage overlooking the shattered

remains of the dome. It was breached in numerous places allowing the enemy into the residential area of the farm complex. Using sensors and infrared, she located the defenders fighting among the ruins. Smoke boiled up from burning buildings adding to the chaos of weapons fire. The resistance seemed well supplied with ammunition. They were lobbing grenades, ineffectually it had to be said, at the gravsleds like there was no tomorrow. Of course, if the Merkiaari had their way, there wouldn't be one, so she understood the sentiment.

She quickly assembled the HTR and loaded it. While the resistance fighters hammered unsuccessfully at the armoured sides and drives of the gravsleds, she chose the open cockpit and the pilots as her target. Laying down and wriggling a little to get comfortable, she carefully targeted the first pilot. He was in range, but the motion of the gravsled as he jinked to avoid fire from the ground, made the shot a challenge. She grinned and squeezed the trigger.

*Zzzzzing!*

The pilot's head exploded nicely, and the gravsled plummeted to the ground. It buried itself hard into the mud and rolled, but apart from the dead pilot, the crew was unhurt. At the urging of their commander, they piled out of the sled and took cover behind broken walls and rubble.

She targeted the commander and took him out before turning her attention to the other gravsled pilots. Both died in the same way as the first, and two more twisted pieces of wreckage were added to the mess littering the ground. Performing another sensor sweep, she found a couple of Merki troopers that were careless about taking cover. She took them out, but then discarded the HTR in favour of her rifle. She laid down some fire before advancing into the dome. Fire and manoeuvre was the order of the day for the next few minutes, but it wasn't long before the resistance gained the upper hand. She left them to finish off the last few troopers, and stopped to check her sensors. She widened her range to max and watched the flashing red icons depicting gravsleds going about their business. They appeared unaware of what had happened here. Good.

"What the hell are you doing?" one of the resistance fighters said, and slapped a fresh magazine into his rifle.

"None of your business," Kate said coldly and without looking in his direction.

In a rage, he lunged toward her.

Kate's hand swept down in a blur of speed and drew her pistol. He froze with the weapon centimetres from his face. With her sensor sweep now complete, Kate turned her attention to him. He was more boy than man; tear tracks were clearly visible on his dirty face.

"Is there a problem?"

"Leave him alone," a woman said from behind her.

Kate smiled. The voice was punctuated by the sound of a round being chambered into a hunting rifle—slug thrower she assumed by the sound. Her sensors had detected the woman some time back. She had all of the resistance on her display, and a single silent command from her was all it took for her processor to target this one.

"Point that rifle at me," Kate said smoothly. "And I'll cap him and then you."

"Stop it all of you." An older man came forward and dragged the boy away from her. "Haven't we got enough trouble? We have to stick together."

The boy shrugged off the man's grip on his arm and stormed off. His girlfriend hesitated a moment, but followed him after aiming a glare Kate's way.

Kate holstered her weapon.

"I'm Ben—your contact for what it's worth." Ben's grimace made Kate doubt it was worth much at all. "Follow me... Captain isn't it?"

Kate nodded. She hefted her kit and followed him into one of the buildings.

\* \* \*

# 15 ~ Simulations II

Kate was led into one of the few houses still standing. Ben led her upstairs and into a room where a woman awaited them.

"This is Erica Rhodes, Captain," Ben said ushering Kate inside. "She leads us."

Kate shook the woman's hand. "Kate... I mean George Burgton, Captain 501st infantry."

"I can see that," Erica said coldly. "I have three dead because Fleet wanted us here to meet you," she said bitterly. "Three lives *wasted*."

"Only three?" Kate said sarcastically.

"You bastard—"

"Don't bother with your insults. I'm here to do a job. You're here to help me do it."

"A job that amounts to suicide. No one can get in there. It can't be done."

"It will be done," Kate said instantly. "Fleet can't come in until it is. How many more will you see dead through your cowardice?"

Ben stepped forward. "Erica's no coward, Captain. She saved us all and led us—"

"He doesn't want to hear it, Ben." Erica sighed. "He's a cyborg remember, just a machine. Isn't that right, *Captain?*"

Kate was hardly impressed. She had said much worse herself. "If thinking that gives you comfort, go ahead and think it."

"*It does,*" Erica snapped with eyes blazing in anger.

"Fine, glad that's sorted out. I need a map of the building they're using for their HQ, and any first hand observations you've managed to bring out."

Erica scowled but turned back to the table.

Among the dross—dirty plates and the like—Kate could see what seemed to be a street map and some hand drawn schematics. She advanced without being asked and snatched up the drawings. She ignored the street map entirely, already having one similar within her database, and concentrated on the building plans.

"Who drew these?"

"Why?" Erica asked sullenly. "They're accurate."

Kate glared, silently waiting for an answer. Erica shuffled her feet nervously but didn't answer. "*Who?*" she asked again, but this time she barked it as an order. Damn civs had no discipline.

Erica jumped in surprise and answered. "Ben worked there before—"

Kate turned to Ben and asked her questions. "This is accurate?"

"Yes," he said not liking her treatment of Erica. "I worked as a loader operator."

"What of this access way? Is it straight, or does it curve like it's drawn?"

"Curves. It's even more obvious when you see it for real. I heard they built it that way to avoid an underground lake that—"

"This elevator," Kate broke in. "Where's the maintenance hatch?"

"There's one in all the cars."

"No good. I'll have to open the doors to enter them and they'll know. Any other way into the shafts?"

"Yeah, in the basement stores, but you'll have to climb almost four stories from there just to reach them."

"Let me worry about that. You haven't shown air conditioning ducts. Why?"

"I told you, I was a loader operator not maintenance," Ben said in an aggrieved tone.

"Then how can you be sure about the basement hatch?"

"Coz I have to go down there a lot to get stuff. I've seen the hatches, and the maintenance crews using them."

Kate nodded. She was well pleased with Ben. "Good. Are the hatches locked or secured in any way?"

"No, there's a simple latch."

Even better. "If I were to say I wanted to get into the basement, what would you say?"

"That you're crazy."

"Why?"

Ben pointed to the map. "Because the only way in is via the loading dock. They're using it as a motor pool. It's guarded like Alliance HQ."

That was interesting. "You a Marine?"

"That was a long time ago."

Kate shrugged quickly losing interest. If he didn't want to talk about it, that was fine. "Draw me another of these showing the loading dock and the way to the basement stores."

"All right, but it's a waste of time," Ben said reaching for a pen.

"He's right," Erica said. "You'll never get in."

"I will be inside this night, and you're going to help."

"How?" Erica asked suspiciously.

"I need you to draw attention away from the loading dock for a few minutes."

Erica was already shaking her head. "The only way to do that is show ourselves. They'll kill us for sure."

"Not if you're careful," Kate said privately agreeing with the woman. "A little shooting should attract the guards away from their posts. You can fade away and lose them in the city."

"I don't know…" Erica said and bit her lip worriedly. "They have electronics and we don't."

"War is dangerous. Chances have to be taken."

"But not *foolish* chances."

"We have to do it," Ben said quietly to his friend from where he was drawing the map. "We have to kill their leaders if the Alliance is to have a chance against so many. We have to do it, Erica."

"I don't know…" Erica whispered uncertainly.

Kate was about to try a little more persuasion, but a glare from Ben gave her pause and she missed the opportunity.

"All right, but I'll do it alone," Erica said finally.

"Now wait a damn minute," Ben said. "I didn't mean—"

"I said *I'll* do it," Erica said glaring at Kate and Ben equally now. "End of discussion. You will lead the others away from here, and don't stop until the Alliance finally lands. That's an order."

Kate didn't expect Ben to obey, but he surprised her. "All right, but I expect to see you tomorrow night without fail."

"I'll be there."

Wherever *there* was, had no bearing on Kate's mission as far as she could see. She dismissed it from her mind and watched the map flowing from Ben's pen. She could already see a way in, but then he started adding crosses to represent guards, and she scowled in annoyance. They were going to upset her plan.

"You're sure about the guards?" Kate said.

"Positive."

"How do you know?"

"I tried what you're about to try a week after the invasion. There were seven of us. I survived."

"That's how we know it's suicide," Erica said. "My husband… he was one of them."

That explained the anger then. Kate hesitated a moment, but she really didn't need it where she was going. "Here, you can use this from much further away. It will give you more options." She offered the HTR to the woman.

Erica took the weapon and examined it. "I've never seen one quite like this."

"viper issue, but it will still work for you."

The HTR was modified to talk to a viper's targeting software, but the scope was fitted as a backup. Anyone could use it, but not as quickly or as efficiently as a viper of course. Erica played with the rifle while they waited for Ben to complete his map. Kate watched over Ben's shoulder occasionally asking for more detail, but on the whole she was satisfied. As soon as he was finished, she held the map before her and studied it. Her processor automatically filed a copy of it in her permanent memory. She discarded the drawing and had her processor display a map of Corigin City.

She nodded in satisfaction when the command was accepted. With another coded thought, she ordered the map zoomed and centred over grid F6 of the city. She found the shopping arcade and zoomed in again until the building was the only one visible. One more command, and her copy of Ben's drawing was superimposed over the arcade, but the fit wasn't anywhere near perfect. She ordered Ben's drawing rescaled.

Much better.

The building was still clear behind Ben's drawing, but she added another little touch by colouring his lines blue. She followed the loading dock into the building and down into the basement. The elevator shaft hatches were easy to find from there.

"You said they're using the fourth floor?"

"Yeah, but that's a guess." Before Kate could argue, Ben explained. "They obviously won't use the arcade or shops, and the basement is out. That leaves the fourth floor—it's like a palace. The high and mighty execs had their rooms up there. I swear it's just like a hotel."

Kate reluctantly agreed with his assessment, but she had to point out something.

"How do you know they don't like living underground?"

"I…" Ben frowned. "I don't, but…"

Kate smiled. "It's all right. I agree they're most likely up on the fourth floor. How many floors are there by the way?"

"Six."

"What's up there?"

"More offices mostly. There's a landing pad on the roof as well."

The landing pad was of no interest, or was it? Could she figure out how to use a Merki gravsled? No, better to ignore it. She could easily find herself trapped up there.

"Okay. How long to get there?" Kate asked knowing that Erica would slow her down.

"Two hours," Erica said confidently. "We have transport."

"The Merki—"

"Won't detect it. It has no electronics."

Kate nodded, feeling better about the situation. "Good. Very good, we go now."

Erica scowled, but she made no protest at the order. She hefted the HTR and led the way outside. Ben trailed along looking worried, and soon the entire group had assembled to see what was happening. Kate shook her head at their stupidity, but said nothing about it. They should have sentries set and be spread out. A single mortar round would kill the lot of them. Seeing their ineptness lowered her opinion of Ben's military expertise. It wasn't surprising he was no longer in the Corps if this was how he deployed his people.

"Ben will take you to join the others," Erica said addressing her command. "The Captain and I have something to take care of. I'll rejoin you in a couple of days. Until then, Ben is in command."

Erica led the way around the side of the house and climbed into the cab of a waiting truck. It was a battered and abused Mitsushima GX4, the one with the three axles and the flatbed extension. The hood was missing, as was all its glass. It looked fit only for scrap. Kate climbed inside and noted the wiring had been ripped out. She turned around and saw a few of Ben's people getting ready to push.

"Gas?" Kate said. "What about ignition?"

"Not gas, diesel."

"Diesel?"

Erica grinned. "We don't have to worry about pollution here, Captain. A lot of the smaller farms save money by using fossil fuels to generate power. We ripped the turbine out of this and stuffed a diesel in her." She shrugged. "It works—kind of."

Erica pulled on a pair of night-vision goggles, and gave the signal to start pushing. The truck needed a push to raise the compression for ignition, but once it was running, it drove like any hydro-turbine powered truck. Erica gunned the engine and launched the truck toward a hole in the dome. Kate grabbed the door handle to steady herself and winced as the truck glanced off a broken dome support.

"Hey, take it easy!"

Erica laughed and cranked the wheel hard right. The truck slewed sideways and almost onto three wheels, but it didn't roll. It crashed back down onto its balloon tyres and accelerated down the road like a missile. Kate gave Erica a dirty look and switched to light amplification. The night receded to a point where they might have been moving through an overcast day. In reality, they were racing at breakneck speed through utter darkness. Garnet was devoid of moons. The only light came from the stars, but it was enough for her systems to work with.

"How did you join up?" Kate yelled over the rushing wind.

"We fought back when they first came down. Not many of us survived, but those that did became the Corigin resistance. When my husband died, I took over from him, when I die, Ben will and so on until there's none of us left."

There wasn't much Kate could say. Erica obviously didn't believe in the Alliance's promise of liberation, or in her own survival. Millions had already died in the fighting. It was hard to blame her.

In the early hours of the morning, Erica pulled off the road and stashed the truck where it wouldn't be easily found. "We walk from here."

Erica led the way. Kate followed far enough back to keep her in sight, but not close enough to get caught up in an ambush with her. Her sensors were sweeping ahead of both of them, and twice she had to direct Erica wide to avoid enemy patrols. The Merki troopers had chosen the obvious demarcation point of the main dome as their patrol radius. It wasn't hard to get inside; they simply waited for the patrol to pass by and then slipped in. Most of the buildings on the outskirts of the city were in ruins. The city's defenders had chosen the area near the dome as their battleground; it had taken heavy damage. Rubble filled the streets and most of the buildings were burned out shells. Erica chose one at random and they went to ground to discuss the situation.

"I'll leave you here," Erica said. "I need to get in position."

"Give me a time."

Erica checked her wristcomp. "Three."

Kate checked the time legend on her internal display. "Don't be late."

Erica nodded once and hurried away.

Kate waited a few minutes then moved out. She made good use of the city's rubble choked streets and alleyways to mask her presence from the occasional patrol. Merkiaari were over confident, but they weren't completely stupid. The patrols, though few in number, were thorough in their sweeps. More than once she feared her plan was blown, but they always went by without spotting her.

When the time came, she was in position overlooking the shopping arcade. She was keeping an eye on the guards standing just inside the loading dock, when suddenly, the guard on the right fell backward with his face a bloody ruin. She glanced at the time and found it was just after three. Erica was as good as her word. A moment later, the other guard died. Silence descended and Kate held her breath, but as she had hoped, the Merkiaari reacted as predicted. Two squads trotted out of the gate and into the city looking for the culprit.

As soon as they were clear, Kate dashed through the gate at top speed and jumped into one of the parked gravsleds. Another squad trotted out of the building and into the night. She waited with her sensors pulled in tight. Slowly, carefully, she extended her awareness outward and breathed a silent thank you to Erica who was no doubt running for her life.

The way was clear.

Kate ran in a crouch into the loading dock. It was littered with abandoned loaders and stacks of crates. She hunkered down behind a tower of boxes to listen and scan the area. All was quiet. She easily located the entrance Ben had told her about, and the curving corridor beyond led her deep into the guts of the shopping arcade. This was an area never seen by customers. There were boxes stacked in front of locked fire escapes, and empty trolleys left haphazardly in the corridors waiting for employees who were probably long dead. The cross corridor on her map came and went, and she descended with more speed and confidence.

Her first mistake.

It didn't kill her, but it could have, and Kate was snarling at her own overconfidence even as she pounced onto the Merki's shoulders. He staggered back from the boxes he had been investigating, and roared loud enough to wake the dead. Grabbing the monster's head with both hands, she twisted with all her viper enhanced strength.

*Crunch!*

The monster fell dead in mid roar, and Kate dropped to her haunches to scan for others. Nothing. Using the boxes of... chocolate bars? Well what do you know; even Merkiaari liked chocolate. They couldn't be all bad. She stacked the boxes over the corpse. Stepping back, she scrutinised her work and nodded once before trotting off to find the hatches that had brought her down here.

As it turned out, Ben was both right and wrong about the security of the hatches. There were no fancy security locks, but they weren't latched as he had maintained either. Instead, an enormous padlock decorated each one. Kate smiled crookedly and ripped one off with her bare hands. She really liked being a viper.

She went to light amplification mode inside the shaft and shut the hatch.

When discussing the possibility of using the elevator shafts to reach the fourth floor, Ben had said no way. Kate had secretly thought he might be right. She was strong, but if the shafts had been smooth, her strength wouldn't have helped her. That was no longer a concern. The shafts weren't smooth and could be climbed, but she didn't need to. There was a metal ladder running down the side of the shaft that disappeared into the darkness overhead. As she climbed, she realised she should have known there would be one. Ben said he saw maintenance people entering the hatches, and of course, they needed a way to reach a broken elevator car. She climbed around it at ground level and continued on with her rifle swinging behind her from its strap. She didn't want to be parted from the weapon, but it was annoying having it bumping her back. She ignored it and the third floor doors that enticed her to open them, on her way to her target.

She halted her climb at the fourth floor, and scanned the corridors beyond the doors with her sensors set at low intensity. She tensed as red icons splashed themselves across her display, but then she relaxed with a grin. These must be her targets. She studied their positions and noted that most were unmoving. Asleep? She hoped so, but she didn't take it for granted. Although Merkiaari were diurnal as Humans were, it didn't stop them from having sentries up and about. She studied the problem but could see no way around opening the door to see if any were awake. There shouldn't be any guards up here, she mused as she struggled to open the protesting elevator doors. Their officers should be confident enough with all their troops between them and the ground.

The doors finally succumbed to her prying fingers and she stepped into a dimly lit corridor. She deselected her light amplification, and stood still as a statue with her back against the wall. Beside her, the doors slid slowly shut.

So far, so good.

Moving carefully down the corridor, she came to the first door. Her sensors insisted there was a target in there, but even with her audio's gain at max, she couldn't hear anything. Hoping that meant they were asleep, she opened the door silently and entered. The room was pitch black, but she didn't bother with light amplification. TRS

(Target Recognition Software) instantly outlined the prone figure in red. Her hand swept down and came up with her pulser in hand, but she aborted the instinctive urge to fire.

She glanced around the room and her eyes narrowed. His armour and uniform were on a chair near the bed. The single sunburst insignia prominently displayed on the armour's breastplate, told her all she needed to know. He was a high-ranking target—a Strike Commander. He probably led in the region of a hundred thousand troopers. Fifteen Marauder class transports were committed to the Garnet incursion, which meant he was one of fifteen targets she needed to kill. She was about to take out the equivalent of an Alliance five star general.

She crept forward, utterly silent, not even breathing. She moved her pistol to within millimetres of the monster's head. She licked her lips and moved it forward to touch the furred head. His eyes flew open and she squeezed the trigger. The recoil was intense, but she was a viper. She held steady. The hiss-crack was muffled by the contact. The smell of singing hair and brains made her want to gag. She stepped away from the corpse listening for any outcry.

Nothing.

She swepped her sensors on low power beyond the room and was satisfied that she hadn't been detected. She opened doors and found closets and bathroom. Nothing. Outside in the corridor, she moved to the next target and then the next, methodically killing each of the aliens with a headshot from her pistol. Fourteen died quickly and silently as she made her way from one end of the building to the other, but then came the last one.

Her sensors reported movement inside, and she hesitated. She watched the icon on her display resolve into two, and knew she was in trouble. The dirty beggar had a female with him, and they weren't playing poker. Should she wait for him to finish, or should she go in and hope to kill them both silently? She opted to go in.

Her first shot blew the female's head into a bloody ruin, but the male was fast—he snatched up a weapon and fired. Kate's pistol was still moving toward him when a searing agony erupted in her shoulder. She spun around and crashed to the deck grimacing in pain. Fighting shock and snarling in hate, she brought her rifle up and laid the room waste on full auto. The Merki disappeared into red mist.

*That's torn it.*

Kate struggled to her feet. A diagnostic alert was flashing on her display. As soon as she noticed, it changed into a wire frame representation of her body, and zoomed in on her left arm and shoulder. A list of text detailing the damage scrolled rapidly by, with her processor's conclusions appended to it.

CRITICAL DAMAGE TO LEFT SHOULDER/ARM.
LEFT ARM NON-RESPONSIVE. COMBAT IMPAIRED 25%.
RECOMMEND HOSPITALISATION AT EARLIEST OPPORTUNITY.

No shit.

Kate blinked stupidly down at her severed arm where it lay on the carpet at her feet. She checked that her IMS was handling the blood loss—it was coping well and had damped the pain to tolerable levels. She staggered into the corridor just as a Merki squad appeared. She hosed them with her rifle set on max power and full auto when they charged her, and managed to take them all down, but as she turned to run the other way, another squad appeared around the corner.

They fired.

\* \* \*

"Weird how history repeats itself in the sims, isn't it?" Rutledge said as they watched Richmond.

"Not really." Stone thought it would be more unusual if a download didn't proceed in that manner. "We're good, but even we can't program every option and contingency into the simulator's matrix. It's bound to follow the download parameters… at least in a general way."

"In a general way, yes," Rutledge agreed. "But look at her."

Stone *was* looking, and he liked what he saw. Anyone else would have quit and waited for them to finish her, but not his Kate. If and when the General's prediction came to pass, he might have a serious competitor in Richmond.

As if by magic, Rutledge divined Stone's thoughts. "How many at your last count?"

"Merki?"

"Yeah."

"Four or five thousand."

Rutledge snorted. "Four *or* five thousand?"

"All right, it is five thousand… plus however many I took out indirectly with artillery and the like."

"Oh, of course," Rutledge said in amusement. "Richmond looks set to follow in your footsteps."

"Yeah," Stone said grimly, which elicited a strange and considering look from Rutledge. "Gordon has a clean sweep it looks like. That boy has the moves, no question."

"He's free and clear," Rutledge said shaking his head in admiration. "We could have used him back in the war."

Stone nodded. "Disconnect him would you?"

"You're the boss," Rutledge said and went to do that.

Zack Gordon had a perfect score. No dead resistance fighters, fifteen dead Merki commanders and dozens of other lowly males dead on his way in. Not only that, he had escaped unscathed *and* undetected. He had led a charmed life in the sim. He hoped it extended to waking life as well.

Stone watched Richmond blast the Merkiaari into next year and smiled grimly. Just as Rutledge said, it was uncanny how her performance had matched his own run in the simulator—almost move for move. Her plan was a good one. So what if it was similar to one he had used to test the simulation? It didn't have to mean what he thought. She might be just that good. Without question she *was* that good, but maybe her previous experience with his download had something to do with it. She did still use retro on occasion. Marion had mentioned it to him more than once. Maybe his download at HQ had a greater impact upon her than he had first thought. Watching her was almost like watching himself... except she was prettier.

He pursed his lips. It would probably be better not to share his suspicion with the others. Scratch that. It would definitely be better not to share it. Besides, he hadn't lied when he told her the effect would wear off with time.

Richmond turned to run just as another enemy squad appeared. She went down under a hail of gauss slugs and plasma, still firing her rifle, but it was the action of someone already dead. He stared into her lifeless eyes on the monitor and shivered. He ignored the legend that appeared. He already knew what it said.

## SUBJECT TERMINATED

The screen cleared and began detailing the mission and Richmond's stats. He ignored the data and went to disconnect her from her rig. The computers would automatically store her run in the archives.

Richmond started disconnecting the sensors as he walked up. "You had me worried there for a minute, Sarge. I almost believed it was real."

He grunted. "Wait until you try one of my interactive simulations."

"Interactive? All simulations are interactive."

"Mine are more so. Direct connection via your node gives me the ability to link the simulator rigs into one programme. You might find yourself leading your squad on a mission, but they won't be constructs, they'll be other recruits on the link."

"Sounds interesting," Richmond said. "When do we do that?"

"After you've learned to use a few more of our toys."

Richmond helped him remove the sensors from her body and then slipped into her uniform. Gordon was already with the others receiving congratulations. Richmond went to join him.

"Listen up," Stone said and the recruits quieted. "You have time for a meal before we head over to the range. It's time you used a real rifle."

"Sergeant?"

"What is it, Cragg?" Stone sighed. There was always someone with questions in this bunch. Why couldn't they wait?

"When will we get our V2s?"

"Why? Have you someone you want to shoot?"

"No, Sergeant," Cragg said seriously. "I want to practice my target acquisition. I'm not happy with how long it took me in the sim."

"You could always go back in... no?" Stone said with amusement. "You will all be issued your rifles and pistols when I'm sure you won't blow someone's brains out by accident. Until then, you'll use what I give you and be satisfied. Clear?"

"Yes, Sergeant!" the recruits shouted as one.

"Good. *Move it out!*" Stone roared and they double-timed to the mess hall.

\* \* \*

### Target shooting range, Petruso Base

Kate opened her present with the others of her squad. The box held a viper's side arm, a plasma pistol quite unlike any she had ever seen outside of the simulators. The butt of the weapon had a modified grip to accept targeting data from her data bus, an oversize magazine she estimated must hold sixty rounds or more, and looking at the housing for the power cell, she estimated that she could fire it non-stop for an hour. She pulled it out of the box and raised it to sight on one of the targets down range.

"Don't even think of pointing that in my direction, Recruit," Sergeant Rutledge said glaring at her.

She laughed along with her squadmates.

"Sarge?" Cragg said. "What gives with the serial numbers?"

"Well now," Rutledge drawled rolling his eyes. "What do *you* think?"

"So only I can use it?"

"Give the boy a cigar." Rutledge shook his head as if wondering what his beloved regiment was coming to. "The General has a thing about leaving weapons lying for the bad guys to pick up. He got himself shot like that once. He didn't like it. So he says, why not key the fu… why not key them to an individual unit? Everyone looked around scratching their heads for a little while, and then said why not? Your pistol talks to your processor all the time anyway, the mod was easy."

"What happens if they get mixed up?" Gordon asked innocently.

Rutledge studied the ceiling and shook his head muttering about fool questions. "Make sure it *doesn't*," he roared. "If anyone depresses the trigger without the weapon receiving the correct serial number, its innards will fuse and likely blow your hand off. Now, we can give you a new hand no problem at all, but a sidearm like them pistols costs a lot of money. Don't mix them up!"

Kate liked Rutledge. The sergeant knew how to get his point across without going into hysterics like some others she had known. Some would fly into a spittle spraying rage, and look close to having a seizure when confronted by a new batch of recruits.

Rutledge pulled his pistol from the holster on his hip, and held it up for the recruit's inspection. "This here is a M2911-V2. The V2 is a handheld pulser with a range close to a klick, and a killing range of about half of that. This here," he pointed to the magazine projecting down just in front of the trigger guard. "This here is your magazine. Sixty round capacity as standard, but there is an extended capacity mag available taking you to ninety rounds of caseless AP blaster ammunition. We don't use them often—they interfere with a quick draw. However, it is *remotely* conceivable that you lot will graduate. If that happens, you might need it for an undercover op where the restriction will not apply."

Kate nodded. No one on such an op would display her weapon by wearing it in a holster. She would hide it within her clothing, or something similar, and lose speed anyway. If speed wasn't a consideration, firepower might be.

"This," Rutledge said popping open a small hatch at the rear of the pistol. "This is your power cell compartment. It takes the standard cell of course, but it's prone to fouling. We've been unable to neutralise the problem completely. When replacing the cell—it's good for an hour when firing at medium settings by the way—make certain the hatch is downward and that the contacts on the cell are free of any garbage. Do not put your fingers inside." He glared around. "The contacts are resilient, but nothing is perfect. If you get any crud inside, you'll have to strip the whole thing down to get it out. Clear?"

"Yes, Sergeant," Kate said along with the rest of her platoon.

Rutledge didn't look convinced. "You will note there is no safety. Wrong. There *is* a safety and it's built into you. The weapon will take its orders from you via the bus. It's always safe until it's in a viper's right hand. Then all bets are off.

"In your box, you will find a magazine. Load it with one; that is *one* round of AP ammunition. Do it now." He watched the recruits do that. "Well done," he said sarcastically. "With the weapon in your right hand, and the mag in your left, load the weapon. Take note of your display. It will show your pistol icon at the top right corner in red. As you load, it should change to green and display the numeral one. This is your ammo indicator, and it's located just below the charge indicator that should say one hundred percent. Anyone who does not have the display as described, tell me now."

"I don't, Sarge," Gordon called raising his hand.

Rutledge shook his head. "I said in your *right* hand, Gordon. That's the one with the gold thing in your palm. Got it?"

"Sorry, Sarge," Gordon said and beamed as his display lit as described.

Rutledge sighed and turned back to his recruits. "Now then. This is the fun part. Keep your weapon pointed at the ceiling and do what I tell you. Access your weapon display—you all know how from the classroom demo. Set the weapon to minimum. If anyone fires at max I'll chew him a new arsehole, and I'll know—*believe* me." Rutledge locked eyes with each of the recruits and then nodded. "With the weapon pointed *up*, fire one round."

Three squads, each containing ten units, fired into the plascrete ceiling. Kate beamed as if at an old friend, Gordon was examining the burn on the ceiling and noting the scarring, but Kate was more interested in her display. It read zero ammo now of course, but the charge indicator hadn't even twitched. Economical in power use was good. In the field she might need that.

"The ceiling is still there, so I know you all did what I told you," Rutledge said. "I like that. Load your magazines to capacity this time; that is *sixty rounds* of AP ammunition for those of you with defective hearing. Do not load your weapons. When ready move to your assigned lane and wait."

Kate quickly loaded her magazine and moved to her lane. The long narrow tunnel went off into the distance. Remembering Rutledge's claim that the V2 had a range of a full klick, she bet the lanes went at least that far. That meant the bunker must extend well under the woods to the west, but not under the foothills and mountains beyond. Not unless there were other, longer ranged, toys to play with. Knowing the regiment's reputation, she was suddenly sure there were.

"Facing down range, load your weapons," Rutledge said loudly from behind her as he walked by her. "Increase magnification on your visual sensors…"

Visual sensors? That was one way of saying it, but it was a little strange calling her eyes sensors. She zoomed down range and found the target easily. Her range finder said it was exactly five hundred metres away.

"Aim your weapon," Rutledge said. "When you're on target, you should have a revolving diamond displaying that fact, just like in the sims. Your pistols are not self-seek weapons. The diamond does not indicate lock-on as it would with some of our other toys. In this case, the diamond indicates where your shot will hit. Move your weapon to the head of the target, and note the diamond moves to show the new location."

Kate moved her weapon in a rock steady hand, and watched the reticule dance and revolve. She moved it off target altogether, and the diamond swung out of view, briefly fixing on something out of sight before disappearing. She ordered her processor to magnify the current view and zoomed beyond the target. There was a maintenance hatch in the wall of the tunnel. That was what the diamond had found. She quickly zoomed out and moved her pistol back on target.

"…your weapon at semi-automatic, and fire a three round burst to the head of your target," Rutledge was saying as he walked slowly behind the recruits again.

Kate depressed the trigger and watched the silhouette of the Merki trooper begin to disintegrate. She was pleased with the accuracy. A plasma pistol wasn't usually so good, but with targeting like this, she couldn't miss. What would a single shot on maximum do? A lot more than the minimum setting they were using now she bet.

"Good," Rutledge said. "Switch to fully automatic and empty your magazines into the target. Do it now."

Kate gave the command to her processor and her weapon's status icon confirmed the change. She squeezed her trigger and held firm as her pistol emptied itself into the target. The recoil this time was excessive, and she found herself wanting to correct a rightward drift. The moment she noticed it, it was corrected, but she wasn't surprised. Her new body was learning.

"Your ammo indicator should now read zero, and your charge indicator will read ninety-nine percent," Rutledge said. "Anyone not have that—Gordon?"

Everyone laughed, but they did indeed have indicators as described.

"You will have noticed your processor adjusting your aim. This is automatically handled when your target recognition software, or TRS, is online—as it is now. Your processors have stored the new data and have recalibrated your servos."

"Sir?"

"What is it Cragg?" Rutledge said.

"Will my servos remain calibrated with TRS *offline*?"

"Well now. Who says TRS can be taken offline?" Rutledge said in amusement.

"I just thought I could."

Rutledge stared at him for a long moment then smiled. "It just so happens that TRS can be taken offline, Recruit, but not by you just yet." He turned away to address the platoon. "All your systems will be activated and under your control, when you graduate and not before. And yes, your servos remain calibrated in all situations. Your processor never forgets once it has learned something."

That was good to know. Kate didn't want to mis-aim her weapon in an unneeded attempt at compensating for full auto.

"Holster your weapons and follow me," Rutledge said and headed for the exit.

The squad automatically fell into a column of two's and followed Rutledge into another training area. This one was different. Instead of lanes, a huge area had been set up to provide training in an urban setting. The buildings were only two stories, but the layout was reminiscent of a city block on some Alliance world. Kate could almost believe the buildings were occupied.

"This is where the fun begins," Rutledge said and picked up a plasma rifle from a rack of them. "Richmond, front and centre."

"Sir." Kate double-timed it to the sergeant.

"Do you know how to use one of these?" Rutledge asked.

"Yes, sir."

"You're sure? Better examine it," Rutledge warned and handed it over.

Kate hefted the weight. It was like an old friend. "It seems to be a M18-AP rifle with modified grip. The grenade launcher is unfamiliar to me, but not unlike my old P100. My processor indicates the weapon is assigned to me, sir."

If the weapon had not been hers, her serial number would have been rejected and her display would have remained dark.

"It seems to be an M18-AP, does it?" Rutledge said and handed her a magazine. "Load and take out that door." He pointed at a building close by.

"Yes, sir," she said and fired.

*CraAAAAacK!*

Her shoulder was throbbing with the recoil but that was nothing compared to the damage she had inflicted on the building. The door was gone—vaporised.

"Maybe I should have told you to set it on minimum." Rutledge smirked. "What do you think?"

"I think this might look like an M18-AP, sir, but it's not."

Rutledge snorted. "Back in line, Richmond, and take that with you. It's yours."

"Yes, sir," Kate said and did as ordered.

Rutledge picked up another rifle from the rack and held it up horizontally before him. "This here, is an M1862-AP assault rifle with integral grenade launcher." He popped open a hatch cover in the stock. "It uses a pair of standard energy cells, not one, and needs them both. It's an energy hog, but can fire non-stop for a quarter of an hour on medium settings." He closed the hatch and opened another on the opposite side. "There is room in the stock to store four spare cells, but I always, *always,* carry some with me on my belt," he said tapping the single leather case on his left side. "You will notice the General does also."

"Sarge?"

"What is it Richmond?"

"Where can I get one of those cases?"

Rutledge smiled. "Smithson's Armoury in Petruso City supplies the regiment with uniforms. They have quite a few odds and ends you might find useful."

Cragg exchanged a glance with her and nodded almost imperceptibly. The instant they received leave to enter the city, they would go there.

"...our own ammunition," Rutledge was saying. "A mission can go down the crapper fast. It's sometimes impossible to anticipate what will happen and you might find yourself using scavenged ammo. Remember this recruits: when using standard ammo, your rifle must, I repeat *must*, be set to fifty percent power or less. If you use any setting above that you will find your ammo cooking off in the barrel. You don't want that, *believe* me." Rutledge glared around. "Now then, as Richmond pointed out, it looks like your old M18-AP. It isn't. The reason it looks so much like your old rifle should be obvious. Richmond?"

"Sir?"

"Why is this here rifle so similar to an M18-AP?"

Not having any idea, she scrambled for an answer. "Because... because the General likes it?"

Her platoon mates laughed, but Rutledge did not. "Very funny. The General does like it as it happens, but that's beside the point.

The Alliance uses millions of M18 pulsers. It's the standard rifle in our military. The regiment has always lacked numbers, but we make up for it with firepower. The M1862-AP uses the chassis, magazine, barrel, and stock of the standard rifle—the stock is slightly modified to provide extra storage. As I said, it can fire standard ammo in a pinch, but our own ammunition is more effective. The circuitry, coils, and nearly all of the internal components of these rifles are manufactured right here on Snakeholme and assembled into the standard casing. The result, as we all saw, is something other than an M18-AP can produce."

Rutledge was being conservative. The results Kate had obtained with a single shot was closer to what she would expect from an AAR.

"Sir?" Dolinski said. "What about the launcher?"

"The grenade launcher is exactly what it looks like—a P100. Unlike the P100s you may have used before, this one is integral. That means it doesn't come off, Gordon, so don't try."

Kate laughed along with the others. Gordon was going to be the target for a lot of jokes later today.

"It uses a standard pump action design," Rutledge went on, "and can be loaded with a maximum of ten grenades. We have a few to choose from; incendiary, high explosive, and fragmentation. Any or all may be loaded in any combination you choose. I prefer using all H.E myself. They're good for taking out Merki infantry as well as lightly armoured vehicles. Any more questions?"

There were none.

"Right. This one belongs to you, Takeri," Rutledge said holding the weapon out to her.

Selinia stepped forward to receive her weapon then returned to her position.

"Cragg…"

A few minutes later, the rack was empty. Kate's platoon was armed and ready for whatever may come.

\* \* \*

# 16 ~ The City

Gina smiled and rolled over. She yawned lazily and opened one eye to peer around. She was no longer in the treatment room. She sat up and squinted at the light shining through the window into her room.

Outside, she could see some of the recruits exercising on the parade ground, and beyond them, the mountains she was going to climb with Richmond. She swung her legs out of her rack, but became entangled in the vine-like wiring connecting her to the bedside consol. She started picking irritably at the tape holding the wires and sensors in place, but as she did so, she saw a flash of gold. She stopped and stared at her clenched fist. Slowly she opened it to reveal a weapon's data bus, *her* data bus.

"Damn me, that was quick," she mumbled to herself in surprise.

"Actually it wasn't," Captain Penleigh said from the open door.

Gina saluted from where she sat in her backless gown. She tried to stand, but she had to take some time to remove the rest of the sensors. She was pleased to note there was no sign of the work carried out on her body. Although her eyes were biomech replacements, she viewed the world as she always had and was relieved. She had gone through enhancement within an eye blink of time. No one said it would be like that. She didn't feel any different... or did she? She did feel different in one way, but it was a good difference. Gravity no longer dragged at her as it had before. She felt energetic and as light as a feather, as if she could jump into the air and fly away. The gravity of Snakeholme was significantly higher than Earth's 1g, but she hardly noticed it now.

"Stay there, Gina." Penleigh stepped further into the room to clear the door.

"But—"

Half a dozen doctors came running in. They were a little upset when they realised why every alarm in the monitoring station was screaming.

"As you were, people," Penleigh said. "She's fine. Give the girl a little room to breathe." He explained the situation, and everyone left with smiles on their faces.

"You said it wasn't quick, sir," she said when they were alone again.

"No it wasn't. You've been out of it for quite a while."

"How long?"

"Almost five weeks."

"Five *weeks!*" Gina squeaked in shock. "The process is only supposed to take eight days at most."

"I'm quite aware of that. It seems your old bots didn't want to leave, Gina. They put up a bit of a fight. No one quite knows why, unless Patel was right. You were close to death when he hit the panic button."

"I see."

"Yes... well," Penleigh said sounding a little put out when she didn't make a fuss. "Have you ever had Grendel's Syndrome?"

Gina nodded. "I caught it pretty bad on a training mission. I nearly croaked then too."

"I'm not surprised, but that episode is probably the reason for this one. It wasn't in your file, Gina. If it had been, a different batch of stage one bots would have been used. When they started work on you, your old bots attacked as if the intruder was a Grendel virus."

"How do you know all this?"

Penleigh shrugged and crossed the room to look out the window. "Patel clued me in. He suspected it, but you couldn't answer when he asked if you had caught it before." He turned back to regard her. "Nanobots learn from experience, Gina. It's part of what makes them so good. They knew how to defeat Grendel virus, and went to war in a big way. You went into cardiac arrest more than once."

Gina shivered at how close she had come to ending her life and career without doing anything with it. Yes, but she hadn't died and the surgery was now complete. She was a viper; it was time she went to work.

"Can I get out of here, sir?"

"I came to get you." He pulled open a drawer and handed her a uniform. "You're a little behind your squadmates, but you'll catch up.

I've seen your work, remember?"

"How could I forget?" she muttered as she stripped out of the hospital gown and climbed into battle dress. It felt good.

Penleigh handed her a new wristcomp; it looked the same as his. She remembered Richmond playing with hers in the barracks when she came back from her own enhancement. There were a lot of new functions to learn. She strapped it on her wrist.

"Ready?"

Gina glanced around the room and then at him. "I'm ready, sir."

She decided he looked good in his class-B uniform. He had a lot of colour on his chest, with campaign ribbons speaking of many well known battles. She absently wondered about the missions that weren't shown. Thurston was not there for instance.

"You said I have squadmates now, sir?" she asked as they made their way outside.

"You and your friends have been assigned to Alpha Company."

Alpha Company? It didn't really mean anything to her, not yet, but once she joined her squad and got to know the others, it would begin to mean a lot more. It would be home to Recruit Gina Fuentez, and hopefully it would later become part of her command. She grinned.

"What's funny, Recruit?" Penleigh said as they left the building.

"Sir, I was thinking how nice it will be when I'm a major, sir."

Penleigh raised an eyebrow. "Why major and not colonel?"

"Majors have more fun, sir."

"Don't be too sure. Stein didn't enjoy sending people out to fight while he stayed home did he?"

"No, sir, but it seems to me that the 501$^{st}$ does things differently. It's unlikely we will ever need to send a battalion of vipers to a world like Thurston. Sending a pair of vipers is more likely… in my opinion, sir."

"You're right of course, but what makes you think the General would send a major when he has, or will have, a full regiment to choose from?"

That stumped her. Why would Burgton send a major? "He… he would send his best. Surely he would promote on merit, so higher ranks will be sent out more often, sir."

Penleigh grinned and shook his head. "As it happens, the General does promote using the merit system. He doesn't like officers who reach high positions through money, or influence, or both. So you're right up to a point. But again, with a full regiment in mind, he would likely send out different units each time to let them gain experience. Not so?"

Gina nodded glumly.

"Don't worry about it. You have a lot to learn before graduation. You can worry about promotion later. I told you once that rank isn't everything."

"I remember, sir, but I told you it's a way for me to keep score."

"We keep score in other ways," Penleigh said grimly. "Survival is my personal favourite. As in how many times can I go in alone and come back out alive. Stone's was always how many Merkiaari he could take down, but now," he shrugged. "Who knows? Rank doesn't mean much after the first fifty years, Gina, you'll see."

Gina hoped not. Striving to become better, to gain rank in her chosen profession, was what had always driven her... and getting her people home alive of course.

"I'll take that under advisement, sir. I prefer to think otherwise."

"We all did at first," Penleigh said, and that was all he would say on the subject of rank from then on. He led the way to one of the many classrooms set aside for training viper recruits.

Gina's entire platoon was being taught how to use their internal sensors and targeting displays. Roscoe was teaching the class. Gina was pleased to note that not only was Kate Richmond in her squad, but that both Martin Cragg and Ian Hiller were also. Seeing them made her feel half way toward having a new family. She nodded to Selinia Takeri and sat next to her, while Penleigh had a quiet word with Sergeant Roscoe.

"It's good to see you up and around," Takeri said quietly.

"Thanks, Selin." Gina looked around noting faces. "Where's Jamie? Don't tell me they assigned him to another platoon."

Takeri's eyes darkened. "He didn't make it."

"But..." she said in confusion. Jamie had been fine when Gina went for enhancement. He had already undergone the process and couldn't wait to start practising his new abilities. "What happened?"

"Officially he died in a training accident, but you know what that means."

Gina swallowed sickly. The regiment always used the fiction of a training accident to cover a whigout. "Who else?" She prayed that no more of her friends were numbered among the washouts.

"You've been gone a long time, Gina. We've had a few... problems," Takeri said, and frowned as she remembered. "Jamie shot himself in the head with his V2. No one knows why he did it. The others," she shrugged. "They were in their bunks at lights out, but the next morning they were gone, and their names were deleted from the duty roster. MJ was one of them. You remember her?"

Gina nodded remembering a tall Anglo woman with dark brown

hair and grey eyes. Her name was Mary Jane Ferguson, and she was recruited by the Colonel from Garnet's militia. Gina had only spoken to her once or twice. MJ was quiet, but she had seemed to know her business where soldiering was concerned.

"Who else?"

"Compton, Middleton, and… and Kent. They were all missing that morning. We asked about them, but were told they had died in a training accident like the others."

Gina groaned. Kent was a friend of hers. She couldn't believe he was gone. She could still see that cheeky grin of his when he followed her into the showers, and offered to give her a massage. Roscoe had taken them on a cross-country run that morning, and had pushed his unenhanced charges to their limit. Gina had returned to the barracks, exhausted in mind and body, but Kent still had enough energy to try wooing her. She wished she had let him now.

"I'm sorry, Gina," Takeri said, and rubbed Gina's back in an attempt to comfort her. "I know you liked Kent."

"It's not just him, Selin. How many have we lost now? Ten? Twenty?"

Takeri shook her head. "Sixteen I think."

"That's almost eight percent, Selin. And we aren't all enhanced yet."

Takeri nodded solemnly.

Gina turned her attention to the front of the classroom. She couldn't hear what Eric was saying to Roscoe; it probably had nothing to do with her in any case. A short time later, Roscoe left the room leaving Penleigh to continue the class.

Penleigh surveyed the recruits and found Gina. "Takeri, help Fuentez connect to her consol."

"Yes, sir," Takeri said.

Takeri placed her right hand flat down in the palm shaped recess in the desk, and punched a sequence of numbers and letters into the keyboard. "Password," she said to Gina's questioning look. "Our processors have their own unique identities on the net. That's important for a number of things. In battle, your processor can make reports to your squad leader about your physical status, or you might ask it to up-link to the net and download the current tacsit. Whatever, there are many things it can do on its own, but that means it has to have its own identity or else we risk confusion. Your net password will be encoded within your processor for quicker access, but to use these consols you have to input it manually. Roscoe says they were designed that way back when the base was just a research facility. Something about wanting the viper prototypes to be physically present to use the equipment."

"Yeah?" Gina said. "I thought the General founded Snakeholme."

Takeri shook her head. "Roscoe says vipers were developed here in secret."

She didn't have time to think about that now. "How do I get my password?"

"The default is always *admin*, but you'll have to change it first thing. It's easy. Just put your weapon hand in the recess and follow the prompts. If you close your eyes it's easier."

Gina closed her eyes and put her hand in the recess.

#### Password Required: >_

The words seemed to hover before her. She opened her eyes again, but they remained at arm's length waiting for her input. She typed the word admin as she had been told, and the prompt was replaced by more instructions.

#### First logon detected.

#### Please change your password, Recruit Fuentez.
#### Enter your old password: >_
#### Enter your new password: >_

Gina chose something she would never forget for her password. Something ingrained upon her soul and that of every Marine since the Corps' inception on November 10th 1775. *Semper Fidelis*. She was no longer a Marine, but in her heart, she would always be one—always faithful to what the Corps stood for.

#### Password accepted... Connection achieved.

"Have you got it?"

"Yeah," Gina said. "Thanks, Selin."

"You're most welcome, Gina," Takeri said with a warm smile.

"Now then," Captain Penleigh said. "With Fuentez in mind, I will recap what you know about your systems. I want you to follow along. A refresher won't hurt."

He placed his hand into the recess in his desk and typed rapidly. Before Gina's eyes, an amazing amount of information appeared. She waved a hand in front of her face and blushed at the laughter from the others.

"We all did that the first day," Takeri whispered.

Gina nodded. She could see the room through the clutter of icons and indicators, but it was distracting. If she wanted to use the data, she had to focus on one part of her display and read it. The display was similar to that of the HUD used in Marine mechs (powered armour). She had always used mechs without a problem, and was sure she would get used to it.

"I'm sending you all a Merki trooper as a target. Seeing as we haven't got a real one for you all to play with, he should appear as an animated character."

A few chuckles sounded through the room.

"For those who know how, target the male. Fuentez, look at your top left indicator. You will see a range to target icon, focus on that and instruct your processor as follows. *Target: Range five hundred metres.*"

Gina did that, and noted her range finder indicated the cartoon was five hundred metres away. She watched the targeting diamond swing in and lock on. It pulsed redly once and revolved to show it was locked on.

"If you have a revolving diamond locked onto the trooper, you have performed correctly. Now, I want you to disengage target lock by telling your processor. Fuentez, how do you think that's accomplished?"

Gina finished disengaging. "Sir, the system seems intuitive, very much like my old mech armour. I disengaged using this command: Disengage target lock."

"Very good. If you ever need to use a function that you're unsure of, it's simply a matter of either doing it the way you would in armour, or telling your processor to do it. If you use the wrong command, your processor will tell you."

"Thank you, sir."

The lesson progressed with various simulations passing before her eyes. At first she doubted she would remember it all, but Takeri said a viper never forgets. During a spare moment, she reviewed what she knew. Takeri was right. Everything she needed was in her memory waiting to be tapped and used. She practised every function her display had at least once, and then began learning how to use them in conjunction with each other. She enjoyed the lessons and was a fast learner. Takeri said they were moving much faster with Captain Penleigh as their instructor.

"Have I caught up yet?"

"Not quite," Takeri said. "You still have communications and the net, and then there's the range. We began weapons training just last week."

"How long have you been attending these classes?"

"Almost three weeks."

Gina couldn't discuss it further; the captain had noticed her inattention. She bent her head and performed the simulation. She had to target a series of Merki troopers at the same time, and keep another group in range of her sensors. It was hard work, but she managed. Two hours later, her display cleared. She looked up to find the others sighing and working tired shoulders. When she removed her hand from the recess, her display winked out. She tried to reactivate it, but a voice for her alone told her off.

**"Access denied. No access to cybernetic enhancements will be granted. Warning: attempting to bypass this order will result in disciplinary action."**

"Okay already," Gina said in embarrassment.

Richmond looked over and grinned. "Naughty, naughty."

"How did you know?"

"I tried that my first day. Nasty critter that processor."

Gina nodded. "It sounded like my dad."

"Yeah? Mine sounds like Whitby. I'm going to change it as soon as I figure out how."

Gina grinned and followed her friend out of the classroom.

"Glad you're back, *Major*," Richmond said.

"Thank you, *Captain*. It's good to be here."

"Amen to that," Cragg said as he dodged by.

Gina exchanged glances with Richmond and they laughed. It was good to be back.

* * *

## Alpha Company's barracks, Petruso Base

Kate squared away her kit, and frowned at the wrinkle that had materialised as if by magic on the blanket covering her rack. She tugged at it, and tucked it in again. Looking at her rack with narrowed eyes, she dared the wrinkle to reappear.

It didn't.

Fuentez snorted behind her back. "I love it when you do that. That glare can strip paint. You do know that don't you?"

Kate grinned. "It comes in handy on occasion."

"You should be ashamed of yourself." Fuentez laughed. "That poor boy."

Kate growled under her breath. Jacobs was not a boy, but he did act like one. He was still in the queue for enhancement, yet he was already trying to lord it over everyone in sight including one Kate

Richmond. That was a mistake. She had never responded well to people who thought themselves better than her. If Jacobs didn't watch his step, he would find himself wearing his face on backwards.

"He annoys me." She shrugged. "I don't like his kind. Hiller doesn't like him either."

"Yeah. Hiller isn't the only one. Where the hell did Stanbridge dredge him up from?"

"He's from Bethany as you well know. I heard a rumour that he scored in the low nineties."

Fuentez raised an eyebrow at that. "Yeah? You could have fooled me."

Kate snorted and opened her locker. Checking her appearance in the mirror attached to the door, she fluffed her hair a little before pulling on her beret. She tried to get the edge perfectly horizontal, with the viper badge in line and directly above her left eye, but it refused to co-operate. She was about to pull it off and try again, when Fuentez intervened.

"Here, gimme."

"It always gives me trouble," Kate said sheepishly.

"That's because you have no patience." Fuentez lowered the beret onto Kate's head in the perfect position, and flattened it down on the right side. "There."

"I'll get the hang of it eventually. At least I can put my helmet on without help."

"It would certainly be something to see if you couldn't."

Kate grinned and said in a silly voice, "Please General, I can't come to the war until I get my helmet on straight. Will you help me please?"

Fuentez cracked up.

"Atten-*hut!*"

Fuentez jumped and dashed to stand at the base of her rack. Kate was closer to hers—one pace sufficed. Everyone snapped to attention as the General himself stepped by Roscoe and into the barracks. This was a very high honour. General Burgton rarely mixed with the recruits. They only saw him when he held a lecture. Those lectures had standing room only. Everyone wanted to learn from him.

"At ease," Burgton said and there was a barely perceptible lessening of tension in the room. "I have just learned of a situation that may, I repeat *may*, require a response."

Kate stiffened and the others murmured questions. The General would not be telling them all this unless he had something in mind. The only thing she could think of excited her beyond all measure.

"Simmer down people. I have no orders to mobilise the regiment, and I don't expect any such orders, but I take no chances. Accordingly, the enhancement and training schedules have been revised with activation of first battalion at the earliest opportunity a priority. As you can imagine, this will cause some disruption.

"Alpha and Bravo Companies are the furthest ahead. All three hundred and twenty units are enhanced, and I'm informed that training is well in hand. Unfortunately, Charlie and Delta Companies have the greatest percentage of unenhanced units. This will slow their training efforts. As I said, measures are being taken to redress this. Now then, how does this affect all of you? Firstly, with the aim of freeing up training resources for Charlie and Delta, I'm authorising a five day pass for Alpha and Bravo Companies. When you return, you will have your systems fully activated."

That caused a stir, and Kate exchanged a meaningful look with Fuentez. The schedule had called for full activation in six weeks time. Immediately after that, a series of live fire exercises had been planned to test their reflexes and abilities. Now all that planning was out the airlock.

Burgton was still speaking. "I will be calling on one or two of you to help with the training of Charlie and Delta. Those at the top of their class in artillery will take over from Sergeants Rutledge and Roscoe to free them for a third and fourth class that I'm arranging. Sergeant Stone will increase his efforts at the Complex with the aim of passing as many recruits through the simulators as possible. He will require some help with basic programming and monitoring. Those of you that have shown yourselves the best in other areas, will take on groups to train as needed."

The General reached the end of the barracks. He turned back and made his slow way to the door with the eyes of the recruits following him.

"I know all this sounds a little half-arsed," Burgton went on. "But I assure you I have considered this from every perspective. I've learned that things can and will go downhill fast if you're not prepared. In my opinion, it's better to have a full battalion of vipers that still need some work, than a highly polished *half* battalion. Not so?"

"Sir, yes, sir," the recruits roared in one voice.

"Good. Alpha and Bravo Companies are on a five day pass from this moment. Carry on."

The General left then, but Roscoe stayed behind. "Things are going to be a little hectic over the next few months so I'm warning you now. If I hear of any recruit abusing his position as temporary instructor, I'll have him scrapped."

No one reacted, least of all Kate. They all knew Roscoe's bark was worse than his bite.

Roscoe smiled. "Now that's out of the way, you had better get out of here. You're wasting party time," he said and made to leave, but stopped short of the door. "One last thing. When you return, you'll be required to check a terminal for new orders at zero-six-hundred each morning. Those with nothing special to do are still mine."

Roscoe left.

Everyone milled around discussing when or if they would mobilise. Kate went to join Fuentez who was chatting with Cragg.

"So, what are we doing?" Cragg said. Takeri wandered over followed by Hiller. "How about having a look in Smithson's Armoury? I want one of those belt pouches."

"Yeah, me too," Kate said thinking that she might need it soon.

"Come on guys, you can do that later. I want a drink, and some real food in a real restaurant," Hiller said plaintively, and the others laughed.

"You're too soft," Kate growled but she was grinning as she said it. "You're not yearning for the old days on Bethany are you?"

Hiller sobered. "No," he said solemnly but then he brightened. "I bet Jacobs is."

"Oh him," Takeri said and surprised everyone by the disgust in her voice. She got along with everyone. "He is not a nice person."

That was a strong condemnation from her. No one knew what had prompted it, but Jacobs must have done something to upset her. She had a good word to say about everyone.

"Okay, listen up," Fuentez said taking charge. "First Squad will immediately leave the base for a good meal in a *real* restaurant, and then head on over to Smithson's place to buy a few goodies."

Kate saluted sloppily and everyone laughed. "Do you think we can steal... err I mean *borrow* an APC?"

"Nah," Gordon said. "Who wants to drive?"

There were no volunteers and it was decided to go by maglev. Petruso City was too far to walk for the unenhanced, which is what they would remain until they returned. Deactivated enhancements might as well not exist.

The maglev consisted of two carriages, a power car, and a single rail that connected the base to Petruso City. It was originally a spur off the main maglev monorail line. In the years since, it had been physically disconnected from the main system leaving a straight run to and from the base. The regiment had exclusive use of it. It used to be for soldiers that wanted to visit their families in the city. Kate hadn't seen it running since arriving on Snakeholme, but she was sure it would be operational. The General wouldn't allow anything to fall into disrepair.

The barracks emptied en masse, and everyone headed for the maglev station.

When they reached it, Kate climbed up into the cockpit of the train, and leaned out of the open door. "Who knows how to work this thing?"

Christine Roberts of Fourth Squad raised a hand. "I might be able to."

"Hey, Chrissie," Gordon called over the heads of his squadmates. "I didn't know you were a train driver before this."

Everyone laughed and shoved Roberts forward.

Kate pulled her up into the cockpit and leaned out the door to glare at the onlookers. "All aboard... what are you waiting for?" She shook her head as everyone stampeded for the two passenger cars. The carriages were small and would not have enough seats for everyone. The unlucky ones would have to stand. "Have you figured it out?"

Roberts nodded and waved a hand at the controls. "It's a straight run from here to the city. There's even an autopilot."

"Great. It's time to party, Chris. Let's go."

Kate sat in the corner. There was just the one seat and Roberts needed that to monitor the controls.

"Here we go," Roberts said and eased the throttle forward.

The ride was smooth and Kate enjoyed it. She hadn't been allowed off base other than for training since arriving on Snakeholme. The countryside was a pleasant change from the base. She looked ahead to see the city seemingly rise out of the ground as the train sped toward it.

Petruso was a small city by Alliance standards, but it was the largest on Snakeholme. It was built in a bowl-like depression beside a crescent shaped lake. That was why it seemed to rise out of the ground as they approached. A wide and peaceful looking river fed the lake with mountain fresh water, but the lake's runoff was another matter; it was turbulent with plenty of white water and spray thrown up as it sped its way to the sea in the west.

"I wouldn't mind taking that on," Roberts said.

"What, the river?"

"Yeah. Ever done any kayaking?"

Kate shook her head. "Not me. I have wings not fins."

"It's great. Running the rapids, pitting yourself against nature really gets the adrenaline pumping. You should try it."

"I might just do that. Gina agreed to do some climbing with me when we're activated. Maybe you could come along."

Roberts nodded eagerly. "That would be great. I used to do a bit of climbing before I joined the service."

"Anything since?"

"Nah. I'm out of practice, but it will come back to me," Roberts said staring out of a side window. "They chose a good site for the city. Look at that view."

Kate *was* looking. The surface of the lake was like a mirror as it reflected the mountains and sky. The towers of the city were doubled in number as they too were mirrored in the waters of the lake. The layout of the city was pleasing to her. The buildings weren't crushed together like many other cities she had visited, and there were wide strips of green between the lanes of the few roads. Parks and trees were numerous. She could almost feel the General's influence over the design.

Vehicles were few in Petruso City. Travel was by elevated monorail or by foot, and the city benefited enormously from that policy. Burgton hadn't let the city planners destroy the countryside either. The woods and forests outside the city limits probably looked little different to the way nature intended, though she was sure the Ranger and Forestry Commission had a lot to do with that. Land for cultivation was plentiful on Snakeholme. With the maglev system connecting every city and town, there was no need to clear land close to the Petruso for farming. It looked great.

"There must be kayaks for rent here," Roberts mused. "Look there."

Kate nodded. She could make out a few sails way out on the lake. "Boats seem popular."

"Not boats—*yachts*."

"What's the difference? They all float don't they?"

Roberts spun around indignantly. "You're joking. What's the difference between a hang glider and a space plane?"

"Oh well, if you're going to be silly about it," Kate said a little huffily. Everyone knew the difference between a non-powered hang glider and a rocket motored space plane.

"I'll ask Gina if she wants to get wet," Roberts mused. "There must be somewhere I can rent a couple of kayaks."

Kate grunted still smarting from Roberts' comparisons. "I'll give it a go if you agree to try hang gliding with me."

"Looking forward to it."

Roberts eased back on the throttle, and they coasted into the station. She powered down the train and then joined Kate and her squadmates as they trotted off excitedly in search of a restaurant that could pass Hiller's fine eye for culinary excellence. They attracted a great deal of attention as they made their way toward the centre of the city. Pedestrians stopped to stare, and a good many interrupted their journeys to shake hands and chat. One elderly gentleman, who introduced himself simply as William, shook hands with Kate and enquired about her home.

"I'm from Bethany, sir," she said aware of the sudden silence that fell over the civs.

"Bethany! Bless my soul that's good to hear. So they finally saw sense, who would have thought it?"

"No, sir. My people are still the same. I doubt they will ever change."

"Oh," William said downcast. "That's a shame. Still, you're here Katherine. Might I ask where you and your friends are going?"

Kate smiled. Her brother had always called her Katherine. "I don't really know, sir. This is our first time in Petruso City. We were hoping to find a good restaurant."

William brightened at hearing that. "My dear, I have the perfect place for you. Sovereigns is the best place in the city. I guarantee you will enjoy the food and the surroundings."

Kate was unsure, but all the nodding heads convinced her. The civs all agreed that Sovereigns was the place. "Thank you, sir. We'll try there then. I hope they have room for us."

"Oh, I don't think you need to worry about reservations or anything," William said in amusement. "Just drop in and you'll be welcomed I'm sure."

The civs laughed at something, but Kate had no idea what it was about. William gave her directions and then left her to find Sovereigns.

"What do you make of that?" Fuentez said.

"Don't know, but everyone seems very friendly," Kate said.

They were more than friendly; they were treating the recruits like celebrities. Kate was a little puzzled by all the excitement, and distrusted it. They should be used to vipers, but instead they seemed almost honoured to see them.

Sovereigns turned out to be very busy. Kate doubted they would have room for two squads of boisterous recruits, but when the manager caught sight of their black uniforms, he erupted into a dervish of activity. He immediately ejected a sizable group of his patrons, taking no notice of the recruit's protestations. It made them all uncomfortable to be the cause of such strife, but far from being unhappy, those being ejected seemed proud to give up their places.

Fuentez went to investigate and came back with a rueful look on her face. "Francisco... that's the manager. Francisco promised them two free meals."

That explained their willingness to leave, and incidentally made Kate and the others feel much better. While waiting for their table, she became conscious of the remaining diners craning their necks to see. She stood taller, trying not to make eye contact, and pulled her carefully folded beret through her belt. She was feeling very exposed under the eyes of so many strangers.

The highly trained staff had things ready in no time, and Francisco himself led them proudly into his restaurant.

Kate sat opposite Fuentez, with Cragg joining them to sit opposite Takeri. Two platoons nearly filled the restaurant. Eighty vipers had a large collective appetite and it wasn't long before they were eating and enjoying themselves. Fuentez and Takeri chose a light soup to start, and Kate did the same.

Fuentez raised her glass in a toast. "I give you The Regiment."

"The Regiment."

"The Regiment."

"The Regiment and General Burgton," Kate said a little self-consciously.

They all drank to that.

They began tucking into the main course. Hiller sighed with pleasure at the table behind, and Kate grinned. He had chosen duck in orange sauce for his main course, and it tasted wonderful. Cragg winked, he had ordered the duck for both of them, and Kate ate it with gusto. It tasted so good after the plainer meals they ate on base.

"You should try this, Gina," she said. "It's great."

"I do like duck, but I prefer my chicken."

Takeri shook her head. "Barbarians."

"We can't all be vegetarians, Selin," Cragg said.

"Why not?"

"Because... just because," he said with a frown and Kate laughed.

Francisco came back just as they were finishing the main course and asked if everything was satisfactory.

Kate had just eaten the best meal of her life. "It was great! I mean... thank you Francisco. It was very nice."

Francisco smiled in polite amusement. "Great is good, I assure you. Are you ready for desert?"

"I think so," she said and the others nodded. "What would you recommend?"

"Something simple I think. Our apple crumble with a dollop of vanilla ice cream."

"I'll have that," Kate said and the others murmured their agreement. "Thank you."

"You are most welcome," Francisco said and a few moments later four deserts arrived. "Enjoy."

"Thanks." She watched Francisco move to one of the other tables. "Seems like a nice man."

"Yeah," Fuentez said. "And his ice-cream is superb."

Everyone laughed and tucked in.

The last surprise came when it was time to leave. Fuentez politely asked a waitress where to pay, but the girl just smiled and said the bill had been taken care of. Not one to take charity, she wouldn't leave it there. Kate and the others waited in reception while Fuentez sought out Francisco. When she came back, she had a puzzled frown on her face.

"What's wrong?" Cragg said.

"He said the regiment would take care of the bill. When I said that I wanted to pay, he laughed and asked me if this was my first time off base."

"What did he mean by that?" Takeri said.

"He said everything is free for vipers."

"Free, everything?"

Fuentez nodded. "He said the regiment always covers the bills, and it's not just here either. Francisco says anything we buy in Petruso is covered by the regiment."

"That doesn't make sense," Takeri said. "They would have told us... wouldn't they?"

They all looked at each other then sighed. "Roscoe."

"I knew that smirking basta—ah, I knew that smirking *sergeant* was up to something," Kate said. "You said the regiment pays?"

Fuentez nodded.

"That means the General then."

"Must be, but your point is...?"

"My point is that we had better not buy anything too extravagant." Kate cringed as she imagined being called before Burgton to explain why she had bought the entire squad a hang glider each. "I don't think the General would like that."

Cragg nodded. "Good point, but how do we know what's too much?"

"We'll know our limit when someone gets in trouble with the General," she said, but she would have a word with Stone when they got back. He would know what was permissible.

"Oh great," Gordon said. "It will probably be me."

Fuentez laughed and punched Gordon playfully on the shoulder as they left the restaurant. First Squad separated from the others outside Sovereigns, and went in search of Smithson's Armoury. They found it easily. There was no end of helpful people willing to stop and chat or offer directions. Perhaps twenty minutes of sightseeing saw them trooping through Smithson's door intent on buying a few little extras.

* * *

# 17 ~ Activation

Gina stood quietly in the padded room with her weapon hand pressed firmly into the palm shaped receptacle in the desk, and watched Doctor Patel study the data being displayed on his monitor. He was hunched over the desk on a level with the screen, and must have been uncomfortable, but he didn't show it. Gina looked around the room, but apart from the desk and the padded walls, there was nothing he could use for a chair. She had heard about padded rooms before this, but she had never dreamed she would become the occupant of one. Patel typed a command into the recessed keyboard in the desktop, and nodded approvingly when fresh results appeared. Gina tried to guess what he was thinking by watching his expression, but it wasn't working. Patel was her judge and jury. As head of Medical, he had to sign off on her fitness for graduation.

"Try to remain absolutely still, Recruit."

Gina turned back to watch him, and tried not to fidget. She had worked toward this for months, but now the waiting was over, and she found herself almost floating off the floor in anticipation. Any second now she would become a viper in full measure. She watched Patel intently as he reviewed the data so recently downloaded from her permanent memory. She had no idea what the individual bytes of data meant, but there was an awful lot of it. Could he actually read real memories from just a bunch of numbers? Was he seeing images in place of those figures?

"Sir?"

"Hmmm?" Patel said, still concentrating on the data dump. "You have a question, Recruit?"

"I was just wondering... I mean if you don't mind telling me..."

"Out with it, Recruit. I'm a little busy here."

"Sorry, sir," she said and bulled ahead. "I was wondering if you can actually decipher the data dump."

Patel smiled, and he looked up at her. "Can I see everything you did since day one of enhancement?"

"Well... yes, sir."

"Of course I can."

She gaped. "You *can?*"

Patel smiled. "Certainly. Think it through, Recruit. How would it be possible for a viper unit to download an experience into the simulators for others to use, if I couldn't do something similar here?"

Gina frowned. She knew about downloading recon data from her lessons in the classroom, but she hadn't thought to apply the knowledge here. She was annoyed with herself. She shouldn't need to be told to think problems through. She should have remembered her lesson and applied it.

"Don't worry, I'm far more interested in your system parameters, than I am in your expertise at climbing or canoing." Patel pointed at the lines of data currently displayed on the monitor. "You should have worn a life preserver. Your enhancement doesn't mean you can't drown."

Gina smiled sheepishly.

"Don't feel too bad, Recruit. This sort of thing does take getting used to."

It did, but now she was thinking, she realised something else. "This is how the archives were created."

Patel nodded solemnly. "We never truly die, Recruit. Our memories live on in the archive. We mourn our dead, but we especially mourn those that were unrecoverable. We honour their memory."

Gina shivered. In this instance, unrecoverable meant they had been damaged so thoroughly, their core memories and processors were beyond recovery. She didn't know how many vipers were missing in action—she hoped it was none, but she doubted it.

"Now then," Patel said turning back to his work.

Patel placed his weapon hand in the second palm-shaped recess, and began typing rapidly. A viper's neural interface was much faster than using keyboards, but they only used them to access Snakeholme's Infonet or the regiment's TacNet. He typed another command, and nodded in satisfaction at what he read.

"This is the last time we will need to do this, Recruit. This session will activate all of your cybernetic enhancements, and put them under your control. I'm requiring you to be still for the same reason this room is so heavily padded. Accidents will happen, they always do. Your servo assisted musculature is currently set at unenhanced, but in a moment you will be at full combat readiness."

"Do I need to be aware of any special problems?"

"Not special, no, but you will feel different. Powerful, very light on your feet. Both of those sensations have been reported to us time and again. My own enhancement was particularly embarrassing as I recall." Patel shrugged. "In any event, there is only one rule: Move slowly and deliberately. You will soon see why. I will initiate your systems now, but don't move until I've left the room. When you feel confident enough to move safely, you may return to your squad."

Patel tapped in his commands, and moved to the door. Gina realised what he meant the moment he hit the enter key. Gravity seemed to have diminished to a point where it barely held her to the floor. She didn't move as Patel opened the door, but called a question.

"Sir?"

"What is it?"

"You initialised everything via the link, can a bad guy do the opposite?"

"No," Patel said firmly. "Contrary to the popular myths about us and the danger we pose to the Alliance, no one has ever successfully hacked a viper's systems. Not even Walden himself could control one of us. Your internal security prevents tampering; even I can't do it without the consent of your processor. Only you can order it to allow access now that all your systems are online."

Gina shivered at the mention of the hated Douglas Walden. What would it be like to have a hacker trying to get into her mind? She shuddered as her imagination supplied all kinds of nasty scenarios. Anyone who tried to hack her systems wouldn't live long. She would see to that.

"Thank you, sir."

Patel regarded her for a long moment. "You're the first recruit to ask that question, Fuentez. I'm impressed."

"Impressed?"

"At the depth of your paranoia," Patel said and left.

It wasn't paranoia. She merely wanted to be sure of her body's abilities. If someone could turn those off, she couldn't be sure of anything. With Patel's warnings in the forefront of her mind, she tried to take a step.

"Yeee aaah!" she yelled in startlement as her single step hurled her across the room to slam into the padded wall.

She shook her head at her own stupidity. Patel had told her to be careful. She turned on the spot until she was facing back the way she had come. With Patel's admonitions in mind, she took another step and flew across the room as if someone had turned off the planet's gravity. She landed with her leg striking the desk. She rubbed her thigh; there was sure to be a bruise tomorrow.

"Dammit," Gina hissed, and thumped the desk in frustration.

*CRUUNCH!*

"Oh shit." She stared at the broken corner, and then guiltily at the door before trying to pull the padding over the damage.

*SHRRRTTT!*

"Damn," she mumbled with a long length of padding dangling in her hand.

\* \* \*

"Ha, ha, Haaaa!" Stone howled in laughter. "That was a classic. Did you see her face?"

Flowers smiled, but there was a serious side to this. Up until now the recruits had used their systems in various ways, but they hadn't lived with them every moment of every day. Before each session, the recruits would have the necessary system activated, and at the end, deactivated. It was a safety precaution, but now it was time to become vipers in full.

"She doesn't seem too upset," he said.

"Nah, Fuentez can handle it."

"I tell you, Ken, I'm worried."

"Why?" Stone said in surprise. "Everything has gone as smooth as can be."

"That's what worries me. Only nineteen scrapped out of two hundred and twenty... I don't like it."

"Pardon me, sir, but that's good!"

"Don't get me wrong. I'll be pleased if we don't have any more washouts. What worries me is that we might have a bunch like Robbins here."

Stone went quiet at the mention of Robbins.

Robbins had been the best of them, a natural leader and looked it. Everyone gravitated toward him and wanted to be in his squad. Then one day he ran off base at full speed. He had snapped. It took a full squad of ten units to track him down, and take him out.

Flowers squeezed his eyes shut trying to shut out the memory, but his processor insisted on finding and displaying it.

Robbins was down. One leg was shot away, but still his weapon hand came up holding his pulser.

"Please don't," Flowers said to his friend. "Don't do it. I don't want to kill you."

Nothing he said made any difference. Robbins was no longer in there; instead, the machine his friend had feared he would become looked out of his eyes.

Flowers snatched his pistol in a servo-assisted blur and blew his best friend's head off.

"Sir?" Stone said.

"What is it?"

Stone looked at him for a long moment, perhaps guessing what had been going through his mind. "She seems to have figured out her own method."

He turned his attention to the monitor and laughed. "Full bore. I like her style."

* * *

Gina muttered to herself then cursed her stupidity. Her strength was so distracting, she had ignored her other abilities. Using her sensors and range finder, she noted the dimensions of the room. With her back near the wall she leapt...

...and landed to slap the opposite wall with her outstretched palms. She did that a few times pushing off with less power each time. Gradually she learned how much was necessary for the desired effect. In the end she found a small hop forward took less than a tenth of the effort she would have used while unenhanced. Knowing how much stronger she was, she tried walking and found she could do it if she concentrated on keeping her movements small and economical. Wandering around the room gave her greater confidence, and perhaps twenty minutes later, she decided she was ready to leave.

As she made her way carefully outside, she realised why vipers always looked like they were walking on air. The gliding movements were the best way to move for an enhanced person. She tried to copy the way Eric and the other veterans moved, and felt herself slowly relaxing.

Gina was greeted with applause when she reached the barracks. She waved away the silly beggars, and the other squads moved off, but her own squadmates stayed to chat.

"First squad is complete," Richmond said in satisfaction. The entire squad was enhanced; the entire platoon for that matter.

"You were quickest to come out," Cragg said. "What's your secret?"

"Jumping," Gina said and explained how she had figured out how much stronger she was by leaping about.

"Wish I'd thought of that," Richmond said ruefully. "I kept racing from one end of the room to the other until I figured it out. Not as quick, but it worked."

Gina nodded and decided not to mention the broken desk. "What's next to do?"

"Training, recruit; lots and lots of lovely training," Sergeant Rutledge said as he entered the barracks. "Roscoe tells me you lot are in need of a workout. I can see he was right. Flabby recruits we do not need. It's First Platoon's turn at the crusher. You have two minutes to fall in with full kit."

No one moved.

"One minute fifty seconds," Rutledge said, and everyone dashed to get his or her kit. "One minute forty," he said as he went out the door.

Everyone moved—viper fast.

Gina's armour was stored in her locker in the order she needed to put it on, but it still took almost a full minute to don. She buckled her belt with its holster for her pistol, making sure to strap it securely to her thigh. She checked the pistol was loaded with training rounds—it was. She settled her webbing over her shoulders, and anchored it in place on her armour using the cleats. The loops on her webbing contained flares, extra magazines, her knife, and a dozen training grenades that everyone called whiz-bangs for the sound they made when they went off. The case on her belt contained extra energy cells for her rifle. She didn't need to check that, she had filled it that morning. Her beret went into her locker, and her helmet went onto her head. Her pack was always ready, and her rifle was near to hand, she snatched them both up and joined the rush to the door.

By the time she reached the parade ground, her pack was on her back as it should be, and her rifle was by her side.

"Attennnnnn-*hut!*" Rutledge barked, and everyone snapped to attention as Captain Penleigh came to inspect the platoon.

It was a simple inspection. He murmured the occasional question in an effort to get a feel for what they knew, and what they didn't, but finally he moved back to a position central to the platoon and turned to face them.

"Sergeant Rutledge," Penleigh said in a loud voice.

"Sir?"

"Is your platoon of recruits fully online?"

"Yes, sir."

"Have they been fully prepared and trained in the use of their enhancements?"

"Yes, sir." Rutledge said. "First Platoon, Alpha Company is ready for war, sir."

Penleigh smiled crookedly and Gina tensed. She had seen him smile that way before. Most notably, just before he shot dead a prisoner. Whatever he had in mind today, it was likely to push them all hard.

"In that case," Penleigh said and looked directly at Gina in the front rank. "I think we should give them a little assignment. First Platoon will make its way to field firing range Bravo by foot, and will reach there no later than fourteen hundred today."

That was less than an hour to travel a hundred klicks. Gina frowned; it was a hundred by road, but cross-country it was more like seventy.

"Upon reaching the objective, you will take out the enemy by any means you deem suitable. Use of natural cover, and weapons captured on site, is permissible. If you're successful, a second target will become apparent and so on. Sergeant Rutledge and I will be along as observers only, and Master Sergeant Stone will join us at the range. At no time will you look to us for help or advice. As far as you're concerned, we are not here."

Penleigh nodded to Rutledge.

"You heard the Captain. Your time starts now."

There was no sudden rush to leave. Gina and her squadmates joined the huddle created by the other three squads to decide their best course of action. Penleigh and Rutledge looked on in silence, and listened to the discussion.

"We need to go through Petruso then cross-country bearing east. Agreed?" Gina said.

"It's the only way," Gwen Wevers of Second Squad said.

"It's not the only way, but it's the best," Roberto Callendri added for Third Squad.

"Okay, let's do it," Gina said and dashed toward the city.

The others fell into formation by squads, and ran with her in the lead position. A few minutes into the run, Cragg increased speed and joined Gina. He suggested they increase the pace to forty klicks an hour, but she said not until after they were through the city. She didn't want to hurt anyone.

"Okay, but we'll have to make up the time," Cragg said, as he ran by her side.

Gina grinned. She was looking forward to it. "It's not a problem.

The first section is open country.

They entered the city running along wide roads and avenues. People stopped and waved, some even cheered to see the black uniform on so many new vipers. The city was well laid out. They made it through in excellent time. When the moment came to leave the road, everyone did that without fuss or bother not missing a step. Down the embankment they went and into open fields.

Gina accelerated until her legs were a pumping blur. "Let's make up some time, people!"

With a coded thought, she accessed her processor and gave her commands.

*Access satellite Alpha one-niner. Locate and display current location.*

An aerial view of the city, and the open ground to the east, appeared on her display. A blinking icon showed her location.

*Increase magnification factor two… factor three. Plot fastest course from current location to field firing range Bravo, and display in green.*

A line appeared. Gina adjusted her course, until her icon followed it. Time elapsed was twenty minutes, but that was not a concern. Following the course plotted by her processor, they would reach the range in another half hour.

The run was pleasant, and the speed exhilarating. Gina grinned into the wind as she led her squad to the designated target. According to sensors, the other three squads were following her lead. The observers were to her right, and a hundred metres back.

Richmond increased her speed to come alongside. "The stream is coming up. Jump or swim?"

"Jump I think. It's not wide. It shouldn't prove a problem."

"Good enough." Richmond dropped aback slightly.

"When we get there," Cragg said. "I think one or two of us should scout the place. Stone being involved makes me nervous."

Stone had a way of doing that to people. Gina glanced at Richmond. "Kate, you know him best. What's he likely to do?"

"Frag our arses. On his own, he would probably set mines and traps. With friends, he might set the mines to herd us to a prepared position and ambush us."

"Which is it?"

"Could be either, but the second is more fun from his point of view. I vote the second."

"Me too," Cragg added.

Gina agreed. "It's unanimous. Kate, you're our best scout. Take

Takeri and recon the place, but report back before engaging."

"Right."

"Once we have decent information, we can try for an encirclement. The other squads might not follow my lead, but if they do that's what I want to try."

"Sounds good," Cragg said.

It did, but Gina was well aware that nothing goes exactly to plan. Stone was bound to have something sneaky up his sleeve.

The stream came into sight. She targeted the banks and computed that it was only twelve metres wide. Gauging her steps, she slowed a little and jumped as her left foot hit the edge. Behind her, the other squads yelled in excitement as they flew over the water, but she was pleased when her own squadmates remained silent. It *was* fun, but they had an assignment to complete. This was no time for clowning around.

Gina hit the ground and shoulder rolled back to her feet with no wasted motions. She heard one or two splashes, and quite a lot of cursing, as Second Squad hit the bank and not the ground beyond it. She watched her sensors ready to turn back, but they were on their feet and chasing her within moments. When she judged they were close enough to the firing range, she slowed the pace to allow Richmond and Takeri to pull ahead and scout the area. As soon as Richmond was out of sight, Gina ordered everyone to stop and rest. Wevers and Callendri began to muddy the waters almost as soon as they stopped.

"Who said you should lead?" Callendri said. "I don't have to take your orders…"

Kamarl Dolinski, Callendri's best friend, shifted as if about to intervene, but then he relaxed and contented himself with watching his friend. There was something about the way he watched, that sent warning tingles down Gina's spine.

"…I was an LT before this; I should lead."

Gina sighed. "Cragg was a leuey too. Takeri was a staff sergeant, and Gordon was a captain… so was Hiller. It doesn't mean anything. We're vipers now."

"In that case, seeing as it don't mean nothing, I'll take over," Wevers said sweetly.

Callendri and Wevers squared off arguing over which of them was more qualified to lead. Gina sighed and stepped away shaking her head. It took a word from Cragg to shut them up.

Cragg shouldered between the two, but saved his glare for Callendri. "Neither of you is fit to lead. We're on a mission for God's sake. It doesn't matter if it's a training op, and it doesn't matter who gives the orders as long as they're the right ones. This platoon is going to ace this mission—get me?" He glared even harder at Callendri, but he saved some for Wevers too.

When Wevers realised how angry Cragg was, the smirk she had been wearing drained away. She backed off, and rejoined her squad where she sullenly refused to answer questions. Without warning, Callendri took a swing at Cragg. The power behind the blow might have killed him, but Cragg was a viper too. He blocked and grappled with Callendri.

"That's *enough!*" Rutledge roared. "Recruit Callendri, you're on notice. One more like this and we'll deactivate you, *permanently.*"

Everyone stiffened at the threat; they knew what it meant. To be deactivated was to be scrapped. What you called it didn't matter. It was death either way.

"Get back to work all of you."

Captain Penleigh looked on in silence.

* * *

### FIELD FIRING RANGE BRAVO, SNAKEHOLME

Kate shook her head at what they had found. She was disappointed in Stone. If this was all he could come up with, they wouldn't learn a damn thing. She wouldn't have been fooled by this before enhancement let alone after. Stone's setup here was a joke. The traps were glaringly obvious to a viper's systems.

"Really damn sloppy," she whispered to Takeri, but then she frowned. It was *too* sloppy. "Too sloppy to be real."

"How can you be sure?"

"I'm sure," she said uncomfortably. "I know Stone, he's better than this."

Kate studied the ambush site and shook her head. It was too easy. One thing she knew, Stone wouldn't make it this easy. Keeping low, they moved to a new vantage and found the surprise. An automatic grenade launcher was dug in, and aimed to hit anyone sneaking through the so-obvious hole in Stone's defensive perimeter.

"You were right," Takeri whispered with respect. "Where to now?"

"If we work our way around, we should see what he's got. I hope Gina waits for us to find it all."

"If not for the time limit she would."

Kate frowned. Takeri should know Gina better by now. "She won't care about that. Winning the battle is more important."

"But the Captain said—"

"He *said* what he had to, Selin. He wants us under pressure."

"Maybe," Takeri said, sounding unconvinced.

Kate decided to risk going active on her sensors.

Takeri gasped and started to protest when Kate began another sweep—an active sweep—of the area, but then she realised what was done could not be undone. She settled down to wait. Gina had given Kate this part of the mission for a reason. She was good at this kind of thing, and Gina trusted her to do the job right. The ground cover didn't give her licence to be blatant about what she was doing, but it did allow her to do the job—as long as she was very careful.

Kate was careful, and Takeri was careful of Kate.

Slowly, painstakingly, she found the launchers and mines. Stone had used every trick in the book to hide his trip wires. He chose to place mines in positions where tripping would cause intruders to fall on them. The wires were made of some kind of synthetic, almost invisible to her sensors. Sneaky bastard.

"I have something else," Kate whispered and Takeri nodded. She had gone active now as well. "It's faint, it's almost as if..." she frowned. "Let's go back, I have what we need."

Takeri didn't argue.

Kate scooted back carefully, and retraced her path back into the hills. Once she was far enough away, she trotted keeping low, but gradually picked up speed until she ran like the wind. She loved the feeling of flying that came upon her as she topped out at seventy-eight klicks an hour, but it was soon over. Her sensors detected the others waiting in a hollow for her return.

"It's about damn time," Gordon said testily. "You do know we should have been there a quarter of an hour ago?"

"*Shadaaap,*" Kate drawled. "Better late than dead."

"What did you find?" Gina said eagerly.

"Synthetic trip wires that don't show on sensors. You trip and fall right onto his mines. He has auto grenade launchers dug in and hidden from sight. They're zeroed to cover the only open corridor in."

"The *only* one?"

"Yeah," Kate said. "It was so obvious, we looked further and found the launchers. I'm pretty sure I wasn't supposed to find the tunnel so quick."

"A tunnel?"

Takeri nodded. "We picked up a faint trace on sensors. The only reason for that I can think of is a tunnel."

Gina frowned. "Can we take out the defences?"

"Easy," Kate said. "Nothing to it."

"That's good, because that's what we're going to do." Gina went to talk with the others. "I need one squad to take out the grenade launchers for me. Who wants it?"

"We'll take it," Wevers said for Second Squad.

"Okay, talk to Kate. She knows where they are."

Wevers nodded.

Gina glanced at the Captain where he stood observing, and then back to her friends. "That leaves the rest of us to investigate the tunnel, and look for the second target the Captain was talking about."

Callendri just glared in silence.

* * *

Eric watched Fuentez deploy her people; it was reminiscent of Thurston. Oh, the mission was completely different, and so were her men, but she handled the situation confidently as she had back on Thurston.

During the earlier stages of her training, she had become a mascot to First Squad, not that Fuentez saw herself that way, or would have been pleased with the description, but it was true nonetheless. When she survived her enhancement, the superstitious recruits decided it was a miracle, and promptly made her their mascot—quietly and unofficially of course. Then had come the battle to catch up with the others, which she had done with, perhaps not ease, but she did make it *seem* easy. She wasn't a complainer, so she worked on and caught up earning her place as unofficial leader of her squad. She was a natural, and seemed to have fallen into the role completely without prior thought. She was literally doing what came naturally.

He turned away from his study of Fuentez, and targeted Roberto Callendri. His earlier attack on Cragg had been completely out of the blue. He would bear watching. There was something in Callendri's silences that set alarm bells ringing, but anyone could lose their temper. It was no reason to scrap him. Eric watched Callendri glaring at Fuentez and worried. If the man was going to have a whigout, now was not a good time. Training rounds or not, their weapons could still be deadly if they struck an unarmoured target at close range. Eric eased his hand onto his pistol, and watched Callendri intently, but nothing untoward happened barring a lot of hateful glaring.

Fuentez gave the word, and ten units from Second Squad took out the dummy launchers Stone had placed yesterday. The timing was perfect. First and Third Squads moved down the safe corridor, quicker perhaps that he would, but the few extra traps he had ordered set were found and disarmed in short order. Fourth Squad played a covering role on the look out for a sneaky bastard named Stone.

Fuentez raised her arm, and then waved everyone down. "First two men, into the tunnel and secure the entrance."

Cragg and Hiller moved forward. Without hesitation, they fired into the darkness before stepping forward and dropping out of sight through the hatch in the ground. Rutledge grinned. He had warned Eric that the recruits wouldn't fall for a booby trap at the hatch, but Eric hadn't been so sure. He had ordered one placed directly under it. Cragg and Hiller had just fried it.

"Clear," Hiller called, his voice faint and echoing from the tunnel walls.

Fuentez ordered half her squad into the tunnel before joining them. Eric jumped the queue; he didn't want to miss anything.

The tunnels had lighting, but of course, Stone had shut it down. As soon as Eric landed, he ordered his processor to go to light amplification mode, and the recruits suddenly appeared in the monochrome he always associated with his use of it. Fuentez had set a perimeter roughly ten metres down the tunnel, and was scanning the surroundings.

"Richmond takes point," Fuentez said in a hushed voice. "Cragg is rear guard. I want half on the left wall; half with me on the right... don't bunch up people."

Eric stayed in the open with Rutledge of course, and received a very annoyed glare from Fuentez and Richmond. He supposed it was a little unfair giving the game away like this. He moved to the right wall while Rutledge took the left.

"Move out," Fuentez ordered, and the recruits crab-walked with their backs firmly against the plascrete following Richmond.

So far, Fuentez had handled the platoon well, but then she should. Her promotion to lieutenant, though of short duration, had been well deserved. She was doing what she knew to do, and doing it well. All the recruits were good; many had been non-commissioned officers in their regiments or gifted PFCs. It was a shame there weren't more slots for officers available, but a single regiment needed only so many. The others would have to be satisfied with doing the job. Not many would be satisfied, but they had years to get it out of their systems. It would take a while for them to realise that rank meant nothing when you had centuries ahead. Only the job and the Alliance mattered as the years rolled by.

Richmond raised a clenched fist and everyone froze. "I have something on sensors... very faint," she whispered. "Like something trying to hide, but poorly shielded."

"Check it out," Fuentez ordered.

Richmond didn't respond. Instead, she went to her belly and eased forward to look around the next corner. She kept very still for a moment then eased back.

"Merki squad. Ten males and three females, all heavily armed. They have a combat gravsled armed with a twin barrelled extended range pulser."

"Manned?" Fuentez asked intently.

"Yeah, but it's targeted the other way.

"Range?"

"Seventy five metres."

"Okay." Fuentez turned to evaluate the recruits. Her eyes skipped over Roberto, but then almost reluctantly came back to him. "Callendri, you and your squad take them out. Second Squad will cover you."

"What about First Squad?" Callendri sneered.

"We'll cover this tunnel."

"There's nothing here."

"Just do the damn *job*," Fuentez said, fast losing patience.

Callendri clutched his rifle angrily. A moment later, he led Third Squad around the corner in a rush. The move took Wevers completely by surprise, and her squad belatedly moved to cover him. The moment Third Squad opened fire, all hell broke loose.

Callendri had advanced forward of his people, and was firing his rifle from the hip on full auto when the flash-bangs went off to blind him and his squad. Wevers was lucky. Due to the suddenness of Callendri's foolish move, her squad was farther back and survived unscathed. Third Squad however was killed to a man, evidenced by the green fluorescent dye spotting their body armour and uniforms. Eric could almost hear Stone's laughter as his paint-filled simunition rounds annihilated Third Squad. Wevers and Second Squad went to ground, and hammered the Merki-shaped targets to splinters. They never lost a man.

Back in the tunnel, First Squad had their own problems to deal with. Cragg, still facing back the way they came, was rear guard and saw the enemy coming. He opened fire while calmly informing his squadmates that some kind of vehicle was approaching. In fact, the vehicle was an old mine car fitted with an auto guidance system set to follow the tunnel walls. It had two automated splat guns, mounted fore and aft, to simulate Merkiaari gauss cannons. Had they been real, the entire platoon would have been in serious jeopardy. Ten rifles opened up, and the splat guns were turned to slag before they could fire more than a couple of their paint filled simunition rounds. The mine car glowed red; the metal of the car was thick, and it took a lot of punishment before Cragg blew off a wheel to stop it. The two dummy troopers were turned to ash a moment later.

"Cease firing!" Fuentez shouted, and the hiss-crack of pulser bolts stopped on the instant.

Eric quickly stepped forward. "Dead recruits will remain out of the way while observing the rest of the mission. You know who you are."

First Squad had one man hit. Cragg had taken a paint pellet early in the fight, but he had a point of view about being left out of the rest of the mission.

"It's a flesh wound, sir," Cragg protested.

"You heard the order, Cragg," Rutledge growled.

"But sarge, it really is only a flesh wound. Look."

Rutledge made a show of inspecting the 'wound', and glanced at Eric.

Eric smiled briefly, and eyed the single splat of paint on Cragg's shoulder. "Hmmm, might have been a railgun, Cragg. It would have taken your arm off, or it might have been a rocket or incendiary."

"Yes, sir," Cragg said visibly crestfallen.

"However, I'll give you the benefit of the doubt." He raised his voice to announce the decision. "Cragg has a light wound, upper left shoulder."

Fuentez went back to work. "Gordon, Takeri, check Third Squad for wounded. Richmond, Hiller, move up and check the Merkiaari for anything useful. Wevers, move your squad up and cover them."

"Copy."

"Affirmative."

"Copy that, we're moving."

Eric followed along and heard some commotion ahead. Pushing between the recruits, he found Callendri arguing with anyone who would listen. No one did. Most moved by the paint spattered and infuriated recruit without twitching an eyelid, but when Fuentez appeared everything went to hell.

"You set me up!" Callendri roared at the sight of her. "You sent us out here to draw their fire!"

"Don't be a fool," Fuentez said, sounding disgusted with his whining. "You walked into it after Richmond told us there was a heavily armed squad here. You took no precautions at all."

Callendri angled his rifle up at Fuentez before Eric could think to intervene.

Kamaral Dolinski, a well liked member of Third Squad and Callendri's best friend, reacted instantly. He drew his pistol in a servo-enhanced blur and pressed it hard against Callendri's ear. "Don't you *fucking* move."

Everyone backed away, but Callendri kept his rifle centred on Fuentez. He stared coldly at his nemesis, taking no notice of the pistol in his ear.

"You won't shoot me, Kamarl. I'm your friend... remember?" Callendri said without a flicker of fear at what his friend might do. His face was coldly calm. If he was feeling anything, it didn't show on his face.

"I remember a good man named Roberto. I don't know who the hell you are, but you ain't him."

Eric was moving when the decision came into Callendri's eyes. "*Shoot him!*" he roared even as Callendri fired. Fuentez leapt aside, but too late.

*Hiss-crack!* Both weapons went off together.

"Damn me, the bastard shot me," Fuentez gasped as she fell. "... it hurts..."

Fuentez was down with a pulser burn over her hip. She was panting wide-eyed at the pain and shock of being shot by one of her own people, but at least she was alive. Her armour was burned away where the fringes of the shot had caught the lower edge, but it had stopped most of the charge. Roberto however, was dead. He didn't have a head.

Dolinski stood exactly as before with his pistol levelled, staring as if still seeing the moment he had shot his squadmate. Everyone stood frozen for an endless moment, but Richmond ended it by jumping forward to give aid to Fuentez.

Eric looked down at the rogue unit that had been recruit Callendri, and shook his head sadly. Roberto had been a good man before the General took him into the regiment. He had been a lieutenant with many citations for bravery. He was awarded the bronze star twice for performing above and beyond the call of duty. Now he was dog meat.

Eric sighed, how many more would die before they were done? "Dolinski, put up your weapon."

"I had to... I had to do it, sir. He was my best friend, and I had to do it," Dolinski whispered in shock.

"I know. You did the right thing. Callendri wasn't in there any longer. He just cracked. It happens. Try to put it behind you." The recruits were staring at what was left of Callendri. He knew what they were thinking: *that could have been me. It might be me next time.* "This exercise is over." He contacted Stone to give him the word. Stone acknowledged the order and said he would come in. "Pick up Fuentez and let's get the hell out of this stinking tunnel. I'll send someone back for Roberto."

Fuentez had quieted, but she yelled and cursed at the pain when her squad lifted her into Cragg's arms to take her to the surface. Eric glanced at what was left of Callendri, and then resolutely turned away to follow the recruits.

* * *

# Part III

# 18 ~ Sol

Sol, the centre of the Human sector and capital system of the Alliance was a busy place to say the least. Earth, overpopulated homeworld of man was the centre of attention of course, but Mars, first colony and independent world was popular with out-system visitors as well. Space habitats bustled with Humanity, civilian liners and merchantmen entered and left the system in a continuous and unending stream, shuttles flitted from ship to ship and planet to station often courting disaster as they skimmed close to jump capable ships jockeying for position in the queues for outbound lanes. And then, there were the warships patrolling the system and, many insisted, generally getting in other people's way.

Such was Sol on a normal day, but the day was far from normal for Tei'Varyk who was just now receiving his first impressions of the first Human system he had ever seen. Translation had been smoother than predicted, or so he was informed by the weak smile directed his way from Tei'Colgan. The wondering and speculation that had run rampant through *Canada* was now laid to rest.

Shan did not handle translation any better than Humans did.

Tei'Varyk clamped his muzzle shut and repeatedly swallowed bile determined not to embarrass himself before the Humans. He concentrated on observing them as they struggled to throw off the disorientation induced by jump translation to normal space. Gradually his sickness subsided and he was able to take a greater interest in what he saw.

"Referent," Tei'Colgan said removing his helmet and setting it down in the rack attached to his station. "Where the hell are we?"

"Scanning... referent attained. We're in the zone—Sol system confirmed, Skipper," Francis said.

"We have a beacon query, Skipper," Lieutenant Ricks said. "It's repeating."

"Send: *ASN Canada* declaring an emergency. Request an immediate priority routing to Gateway."

"Aye sir, transmitting now."

"Gateway?" Tei'Varyk said.

"We could dock at almost any station really, but Gateway is the best one for us. It's in Earth orbit for one thing, and it's only a short hop to HQ from there. Besides, *Canada* needs a lot of work and Gateway controls the best yard facilities in the system."

Tei'Varyk understood that Colgan wanted his ship repaired quickly, but more importantly, being close to his homeworld would allow them to meet with Colgan's elders that much quicker. Speed was essential; he tried not to think that it was already too late.

"Docking at Gateway is approved, Skipper. They're clearing a lane for us," Ricks said.

"Thank you, Mark, pass the lane assignment to the helm. Janice?"

"Sir?"

"I don't want any accidents, but we need to get in and dock fast."

"Aye sir," Janice grinned. "Best speed to Gateway station."

"Good."

*ASN Canada* swung into her assigned lane and accelerated on her two operational n-space drives at her maximum attainable speed. The third drive had proven beyond repair and would need complete replacement at the yard.

\* \* \*

EARTH, CAPITAL OF THE ALLIANCE

"Order!" President Dyachenko said, not quite shouting.

Not for the first time did he regret running for office. If only he had known what he was letting himself in for, he wouldn't have come anywhere near the place! That was a lie, he grudgingly admitted to himself. Being President of the Alliance was a great honour and responsibility. Unfortunately, it was also a heavy burden. It did have one redeeming feature—it gave him the power to make what was wrong right again. He still believed that, but in all too many cases it was proving tricky to do.

"Order!" he shouted, slamming the gavel down so hard he felt the handle loosen.

"This is your fault!" Councillor Whitby went on. "One of our survey ships has been trapped by the aliens; it could well have been captured or destroyed by now. Destroyed is one thing, but what if it has been captured? Think of the data on that ship in alien hands! The other ship was so badly damaged it barely made the jump to Northcliff, and it was a warship!" She waved a sheaf of papers in the air theatrically. "I have here a list of the dead and injured. The entire crew was nearly lost and the ship will cost millions to repair. I warned you this might happen, but did you listen, did any of you listen? No, and this is the direct result of your foolishness!"

This was the third day of the Council session called to discuss the significance of *Invincible* jumping into Northcliff badly mauled by the Shan. As far as Dyachenko could see, and despite Admiral Rawlins' testimony aimed at lessening the impact of the dreadful news, the session had produced absolutely nothing in the way of productive results. Paul Rawlins had done his best, but the entire thing had been a colossal waste of time. Worse than that, it had inflamed passions, making the Councillors second guess the original decision to contact the aliens.

"—result of your *incompetence!*" Councillor Whitby raged, slamming the now badly crumpled papers onto the desk in front of her. She continued haranguing the Council but her rhetoric was aimed increasingly at the President himself. "Your stupidity, yes *stupidity,* will doom us all!"

Gasps of shock went around the Council chamber at the insult so openly expressed. Many of the Councillors might agree with her sentiments, but to do so verbally and in public like this was just not done. It lacked finesse, and showed a deplorable lack of control—a fatal failing in politics. A goodly number of Councillors jumped to their feet to shout her down, and tempers frayed. Perhaps realising she had gone too far she sat down, but the arguing continued unabated. A light began blinking on Dyachenko's desk comp, signalling Councillor Mindel's wish to speak. It was one of many, but Dyachenko chose to take a chance.

"Order!" he shouted, rising to his feet. He gave up using the weakened gavel and bellowed for quiet. Eventually he received a lower level of noise, but not the quiet he had demanded. "The chair recognises Councillor Mindel of Northcliff."

"Let us not stoop to name calling. This august body is surely above such things." Nathan Mindel said and calmed things a little by reaching for a carafe of water. He took a small sip, and others took the chance to do the same. When he began again the temper of the Council had cooled considerably and quiet was restored. "I have the President's personal assurance that the Shan do not pose a threat to the Alliance. As Admiral Rawlins explained not long ago, they have no jump technology. However, there is the matter of one of our ships stranded and in need of aid.

"I, and I'm sure all of you, wish to support our forces to the maximum. Indeed, I would be a fool if I did not." Nathan looked directly into the President's eyes for a long moment.

Dyachenko inclined his head acknowledging the debt he had just incurred. He new Mindel would come to collect someday, but someday was not now, and he was grateful to him for calming the situation.

"We of Northcliff know only too well what could happen if Fleet were not there to protect us. We must endorse Admiral Rawlins' proposal to send a task force to extract *Canada* and her valiant crew. It's the only honourable thing to do."

There was a good deal of applause for Mindel's speech, but those applauding were barely in the majority. It would take a count of heads to be certain, but it was already obvious to Dyachenko that the Council was split.

"We have debated the issue for days," Councillor Hartman said. "I believe we know all we need to know. Admiral Rawlins has every right to send the task force as long as doing so does not impinge on the Council's prerogatives. I think we can all agree that the rescue of *Canada* and her crew does not do that. Our place is to make policy, the military's is to defend the Alliance. We should let them do their job, and get on with ours."

"Here, here!" Councillor Demkakova said and patted his table in quiet applause. "The rescue is obviously a concern of Navy Department planners and the Fleet, not ours. I think our time would be better spent on..." Demkakova trailed off as the doors to the Council chamber burst open and slammed against the wall as a white-faced Jerry McCartney hurried in.

The Council erupted in whispering as the members craned their necks trying to see what the President's chief of staff was doing here. Dyachenko's stomach began to churn as Jerry made his way down the red-carpeted aisle toward him. The look on Jerry's face told him it was going to be bad news, but not how bad.

"Admiral Rawlins just informed me, Mister President," Jerry whispered.

He switched off his microphone before answering. "Informed you of what?"

"*Canada* just came in shot to hell, but Shan ships didn't do it. A Merki squadron did."

"What!" Dyachenko yelped. He just couldn't help it, and the shock on his face silenced the Council. It was so quiet he could hear the faint hiss of the air conditioning overhead. "The Merkiaari?" he whispered.

Jerry nodded. "The Shan fleet has been wiped out, and the Merkiaari are in the process of cleansing the twin planets of their system."

"Oh my God," he said feeling sick. "Genocide."

"That's not all. Captain Colgan blew away a substantial part of the Merki squadron before jumping out system."

"Serves the bastards right! I'll give him a medal—a box of medals!"

"As you say, but there's more."

"What else?"

"Paul Rawlins said to tell you that he's put our forces on Red One alert. He expects an incursion to follow the destruction of the Shan homeworld. He said, and I quote: Burgton was right in everything but the time, he was five years out. What does he mean, Alex?"

"Never mind that now. Do we have any idea how long we have?" Dyachenko asked, thinking about Burgton and his recruits. They needed those five years dammit!

"No, but there's more. Captain Colgan informed the Admiral that friendly relations have been initiated with the Shan elders, and that they assigned an ambassador to us before the attack. It seems the task force was not needed."

"Why didn't he send a drone?" Dyachenko hissed under his breath. "If only we had reached them sooner!"

"Colgan sent thirteen drones, but only three reached fold space. He says we'll receive them in the next few days. *Canada* must have overtaken them on the way here; you know how slow they are."

Slow was an understatement. Urgent messages were sent by courier ship not drone, but of course, a ship big enough to carry a jump capable courier wouldn't have been trapped in the system in the first place.

"God, what a mess," Dyachenko said holding his head. "Did Paul give you his recommendations?"

Jerry nodded and glanced at the silent and suspicious Councillors before turning back and whispering. "The Admiral is with the Shan ambassador now. He wants to order the—" Jerry lowered his voice still more. "He says time is critical. He wants your permission to order the 501st to join the task force."

"Against the Merkiaari?"

"Yes. He says the task force is strong enough for the preliminary fight, but Admiral Meyers will need troops to take out the Merki ground forces already deployed. Vipers were designed for this very thing."

"Doesn't he know I need Council approval for that?" Dyachenko hissed in frustration. "It's not a rescue mission any longer, it's a war!"

"He said you would say that. Here's his answer: We are already at war, Mister President, and have been for centuries. We can fight in the Shan system now, or in Sol system a few years from now. That was a direct quote, Alex, and he means it."

"Schedule a Cabinet meeting for tomorrow morning—early—but I want to talk to the Shan ambassador first. Get me up there as soon as possible."

Jerry nodded. "What should I say about the other thing?"

"I'll tell him myself." Dyachenko leaned forward toward his microphone and switched it back on. "Councillors, I have grave news. The Merkiaari have attacked the Shan with heavy loss of life."

The uproar was deafening. Everyone shouted questions at once and he was unable to answer any. "I have been advised to commit the task force readied for the rescue mission in a... *delaying action*, while our forces mobilise to confront the threat."

"Delay? What good is a *delay?*" Councillor Whitby shouted, visibly afraid. "Send the Fleet! We must order the Navy to destroy them all!"

Councillor Mindel clapped his hands slowly and sneered. "Very good. How?"

"I'm not a soldier! Tell them to do it and leave the details to Admiral Rawlins!"

Mindel pounced on the opportunity handed him. "What we need is more vipers, but people like you—just like you actually—forced this Council not to build more of the only weapons we have worth a damn against Merki ground troops! They are coming just as General Burgton said they would, and we might as well be *naked* for all the good our troops will do!"

"How dare you speak to me like that? I'll—"

"You'll what? You'll be too busy hiding in your embassy's basement."

"Please Councillors," Dyachenko said. "We have no time for this. I need a vote on Admiral Rawlins' recommendation to deploy the task force and *sundry* units to combat the Merkiaari. Please Councillors, this may be the most important decision ever to come before us. Green for yes, red for no."

All but one light burned green. The big screen on the wall above Dyachenko's chair told the tale for all to see. Everyone turned to look at Councillor Mindel who had yet to cast his vote. Dyachenko knew Mindel hadn't missed the way he had attached *sundry* units to the task force before calling the vote. In effect, the Council had just given him a free hand. He could order Admiral Rawlins to send every man and ship under his command and still claim that he was following the Council's will. Not that he was going to do that of course, but it did give him a legitimate way to send Burgton's men.

Mindel smiled knowingly and pressed his green button, making Dyachenko's decision to send the vipers to war completely legal.

"The vote is unanimous." Dyachenko said with relief. "This meeting is adjourned until the same time tomorrow. I will report back to the Council with all we are doing to combat this threat. Until tomorrow."

Dyachenko stood and hurried out of chambers with Jerry trotting at his heels. As soon as he reached the exit, his security detachment fell in around him and escorted him to the car.

"Where are Paul and the Shan ambassador?" he asked Jerry as the car pulled away.

"Alliance HQ. It's the only place we can keep the media out of."

"Christ, they'll have a field day! Get me up there fast!"

"It's all arranged, Alex. We board your shuttle in less than five minutes."

"Destination?"

"Gateway, sir. From there we transfer to a navy shuttle—faster than civilian models—which will take us direct to HQ. You'll be with Paul in less than an hour."

"Good," he said and stared out the window at nothing.

## ALLIANCE HQ, LUNA, SOL SYSTEM

"—And you are feeling better now?" Paul Rawlins asked. "You're sure?"

Tarjei flicked her ears in agreement. "Ambrai healer very good," she said, carefully enunciating the words in English. "He said..." she looked to her mate helplessly.

Tei'Varyk's jaw dropped into a smile. "Doctor Ambrai told me your nano technology dealt with the problem. I was very concerned, especially when the crew fell sick, but the little machines learn quickly."

Paul nodded. "So, all is well on that side of things. Maybe we can programme them for Shan physiology, but that's a task for the future."

Tei'Varyk flicked his ears in agreement. "Even those used for surgery would be a boon to my people."

It seemed the Shan had not developed nanotech. Their interests had so far been directed outward, into macro rather than micro issues. Rawlins could hardly blame them for that. With the Merkiaari a constant threat, their first order of business had been building a defence net for their worlds followed by a fleet to protect the wider system. Health issues such as the prolonging of life with nanotech had not occurred to them.

When *Canada's* crew fell ill from an unknown virus, their bots had struggled at first to purge their systems. As one after another fell ill, Captain Colgan had feared for ship's operations. It was touch and go, but the crisis had ended with Doctor Ambrai apparently much the wiser. He had even written a paper on the experience. The first of its kind, it was sure to be hailed as a datum on cross species infection.

"These Keeps you mentioned. Can they be detected from orbit?"

"No," Tei'Varyk said. "We designed them not to be, but who knows what new technology the Merkiaari have developed since the war? Our own ships cannot detect them, we made certain of it, but theirs? I don't know."

"I can verify that, Admiral," Colgan said. "Our scans of the surface turned up no trace of the Keeps. They are dug into the mountains so deep no emissions escape."

"That's good news."

"It is," Tei'Varyk agreed. "but you must realise that my people have been through this before. We hid in the deep forests and in caves. Many were discovered and killed, but enough of us survived to rebuild what was lost. They will not let that happen again. They will stay until none of us are left alive."

"Surely you don't think they would use an orbital bombardment!" Rawlins felt sick at the thought of such lovely worlds destroyed by nuclear strike.

"I do not know what moves them," Tei'Varyk said. "Do they want our worlds for themselves? If they do, they will not destroy them utterly, but if that is so, why did they not attempt to colonise last time? If all they want is us dead, I put nothing beyond them."

Rawlins frowned. It had always been a puzzle. The Merkiaari fought and died for a planet, but instead of colonising their conquered worlds, they merely left garrisons and moved on to the next target.

One of the most popular modern beliefs was that they did indeed intend to colonise captured worlds, but not until they had created a buffer around the captured territory. Preventing that had been a Fleet priority during the Merki War. Once colonised, liberating a captured world would have been close to impossible.

General Burgton knew them best, yet even he was only guessing when he said they lived only to fight. Surely they had other pursuits. What of family? What of art and literature? They must have these things; they certainly had industry and technology. Without advanced technology and education, they could not wage their wars. Burgton believed that Merkiaari society was geared to support its military and not the other way around. He was of the opinion that everything was subordinate to their war effort, and that colonising new worlds was a means of claiming new resources. He might well be right.

If Rawlins was honest with himself, he would rather not think of reasons for their behaviour except where it pertained to battle tactics. He preferred to kill them wherever found and would not try to paint them as other than they were. The Shan had it spot on, as far as he was concerned. The Merkiaari were genocidal maniacs, murderers on a massive scale, and that's all they were.

He was happy with that.

The Alliance Council had officially accepted what most people, including top scientists, believed. That the Merkiaari as a species were inherently xenophobic in nature. Researchers were satisfied that there was nothing to be gained by further study, and had moved on to more interesting projects leaving the military to deal with Merki xenophobic tendencies.

A fleet of dreadnoughts had always worked quite well.

Rawlins leaned forward in his seat and clasped his hands on his desk. "What they want is a question our people have been asking for centuries. I will leave such questions to people who are better suited to answering them. My response to them is overwhelming force. That's all they understand."

Tarjei growled low in her throat making Rawlins' short hairs stand to attention. "Yessss," she said with her muzzle still rumpled. "We should hunt together. We will find their lairs and destroy them all."

Tei'Varyk flicked his ears in agreement.

A knock on the door heralded Joseph's arrival. "The President has just landed, Admiral. He will be here momentarily."

"Thank you Joseph. Best arrange for some refreshments."

"Yes sir," Joseph said and quietly closed the door.

\* \* \*

President Dyachenko strode out of the tube and onto the concourse proper in a flurry of harried secret service agents. They were not happy with the suddenness of his decision to travel to Alliance HQ, but they were dealing with it.

"Let us at least clear the concourse, Mister President," Agent Carstens said, trying to look everywhere at once.

"If I'm not safe here, Andrew, I'm not safe anywhere."

Carstens gave up and ordered his people to hold back the crowd as best they could. A dozen men in dark suites and wearing comm moved out and surrounded the President at a distance. They provided a globe of seeming safety for him as they moved along the concourse trying to keep their spacing.

Alex kept his face neutral, denying the spectators anything to base their rumours on. He had no doubt the rumours would fly from his visit regardless, but that was better than allowing them to see his fear and learning the truth.

"Here, Alex. In here," Jerry said, diverting him toward the elevator.

He stepped inside the waiting car without pause and his security detachment bundled inside. Jerry selected sub-level five and the car descended.

"Mister President?" A quiet voice said, interrupting his reverie.

"Yes," he said, turning to find the source of the voice.

In the corner were two women. Both wore the uniform of ensign, and were quite pretty, he thought. Both were squished against the car held there by two agents.

"Stop that," he said quietly and was instantly obeyed. "Let them out of there."

The disgruntled agents did as they were bid, but they hovered behind the two women ready to intervene should either one pull a nuke out of her pocket.

"Thank you, sir," Ensign on the right said and the one on the left saluted him. The first belatedly realised she should do the same. After all, she was in the presence of the Alliance's supreme commander.

Alex smiled and returned it, though he was very aware that his effort fell far short of their snappy movement. "Your names?"

"Ensign Collier—Sandra, sir."

"Ensign Newman, sir. Everyone calls me Kim."

"Kimberly?"

"That's right, sir."

"Been in the service long?"

"Six years, sir." Kimberly said.

"And you?"

"The same, sir."

Ping! The elevator stopped and the doors slid open.

"How do you like it?" he asked as the detail trooped out of the elevator to guard the corridor.

"It's all right, sir," they chorused.

Dyachenko ignored Jerry's pleading look to hurry. "No more than that?"

They seemed embarrassed, but Kim braced up and explained. "We wanted to work aboard ship, sir. Instead, I'm a glorified secretary. I'm getting out."

"Hmmm. You feel the system has failed you?"

"It has, sir. I'm not the best officer, I know that, but I am good. Why should I spend my entire career filing reports?"

"It's an important job, I should think," he said, shuddering at the thought of a lifetime of paperwork.

"I suppose so, sir. But can't they rotate the position?"

"I don't know. I'll ask Paul about it."

Twin gasps and stammered denials. "Don't do that!"

"Not the Admiral!"

He grinned, and stepped out of the lift. "Not to worry. He owes me a favour or three."

"But—" Sandra began, but the elevator door slid shut.

Dyachenko chortled as he followed Jerry to the Admiral's office. The look of horror on their faces had been something to see. He smiled and wondered if Paul knew his ensigns were afraid of him. Fancy anyone being afraid of Paul Rawlins.

"Hello Joseph, is he in?"

"Yes sir, Mister President. You'll be needing this," Joseph said and handed him a headset.

"I will?"

"Yes sir. I was told to make sure you put it on before entering."

"I had better do that then."

Dyachenko smiled, put on the device, and then nodded to Joseph before going through into Rawlins' office. He stopped abruptly on the threshold as he realised there was not one but two aliens present. This was a great day for him. Just think, he was meeting an alien representative of an alien race, perhaps the first such race to join the Alliance.

Rawlins stood. "Mister President, may I introduce ambassador Tei'Varyk and his mate Tarjei?"

Dyachenko closed the door separating himself from the distractions he had brought with him. He would catch hell for it later, but he didn't want Andrew trying to search the aliens.

"This is a very great honour," Dyachenko said, bowing in the most formal greeting he knew. It seemed the right thing.

Tei'Varyk and Tarjei bowed and then held up their right palms.

"Press your right palm to theirs, Mister President," a man in the uniform of a Fleet Captain said.

"Ah, a handshake?"

"Similar, Mister President."

Dyachenko pressed his palm to Tei'Varyk's and then Tarjei's palm... paw? He noted the claws and the pads. The pads felt rough like the paw of a dog. Did they go on all fours sometimes? It was fascinating.

"I greet you on behalf of the elders," Tei'Varyk said formally.

The translation came through the headset clearer than Dyachenko had imagined it would. "Thank you. Welcome to the Alliance. Let us be seated so we may discuss your news."

Rawlins introduced him to Captain Colgan and they shook hands. "Well done, Captain. I'm sorry for the loss of your crewmen. You and yours have done a very great service for the Alliance."

"Thank you, Mister President. It will mean a lot to them."

Dyachenko took a seat. Colgan had not said it meant a lot to him, only his crew. It was always hard losing people you cared for, but it was worse when they died because they had followed your orders. How well he knew that.

"I received your message, Paul. The Red-One is in effect?"

Rawlins nodded. "Throughout the system, yes sir. The rest of the Alliance will receive the order as the couriers arrive. The effect will ripple out from the centre and gain momentum. A month or so will see every ship and world on Red-One alert. Movement orders will go out no later than today. I must consolidate my assets in key locations."

"I understand, but I trust you will not uncover our worlds."

"I can't guarantee that. I must plan for an incursion within the year, two at the outside. I have already ordered the shipyards to ramp up production of our *Washington* class cruisers as well as our production of cap ship missiles. We're going to need them."

Dyachenko nodded. Such things were within the First Space Lord's authority, though his budget would not cover the cost. It was the Council's job to provide the Navy Department with the necessary funds and it would be high on the agenda for tomorrow's meeting.

"We need to plan for an increase in fuel expenditure and attrition in ground forces," Rawlins went on. "Recruiting has never been a problem for us, but we need to treble it if we can. I'll need your permission to raise the age limit."

"Why my permission? You have the authority, though I should think lowering it would be in your interest not the other way."

Rawlins shook his head. "Twenty is as low as I will ever go, but that has nothing to do with the Merkiaari. I just think the kids of today are too immature below that age. They live their lives in luxury filling their heads with Zelda and the Spaceways and think that's all there is to life. I would like to send them to live on the Border Worlds for a while. Might wake them up."

Dyachenko snorted. "So you want to re-activate the old-timers?"

Old-timers were ex-army and ex-Marine. They were not truly in service any longer, but they played a role as a territorial army or what used to be called a national guard. They trained together for the sense of comradeship and liked to play soldier on weekends. It would take much less time to bring them up to speed than a batch of green recruits.

"Not necessarily. I want to offer them positions in their old branch of the military whether Navy or regular army, but I especially want as many trained people with rifles in their hands as I can get. You know we can't stop them making landings if they're determined. Remember Garnet?"

"How could I forget?"

"I would hate to see that kind of thing happen again."

Garnet was a core world. Its population had nearly been wiped out, but the resistance had taken a great toll on the Merkiaari and had survived long enough for the Alliance to bring enough ships to the system to annihilate the aliens. Garnet was re-taken, but the cost in lives had been astronomical.

"I could increase the available ground forces by almost twenty-five percent if I use the old timers in a guard position. They will free up a good many of my men for redeployment," Rawlins said.

"Do it," he said but then added a qualifier, "Quietly."

"The media will find out, sir, you know that."

"I know, but I need time to arrange matters before they start asking questions I can't answer."

"I'll do my best."

"Now," Dyachenko said. "You want me to sign off on you sending the task force to help?"

"Not just that. I want to send the 501st."

"Hmmm, Jerry mentioned it."

Rawlins leaned forward. "If we can kick their butts out of the system and hold them out long enough to establish a strong defence, Tei'Varyk assures me the elders will join the Alliance."

"That is so," Tei'Varyk said. He had been following the

conversation with interest. "I am the eyes and ears of the elders—you say ambassador. My voice is theirs."

"You have that kind of authority?" Dyachenko asked, surprised but glad to hear it.

"To be the eyes and ears for the elders is a great honour," Tei'Varyk said and his mate flicked her ears in agreement. "The elders will never leave our system. I am their representative to the Alliance. The elders are bound—as I am bound—by my word."

"Have you discussed joining the Alliance with them?"

"I had many meetings with them. We discussed the future and the past. It was decided to join your Alliance if certain things came to pass."

"What things?" he asked, still feeling a little sceptical—an ambassador with power to bind his entire race?

"We were not sure of Humans. It was decided we would be friends, but no more than that. We would not join you until we saw for ourselves that what we were told by James was true."

"James?"

"Professor Wilder, Mister President," Colgan said. "He more or less led the contact team after the first few months."

"I see. James told you of us then, he told you of the Alliance?"

"We spoke for many cycles—days," Tarjei said.

"He is a good friend," Tei'Varyk agreed. "He spoke of the Merkiaari attacking Humans, of uncountable millions of Humans inhabiting over two hundred worlds, of vast fleets of ships, of... of many things. We did not believe all, but I have come to see the truth. If I could, I would tell the elders what I know, but that is not possible. If they still live, they would order me to join the Alliance and free our worlds. I know this as I know my clan name."

"Tei'Varyk speaks truth," Tarjei said. "He is elder for all our people here."

Tei'Varyk's ears flattened. "My mate does not speak my words."

Dyachenko cocked his head. What was happening now? Tei'Varyk seemed upset by his mate's support. Colgan had a look of speculation on his face as if he had an idea and was waiting to see it borne out. Dyachenko listened to his translator and concentrated on making sense of what he heard.

"I speak the words of those here with us. We all agree, Tei," Tarjei said.

"But I do not want this!" Tei'Varyk protested. "I want a ship, a crew, and a mate who loves me as I love her. Nothing else."

"You will have all these things again. You have me already, but now you must be elder. For the good of our people, you must be elder.

Who else sees the future so clearly—Kajika?"

Tei'Varyk dropped his jaw in a laugh. "I do not think so!"

Tarjei flipped her ears in amusement.

Tei'Varyk turned back to his audience. "The twin worlds of harmony will join the Alliance."

Dyachenko nodded. "And we will take care of the Merkiaari," he said and turned to Rawlins. "Send in the vipers."

* * *

# 19 ~ Red One Alert

"Rawlins did this on purpose," Alice Meyers, one-time Admiral of Fifth Fleet's third squadron, said as she surveyed her new command.

"I doubt the First Space Lord shook you loose of Fifth Fleet on a whim ma'am," Lieutenant Pike, her flag Lieutenant, said with a straight face.

She snorted, but Joshua was right. Paul Rawlins might be many things, but one thing he wasn't was an alarmist. Her orders to go in ready for bear meant he believed shooting was in the offing. She looked forward to it, but how much action was she likely to see when he deemed a scratch-built task force like *TF19* was suitable for the mission?

"I ought to be getting the squadron ready for the war games, not dicking about with this pitiful excuse for a task force. Why am I in the back and beyond? There are other admirals he could have sent."

Joshua wisely remained silent.

"Sorry," Meyers said. She really shouldn't put him in a position where he either agreed with her thereby showing disloyalty to the First Space Lord, or disagreeing with her and pissing off his CO.

"No problem, ma'am," Joshua said. "If you've seen enough, I'll make ready to dock—" he broke off as he received a transmission over his headset.

"Problems?" she asked, already expecting some kind of trouble.

"*Victorious* just went to Red One, ma'am!"

*Red One!* "What reason did they give?"

"None, ma'am. I was receiving docking instructions when I heard the announcement, but nothing since then."

"Take us in, Joshua, quick as you can."

"Aye, ma'am. *Victorious* this is Bravo-two-four requesting immediate docking."

"Cleared to dock Bravo-two-four; bay four."

"Roger, bay four."

Joshua handled the shuttle with the finesse she had come to expect of him, but she could still admire his skill. He pushed the throttle through the stops and the shuttle surged ahead pressing her into her acceleration couch. She grunted, but said nothing as he manoeuvred between *ASN Neptune* and *ASN Vigilant*. Both destroyers were at station keeping, making the manoeuvre look easy, though of course it wasn't. Joshua's course—laid down by eye she noted—threaded the needle as if he did this every day.

Destroyers were not large by Fleet standards, but a shuttle was still tiny in comparison. Meyers watched the armoured hull of *ASN Vigilant* passing a few metres to starboard and leaned forward against the accel trying to see the top of the huge letter G of her name as it receded rearward. A stupendous letter I took its place quickly followed by the V.

Destroyers were small ships, but still vast in comparison to a tiny Admiral gaping out the window like a tourist. She shivered in delight as the shuttle shot by *Vigilant's* forward batteries. She noted the maintenance work ongoing inside one of her two forward firing missile tubes.

"Hmmm, remind me to get an update on ship's readiness when we've settled in, Joshua. Looks like *Vigilant* might have rail problems," she said, noting a new section of launch rail being manoeuvred into place through the open outer door of her number two launch tube.

"Aye, aye ma'am," Joshua said, keeping his eyes glued to his instruments.

*ASN Victorious* loomed up ahead of them broadside on to their approach, which gave Meyers a wonderful view of her white painted and armoured hide. Any heavy cruiser was an awesome weapon, but the *Washington* class cruiser was the pinnacle of current cruiser development. Armoured to take punishment from any ship up to and including a Merki dreadnought, she had enough firepower to take out ships double her mass while retaining the speed and manoeuvrability of cruisers half her size.

Dreadnoughts of course, were superior to battle cruisers at soaking up enemy fire while dishing out horrendous storms of missiles, but for all of that they were still too slow for anything but system defence, which is what they were used for in the main. Defending was fine by her, but she liked to hit hard and first if possible. A heavy cruiser squadron was perfect for the job, more than one and she was in heaven. A fleet would come to her in time, but for now, she had other concerns to think about.

Although she had left ten heavy cruisers behind at her last posting in Forestal, it was impossible to be blasé about having this one under her command. A *Washington* class heavy cruiser like *Victorious* in her task force made up for a hell of a lot. Rawlins had probably given her the ship as a kind of apology for boosting her out of Fifth Fleet. Whatever it had taken to get *Victorious* here, she *was* here and Meyers thanked God and Paul Rawlins for it.

She gazed at the ship, ignoring the mountainous carrier in the background that made even a heavy cruiser look puny by comparison. She had a great deal of respect for battle group carriers and those who crewed them, but she still found their weak armour and lack of offensive punch a turn-off. Carriers could be effective if used correctly, but they needed to be constantly protected by sufficient force to see off an aggressor. That kind of thing was a serious handicap to an admiral with very few ships to begin with and a penchant for offensive tactics.

"What a beauty," Joshua said, meaning *Victorious*. "Shame we haven't got a few more, ma'am."

"Give us time, give us time. Her class is still new. I don't think we've reached double figures as yet, but we will."

"I heard they have a new battleship in the works," Joshua said.

"I doubt that. There's really no need for another class. We have everything pretty much covered. Destroyers and frigates for hard-hitting quick actions, light cruisers to screen the heavier units and safeguard the carriers, heavy cruisers for striking at the enemy, and dreadnoughts for when the enemy won't take no for an answer. Battleships can't provide anything we don't already have."

"It was a pretty solid rumour, ma'am."

"From where, from whom?" she asked with a frown developing between her eyes. Building battleships was fine with her, but what need? Surely the money was better spent on improving current designs.

"I'd rather not say, ma'am," Joshua said uncomfortably.

Meyers considered her flag lieutenant, debating whether to order him to speak, when they finally arrived and began docking procedures.

"Saved by the bell," she whispered and Joshua flushed as he worked to bring the shuttle into the docking cradle smoothly.

Gravity resumed as they crossed the threshold and Joshua, ever the perfectionist, lowered the shuttle with nary a bump.

As the bay pressurised, Meyers stood and straightened her tunic. Taking command of a new squadron, or task force in this case, was something of an event. Already she could see her captains entering the bay accompanied by one or two officers from their ships.

"I hope they left someone in charge when they decided to bring all that lot to meet me," she muttered under her breath.

"I'm sure they left someone aboard to turn the lights out, ma'am."

She smiled and made her way out of the cockpit and into the main cabin. Joshua preceded her and keyed the hatch open so that she might descend without waiting.

"How do I look?" she asked.

"Like a very important admiral, Admiral."

"That's good," she whispered and stepped through the hatch.

As soon as she appeared at the top of the ramp, the side party snapped to attention and saluted. She returned the salute and began to descend even as the computer-generated boson's pipes sounded her arrival.

"Honour guard, attennnnnn-*hut!*" the Marine gunnery sergeant barked, as she set foot on the deck of *Victorious'* bay. The Marine detachment snapped to attention slapping their rifles in perfect synch. The pipes faded and the ship's computer announced her arrival.

"Admiral Meyers arriving," the feminine contralto said.

Meyers turned to face a Commander she didn't know and returned his salute with one of her own. "Permission to come aboard?"

"Permission granted, Admiral," he said and introduced himself. "I'm Commander Hanson, *Victorious'* XO. If you will permit me?"

Meyers nodded. "Certainly, Commander," she said, going through the motions that courtesy dictated at such times, but all the while wondering where her flag captain might be.

Commander Hanson walked on her left and introduced her to the officers standing at attention waiting to meet her. She had been correct in her assessment; they were her Captains. As she moved along the line, she itched to know where Thomas Fernandez—*Victorious'* Captain—was keeping himself. What was he doing that was more important than greeting his Admiral?

Meyers moved along the line memorising faces and names, all the while wishing she knew what was happening. The courtesies were soon over and she could be herself. The Marine detachment was dismissed leaving her to speak with the Captains of *TF19*.

"Commander Hanson, where is my flag captain and why isn't he here?"

"He's decoding the Red-One message, ma'am. He asked me to apologise for his absence, but he felt it necessary to read the news as soon as possible."

"I see."

Meyers didn't like what it said of her other Captains. They were here and not on their ships during a Red-One alert. Red-One was as close to war as the Alliance ever came short of the first missiles being fired. These men and women should be aboard their own ships. Their execs could have paid their respects in their places.

"I expect you all to attend a briefing in one hour," she said then looked to Hanson to show her to her quarters.

"This way, ma'am," Hanson said, and led her to the elevator.

"Inform Captain Fernandez of the meeting, Commander, and I would appreciate a copy of that Red-One."

"Certainly ma'am, there should be one on your comp."

"Good," she said, thawing a little at Hanson's obvious competence.

Once in her quarters, she made directly for her office and its comp to bring herself up to date. Keying in her I.D and pass phrase, she read the Red-One alert message, and nothing was ever the same again.

"My God!"

"Ma'am?" Joshua asked from across the cabin.

"Merkiaari have attacked and wiped out the Shan fleet. Our survey ship, *Canada,* came in badly shot-up with the news."

"Our mission is scrubbed then, Admiral?"

"Looks like it—" she began, but lost her train of thought when a password request popped up on her screen.

Meyers frowned in consternation. Why require a second phrase when the message was already decoded by application of the first? Obviously there was more to the message that met the eye, and more to the point it was directed specifically at her and not Captain Fernandez. Only officers of flag rank had the clearance to decode this message further.

"Leave the room for a moment, Joshua. I'll call."

"Yes, ma'am," Joshua said, his puzzlement obvious.

Meyers turned back to her comp after she heard the hatch close, and input her second pass phrase. The screen cleared and another more extensive message was revealed.

"Oh, boy," she hissed as she read the communiqué.

The bulk of the message detailed a revised mission for *TF19* including threat assessment and detailed notes on the system as well as planetary targets the Merkiaari would be interested in. The destination was the same as her original mission, but the objective...

*Admiral Meyers. You will, upon the receipt of this message, assemble TF19 and jump out system immediately. Your destination is NGC 1513-4964. Upon arrival, you will rendezvous with your ground force and immediately jump out system to fulfil your mission within the target system.*

*The Shan have been declared an allied power and will be protected to the utmost of the Alliance's ability. Seek and destroy all Merkiaari in the system preparatory for arrival Fifth Fleet. Fifth Fleet will be augmented heavily with divisions comprising: Alliance Army, Alizon Rangers, Alliance Marines, Bethany Airborne Rangers, Faragut Airborne Strike Force...*

Meyers whistled at the list of units being sent in the second wave. Was that because they thought she would fail, or was it precautionary? She was determined not to fail, but maybe HQ knew something she didn't.

She keyed her comm. "Computer: page Captain Fernandez," she said and smiled as he appeared on screen. "I assume you're having trouble decoding the Red-One, Captain."

"How did you—yes ma'am, I am. The stupid thing keeps requesting a second phrase."

"I'm aware of that, Thomas. The second portion of the message was addressed to me, but you need to see it. Meet me in the briefing room in..." she checked the time. "In thirty minutes. The others will be there."

"Yes, ma'am, I'll be there."

"Good, until then," she said and cut the circuit.

At the appointed time, Meyers entered the briefing room followed by a harried Joshua carrying a case full of compads that he had hurriedly updated with their revised mission. Thomas stood as she entered as did her other captains.

"As you were," she said, and they all took their seats. "Pass those around, Joshua."

"Yes, ma'am."

Meyers found her place at the head of the table while Joshua handed the compads to her captains. Captain Monroe of *Invincible* was on her left, third from the end. Meyers watched the Captain's face as she received her compad from Joshua. There was shock at first, and then puzzlement. Monroe looked around at her fellow officers then turned to her admiral.

"You cannot be serious!"

Meyers smiled. "The First Space Lord is very serious, Captain, and so is the President. The Shan are our allies now. The Council ratified a treaty with them and signed a mutual defence agreement just a few weeks ago. If we are successful, they will become full members of the Alliance."

"I understand that ma'am," Monroe said. "I applaud the decision, but eight ships against the Merkiaari?"

"That is one of the problems this meeting will address." Joshua had finished handing out the compads. He was waiting at the holotank controls for her. "If you would, Joshua?"

"Yes ma'am," Joshua said, lowering the lights and activating the tank. "The plan was to extract *Canada* from the system without firing a shot. As you can see that is no longer the mission. This data was obtained by *Canada* while in the system and fighting for her life against a squadron of Merki ships."

Everyone leaned forward to study the new data. They keyed personal compads to life and began making notes, but all eyes were on the battle raging in the tank. The Shan cruisers were dishing out horrendous storms of missiles, but few of them were reaching their targets. As many as eighty percent were decoyed off target or destroyed by point defence.

Meyers watched one brave ship battered and barely making way trim her course and ram a stupendous Merki dreadnought. Both ships blew up in spectacular fashion, but more ships were coming. The holotank blanked for a moment as another log was uploaded. This time there was a gasp from all those watching.

"Hold the playback, Joshua."

"Yes, ma'am."

"This data gentlemen, was taken from the log of a heavy cruiser. The Shan call them heavy fangs by the way." Meyers aimed her wand at the figure at the centre of attention. "This is Tei'Varyk, Captain of *Naktlon*. I am told the word Tei means leader or commander. This portion of *Naktlon's* log begins just as Tei'Varyk makes his run against the Merki ships. They outgun him four to one. *Canada* and *Naktlon* are the only friendlies remaining in the system."

"Excuse me ma'am, but where is *Canada*?" Thomas Fernandez asked.

"Captain Colgan has withdrawn his ship at this point. *Canada* has taken critical damage to her aft shields and engineering. I might add that *Canada* is a survey vessel ill equipped to fight a concerted Merkiaari attack. Colgan believed otherwise and fought his ship with distinction. He destroyed two ships outright—destroyer class I believe. Am I right, Joshua?"

"Yes ma'am. Two positively identified as kills. One or two more that were heavily damaged and later destroyed by our allies. She also finished off a heavy at the close of the action, ma'am."

Meyers nodded. "Captain Colgan had planned to rescue the contact team and jump out system, hoping to bring the Fleet back to help. That was the plan, but fate dictated otherwise—observe."

Joshua activated the holotank and everyone sat still to watch. The audio was frighteningly real and made Meyers jump as warning sirens blared from the speakers. Crew yapped and barked orders, sounding like a pack of hunting dogs on a scent, but over it all came a translation in quietly spoken English.

"I hear," Tei'Varyk said. "*Open fire!*"

Meyers smiled grimly at the hisses of shock coming from her captains as *Naktlon* erupted in fury. Torpedo launchers went to rapid continuous fire attempting to saturate the defences of Tei'Varyk's chosen target. As the range closed, his beamers and particle cannons spoke.

The Merki heavy cruiser blew apart, but even as it did, missiles infinitely more powerful than any Shan torpedo hammered *Naktlon* closer to destruction. Closer and closer, but finally the fire ended and he was still there. Though battered and bleeding atmosphere, he continued to pour fire into the remaining enemy ships.

"Magazines destroyed or depleted!"

"I hear. Continue with all remaining weapons. Kill them all!" Tei'Varyk snarled as his ship slowly died around him.

The holo image became shaky and hard to make out as *Naktlon* bucked and reared at the centre of nuclear fury. Fires had broken out in some of the bridge consols, but no one took any notice except to close helmet visors to keep the smoke out. Meyers kept one eye on the scrolling damage report on her compad. She was trying to keep it coordinated with the holo tank. *Naktlon* was blinded to starboard, and nearly so on her portside, but her great engines continued to propel her into the heart of the storm to kill her enemies even as she was hammered into uselessness.

"Take out those honourless light fangs!" Tei'Varyk snarled as they pecked away at *Naktlon's* armoured hide.

*Naktlon's* particle cannons swivelled and targeted first one, then a second light unit. Both blew apart as energy beams designed to strip the hide from a Merki dreadnought ripped through them.

Meyers made a note to find out more about Shan particle

cannons. They seemed similar to an Alliance PPG, but the output was much higher. She wanted some of them for the Alliance. BuShips was working hard to increase the numbers of heavy cruisers, notably the new *Washington* class. She was sure BuWeps would jump at the chance of adding such powerful particle cannons to their arsenal.

"Target the next—" Tei'Varyk began, but that was as far as he got.

*Naktlon,* broken and barely making way with a single drive, was hit amidships. The beam sliced through deck after deck killing Tei'Varyk's crew and severing control runs. His particle cannons locked and fell silent as power cables were turned to slag. His remaining torpedo launchers, had they ammunition would have been useless as power runs to the launch rails were cut. By far the worst damage was to *Naktlon's* fusion room. The beam reached the core of its reactor and *Naktlon* erupted with super hot plasma eating everything in sight. Blast doors slammed and alarms screamed, but it was all for nothing.

*Naktlon* broke in two.

Groans of anguish filled the room as the holotank froze on the image of Tei'Varyk being thrown out of his command station. Meyers had the benefit of knowing what would happen next, but this viewing was the first time for her Captains.

"At this point things become disjointed," Meyers said into the silence. "*Naktlon* was destroyed as you see, but the two Merki heavy cruisers have taken critical damage. Captain Colgan decides to change course and intercept them. He destroys them both while sustaining heavy damage to *Canada*. He loses thirty-eight crewmen plus the dead from the earlier action. All told, he has lost over half of his crew. Continue playback please, Joshua."

"Yes ma'am."

Tei'Varyk flew through the air and would have crashed to the deck had not the internal gravity field failed. It failed because *Naktlon's* aft section including fusion reactors and power generation had just been destroyed. *Naktlon's* forward section, bleeding atmosphere and crumpled almost beyond recognition, was ejected from nuclear fire like a cork from a bottle.

Tei'Varyk hit his helmsman in the back and was grappled to safety, but others were less lucky. A scream of anguish was cut short as another crewmember, a female this time, smashed into the view-screen with crushing force.

"Tarjei!" Tei'Varyk yelled in fear and pushed off to reach the limp figure floating a few metres away. Blood floated on the air and the figure seemed lifeless.

"Tarjei is Tei'Varyk's mate," Meyers said as the holotank blanked. "The next log is approximately an hour or so later. *Canada* has engaged and defeated the remaining heavy cruisers and is closing on the wreck of *Naktlon* looking for survivors."

"Contact!" A voice announced, but there was no answer from Tei'Varyk. He was strapped into his station holding his dying mate in his arms. "Contact Tei!"

"What contact?"

"I have a contact bearing two-zero-five degrees. I cannot be certain Tei, but I think Tei'Colgan has come for us."

Tei'Varyk sat in silence, staring at his one operational monitor. On the screen he watched Merki troopers running through city streets and killing everyone they found. Fires were leaping up and people were falling in heaps or fighting back with nothing but their claws.

"Have the elders responded?"

"No Tei, they cannot hear us."

Tei'Varyk held Tarjei and rocked her gently.

Kajika reached across his board to operate an empty station's controls. A moment later, a fuzzy and rolling picture appeared on the damaged view-screen. The blood running down the screen did not obscure the image too badly. A worried Human face peered at Tei'Varyk from a smoky bridge.

"Tei!" Colgan said in relief. "Hold on, I'm coming to get you out!"

Tei'Varyk blinked and seemed to come back to himself at hearing a Human voice. "Tei'Colgan. You should have left when you had the chance," he said in a dead voice.

"It's okay, we killed the last of the ships for you."

"And what of the ones landing troops on Harmony?"

"What?!" Colgan looked aside at his own screens.

"Do not *Canada's* sensors reach so far? *Naktlon's* are all but destroyed, but we are still receiving transmissions of the landings."

The holotank blanked and the lights came up. "That completes the relevant portions of the logs given us by Captain Colgan and Tei'Varyk," Joshua said.

"Thank you, Joshua," Meyers said. "We do have some more data, but none fit for direct viewing. Your compads have been uploaded with what we know about the target system, but I will go over it with you now.

"Firstly, the Merki squadron was completely destroyed, but those ships merely constituted half the screening units for the Merkiaari landings, which I'm afraid went ahead unopposed. We will be facing troop transports and light screening units. All of the heavies and the few dreadnoughts they sent along were destroyed by Shan fortresses and ships, but I don't trust the thought that this mission will be easy."

"They may have been reinforced, Admiral," Commander Svenson of *Neptune* warned. "May I make a proposal?"

"Go ahead, Commander," Meyers said leaning back in her chair and smiling encouragement. She had already planned the mission, but encouraging juniors to participate in these sessions was part of the job title—besides, she wasn't infallible. Valentin might have a good idea.

"Thank you, Admiral. *Vigilant* and my own *Neptune* are our fastest units. I propose the task force jumps short and we two go in to recon the system."

Meyers smiled. It was a simple but sensible precaution. She had already planned to do it that way, but the task force would not jump short. Instead, she had planned to hang back at the system periphery while her destroyers reconnoitred the system. That way she could receive scan data directly rather than waiting for her scouts to jump back to her.

"*Vigilant* and *Neptune* will advance into the system ahead of the task force," Meyers agreed. "*Sutherland* will use her wings in a wide deployment on the off chance that the Merkiaari are lurking so far out. As soon as I a have definite scan data, we will move in and take out their screening elements. With luck we will catch them napping, but lucky or not we will take them out and give our ground forces a chance at the Merki on the surface."

"About that, Admiral," Thomas said. "Am I right in assuming we will be met by more ships on route?"

"That's correct. Our rendezvous is an uninhabited system known simply by its catalogue number: NGC 1513-4964."

"Do we know who we are picking up, ma'am?"

"Not specifically," Meyers admitted and she was uncomfortable with that lack. "Admiral Rawlins simply stated that our ground force would be waiting. I'm sure it will be sufficient. Once we have the system secured, Fifth Fleet will jump in to hold it against further attacks while helping the Shan rebuild their defences."

"That's a long term project, Admiral. Very long term."

"Agreed, but the Merkiaari have been a long term problem for us and the Shan both. They won't just disappear because we want them to."

"Shame," Thomas said.

"That it is," Meyers agreed. "Now then; regarding ship readiness. On my way to *Victorious*, I noticed some maintenance ongoing in *Vigilant's* number two missile tube…

* * *

# 20 ~ Mobilisation

*Beep!*

Pamela dropped her feet from her control board and put aside the romance novel she had been reading. She was just getting to the good part too. Oh well, no rest for the wicked.

She punched up the live feed from her sensors. "I have a contact, sir."

"Location?" Giles said, looking up from his own book. He had always been partial to a good fantasy adventure.

"Red sector…" she said frowning and refined her data. "Red six. It's a drone. Should I make contact?"

"Go ahead, Pam. Shunt the message straight to my consol; it's probably routine."

Pamela nodded and did that. "I've notified SysSec to pick up the drone, sir."

"Good. I—"

Pam turned and found Giles punching keys rapidly. He looked shaken; he looked afraid.

### GENERAL BURGTON'S OFFICE, PETRUSO BASE, SNAKEHOLME

General George Burgton shuffled the compads that were beginning to pile up before him on the table into order, before finishing his coffee. He could have accessed data far more comprehensive than this, via his processor and an up-link to the regiment's database, but he wasn't interested in the recruits' assimilation of their biomech and cybernetics at the moment. Neither was he interested in their scores on the range, or any of the other hundred and one bits of statistical information he could access. He wanted a more personal take on things, and that could only be supplied by people, not computers. Hence this meeting, and the pile of compads containing notes and personal observations of the recruits, written by their instructors.

Burgton glanced at Stone where he sat at his ease between Hymas and Flowers. The three musketeers... he smiled as he remembered how they came by that appellation. They had been inseparable in the early days of the regiment's inception, and had saved each other's lives many times since. Three closer friends would be very hard to find.

He leaned forward and raised the jug. "More coffee, Ken? Anyone?"

Stone shook his head. "I'm sloshing already. Thank you, sir."

Flowers and Hymas also shook their heads, they hadn't finished theirs. Burgton poured himself a fresh cup, crossed his legs, and sat back to savour it.

"You know, I think this might actually be good for them," Colonel Flowers said, going through the latest data on one of the recruits. "Look here."

Burgton took the offered compad and raised an eyebrow. "Hmmm. I see what you mean. Fuentez' scores have risen almost two points across the board. Is it the competition do you think?"

"Could be, but I think it has more to do with teaching the others. Teaching students always makes you think about things."

"Her scores have always been high, but now..." he shook his head. "Give her another year and she'll be top of her platoon."

"Richmond will always be top, sir," Stone said.

Burgton raised an eyebrow. "Why do you say that, Ken?"

"Richmond is a killer, Fuentez is not. She isn't ruthless enough."

"And you think being ruthless is important enough to make the difference, Ken?"

"I do, sir. Fuentez is good, there's no question about that. Maybe good enough to best me even, but of Richmond I have no doubt."

"High praise," Flowers murmured.

"Just stating the facts, Colonel," Stone said just a little stiffly. "I have no favourites."

"No one is suggesting that, Ken." Burgton tapped a finger against the edge of the compad he was holding. "It's a little early to be talking graduation here, but I would like to get a feel for how the regiment is shaping up. Marion?"

"Sir?"

"You've said very little."

"Sorry, sir," Lieutenant Hymas said. "I was reviewing her record. I agree with Ken. Richmond is a killer, but she always was. Her enhancement has done wonders for her temperament. She used to be a disruptive influence on all those around her, but now she channels her energy toward the benefit of her squadmates."

"Example?"

"The Steiner simulation comes immediately to my mind. Richmond allowed herself to be seen and killed so the others could penetrate the base."

"Hmmm." Burgton frowned not sure he liked that. "Self sacrifice is a noble thing, but is it desirable in an officer? Dare we promote someone like Richmond to a high post when she's prone to heroics?"

Flowers raised an eyebrow. "Are we talking about promoting her then?"

Burgton rocked a hand in a maybe yes, maybe no gesture. The sun winked from the contacts of his weapon's bus at each movement. "Not at this time, but eventually... yes."

Hymas pursed her lips. "There are people, a lot of people, who see you as a hero, sir. Would you say that makes you a good choice or a poor choice to lead the regiment?"

"Are you trying to shrink my head again, Marion?"

Hymas smiled. "It's a valid point, and you know it. A hero is just someone who does the job when everyone else gives up. That, in my opinion, makes for an excellent officer."

Burgton reread the data displayed on the compad he was holding, and frowned. "I suppose... in the right situation, someone as you describe would be an asset beyond price, but should it happen that a glory hound came to lead my men, I would call that an unmitigated disaster."

"Richmond falls into the first, not the second category, sir," Hymas said.

"I agree," Stone said with a nod.

Flowers smiled. "Concur."

"Well then." He made a note on his compad. "Next we have Martin Cragg. Formerly a lieutenant in the Alizon Rangers."

"Undistinguished career to date, but I like his look," Flowers said. "He's quiet, but he's good with his weapons."

Stone nodded. "He's not the best at tactics, the results of the simulations prove that, but he does have a way of making it through. He was a ranger and it shows."

Burgton nodded and made another note on his compad. "You mean he would be best in a lead position... a scout position?"

"Yes, sir. He was born for recon."

"Fine then. Have you anything to add, Marion?"

"Not regarding his fitness to command, but on a general note, yes. Cragg is one of the most even tempered of all the recruits. His adjustment to enhancement has been smooth as well as quick. I would venture to say he is one of those least affected by the enhancement process. His latest psych profile is almost identical to the one taken at HQ. He hasn't changed at all."

"Unusual?" Burgton asked.

"Not especially. Perhaps ten percent of all enhancements leave the recipients unchanged... at least mentally."

Burgton raised an eyebrow. "I've never noticed. I remember feeling cut off from everything I ever knew, everyone I ever..." he cleared his throat. "So, he's stable and would make a good unit for a recon platoon. Anything else?"

Flowers nodded. "He's a good influence on the others. Like the time he stopped a fight between Callendri and Fuentez."

"It didn't help in the long run."

"To be fair, sir," Stone put in. "Cragg was rear guard when that went down. I don't say he would have stopped it, but we'll never know now."

Burgton nodded. Callendri was a great loss to the regiment. He had liked the boy, and still felt guilty for his part in what had happened. His death had hit them all hard. He shook off his sudden dark mood. Regrets were a luxury he could ill afford.

"I doubt it could have been stopped, Ken," he said. "I did review Eric's download of the incident that day. Callendri went over the edge too quick."

"It's rarely any other way, sir."

He nodded. "Callendri is the past; it's the future we need to concern ourselves with. Nothing can replace what we lost in the war, but at least we'll have the regiment strong again—a regiment to be proud of."

"The uniform has always been enough for me," Stone said coldly. "There *is* nothing else."

Flowers and Hymas exchanged a glance over Stone's head. They all felt strongly where the regiment was concerned. It was home. Apart from the Alliance, it was the only thing that endured in a viper unit's life. His very long, long, *long* life.

"Next we have—"

The office door opened and a worried looking Captain Hames entered. "Another drone just came in. It's bad."

"Bad?" Burgton asked reaching for the compad. "Red One? What the hell for..." he broke off as he digested the message's import.

"It's the Merkiaari," Hames said looking around at the others. "The bastards have taken out the Shan fleet."

Stone cursed viciously.

Burgton read the message and offered the compad to Flowers.

Flowers took it and read the message. "Nothing but the Red One, and orders to rendezvous with *TF19*. Where's the threat assessment, the mission parameters... what the *hell* is Rawlins playing at?"

"That will do, Dan," Burgton chided. "A Merki attack is enough for now. Don't forget the drone left Sol weeks ago."

"Who knows what's gone down in that time?" Stone said.

"Exactly." Burgton took the compad back for one last look. He grimaced when nothing further appeared to him. He dropped it casually on the table with a clatter, and stroked his chin with one finger. He could do with a shave. "I'm sure Paul will send us more information as soon as Naval Intelligence makes it available to him, but we have enough to act. Richard, I want us on Red One immediately. Recall all personnel on leave, and order our ships to increase their patrol radius—send them right out to the edge of the Zone. Order round the clock tracking at Uriel. All clear?"

"Yes, sir." Hames saluted, and left to give his orders.

Burgton rose to his feet. "We have preparations to make for the rendezvous with *TF19*. I'm going to call everyone in. I want contingency plans written, and put into place."

"The training?" Stone asked.

"Will continue unabated until the last minute before departure. Can we push Charlie and Delta any harder?"

"No, sir," Stone said emphatically, and Flowers nodded. "I have my best people from Alpha and Bravo already on the problem. At least all the recruits have been activated."

Burgton nodded. "I'm thankful for that."

The meeting adjourned with his officers hurrying out of the office intent upon issuing orders of their own. Burgton accessed his processor, and with a series of lightning fast commands, he up-linked to Infonet (Information Network) to contact his department heads. His Infonet avatar was a simple recreation of reality as was his virtual office. Unlike some, he preferred not to bother with the almost limitless manipulations one could use to improve an avatar or office. He'd had enough real life improvements used upon his mind and body, without inflicting more upon himself.

One by one, his department heads joined him in the virtual environment. The first to respond to his summons was Alfred Kusac. Kusac was head of power generation and supply. He always used the PowerGen logo as his avatar. Burgton would have preferred Kusac to use a Humanoid avatar instead—he didn't like talking to what amounted to an animated depiction of a generator on overload.

Head of transportation Julia Knight, and head of education Louise Spencer, arrived together. They had chosen idealised versions of themselves for avatars. Both were recognisable in their facial features, but they appeared almost superhumanly beautiful in this place. They were elf-like in traditional fantasy garb, complete with sheathed daggers at their waists, and arrow-filled quivers on their backs. They carried bows. They obviously still took their role-playing seriously. Such gaming was popular on many worlds of the Alliance, with Zelda and the Spaceways topping the current hit list.

Roger Massey of the Ranger and Forestry Commission was next to arrive, followed shortly by his brother Derrick who was currently head of agriculture. Roger's avatar was dull in comparison to the elves. Both women grinned at his comical double-take when he first noticed them standing there. Roger's avatar was Human normal, and wearing a ranger's uniform. The rangers doubled as a police force on Snakeholme, but it had been years since Roger had worn his uniform on active duty. His avatar recalled those days perfectly. Derrick's avatar was wearing a stiff-collared business suit—a plain mirror of his real self in an office thousands of klicks away. Burgton approved. Derrick snapped to attention when he greeted Burgton. He was still new in his position.

"Has anyone heard from Liz?" Burgton asked.

Liz Brenchley was head of industry. As such, she was responsible for the maintenance and upkeep of Snakeholme's small industrial complex, which included their single weapon's factory, and its attendant smelters in orbit. It was an important position, and he wanted her in on this meeting. There were a number of projects that she was overseeing for him. It was unlike her to be late.

Derrick stepped forward. "I spoke to her this morning as a matter of fact. She's inspecting that new facility you two are working on. Remember, sir, we haven't the advantage of implants," he said apologetically, and tapped the headset he was wearing with a finger. The unit attached to his temple gave him access to Infonet in his home or office, but unlike a viper's internal systems, it did not provide unlimited access anywhere on the planet. "She'll be along when she gets the word from her people."

Burgton hadn't realised the inspection was today. It explained her tardiness. "Not a problem. I'll upload the meeting to her office comp when we're done. I asked you all to come on such short notice for a reason. A serious situation is brewing that needs attention. The mission will require an extended absence for myself and my officers."

Not surprisingly that caused a bit of a stir. He had only been back a year from his visit to Sol, and the round trip had taken months.

"Can you tell us what's going on?" Roger asked.

He nodded. "Some of it. I received news via drone a short while ago that the Alliance is on Red One alert."

There was shock, but no panic, and Burgton was proud of them. Over the years he had built a good team to run Snakeholme for him. Each department head was autonomous and reported only to him. The system was a good one, based upon tried and tested military doctrine. Politicians and political parties had no purpose on Snakeholme—there was no government. There was only him, the regiment, and then everyone else in that order. Snakeholme had, and had always had, but one purpose—keeping the regiment in fighting trim so that it could safeguard the Alliance. He had never made a secret of the fact, not even all those years ago when he first offered the families of his men a place here away from the Merki advance. Everyone knew and accepted that his loyalty was to the Alliance and the regiment first, Snakeholme second.

"It has to do with the mission I mentioned," he said. "I can't go into specifics, but suffice it to say that it's a tough one. I'll be taking my best people with me including all units of First Battalion. Colonel Stanbridge will be in command of the base, and the recruits left behind to finish their training. I'm leaving him a strong cadre of veterans."

"What are your orders, General?" Roger said and the others mumbled similar things.

Burgton smiled. "Thank you all. Here is what I need you to do…"

They listened to his explanation of what was happening, and quietly informed him that they would take care of everything. There were one or two questions regarding his coming absence—simple matters of procedure and nothing he couldn't easily answer. The meeting lasted less than an hour. When they left, he lingered just long enough to download and send a copy of the meeting to Liz along with her instructions. With that done, he was confident he had fulfilled his responsibilities to Snakeholme. He was leaving her people in good hands. He broke his link to Infonet and quickly up-linked to the regiment's TacNet (Tactical Network) to begin issuing his orders.

Vipers, no matter where they happened to be or what they happened to be doing, froze as their processors flashed an alert upon their displays indicating a priority message was incoming. Minutes later, black clad men and women sprinted for the nearest ground or air transport back to Petruso Base. People stopped to stare as vipers piled out of buildings in cities all over Snakeholme, and ran at top speed for the nearest maglev station.

\* \* \*

# 21 ~ Rendezvous

*TF19* jumped into the system in battle formation. The stupendous bulk of *ASN Sutherland* was central to the formation and protected from all sides by her escort. As the only carrier assigned to *TF19*, *Sutherland* was an asset beyond price, but she was also a huge liability. The task force simply did not have enough ships to nursemaid a carrier, but they needed one to perform their mission. It was an insoluble situation, Captain Fernandez thought for the umpteenth time. His repeater displays suddenly blossomed with colour as *Sutherland* launched fighters to supplement her defence. He watched as the fighters piled on the acceleration and raced madly into the void. Most people had sense enough to avoid g-stress. Fighter pilots loved it.

"Contact," Commander Hanson sang out from his position at scan. "Target designate: Alpha one through three. Two tin cans and a troop transport, Skipper."

Fernandez aborted his fumbling attempt to remove his helmet. "Class?"

"The destroyers are *Broadsword* class, the transport is a…" Hanson looked up from the master plot's display with a frown. "It's an old *Hunter* class."

The *Hunter* class of ships had been decommissioned more than a century ago. Before that they were the mainstay of the Alliance's transport fleet. During the Merki war, more than ninety percent of all troop movements were accomplished using *Hunter* class ships.

"Designation?"

"I'm not picking up IFF, sir."

Fernandez didn't like that, he didn't like that at all. "Keep us at battle stations. Try to contact them, Lena."

"Aye, sir," Lieutenant Braun, said and worked her consol. "I have... I have *General Burgton* on the line," she gasped. "He says he would like to join us if that's all right with you, sir."

"Burgton..." he whispered. "*The* Burgton?"

"Yes, sir. Should I put him on?"

"On screen, Lieutenant."

"Aye, sir."

The screen activated to show a man with wide shoulders wearing black battle dress. He was sitting among others wearing similar uniform. It *was* Burgton. No one could ever mistake his face or his uniform. There were no navy personnel present on his bridge—none at all.

"I don't believe I've had the honour Captain...?" Burgton said.

"I... I mean... Captain Fernandez of *Victorious* at your service, General."

"At my service?" Burgton smiled tolerantly. "I rather think it's the other way around don't you?"

Fernandez nodded. "I'm sure the Admiral will want to speak with you, General. Your ships..." he paused to pull himself together. "I'm not reading IFF from your ships, General. Why not?"

"*Swordfish* and *Hammer*, my escort, will be departing momentarily, Captain Fernandez. As for *Grafton's* IFF, none of my ships belong to the navy. They're... they're on permanent *loan* you might say."

*Broadsword* class destroyers on loan; on *permanent* loan? And no IFF? Not even courier ships were exempt. Privately owned or not, Burgton's ships should still be broadcasting identity and registry. It seemed obvious that *Grafton* was crewed by the General's men; he could see them on the screen. That being so, the destroyers were probably crewed by non-navy personnel also.

"I see," Fernandez said thoughtfully. When the Council learned that Burgton had his own personal navy, the explosion would be heard from Kalmar to Northcliff... unless they already knew and approved? "I see indeed. *Grafton* may come ahead, General. *Victorious* out."

Burgton nodded and the screen cleared to show *Grafton* manoeuvring clear of her escort.

"Keep an eye on those destroyers, XO."

Hanson nodded, but then looked up immediately. "*Swordfish* and *Hammer* are moving, Skipper. They're going for jump."

Fernandez nodded as the destroyers jumped outsystem. "Get me the Admiral."

\* \* \*

## ABOARD GRAFTON, AT STATION KEEPING, NGC 1513-4964

"All stop confirmed, General. Your shuttle is ready," Stone said from his position at the helm.

"Thank you, Ken. Eric, you have the con."

"Yes, sir, I have the con," Penleigh said, leaving his place at communications to take the command station.

Burgton stepped into the elevator followed by Colonel Flowers, Major Faggini, and Lieutenant Hymas. He had chosen the three to accompany him for various reasons. Dan Flowers was always with him, and had been since the beginning. Erica Faggini was officially CO of First Battalion; she would gain a valuable insight into the mission by converse with Admiral Meyers. Marion Hymas was along to listen. Burgton valued her advice, and she was a qualified shrink. If anyone knew what was going on in another's head, it was Marion. Knowing the opposition was always a good thing.

They made their way through *Grafton's* meticulously neat, though worn, corridors to the portside lock. *Grafton* was ancient, as ancient as Burgton felt sometimes. She had two small shuttles that rarely saw use in these days. The other pair of shuttles that had once resided on *Grafton's* hull, were now used to ferry personnel to and from Uriel.

Burgton found an empty seat in the shuttle's cabin and strapped in. "Who wants to drive?"

"My turn," Hymas said, and took the pilot's position.

He smiled at her eagerness. Whether it be a tank or a shuttle, she always liked taking the controls. Flowers took the co-pilot's position by her side.

"What do we know of this Meyers? Have you met her?" Faggini said, as she strapped in.

Burgton shook his head. "I don't know her, but I know *of* her. Paul Rawlins mentioned her once… hmmm, it was about twelve years ago as I recall. She wasn't an admiral then of course."

"Captain?"

"No, a commodore I believe. It was just after that business on Flotsam. Paul had a few things to say about Ken making too big a bang in that system… or some such thing." Burgton shrugged. "I really don't care what it was about. We cleared the scum out for a few years anyway."

Faggini grinned. "Ken does have a way of doing that, but you know they always come back. They're like weeds. Pull them up, and another batch grow next year."

"And I'll pull them up again," he said grimly, remembering all the times he had sent his people to do just that—quite often on missions that duplicated earlier ones down to the letter. "It's getting worse you know."

"What? Worse did you say? It's always been like this."

The shuttle undocked and accelerated toward *Victorious*. Burgton took no notice of being pushed deeper into his couch. He was too busy studying the figures he had instructed his processor to display. They made grim reading.

"I said it's always been like this," Faggini said again when Burgton failed to answer.

"Sorry, I was just going over some things. The Alliance is heading for a fall; a big one. Within twenty years we'll have a breakaway—probably led by Bethany."

"You know what I think about that, George. It won't happen, especially not with this Merki attack."

Burgton pursed his lips and considered. Finally he gave a sharp nod. "Perhaps you're right, I hope so. I told Paul they would be back in five years, and I would have stood by that, but here we are off to war before we're ready. Look at the figures. We've had more missions in the last fifty years than in the entire time preceding that—not including the war of course. It's getting worse. Raider ships are no longer patched together junk. They have heavy cruisers now. A century ago, they threatened cargo, now they threaten entire colonies. Back then a single cruiser outgunned them, and easily took them out. Now the navy uses task forces, and they don't always win."

Faggini sighed. "I know, I know, but you realise what you're saying?"

"Of course I do," Burgton said grimly. "Without the Merki, we would be constantly at war with ourselves." He accessed a view from the shuttle's forward sensors, and watched as they slowed for docking. *Victorious'* armoured hide swung into view with her gun ports sealed giving only a hint of the destructive capacity they contained. "What would happen if Bethany and say... Alizon broke away? How many naval vessels are crewed by patriotic men and women? Men and women who still think in the old way, men and women willing to desert the Alliance to go to the aid of their home worlds?"

A crease of worry appeared upon Faggini's brow marring her flawless face. "Ties like that are strong, George, but navy crews are too diverse. Ships are never crewed exclusively from Bethany, or any other world for that matter."

"That won't stop it. Our history is rife with wars. The Merkiaari are an outlet for our baser instincts… a reason not to kill each other if you will, but memories are short."

"Not ours."

"No, not ours, but the unenhanced don't know them like we know them. They live for the present, and only see what's in their short term interest. Even the Council has been guilty of it. I've been trying to convince them to build more of us for years now. I've tried to make them see, but they will not. We need a dozen or more viper regiments, not one."

"I don't know that even a dozen would be enough to destroy the Merkiaari utterly, George, and from what you say, we shouldn't try. Their threat holds the Alliance together."

Burgton nodded, but he was troubled. Hearing his own words used to defend the Merkiaari, to actually *prevent* their destruction, went against everything he was built to achieve. His purpose was to seek and destroy them, yet if he did by some miracle manage to kill them all, he would be sowing the seeds of the Alliance's own destruction… or at least its fragmentation.

"The Council are afraid of me… of us," he said with a wry smile. "They will never build another regiment, and perhaps that's for the best considering how paranoid some of them are. As long as the Merkiaari remain a threat, we are strong."

"As long as that's all they are," Faggini warned. "I have to tell you, George, I'm damn worried. We have six hundred and forty units here, and none of them have been battle tested. They say we're going up against a few divisions and a light cruiser squadron, which I might add, will give Admiral Meyers a run for her money. What if they're wrong? What if they've been reinforced? What if—"

"We can play *what if* all day. We'll know soon enough."

Docking commenced and Burgton made ready to put on his show. He was the hero of Garnet, of Thorfinni… and of San Luis. He was the big bad Merkiaari killer. Was there anything left of the young Human officer he had been at the beginning of the war? After a moment's thought, he decided there wasn't. He was the man that personally oversaw the utter annihilation of an entire world. It was a world of Merkiaari, but still a world.

He closed his eyes as his processor dragged up the well accessed memory file of San Luis. He saw himself standing among the dead, with rivers of blood running down the street and flowing thickly into the drains. The sky was the colour of ash and the noise… he still heard it all these years later. The roaring of the fires, and the crashing of the buildings succumbing to them. They had been badly weakened by the regiment's assault, and the bombing before that. Above it all, he heard the screams of the aliens as they burned.

San Luis had been an object lesson to the Merkiaari; he had decided they needed one after what they did to Garnet and him. He had turned San Luis into a charnel house, a bonfire, a Merki's vision of hell if they had such a thing. Oh yes, he had lit a fire on San Luis all right. He had thrown them on top, and stepped back to watch them burn. That was what the Alliance saw when they looked at him—a larger than life man in black uniform standing upon a mountain of Merki corpses. They wanted the *hero*, so that is what he gave them—always.

"George?" Faggini said, and the vision of San Luis slipped back into the mists of time to wait for his call. "It's time."

Burgton slapped his harness release and stood. Flowers preceded him to the lock with Faggini and Hymas following along behind. As he readied himself to put on his show, his thoughts turned to Admiral Meyers. Did she have any new data on the incursion? *Canada's* report, out of date though it was, indicated that it was a small one—merely two *Marauder* class transports had been committed to it. A *Marauder* was nothing to sneer at under any circumstances, but this incursion *was* small in comparison to say… the Garnet incursion. A fleet of fifteen *Marauders* had hit that luckless world.

The *Marauder* class heavy transport was a huge ship on anyone's scale. Its detachable landers could quickly transport Merki regiments, called fists by the Merkiaari, to any planetary surface within a target system. Each fist was composed of a thousand individuals, each heavily armed. There were typically a hundred such fists per transport ready to be awakened at the press of a button. Ten fists were classed as a division by the Alliance. No one knew what the Merkiaari called them. Two *Marauder* class transports meant twenty divisions. It was as simple as that. Two hundred thousand murderous aliens ready to fight at the touch of a button, two hundred thousand fighting machines needed to die for the mission to be complete.

*Could it be done?*

He had some ideas, but a lot depended on the Merkiaari doing what he expected. He knew them of old. They could hardly be called original thinkers. They always reacted with massive force to any attack or defiance. That kind of mindless aggression could be channelled to their detriment if he was careful. Merki males tended to rely heavily on their gauss cannons, which operated in similar manner to an Alliance AAR. The females were different. They were more intelligent than the average male, and had proven it to him more than once by ruining his plans. They were physically larger than the males—much larger, and they liked to use a dizzying array of weaponry. No two were alike in their preferences. Being so large, they were dangerous whether they were armed or not. He preferred not of course, but his preferences rarely made a difference where Merkiaari were concerned.

Burgton knew what the mission would be. It was the same as it ever was—destroy Merkiaari wherever he found them. Vipers were created for that purpose, but it would take more than a single battalion to liberate the Shan worlds. Of that he had no doubt. *Sutherland's* fighter wings were a godsend. Without them the mission would be untenable. A single unsupported battalion pitted against twenty divisions of Merkiaari? He shuddered inwardly. Enhanced or not, it would be a slaughter. He would not allow that to happen. The Alliance needed him and his men intact. He knew it beyond doubt or question. Admiral Rawlins knew it, and the President knew it.

His vipers were essential to the future of the Alliance. That being so, he had to make Admiral Meyers give him control of *Sutherland*, or at least control of her fighter wings. He needed to know that when he ordered an air strike, it would be forthcoming in timely fashion without the need to wade through red tape or smooth ruffled feathers.

The outer hatch cycled open, and Burgton stepped through it to board *Victorious*. "Permission to come aboard?"

A young ensign stood nervously at attention and greeted them. "Granted, sir. If you would follow me?"

Burgton smiled. Ah, to be that young again. "Lead on, Ensign."

He followed the ensign to her captain who was waiting not far away.

Captain Fernandez stood at slightly over six feet in his regulation boots. His white navy shipsuit was as immaculate as one would expect from one of the Alliance's best cruiser Skippers, and his handshake was unselfconscious. It was a relief. Many people were uncomfortable in the presence of what they called cyborgs. Burgton sometimes felt like staying at home and never venturing off planet because of it.

"May I introduce my officers?" Burgton asked, indicating those accompanying him. "Colonel Flowers, Major Faggini, and Lieutenant Hymas."

"Welcome aboard," Fernandez said.

"Call me Dan," Flowers said and shook the offered hand.

"Erica," Major Faggini said, also shaking the Captain's hand. "You have a fine ship here. I would like a tour sometime... when you're not so busy of course."

"Call me Tomas won't you? I would be honoured to escort you around her personally," Fernandez said, and smiled widely. Anyone who praised his ship was good people as far as he was concerned. He shook Hymas' hand and then turned back Burgton. "The Admiral asked me to escort you to her."

Burgton nodded, expecting nothing else. "Of course. Lead on, Captain."

After dismissing the wide-eyed Ensign, Fernandez indicated the way with a wave of his hand. "May I ask a question, General?"

"Go ahead. I don't promise to answer."

"It's not that kind of question. You must get a lot of that kind."

"You have no idea," Burgton said, barely holding in a sigh. "What's your question?"

"It regards our mission. I understand from conversations with the Admiral that you have only a single battalion with you. Can you really hope to liberate the system with so few?"

"You don't believe in viper superiority and indestructibility then?" Burgton asked wryly, and Flowers snorted. "Haven't you heard? We won the last war single-handed."

Fernandez chuckled, but it was a strained sound. "This is my first mission against Merkiaari. None of us have fought them before. Only you and your men have ever faced them. Have you any advice for me?"

"Hit them hard and fast from concealment. Keep firing until your magazine runs dry or they're all dead, whichever comes first. Give them time to organise and you're dead—period."

Flowers and Faggini nodded grimly, perhaps seeing battles of long ago. Burgton didn't need to look back. He carried his defeats with him every day... and his dead.

"...land war. Concealment is hard to come by in space," Fernandez said querulously. "How would you approach this mission?"

Burgton smiled. "That's what we're here to discuss. Admiral Meyers will handle any enemy ships in the system, but if I was her, I would jump in right on top of them, and let them have everything at point blank."

"You're assuming a lot. What if we jump in and don't find them where we expect—what then?"

Flowers shrugged. "Then we die."

Burgton nodded. "Nothing is certain, Captain. All we can do is plan for the worst and hope for the best."

"Not very comforting."

"You're in the wrong line of work for comfort, Captain," Faggini said, smiling to take the sting out of her words. "You and your crew will do your best, as will we. It will just have to be enough."

Burgton knew the truth of those words. When Merkiaari were

involved, nothing but the best would suffice.

Fernandez stopped outside an unremarkable hatch. It was like any of a dozen others they had seen. He keyed the comm and asked admittance. The hatch slid aside to reveal a very young seeming Admiral's aide.

"General Burgton and his officers to see the Admiral, Joshua," Fernandez said.

"Yes, sir. She's been expecting you."

They entered and Admiral Meyers stood to greet her guests. "It's good to finally meet you in person, General," she said and shook Burgton's hand. She had a firm grip. "And these are…?"

"Colonel Flowers, my aide and Regimental Exec," Burgton said and quickly made up something to cover Marion's presence. "Lieutenant Hymas heads up Intel and coordinates data gathering. Major Faggini is officially CO of First Battalion, but Dan and I couldn't keep away. We'll try not to be a burden."

Major Faggini snorted but said nothing.

Meyers raised an eyebrow at the byplay. "I'm pleased you came along then, General. I have a few questions about your part in the mission. I'm glad Admiral Rawlins saw fit to send you, but I still don't like the odds." She motioned to the hastily arranged seating. "Make yourselves comfortable."

Burgton seated himself and accepted a cup of steaming coffee from Joshua. It was very hot and very strong, just the way he liked it. He drank a scolding mouthful ignoring the alert that flashed in the corner of his vision. His processor was like a mother hen sometimes. Caffeine wouldn't kill him.

"My vipers' part in this mission is simple in theory: Kill all Merkiaari in the target system. Wonderful coffee by the way."

Joshua smiled briefly from the corner of the cabin where he sat in fascinated silence. Studying the legend, Burgton thought with an inward sigh. At least Joshua was discreet, unlike some he had met in his time.

"Theory rarely agrees with reality," Meyers said dryly.

"Not a hundred percent," Burgton agreed. "But in this case it's close enough to serve. Assuming certain things come to pass, we will accomplish what we have been set to do. Firstly, we need to clarify what the mission is."

"Obvious I should think," Fernandez said, glancing at Meyers in surprise.

"Obvious?" Burgton mused. He placed his empty cup on Meyers' desk. "Let us assume they haven't been reinforced. Further, let us assume that you are successful in destroying the Merki ships—a big assumption. Now then, we have upwards of two hundred thousand Merkiaari on planet, and I have precisely six hundred and forty viper units to engage them. That means each unit must kill three hundred and twelve point two Merki troopers. Doable, but not easy."

"Hmmm…" Meyers frowned. "Let's say the mission is to keep them busy until Fifth Fleet jumps in."

"Better," Burgton said, pleased that Meyers saw things his way. "Such an objective allows me to pick my battles and husband my strength. It allows me to kill the maximum number of Merkiaari with the minimum of loss."

"But what of the loss to the natives?" Fernandez said unhappily. "They're dying by the thousands."

"By the millions, Captain, by the millions. It changes nothing. Adding my men to the count benefits no one, least of all the Shan. I can best help them by drawing the enemy's attention. While they try to respond to my presence, they're not killing civilians."

Meyers nodded. "I agree. How do you plan to proceed?"

"Securing a landing zone is a priority. I need somewhere large enough to be occupied by Merkiaari, but not so large that it houses multiple fists."

"Hmmm. A port?"

"Precisely. And that brings me to one of those assumptions I mentioned. I need *Sutherland* placed at my disposal."

Fernandez gasped. "*Are you out of your mind?* Liz will shit a brick when she hears! It's out of the question."

"I cannot proceed with my mission without air support. It would be suicide."

Burgton was adamant on that point.

"And if I order you to go ahead regardless?" Meyers asked quietly.

Flowers and Faggini tensed at the implied threat.

Burgton considered his words carefully. "During the Merki War, my men and I were sent into occupied world after occupied world to take out the Merki garrisons. I protested the orders repeatedly, but I was ignored. I was ignored, and my regiment died a little more each time. And for what? Nothing. Those worlds had been lost years earlier. There wasn't a single Human being left alive to save, yet we went in and died one by one."

"It was your duty—" Fernandez began to say.

"Don't tell me my duty, Captain! I know my duty better than you. Dying to save a few trillion credits of someone's money is not it. There wasn't an iota of military sense in sending us in. The Fleet could have taken out the Merki garrisons with surgical precision from orbit, but of course, the cities would have cost a fortune to replace," Burgton finished bitterly.

"The past is in the past," Meyers said. "I *will* use your men to further the mission, General, and use them up if the situation demands it, but I swear they won't die for no purpose."

"Dead is still dead," Faggini said.

Meyers ignored Faggini's quiet murmur. "I cannot give you *Sutherland*, General. You're not Fleet—you're not even navy for Chrissakes, you're infantry. As Tomas so inelegantly put it, Captain Alston would shit a brick, but I can detach a squadron of her fighters for your use."

"Not good enough," Burgton said.

Meyers' eyes hardened. "It will have to be."

Burgton glared back and knew it was going to happen again. He had told his people on the journey that he wouldn't let them die for nothing, not this time, but here they were having the same kind of conversation he'd had with his superiors back during the Merki War. He could refuse the order. The others would back him, but who would Meyers put in command? He shuddered at the thought of some unenhanced marine trying to lead his people into battle.

"Four squadrons," he said and ignored twin sighs at his back.

The Admiral's eyes bugged. "Two, and not a ship more!"

\* \* \*

# 22 ~ No Quarter

"...we have Merki concentrations in orbit of *both* planets," Commander Linden reported from her position at scan. "The defence grid we were told to look for is gone, Skipper. It looks as if the Merkiaari blew it to hell and gone right at the start. I'm picking up debris, but by the dispersal pattern I estimate its months old. I have twenty plus Merki guard ships in orbit of Child of Harmony. They're similar to our light cruisers in configuration. They look fast and lightly armoured, light on missiles, but heavy on beam armament. We have five... *five* troop transports in orbit of Harmony—*Marauder* class. No heavy stuff, repeat no heavies in evidence. The cruisers weapons are at standby, and their drives are cold. I estimate..."

Lieutenant Commander Pamela Finster, Captain of *ASN Vigilant*, listened attentively to Linden's report. *Neptune* was holding position on her starboard aft quarter. She nodded in satisfaction at the nice tight spacing. She had known her Captain for years, and had even dated him for a while back at the academy. Valentin knew what he was doing. She noted the wreckage of the planetary defence net around the Shan colony world. That was something they had all hoped not to see, but the Admiral had allowed for it. It had been hoped the task force would arrive before the Merkiaari attacked Child of Harmony, but initial indications seemed to show that both planets were under simultaneous assault.

"Update *Victorious*, Harry," Finster said.

"Aye, aye, Skipper," Lieutenant Coleman said, and worked his controls.

Tight beam comms at this distance would be slow, but with the ship at battle stations and her stealth field active, any kind of launch was out of the question. A drone's reactor was too small to power a decent stealth field. The Merkiaari would be sure to see it.

"Steady on course," she said and settled herself more comfortably in her seat. This was going to be a long and nerve wracking day.

* * *

### Aboard ASN Victorious, in the zone, Shan System

"*Sutherland* has deployed fighters, Admiral," Joshua said from his station on the other side of CIC's main holotank.

"I see them, Joshua," Meyers replied watching the battlespace displayed in the holotank. "*Sutherland's* wings will provide her with a warning net."

"Yes, ma'am, but two destroyers to protect a carrier? I don't think I could have made that decision."

"Give it time, Joshua, give it time. In a few years you'll be grey haired with worry, just like me. We haven't the ships to spare to do the job *and* protect *Sutherland* as she's accustomed to. This is the best I can do."

Meyers studied her ship deployments again, not happily perhaps, but she did have enough firepower to take care of the Merki ships in orbit—if they didn't power up and move. It was the Merki troops on the surface that were giving her sleepless nights. She couldn't see how Burgton had a hope of making a dent in the Merki offensive before Fifth Fleet arrived on station. He was outnumbered hundreds to one—many hundreds to one. There were five *Marauders* in the system, *five!* That meant there were half a million blood crazed monsters busily killing people she was sworn to save, and Burgton had six hundred and forty vipers to engage them. It was suicide. They both knew it, of course, but there was nothing to be done about it. The Shan needed help, and she was here to supply it.

*Vigilant* and *Neptune* had arrived back just a short time ago from their recon of the system, and were dogging *Sutherland's* heels for now. *Sutherland* was vulnerable with only two destroyers for protection, but Meyers felt the risk was acceptable. When they jumped, *Sutherland* would be left entirely on her own until the Merki ships were taken care of. Leaving a carrier unprotected was a heinous crime that no admiral in her right mind would perpetrate, but she had no choice and cursed the fact. With luck, it would all be over before the Merkiaari realised how badly a certain admiral had ignored the book and left a carrier to fend for itself.

*God, I hope so.*

"Captain Alston took the news better than I thought she would, ma'am," Joshua said.

Meyers grimaced. The news that there were five and not two *Marauders* in the system had been a major shock. Burgton had immediately gone back on their deal, and insisted they talk. This time he demanded all of *Sutherland's* fighters be placed at his disposal, and he wouldn't budge. She didn't much blame him, and knew she had undermined her own position with that sympathy. She had acquiesced to his demands with one proviso. He could plan his use of air support, and have unlimited use of same, but he must *request* fighter coverage through his liaison. At her request, Captain Alston assigned Commander Heinemann to Burgton's staff. As one of only three COFDO (chiefs of flight deck operations) aboard *Sutherland*, Heinemann was ideally suited for the position. Liz Alston would have to scrape by with the remaining two. Liz had a good crew, they would take up the slack.

"I have Captain Fernandez for you, Admiral," Joshua said.

"Put him on," she said, and her screen lit to show her flag captain. "Well Tomas, here we are. Is everything ready?"

"Yes, ma'am, looks perfect for Sierra Two."

"I concur."

"Orders, ma'am?" Fernandez said.

"None. You may execute Sierra Two at your discretion."

"Aye, aye, ma'am."

The screen darkened.

\* \* \*

## ABOARD VICTORIOUS, AT JUMP STATIONS

"*Vigilant* and *Neptune* report ready to jump, sir… all ships report ready, Skipper."

Fernandez nodded. Trust a tin can jockey to be first. They were all like that. He watched the chronometer cycle down towards zero. "Weps, I want full safeties on your birds. Lock in your solutions now."

"Aye, sir," Lieutenant Benson said from his place at tactical.

By locking in a targeting solution now, he was running a considerable risk of losing target lock if the enemy ships powered up and got underway, but he deemed the situation such that a few misses were worth the time saving. If all went well, he would launch two, maybe even three, full broadsides into the Merki ships under computer control before they knew anyone was there. That was the plan in any case.

"Jump stations manned and ready, Skipper," Jennings said from the helm. Her voice was steady, but her palms were sweaty on the controls.

"Execute as planned."

"Aye, sir. Twenty seconds."

Fernandez slapped his visor closed and panted trying to saturate his blood with oxygen. Friends said it was just superstition on his part, but he found it really did help his jump sickness. Besides, he always did it and would feel uncomfortable not doing it here.

"Five seconds... four, three, two, one... exe—"

*Victorious* jumped, and Fernandez's world turned inside out. He sagged in his harness straps—his brain seemingly disconnected from his body. It was the worst part about commanding a ship. He had an apparently infinite time to worry about his plans and his crew. He knew it was an illusion, but a second in the jump felt like years, and this was worse than usual.

*He was falling...*

*...falling forever....*

*...round and around and down...*

A skip jump was unlike any other. It was really two normal jumps strung together. The first one into fold space using power from the mains. The second jump was back to real space using auxiliary power timed and executed via computer control. He worried about the Merkiaari seeing them ahead of time, about them seeing the jump signature. He worried about arriving in the midst of them with no power available to jump back out. He worried about...

*Whirling and spinning...*

*...round and down and around...*

*TF19* arrived back into normal space. Less than a second later, her ships erupted in fury as salvo after salvo of missiles roared out under computer control to rend the Merki ships. Thousands of nuclear warheads slammed home, and ships began to die. Two Merki cruisers fell out of orbit burning, yet gamely trying to fire back. They failed as *TF19's* second broadside arrived and wiped them out of existence.

The Merki ships writhed at the centre of an inferno created by thousands of missiles, yet Fernandez didn't have it all his own way. He had been right to worry about his detection. One Merki ship had detected the jump signature and launched an attack of its own even as it died.

"Incoming mis—" Commander Hanson began.

The cap ship missiles stormed into attack range and detonated.

Dozens of bomb-pumped energy beams stabbed at *Victorious'* vitals, and atmosphere belched from her torn and bleeding hide. Lieutenant Jennings rolled ship in a lightning fast manoeuvre, but the damage was already done. Breached and broken yet still firing, *Victorious* staggered out of formation trying to put some distance between herself and her attackers.

"Concentrate all fire aft," Fernandez snapped, as his CIC repeaters flared and died. "Get me the Admiral."

"I can't, sir. I think… I think she's gone."

He clenched his jaw. "Send to all ships: I'm assuming command of the task force. Form on me and come to a new heading…"

\* \* \*

## ABOARD ASN VIGILANT

"*Victorious* is hurt, ma'am," Commander Linden reported looking up from the plot his station was displaying. "She's falling out of formation."

"Helm," Captain Finster snapped. "You stick on her arse—keep those bastards off her."

"Aye, aye. Coming port to three-one-zero by three-two-five degrees."

Hearing his captain's order to the helm, Ensign Meier re-prioritised his targets without orders and slammed the commit button flat.

*ASN Vigilant* roared by a Merki cruiser that was even now firing on *Victorious,* and blew it apart with raking fire from every energy mount that could bear on the target.

Finster howled in triumph as her single destroyer whacked a Merki light cruiser. "Yes!" She glared at the cruiser as it broke apart. "Now do it again."

"Yes, ma'am," Meier said happily, but his energy weapons were out of range.

*ASN Neptune* dove into the fray, and added more destruction to that being heaped upon the Merkiaari before taking station on *Victorious'* other side. Together the cruiser and two destroyers turned back to the fight.

"Message from the flag, Skipper."

"Let's have it," Finster said.

"Captain Fernandez is assuming command of the task force, ma'am. He orders all ships to form on him and attack in force. No quarter, ma'am."

That meant the Admiral was dead. The no quarter order was

standard when fighting Merkiaari. They neither accepted nor gave quarter themselves.

"Understood. Steady as she goes, helm. Look out for the others coming in."

"Aye, aye, Skipper."

* * *

### Aboard ASN Victorious

"Damn and blast it to hell," Meyers snarled. "What is happening?"

"We lost power, ma'am," Joshua said, still messing around with the hatch mechanism.

"I know that. I meant with the battle."

She couldn't believe it. She was the first admiral to fight Merkiaari in centuries, and she was missing it. The hit *Victorious* had taken had severed the control runs to CIC—more even than that, it had plunged the entire deck into darkness. That should never have happened. What about emergency power? Where the hell was it?

"How long to get that open?" she asked impatiently.

"Not long, Admiral."

"You said that twenty minutes ago, Joshua. I swear that if I get out of this alive, BuShips is going to hear about this day. This ship is supposed to be *tough*."

Joshua grinned briefly, and then composed himself before his admiral saw it. "It was a lucky hit, ma'am. It could have happened to anyone."

"Oh? Well it happened to me," she snapped in frustration.

Joshua remained wisely silent as he worked on overriding the safeties on the hatch. "I think... yes... that's got it, ma'am," Joshua said.

"Hallelujah!" Meyers jumped through the hatch even as it was opening.

She blinked dazzled eyes, looking around for signs of damage. At least the lights meant this section had power. She found a bunch of gaping crewmen huddled and whispering around a comm station, and went to join them.

"What's going on?" Meyers asked, pushing her way through the crowd. "Why aren't you at your posts?"

A young ensign gaped at her admiral, but then snapped to attention. "We're cut off, Admiral. Captain says to sit tight and wait for damage control to get to us."

"You're in touch with the bridge?"

"Er... yes, ma'am. Ma'am?"

Meyers frowned at the comm's display. "What is it?"

"Everyone thinks you're dead, ma'am."

She grunted. "I'm not surprised, I very nearly was." She watched a Merki cruiser break up on the tiny screen. "Is this real time?"

"Yes, ma'am. Commander Hanson piped a feed down here when he heard we were trapped."

"Did he now… good for him! Right, let me at the controls. I have a worried captain to talk to and a battle to win."

\* \* \*

# 23 ~ Graduation

"Attennnnnn-*hut!*" Master Sergeant Stone ordered.

"As you were," General Burgton said, as he entered the main hold of the troop transport *Grafton*. It was the only place large enough to seat the entire battalion.

Everyone sat as the General and his staff made their way to the head of the cavernous room. Captains Penleigh and Hames were grim faced as were the other veterans accompanying the General. They were looking decidedly uneasy, and the tension level throughout the hold soared in anticipation of bad news. Burgton spoke a few words with the Colonel, nodded at what he heard, and turned to face his men. He stood at parade rest and surveyed the rapt faces of First Battalion.

"I had planned for you all to attend a graduation ceremony back on Snakeholme," Burgton said. "I'm sorry there wasn't time for it before embarkation to *Grafton*, but our mission here dictated a swift departure. Tomorrow you will be making your first combat drops against Merkiaari." He smiled grimly at the eager faces. "I would give much for another year to prepare you... six months even, but that is not to be. People are dying in their millions as I speak. They need us now, not six months from now. It won't be easy, but you are vipers. I *know* you can do the job."

Colonel Flowers keyed the holotank to life and lowered the lights. A diagram of the Shan solar system appeared, complete with all the planets and both asteroid fields.

"Gentlemen, as you can see, this system boasts two habitable planets. One here," Flowers said and the fourth planet flashed red. "And one here," the third planet also started flashing. "The fourth planet is Harmony, and the other is known as Child of Harmony." He pause to let the information settle before continuing.

"Our mission is to neutralise all Merkiaari in this system in preparation for the arrival of Fifth Fleet, which will hold the system after its liberation. Admiral Meyers has made a good start on that as you can see."

The holotank display changed to show a wire frame diagram of Child of Harmony, and the ships in its immediate vicinity. In geosynchronous orbit was a blue icon representing *Grafton*. Surveillance satellites seeded around the planet yesterday by the navy glowed a reassuring green. They were extremely important to the regiment. No matter the cost, the admiral had not stinted in her use of them. A little further out, a large formation of blue icons representing *TF19* stooged about awaiting further orders, keeping a wary eye on the wreckage of the Merki ships.

A stupendous *Marauder* class transport broke in two as Gina watched, and the holo tank updated itself by painting each section with new data. The blinking vectors indicated the ship would burn up in atmosphere, and indeed, the forward section was already beginning its final journey. It hit atmosphere, broke apart, and its red icon faded from the tank's display.

The battle that had destroyed those ships had been costly in men as well as ships. *Victorious* had been damaged, and would need extensive repairs at the yard. She was still combat capable, but the same couldn't be said for other ships of the task force. Admiral Meyers had lost two of her four *Excalibur* class heavy cruisers with all hands: *Intrepid* and *Coventry*. In addition, *Voyager*, an ageing light cruiser, had to be abandoned when repeated attempts to stabilise her fusion reactors failed. Her crew had been taken aboard *Victorious*. *Voyager* was a lonely icon all alone in the holotank's display. She would probably be scuttled at some point, but not just yet. Her captain had requested that they wait for the arrival of Fifth Fleet in case his ship could be salvaged.

"We estimate the enemy's strength at over three hundred thousand troopers on Child of Harmony, with a further two hundred to two hundred and fifty thousand on Harmony. As previously mentioned, this is a *small* incursion."

There was a smattering of laughter at that, but not from the veterans. They were grim and silent. Repeated scans of the surface of both planets made it clear that although the native population outnumbered the Merkiaari by many thousands to one, their weapons were simply not up to the job of defeating their enemy. They were losing, and losing badly. They had nothing to match the Merki interceptors, which meant the Merki had air superiority almost everywhere on both planets. Not only that, the Shan had not developed shielding adequate to withstand Merki weapon's fire. They were being slaughtered in almost every battle they fought.

Burgton took over the briefing. "In consultation with Admiral Meyers and my senior staff, I have decided Child of Harmony needs our immediate attention. Although there are fewer Merkiaari on Harmony, they have met with greater success there. They are now conducting what can only be described as mopping-up operations. Very few people remain alive above ground. On Child of Harmony however, they are meeting stiff opposition. A number of regular military units have been sighted conducting operations against the enemy, and there appear to be strong resistance movements working independently against the enemy in the larger cities. Coordination between the resistance and the remnants of the Shan military is limited, but it's encouraging nonetheless.

"Our immediate task will be to establish a base of operations." Burgton nodded to Colonel Flowers. An aerial view of a spaceport appeared in the holotank. "This is Zuleika Spaceport. It's located on the northernmost continent of Child of Harmony, roughly equidistant between the Kachina Mountain range and the eastern ocean. This spaceport represents the only one still functional on the planet. The others were smashed by the first wave of enemy attacks. Zuleika is therefore *vital* to our operations. These buildings here…"

Gina listened intently as Burgton laid out his plans to take and hold the spaceport in preparation for full-scale operations against the Merkiaari in the nearby city of Zuleika. From there, and with air cover provided by *Sutherland*, they would move on the next concentration of Merki troops and the next until they either liberated Child of Harmony, or Fifth Fleet's arrival necessitated revising the plan.

Roughly an hour went by with Burgton explaining each step of the plan and answering queries. Colonel Flowers fielded questions regarding resupply, while Lieutenant Hymas concerned herself solely with medical matters, including the temporary repair of viper units in the field. Finally, the holotank shut down and the lights came up.

Gina sighed and rolled her head from side to side, in an effort to ease her tight shoulders. She had been watching the General so intently that her neck muscles felt knotted.

Burgton gestured toward four of the veterans standing with him at the head of the room. "Captains Hames, Elliot, Greenwood, and Penleigh are in command of Companies Alpha through Delta respectively, but that still leaves quite a few slots to fill. Let us take care of that now," he said, smiling at the anticipation he read on some of his men's faces. He turned and nodded to Stone. "Master Sergeant Stone, call the roll."

"Yes, sir." Stone turned to address the battalion. "When you hear your name called, stand and approach the General. Higgins John J, Roberts Christine, Hiller Ian G, Takeri Selinia, Singh…"

Burgton returned Higgins' salute and shook his hand. Colonel Flowers stepped forward holding a wooden case containing the rank insignia to be bestowed. Burgton unerringly chose the three stripes and a single rocker of a Staff Sergeant, and handed them to Higgins.

"Congratulations, Staff."

"Thank you, sir," Staff Sergeant Higgins said, and went back to his seat, beaming. He was clutching his stripes as if they were more important to him than a fistful of jewels.

Next was Christine Roberts.

"Congratulations, Corporal."

"Thank you, sir," Roberts said, and left to find her seat.

The next one was particularly pleasing. Ian Hiller was a Bethanite and as such had been thought of as an unlikely prospect to graduate. Ian had proven himself not only able to disregard his upbringing, with its cultural prejudices and hatred for the technology used to create vipers, he had done so in a manner that had seen him thrive.

"Congratulations, Sergeant."

"Thank you, sir," Hiller said, with a smile and returned to his seat.

"Well done, Takeri."

"Thank you, sir," Takeri said, and saluted before returning to her seat.

Burgton shook hands with one unit after another handing them their insignia, and the responsibilities that went with them. Gina didn't keep count, but when no more came forward, she knew the battalion had its full complement of non-coms at last.

"From this point on," Burgton announced. "Those just elevated not only have the rank and privileges; they also have the responsibilities that come with the stripes. We, your instructors and I, have thought long and hard on those who will fill the position of lieutenant for each platoon. Sixteen men and women have been chosen from the entire battalion as possessing the skills and outlook necessary for the position. Using the results and observations taken over a year of testing and training, I have chosen to promote the following units to lieutenant: Erma Dengler, Kamarl Dolinski, Gina Fuentez, Katherine Richmond…"

Gina grinned in delight when her name was called. She jumped to her feet and followed her friends as they marched to collect their insignia. She almost laughed aloud when she heard Richmond cussing under her breath behind her. Dengler took her promotion in stride, but Dolinski looked unhappy. It had to be the thing with Callendri. There was nothing anyone could do about what had happened, but perhaps a word from her would help in some way. She made a note to get Kamarl alone later.

"Congratulations, Kamarl," Burgton said. "I know you feel responsible for Roberto, and you are in a way, but it's a responsibility we all share. I know what it is to kill a friend."

"Does it get better, sir?"

"No, but it does get easier to live with."

"Thank you, sir," Dolinski said, saluted, and took the case containing his bars.

Gina stepped forward and saluted.

"Well done, Gina, especially with the rocky start."

"Thank you, sir," she said, and took the small case containing the two silver bars of a first lieutenant. She shook his hand before saluting again.

Richmond stepped forward, wide eyed with shock.

"Congratulations, Katherine. Surprised?"

"Yes, sir," Richmond said with feeling. "With respect, sir, I don't like officers."

Burgton laughed at that. "You'll find the best officers are the ones who least like ordering others to do the work. I need people who not only know the job, but ones willing to get down in the dirt and do it. A soldier who likes to order others to do what he should have done, has no place in the regiment let alone filling a command slot."

"Yes, sir, I agree. Maybe my problem is that all the officers I knew came from Bethany."

Burgton pursed his lips. "It wouldn't be politic for me to agree with you, but there might indeed be something to that. Congratulations," he said again, and handed her the case containing her bars.

"Thank you, sir," Richmond said and saluted.

Burgton shook hands with each of his new lieutenants and handed them their insignia. Sixteen handshakes later, First Battalion was ready for war.

Richmond still looked stunned. She was clutching the case containing her bars as if afraid to open it.

Gina grinned. "You okay?"

Richmond nodded jerkily. "I will be."

"...duties as well as the privileges that rank confers," General

Burgton said. "Platoon leaders will remain behind, the rest of you are dismissed to quarters. I suggest you take time for an early dinner because we have a lot to get done later today. Dismissed."

"Attennnnnn-*Hut!*" Stone ordered, and everyone briefly stood to attention before leaving the hold.

Gina automatically fell in with Alpha Company's newly promoted lieutenants as they moved en masse to join the senior staff standing around the holotank. Captain Hames was CO of Alpha Company. As such, he was her immediate superior. He gestured for them to join him and they did so.

"Fuentez, I want you to take First Platoon," Hames said and handed her a compad. "Study that. If you have any questions come to me and we'll go over it together. The drop has been scheduled for zero-five-hundred tomorrow. That's just before dawn at Zuleika."

"Yes, sir." Gina quickly scanned the contents of the compad. It was a mission overview, but before she could ask for a more detailed ops plan, she found it. "The terminal building?"

Hames pointed to the holotank that was again displaying the spaceport. The General was studying it, while the Colonel pointed to this or that detail.

"The General has designated the northernmost building as a terminal. It's an arbitrary decision and for reference only. We don't actually know what the natives use it for, but we had to call it something. The buildings to the east look very much like hangars, so as far as we're concerned that's what they are until the natives tell us different."

"I understand, sir."

"Good," Hames said and handed each of the other platoon leaders a compad. "Dengler, you take…"

\* \* \*

## Zuleika, Child of Harmony, Shan System

James Wilder, professor of history turned resistance fighter, ducked as the Merki death squad opened fire on his position. He huddled behind the wrecked ground car, waiting for a chance to fire back, and prayed. He hadn't been one to rely upon prayer before visiting Child of Harmony, but he'd been doing a lot of it lately. He figured it couldn't hurt. He could use all the help he could get.

He hoped his friends had escaped. They had been searching for survivors, as they had done many times before, but this time James had become separated from the rest of his group when the Merki death squad appeared out of nowhere. Tei'Adeladja, their raid leader, had ordered them to scatter. By splitting into smaller groups, he had hoped to lead at least some of the people they had found to safety. He understood Adeladja's reasoning, but if James had been in command he would never have given that order.

James crawled along the ground, trying to find a better view of the enemy, but he had to duck back into cover when a crater was blasted into the road's surface. With his back to the wreck, he looked around for inspiration; an escape route, a clever attack plan, someone to help him... anything! There was no sign of the others, and he couldn't think of anything clever to defeat the Merki troops or escape. He hugged his knees, trying to make himself smaller as the wrecked car slowly disintegrated, gradually reducing his hiding place to nothing. This was it then, he thought, gripping his beamer tighter.

He wished he could tell Brenda he loved her one last time.

James surged to his feet, firing his beamer at anything that moved. The Merkiaari continued their methodical advance toward him laying down a barrage that would have made the Fleet proud. James ran in a crouch across the road, firing without aiming and expecting to die, but determined to go out fighting. One of his shots burned through a Merki female's arm, but it didn't faze her. The sudden flurry of shots from further up the street was another matter. She went down in a charred heap, and the other aliens scattered into hiding.

"Fall back, James," Shima yelled. "I'll cover you."

Shima had come back for him. Thank god!

James ran to her, dodging left and right. Shots sizzled by, but none were close. He managed to duck around the corner where Shima stood tall, firing back the way he had come. The Merkiaari stayed down, acting more like Human soldiers than the Merkiaari of old. It made perfect sense to him to take cover, but they weren't supposed to react this way. In the last war, they had been ferocious killing machines, deadly but seemingly stupid without a leader to tell them what to do.

Something had changed, and it scared James to imagine what it could be. Two hundred years was quite a long while. Even with nano technology increasing life spans, the last war was a distant memory in the Alliance. James suspected the Merkiaari had used the time to analyse how Humans had defeated them and then adapted. He feared what other things they may have learned.

"Let us pull back, James. They are moving through the buildings to trap us."

Although Shima's eyes were weak, the Harmonies were strong in her. In Human terms, she was an empath. Her talent made her an excellent hunter; her tracking ability bordered on the miraculous. No one and nothing could hide from her.

"I hear," James said, and ran as fast as he could, trying not to hold Shima up.

Shan were fast runners on two legs. If they dropped to all four, they were blindingly fast. Shima stayed on two, and kept pace with him until they put more buildings between themselves and the Merkiaari advance.

"Are… we… clear?" James panted. He was much fitter than he had been, but fifty years of easy living wasn't overcome so quickly.

"I think so. We will meet with the others and plan what to do next. Tei'Adeladja has led us well."

"He… has, but I still think we should… contact the other fighters, and try to kill the Merki's First Claw."

"But you have seen that it will do no good. Kill him and another will take his place. And besides, he will be heavily guarded. Many of us will fall just to reach him."

"It's true that another will take his place, but will the replacement be as good a warrior as this one? If we kill enough of their leaders, we might have a real chance of taking back the city."

"But to what purpose? The city is nothing, James. Let them have it. My people are all that matters."

"I know how you feel, Shima, but if you let them have their way here, they will spread out and take the countryside from you. Before you know it, they will be breaking into the Keeps. We have to contain them in the cities."

James' breathing settled after a few minutes, and he paced himself to reach the rendezvous without completely exhausting himself. The city was eerily silent one moment, and then shattered by the sound of battle the next. The elders had ordered every city evacuated as soon as it became obvious the Fleet was doomed, but as always, some were either unwilling or unable to leave in time. Most of the city's population had escaped and were hidden deep underground in the keeps. Some, like Shima, routinely left safety to fight and save those left behind. Most did not return from the raids, but there was no end to those volunteering to fight. This was James' eleventh raid. He was becoming used to the constant fear now.

All Shan were trained to fight at an early age. It dated back to the time called the Breaking of Harmony or simply The Breaking. The survivors of that time had stumbled forth from hiding to find their cities devastated, and their race close to extinction. They had vowed to build the Great Harmony anew, but they failed in that. What they created however, was admirable for many reasons. A law introduced in those first years required everyone to learn how to fight; it changed their culture from a carefree and peaceful one into one based on the need to fight and survive another Merki incursion. Until now, they had believed themselves well prepared.

Shima ducked into the residential block designated as the emergency rendezvous for their group. James quickly followed his friend inside and learned their group had been badly mauled. Grief clogged his suddenly tight chest. These people were his friends and comrades; most knew him from his first day in the keep. He looked around hoping to see the familiar kinked ear and spotted fur of Adeladja. The leader of their group had been a crewman on a light fang before it was destroyed. Somehow against all the odds he had managed to pilot his escape pod down safely. He was a good leader.

James' heart sank when he failed to find him. "Where is Tei'Adeladja?"

"Dead," Nadisu said from where she sat slumped dejectedly upon the floor.

Dead. James still needed more practice with the Shan language, but he knew that word very well. It was one he had heard too often on these forays to mistake. It was always spoken when he asked where a familiar face was. If he had to ask, then that person was dead. He looked around at the sadly diminished group, and then at Shima who flicked her ears. She had no idea what to do either.

He crouched down on a level with Nadisu. "Who is Tei now?" Everyone looked at each other and then back at him. "Now wait a damn minute! I can't be Tei, I'm not even Shan!"

"It does not matter. When you die, we will choose another," Nadisu said.

"Thanks a bunch," James said, and then laughed at his situation. A lone Human—an alien visitor to an alien planet, leading aliens in a war against aliens.

His friends watched him laugh with puzzlement that gradually changed to amusement. The wiggling ears and drop-jawed grins made it worse, and James howled with laughter. He sat on the dirty floor and hung his head, gasping for breath until his hilarity faded.

"The others still hold the north?" James asked, thinking about the future. He would not let them down.

"Yes, Tei. They are doing good work. The Murderers have not killed them all."

Not yet, at least. What they really needed to do was join up with the others and make a real effort to hold the city. While the Merkiaari were fighting here, they couldn't be looking for the Keeps. Brenda was waiting for him in one of those sanctuaries. He would do anything to keep her safe.

"We will join forces with the others in the north," he said firmly. "We will throw the Merkiaari out of our city, or die trying."

His order was met with yips and growls of agreement.

\* \* \*

# 24 ~ Going To War

Gina watched Richmond giving one of her team some last minute instructions. She smiled when she remembered the look of horrified panic that had flashed on her friend's face during the promotions. There was no sign of it now. It hadn't taken Richmond long to settle into her new role.

"I'll see you when the company assembles for the push on the city," Richmond said, turning to Gina at last.

Gina nodded slowly and took her friend's hand. "Good luck to us all."

"Luck has nothing to do with it," Richmond said with massive confidence, and trotted up the ramp of the second transport.

Gina, with Lieutenant Dolinski of Second Platoon by her side, climbed the ramp of Viper-One. "Listen up," she said to her platoon as Dolinski continued forward to the other troop hold. "We hit the dirt in less than fifteen. The General will be coming down just two hours later." She closed the ramp behind her and leaned against it. "We do good work. Everyone knows First Platoon is the best in the Company."

"Damn straight!"

"Everyone knows we kick arse!"

Gina spoke over the comments. "I don't want any mishaps. I want the enemy driven well clear of the spaceport before the General comes down. Clear?"

"Sir, yessir!" the platoon shouted in synch.

Gina strapped herself into a seat. It was the closest to the ramp. "First Platoon set," she said over the comm.

"Ten seconds…" the pilot announced.

*Grafton* held position in synchronous orbit over the spaceport. To starboard, *Sutherland* lay not too far off in astronomical terms, ready to deploy her fighters. *Grafton's* bay doors slowly cranked open, and two *Wolfcub* class transports were ejected from her launch rails.

"Shit!" one man cried, as the sudden intense acceleration shook the ship.

Viper-One sped away from *Grafton* riding out on the impetus imparted by the mag cradles. At five hundred metres, the pilot went to max thrust and headed for the LZ.

"Who the hell is driving this thing?" another unit said, grunting as the gees built.

"My pet monkey."

"Yeah…"

Gina ignored the complaints while she concentrated on TacNet. She was pleased when the pilot went to max thrust and bored into the atmosphere. The faster the better as far as she was concerned. Who knew what kind of anti-ship capabilities the enemy still had? Better to get dirtside before they found out.

She listened to comm traffic as the fighter escort joined them.

"Viper-One, Scorpion Leader."

"Scorpion Leader, Viper-One, go."

"Coming up on your six."

"Roger, Scorpion Leader. I have you on scope."

Gina turned her attention back to the mission and her target. She made the mental shift to access her internal processor, and considered what command to give it.

"Access satellite Sierra Zero One," she said hesitantly under her breath, and concentrated on the mental command.

She relaxed when the command worked. Stone and Rutledge had promised that using her processor would become second nature in no time, but it still took her a lot of concentration to get it right. Did the others have the same problem? She shook her head. It didn't matter because she wasn't going to ask them. Doing that would undermine their confidence in her. As their lieutenant, it was something she couldn't allow.

Gina's display cleared to reveal a real time view of the spaceport, and she studied it just as the General was doing on *Grafton's* bridge. The satellites seeded around both planets were accessible by all units including the admiral, but the view seemed little different from Gina's previous access during the briefing.

*Enlarge grid G-five.*

Grid G-five contained the largest building, which was her platoon's designated target. Second Platoon was tasked with setting and holding a safe perimeter for Viper-Two to land in. Viper-Two was carrying Third and Fourth Platoons, along with Alpha Company's supplies. It was vital to the mission.

Gina studied the structure with an eye toward finding Merki heavy weapon emplacements. It would be ideal from their perspective, but if they had such things on planet, she was so far unable to find them. The wreckage of two landers was clearly visible in the open area behind the terminal. The General had asked for, and received, multiple air strikes on those ships yesterday to take out any anti-ship weapons they may have had. Nothing remained of them but scrap.

Gina studied the terminal building, but she found nothing to suggest the enemy were even in possession of it, let alone finding heavy weapon emplacements. She doubted they had abandoned the port without a fight. They were there somewhere. The earthworks and trenches they dug at the perimeter of the port were teeming with them, but that was Captain Hames' concern not hers. Her platoon's mission was to take and hold the northernmost building, and that's what she was going to do.

"ETA one minute. One minute to landing," the pilot announced.

Gina gave another mental command, and her targeting display replaced the satellite imagery. She slapped her harness release, and pulled herself to her feet. The buffeting and turbulence threatened to throw her to the deck, but her enhanced muscles were enough to anchor her to the handgrip beside the ramp controls.

"Thirty seconds," she shouted. "Sensors up!"

Viper-One landed hard and fast with the landing struts slamming down on the pad. The struts were still recoiling on their dampers when Scorpion Wing flew overhead. Explosions shook the air as the fighters fired their guns into the buildings designated as hangars by the General. Flashes of light lit the predawn sky as Merki anti aircraft batteries revealed themselves and fired, trying in vain to track the speeding fighters.

Gina dashed down the ramp, and hit the dirt scanning for hostiles. Her platoon fanned out to protect the transport as Second Platoon debarked and took its place. Red icons began populating her display as her sensors found the Merki troopers.

"Hostiles detected," she said calmly, using her platoon's all-units channel. "Merki in the target building. First and second squads, clear them out. Third and fourth in support."

She stood and sprinted away. The transport lifted and went to max thrust just metres from the ground. She felt the pressure wave at her back, but ignored it as she opened fire on a large shadow that her target recognition software (TRS) designated as a Merki female. The target was blasted back, and she wasn't getting back up. Gina charged forward, leaping over the still twitching corpse. The roar of fighters overhead almost drowned out the sound of booted feet running beside her. The others were keeping pace.

Cragg went to one knee, and Takeri covered him. He targeted an interceptor pursuing an Alliance fighter. Merki interceptors were fast and manoeuvrable fighters. No one wanted one chasing them. The Alliance ship was jinking and trying to shake its pursuer off, but it was stubborn. It wasn't letting go. Cragg pressed the commit button on his rig, and the missile roared away to chase its prey. Ten seconds later, it detonated in the exhaust of the interceptor, and the ship spiralled down onto the taxiway. The explosion was intense, with a ball of fire climbing into the sky. An Alliance fighter flew through the fireball to launch its own missiles at an anti aircraft emplacement that had revealed itself on the roof of a building. It missed badly, and was hit on the starboard wing. It gamely clawed for altitude, but just as it appeared to be safe from danger, the pilot ejected, and his ship detonated in spectacular fashion.

A flash of light to Gina's right was the only warning she had. She threw herself flat, but she wasn't the target. Gordon was. He was struck full in the chest and hurled onto his back.

"Zack!" Cragg shouted and returned fire. The Merki trooper went down as Takeri added her own vengeance to his.

"I'm okay," Gordon mumbled. "I'm okay… am I okay?"

Takeri checked him out. His armour was scarred, but not penetrated. "You're okay. On your feet, soldier. We've got a job to do." She pulled him up.

Gina ducked as a Merki blaster tracked her and fired. She went to one knee, her display pulsed red, and she fired in the space of a single heartbeat. The trooper went down to stay. Ian Hiller stayed standing and fired at full auto as a squad of Merkiaari charged from one of the hangars. Together with Takeri, Gina added her weight to his fire. The troopers took a lot of punishment before they went down.

Gina quickly reloaded and moved out again.

The sky rained debris as more fighters howled overhead. An interceptor died here, an Alliance fighter there. Over it all, the battle chatter of Gina's platoon sounded over her helmet comm and TacNet both. She ducked as a fighter skimmed the ground, and ploughed into the hangar wall. It exploded. The night was lit as bright as day for an instant, and then plunged back into darkness. The flyboys were taking heavy casualties from the batteries located on the roofs of the buildings. She had to knock them out fast.

*Engage light amplification mode.*

Gina carefully entered the terminal building's ground floor as the fighters screamed overhead, and blasted their targets a second time for good measure. Anti-aircraft fire was suddenly cut in half, as a huge explosion announced the deployment of hornet missiles. Flyboys always did like overkill.

Gina's light amplification gave her world a monochrome cast. Her Marine helmet used to do the same, and it was somehow comforting to her. With her back against a convenient wall, she checked her sensors and waved First Squad down the right hand corridor. She added Second Squad as backup. Third squad came up and she deployed it to the left where her sensors reported the enemy moving this way.

"Alpha Four-One, Alpha One," Gina whispered, not wanting to be heard as she watched Rob Maxwell warily lead his squad down the left corridor.

"Alpha Four-One, go," Higgins whispered in reply.

"John, you and yours with me up the ramp."

"Copy."

With her sensors probing ahead, Gina ran up the winding ramp. The natives didn't use stairs. It had something to do with the way their legs worked. Halfway up, she braced her back into the corner created by a convenient alcove. She covered the next section of ramp, while Sergeant Higgins sent three units ahead to sandwich her between the two halves of Fourth Squad. She moved up when Corporal Roberts waved all clear, and stepped onto the second floor. Her sensors insisted there was a large enemy force on this level somewhere ahead.

She found them.

Gina hit the deck and fired in one motion as a Merki squad charged her position. Fourth Squad opened up, and blew them into next year, but they didn't have it all their own way. More fire came from the opposite direction. The corridor ran the entire length of the building, and the dead troopers were at the closer end. Sensors reported no live hostiles there, but in the other direction, there were more than enough to go around as the hail of slugs testified.

Gina rolled to the side and pressed herself into the corner trying to make herself as small a target as possible. Slugs hammered the walls, and debris rained down on her. On the level below, she could hear first and second squads hammering the enemy, punctuated by the thuds of grenades. Thinking that a wonderful idea, she jacked the slide of enade launcher, and fired once then a second time for good ...asure.

*WHUMP! WHUMP!*

The explosions took out a large section of wall and flooring, but fire didn't appear to be a problem. The attack was blunted but not stopped. Intermittent fire still came from the Merki troopers, but they couldn't advance. They would have to find another route around the destroyed section, or chance leaping over it. Gina waited, willing them to try it; they would have to give up their cover, but they didn't risk it. She watched her sensors as half of them pulled back heading for a corridor to bypass the damaged section.

Gina waited until she was positive before giving her orders. "John, two units to clear the room on the left, another two on the right. The rest up the corridor to the next intersection. I want that branch in my hands ASAP. Move out."

"Copy that," Higgins replied.

According to sensors, Gina could work her way around the enemy on this level by using that branch, but they were obviously aware of it. The force they had left behind laid down heavy fire, both slugs and plasma, which was ripping the building to pieces, but had so far failed to stop her people. She vowed it wouldn't.

The room on the left succumbed to a pair of grenades pitched underhanded through the door, but the one on the right caused Gina's first serious casualty. Corporal Roberts threw a grenade into the room, only to have it appear back out of the door when it bounced off a Merki trooper's chest. She yelled and sprang away.

*WHUMP!*

The explosion was close, and Chris went down. Gina killed the trooper herself, and barrelled into the room to blast everything in sight on full auto. The computers died under her fire, and the windows did also, but there weren't any Merkiaari to receive her anger. She quickly went back to check on her friend.

"How is she?" Gina said, not noticing in the heat of battle that Chris' icon was blinking on and off on her sensors, indicating a unit down awaiting pickup.

"Dead," Higgins said coldly, and moved off to see to his squad.

*Dead! But she was a viper...*

Gina knelt to make certain, but there was no point in querying Chris' wristcomp. The back of her head and neck had taken the brunt of the blast. Her head was almost severed. Gina stared sadly into her friend's empty eyes for a long moment and then reached over to close them. She turned resolutely back to business.

The intersection was in Gina's hands in short order. She sent half of Fourth Squad, led by Higgins, to check the rooms while she held the Merkiaari bottled up.

"Alpha One, Alpha Three-One," Sergeant Maxwell said over the comm.

"Alpha One. Go," Gina replied.

"Section secured. No casualties."

"Good. Move up and cover the third level. Do not, repeat *do not* move in without support."

"Copy, we're moving."

Gina changed channels. "Alpha One-One, Alpha One, report."

"Alpha One-One," Hiller replied. "Most of our section is clear, but I have stiff resistance from two squads holding some kind of control centre."

"A control centre?"

"Looks like it. Lots of controls. I swear one of them looks like a fold space navigation board, like on a ship."

"That doesn't make sense."

"Yeah I know—"

"*Break, break,*" the General interrupted. "That board is a Merki comm station. Seize it or destroy it immediately. Top priority. No one is to get within reach of it."

"Understood—" Gina began to say but Hiller broke in.

"Sorry, sir," Hiller said. "I just killed the operator myself, but he was already doing something with it when we went in."

"Understood," Burgton said grimly. "Blow the damn thing and every Merkiaari you find off the planet."

"Yes, sir," Hiller said.

"Understood, sir." Gina went back to what she was doing. "Alpha Two-One, report status."

"Alpha Two-One. In support of First Squad, no casualties."

"Can First Squad finish up alone?"

There was the barest hesitation as Wevers sought Hiller's opinion. "Affirmative."

Gina nodded, expecting nothing less. "I want you to help Third Squad, Gwen. Clear the third level and check out the roof. As soon as you can, I want a fire team set up on the south side to cover the LZ."

"Copy that, moving now."

Satisfied that all was well, Gina advanced down her own corridor shooting everything that moved. She was hit in the chest, and was staggered, but her armour reacted instantly and wasn't penetrated. She blasted the culprit with almost a full magazine. She dropped the spent one, slapped a fresh one into her rifle, and kicked a door open to empty it into the snarling faces of a pair of troopers attempting to break through the connecting wall. Farther along, she heard multiple explosions as grenades took out the last few troopers hiding in the second corridor, and that was followed by rapid fire from the second half of Fourth Squad just now completing their sweep. Her sensors detected movement; she spun to her right as a huge form slammed into her. She lost her rifle as a Merki male crushed her in a bear hug trying to break her back. She pushed back, and managed to free an arm.

"Let go you fucker," she snarled in the monster's face and chopped at his neck.

He grunted as her enhanced strength beat him to his knees, but he wasn't ready to let go. Gina smashed her fist into his face repeatedly. He didn't like that and bit her hand.

"Need some help?" Higgins asked casually as he rounded the corner.

"Nah, I've got him." Gina shoved her hand down the monster's throat, only to rip it out sideways a moment later.

"Ouch," Higgins said. He skipped back from a fountain of blood as the huge monster went into shrieking convulsions.

"Phaw!" Gina shook her hand free of blood and slobber. "God that's disgusting." She tried not to smell it, and shook the worst of the goo off her hand.

Higgins casually pressed the muzzle of his rifle against the dying monster's head and pulled the trigger.

Gina took her rifle back from him. "Thanks. Second floor clear?"

"All done. I have one dead and two wounded."

"How bad?"

"Your hand, my leg, both slight."

A few tooth marks were nothing, and John was still mobile even with blood showing. Their bots would see to both injuries without needing help.

"Alpha One, Alpha One-One," Hiller said over the comm.

Gina finished cleaning the goo off her hand and replied, "Alpha One. Go ahead."

"All clear. Comm station destroyed as ordered."

"Good, Ian. How do things look outside?"

"Pretty peaceful. The sun's just coming up. Not much happening on this side."

Gina nodded in satisfaction. "Okay. Hold the ground floor in case we have visitors."

"Copy that."

She turned to Higgins. "Collect your boys, John. I want to have a look up top."

Higgins nodded and spoke quietly over his comm as they walked back toward the ramp through the mess they had made.

Gina selected a channel and contacted Second Squad. "Alpha Two-One, Alpha One. Report."

"Alpha Two-One. Third floor just about… Third floor now clear. Third Squad on the roof."

"Okay, Gwen," she said pleased with their progress. "Get up there and set your fire teams to cover the LZ. I'm on my way up."

"Copy."

Higgins was waiting for her at the ramp.

"John, I want you to go down and sweep the grounds around the building. After that, send a couple of your boys back to the LZ for a quick resupply, and then take defensive positions. Have a word with Ian about coordinating a decent defence… just in case."

Higgins nodded once, and led his men down the ramp while Gina went up to the roof.

Gina stepped out into the open, and took a deep lungful of the bracing air before looking about herself. Gwen had positioned three spotter/shooter teams along the south side of the roof to cover the LZ and its approaches, but she hadn't neglected the other sides. Third squad was helping her people watch the north and west sides. The east was deemed of lesser risk. According to satellite surveillance, the area had been extensively cultivated, but very few people lived on those huge automated farms. It was of no interest to the enemy.

Gina crossed to the south side of the roof, and nodded to the others. "Anything interesting, Gwen?"

"Captain Hames is ripping them up."

Gina commanded her processor to magnify the scene before her, and X4 strobed on her display. The battlefield rushed closer, and she watched the show. The enemy was dug in pretty good and they were holding for the moment. Captain Hames had positioned his AARs on the wings of his formation and they were strafing the enemy lines on a diagonal. The mortars and grenade launchers were popping their rounds among the Merki troops with frightening accuracy, but they simply stayed put and soaked up punishment.

As yet, only two of the regiment's APCs were down. They had been deployed to help cover the LZ. Hames had a while to wait yet before he could call on artillery. The regiment's self-propelled guns were heavy ordnance, and could only be loaded aboard the landers one at a time. *Grafton* had only two *Wolfcubs,* and they were currently ferrying the APCs filled to the brim with ammo and grenades.

From the west, a wing of fighters screamed by the terminal

building, low enough for Gina to make out the pilots. In a widely spread formation, they strafed the Merkiaari with their guns before climbing steeply. The sonic boom of six SPAF-18 Nighthawks echoed in the cool morning air as they clawed for altitude.

Wevers shook her head. "They missed the damn mines. Flyboys... " her lip curled in disgust. "They can't wait to kick arse."

Gina nodded thoughtfully, and wondered what the General thought about it. She was willing to bet he was not happy. "The mines are stopping us from pushing them completely out of the port. The General will be coming down soon. We need to clear the area and access the city before then."

"We could go and help."

Gina nodded. "I'll ask."

* * *

The ground erupted and showered Kate with soil. The damn flyboys had screwed up and left her arse flapping in the wind. Captain Hames seemed to agree. He spat dirt, and propped himself up on his elbows to evaluate the strike. It was obvious he didn't like what he was seeing.

Hames scowled and turned to give his orders. "Richmond—" his eyes went wide, and he slumped forward as the gauss slug sheared through his helmet.

Kate wiped grey and red gunk off her helmet's visor with a shaking hand. Keeping low, she dragged the captain's body down from the lip of the crater. She checked his vitals as a matter of course, but she didn't need the flat line on his wristcomp to tell he was gone. She glanced around at the others trying to ignore the blinking blue icon on her sensors, but none of them had seen Hames go down. They were busy taking pot-shots at the enemy, completely oblivious to the disaster that had befallen one Lieutenant Richmond. She looked back at her captain for a long moment and shivered. This was not good, not good at all. Hames was, *had been*, the only veteran assigned to Alpha Company. Only he knew what he'd planned to do next. The General's plan was screwed to hell and gone, and the goddamn flyboys hadn't done their jobs...

Kate swallowed her incipient panic and took a deep breath. Okay... okay all right. She didn't need a damn officer to tell her what needed doing, not even one as good as Hames had been. She could handle it. She *would* handle it.

She selected a channel, and took a deep breath. "Gold One, Charlie One."

"Burgton, Charlie One. Go."

"Sir. I have a situation here. Captain Hames is dead, sir. Orders?"

There was a long silence, but then, "Richard is... Hames is dead you say? You're sure?"

"Positive, sir," Kate said looking into Hames' dead eyes. "I believe he was about to order another air-strike. At least that's what I'd like to think he was going to do. Are you monitoring our situation?"

"Affirmative," Burgton said. "They have you pinned."

"Exactly right, sir. They have us pinned down, but we have them pinned down too. It's a stalemate, sir."

"Not acceptable," Burgton said coldly.

"No, sir, I agree. We need those mines cleared."

"Katherine, here is what you will do. First of all, call the other platoon leaders and inform them of the situation. Secondly, hand over command of your platoon to Brice. He can handle it... you agree?"

Kate nodded to herself. "Yes, sir, Martin would be my choice. He knows what to do."

"Good. I'm raising you to temporary command of Alpha Company effective immediately."

Her mouth went dry. "Yes, sir, I understand."

"Order your strike, Captain. Gold One clear."

"Charlie... *Alpha Leader* clear," she said feeling almost dizzy.

Burgton wouldn't make her elevation permanent would he? He wouldn't do that to her... would he? Kate shook her head and got to work. She couldn't worry about it now. She called Brice and Dengler in to inform them about Hames' death, and the General's response to it. Brice was unconcerned about his promotion to command Third Platoon. He was more than competent.

Dengler frowned at Hames' corpse and then at Kate. "You gonna order another strike?"

"Yeah." Kate changed channels. "Jaguar Leader, Alpha Leader, come in."

"Copy, Alpha Leader."

"Jaguar Leader, you missed."

"Come again?" Jaguar Leader said in surprise. "Er, I mean repeat please, Alpha Leader."

"The minefield is still here, Jaguar Leader. I want it *gone!* The Merkiaari are not your target, what do you think I'm here for? Now listen: I want another run to take out those mines. If I don't get it, I'm coming up there, and taking it out of your hide, *personally!*"

"Jaguar Leader copies," the pilot said stiffly.

Kate waited for the strike while her people used the mortars to keep the enemy's heads down, and the AARs to kill any that popped up for a look see. There weren't many of the latter, not after the first few times.

"We should have landed a squad on the other side," Dengler mused.

"No. The city is infested with Merki infantry. Vipers we may be, but we're not invincible." Kate nodded at Hames as proof. "Landing between two forces is not a good idea."

"Maybe we should wait for Arty."

Kate shook her head. When she had mentioned the possibility earlier, Hames told her the guns would take hours to get here. She wanted this over long before then. There was no way she would be responsible for the General landing in the middle of a battle.

"Alpha Leader, Alpha One," Fuentez said over the comm.

"Alpha Leader. Go." Kate ducked again as a persistent trooper popped up and fired at her.

"The terminal building is secure, and Second Platoon holds the LZ. All hostiles eliminated, but I lost a man."

*Shit.* "Who?"

"Chrissie Roberts."

Ah hell, why did it have to be Chris? They had been so damn lucky so far, and now this. Perhaps it wasn't so surprising they had another casualty, not when considering the opposition they were facing. It was a damn shame, but people died in war.

"Copy that, Gina. I want you to hold the terminal and keep an eye on the satellite feeds—especially over the city. Sing out if you see something I should know."

"Copy that, but I could come over and support your right…"

"Negative, Alpha One. Sit tight and wait for the General."

"Copy, holding position."

Kate watched as the fighters bore in. This time they attacked the correct target and the minefield erupted.

*WHUMP! WHUMP! WHUMP! WHUMP! WHUMP! WHUMP!*

She nodded in satisfaction as a path three hundred metres wide was blasted through the minefield all the way to, and through, the Merki's lines.

"Alpha Leader, Jaguar Leader."

"Copy, Jaguar Leader," Kate replied.

"Returning to rearm. Jaguar Leader out."

"She's in a bit of a snit isn't she?" Brice said.

"Too damn bad," Kate said, and answered the call. "Alpha Leader copies." She turned back to business. "On my signal, clear?"

Brice and Dengler nodded, and ran in a crouch to rejoin their platoons. Moments later the mortars and grenade launchers left off their methodical attack to go to rapid fire. The AARs laid down covering fire as both platoons moved up ready for her signal.

"Go," Kate said simply and ran forward.

The enemy stayed down at first, but one brave troop must have poked his head up long enough to realise they were coming, because suddenly the entire Merki force opened up. Kate sprinted at full speed jinking left and right to avoid being hit. She leapt into a convenient crater, and then jumped out and ran forward to dive head first into another one.

"This will do nicely," Kate murmured to herself and raised her rifle. "Hmmm, where are you? Ah…"

She squeezed the trigger and took the top of a Merki's head off. Her targeting reticule hesitated a second, and then tentatively settled on another target, this time the barrel of a plasma cannon. She dropped onto the target and fired a three round burst and watched the cannon explode into its operator's face.

Kate chuckled. "Lovely."

Looking around, she found her people moving from crater to crater, closer and closer. Time to move up again. She crawled out then sprinted forward a few yards. The first she knew she was hit was when she fell face first into a crater. She grunted as the air was blasted from her lungs, but the fact it hurt was reassuring. If it hurt, then she must be alive. She realised her armour was cracked over her ribs, and that her damage indicator was blinking pale yellow over her left side. It hurt like a sonofabitch, but it was nothing to worry about. No doubt she would sport one hell of a bruise tomorrow. She leapt out of her crater into the next one.

"Now then, what's the range?" Kate checked her range finder. "One hundred?" She poked her head up for a better look, and ducked as the rim of the crater eroded from incoming fire. "Yep, one hundred. Delta One, Alpha Leader. Report status."

"Delta One," Lieutenant Dengler answered in a distracted tone of voice. "Still moving forward. I make it two hundred metres to target."

"Copy that. I'm at one hundred. Move up in line, and call off the barrage in exactly five minutes… *mark.*"

"Copy."

Kate looked to her left but couldn't see Brice. "Charlie One, Alpha Leader. Report status."

"Charlie One. I'm bogged down," Brice said.

"How far back?"

"Three hundred metres."

"Three hundred is unacceptable, Lieutenant," she said knowing that Brice wouldn't like that. "Move your people up. In exactly four minutes, the barrage will lift and we go in. *Be there.*"

There was silence for a few moments. "Copy."

Exactly four minutes later, Kate ran forward at top speed hearing the last grenades and mortars detonating ahead. It was a relief. She would really hate it if her own launchers killed her. She grinned into the wind, and fired at the Merki troopers in front of her. Both males went down as she jumped into their foxhole.

"Woof!" Kate was body checked by a trooper before she could fire. He began to throttle her.

She had a flashback of the simulation back at Alliance HQ for an instant, but this time she didn't mess about. Her rifle came up in her right hand, and she selected full auto even as she pulled the trigger. She staggered back from the collapsing monster, drenched in alien blood, and reloaded her rifle.

One of her men jumped into her foxhole, and immediately swung left to fire along the enemy lines. Thinking that a fine idea, Kate did the same on the right before climbing out and heading for the next position. With her sensors sweeping ahead of her, and her targeting software locking up one Merki trooper after another, she became a walking killing machine. The next enemy position appeared before her, and a grenade arrived in her hand as if by magic.

"One... two—"

*WHUMP!*

"Three." Kate grinned and dropped into the foxhole already firing. She stared at the corpses, and shook her head. "Waste of ammo." She climbed out looking for something else to kill.

All along the Merkiaari lines, her sensors reported blue viper icons swarming over, and slaying, the glaring red ones denoting enemy troops. She found herself too far away to do any good, and watched the red lights wink out one after another without firing a shot. With nothing else to do, she called for satellite imagery of the battlefield.

*Access satellite Sierra Zero One. Enlarge sector G-five.*

Everything looked quiet now. The satellite showed the port facilities and the surrounding area. The hangars were still burning, and she could see activity on the roof of the terminal building, which had gaping holes in the walls and many windows broken or missing. Fuentez had set up a squad on the roof to overlook the LZ, and another was patrolling the grounds around the building.

*Centre grid G-six.*

The image was replaced with another showing Zuleika. The city seemed quiet, too quiet. There was no obvious enemy activity, but

Kate knew they were there. The General said the control room found by Fuentez's First Squad, was some kind of communications centre. She could expect to receive another attack at almost any time.

"Alpha Leader, Charlie One," Brice said over the comm.

Kate ordered her processor to clear the image. As the view of the city disappeared to be replaced by her targeting display, she began making her way back toward the LZ.

"Alpha Leader. Go," Kate said as she crossed what had been the Merki line of defence.

"Sector secure, no casualties."

"Copy that. Set the perimeter alarms and move the launchers into the dugouts. We might be receiving company from the city."

"Copy Alpha Leader."

"Alpha Leader, Delta One," Dengler said making her report.

"Go," Kate answered.

"Sector secure. No casualties."

"Copy that. Set up your spy eyes, Erma, and bring the mortars into position. Send someone back to Viper-One to re-supply your platoon."

"Copy that."

Kate contacted Brice again to order a similar resupply for his platoon. She didn't tell Fuentez to do the same; there was no point. Her friend would have seen the need, and already have done it. Kate decided it was time to give the General a sitrep.

"Gold One, Alpha Leader."

"Report," Burgton said instantly.

"Spaceport secured, sir. No activity from the city as yet, but I've ordered alarms set to give warning, and a defensive perimeter is now in place. You may make your landing at your convenience, General."

"Outstanding Katherine. Casualties?"

"Captain Hames and one other, sir. Chrissie Roberts bought it."

Burgton sighed. "Copy that, Katherine. Meet me at the LZ."

"Will do, sir. Alpha Leader out."

"Gold One out."

* * *

# 25 ~ Resistance

James searched the empty sky for the source of the sound. Thunder? No, it was getting louder. Shima pointed behind him and he turned in time to see a pair of Nighthawks fly subsonic over the outskirts of the port. He flinched as the fighters accelerated through the sound barrier, the sonic boom echoing over the busy port as they climbed steeply. He watched the neon blue light of their twin afterburners until he lost them to distance.

"Professor Wilder?"

James recognised the black battle dress uniform of a viper Colonel. "Yes, sir," he said to the approaching man, coming to a rough attention.

"Let me introduce myself, Professor. I'm Colonel Flowers, Regimental Exec." Flowers smiled and shook hands. "Call me Dan if you like. And who is your companion?"

"Colonel, this is Shima." James turned and translated for his friend. "Shima, this man is a Tei among the vipers. His name is Dan."

"But James," Shima protested. "You have told me of the shock troops called vipers. You said the Alliance had no more."

"It seems I was mistaken my friend, and thank the harmonies I was."

"Tei'Dan, I... *pleased* am you here are," Shima said in halting English and held up a paw.

"Like a handshake, sir," James explained. "Press your right palm to hers for a few moments."

Flowers did so without hesitation.

"I greet you, Shima. May you live in harmony," Flowers said in passable Shan, and James grunted in surprise. "I'm glad to finally meet one of your people face to face. Tei'Varyk's brief went a long way to help us, but there's nothing like the personal touch."

"Colonel, if I might ask," James said. "How is it you speak Shan so well?"

Flowers smiled ruefully. "Not so well, as you no doubt noticed, Professor, but good enough for now. My men and I uploaded the language on our way here."

He nodded, intrigued by the idea that Binder's translation could be used by a viper's internal computer system. It would be like having a built in translator.

"You said Varyk is alive?"

Flowers nodded. "Very much so. *Canada* picked him up from the wreckage of his ship. He was instrumental in arranging our presence here."

"And Tarjei?"

"His mate?"

James nodded.

"She's well. Tei'Varyk and the remnants of his crew received nano treatment before reaching Earth. There was some concern over cross-species infection I understand, but *Canada's* surgeon took care of it."

"That's great. I barely had time to get to know them both. They were the first Shan I ever met. I'm glad they survived."

James quickly translated for Shima. She was delighted and spoke rapidly to the others to tell them the good news. He listed for a moment before turning back to address the reason for his presence at the spaceport.

"I know you've seen some fighting here, Colonel, but I have to warn you that the Merkiaari here are nothing compared with the new troops in the city."

"New troops?" Flowers said with a frown. "I don't believe I understand, Professor."

"Call me James. My friends and I have been fighting here for months. The new troopers are extremely hard to kill, sir. They fight smarter than those you fought before. They have learned a lot from their previous defeat, Colonel. Too much for my peace of mind."

"Come with me. The General needs to hear this."

"But my men," James said glancing back at what was left of Zuleika's resistance movement. There were perhaps three hundred bedraggled people gaping at their surroundings, and flinching as the fighters screamed overhead on their way to bomb the known Merki infestations.

Flowers' expression softened. "I'll assign you a couple of men. Take a half hour to get them settled and fed."

"*Weapons* Colonel, we need *weapons*. Our cell charger is in the city and what we have with us won't last long."

"We'll discuss that later. For now, get them bedded down in the east wing. I'll come get you when the General has time for you."

James would have protested, but what was the point? He was in the presence of one of the Alliance's greatest heroes as well as in the middle of a camp full of its elite troops. He nodded slowly and turned back to explain to his people.

A few hours later, James was sitting at a table in a large room on the terminal building's ground floor. Burgton was there along with his officers. Flowers was sitting next to the General, and both had worried faces. He didn't blame them. He had learned since his arrival that there was only a single battalion of vipers in the system. Worse than that, they represented every combat capable viper the Alliance had available. Shima and James' team leaders sat with him. He had explained that he wanted them nearby to back him up, and would go over what was said after the meeting. Their English was still too poor to make understanding easy, but he felt better facing so many vipers with a few of his own men with him.

"Firstly," Burgton began. "I am ordered to offer you a ride up to *Victorious* to rejoin the rest of the contact team, but I don't think you'll take it. Will you?"

"No," James said without hesitation. "I have responsibilities here."

"He is our Tei," Shima said in heavily accented English, but the words were understandable.

Burgton nodded. "As I thought. Now that's out of the way, let us get down to business. Dan has briefed me on your claims—"

"Not claims, *facts*," James interrupted.

"*Claims*," Burgton said firmly. "They are claims until one of my people examines an example of your new Merki troopers. Having said that however, we will proceed on the assumption that they are indeed something new. Caution costs little. I need everything you have regarding them, Professor."

James nodded. He was relieved that Burgton was willing to listen. He interlocked his fingers, and leaned forward intently.

"I don't know if you know this, but one of my fields is history. I assure you that I know what I'm talking about, General. The troops you fought were tough, there's no disputing that, but they were also stupid. You agree?"

Burgton smiled. "Up to a point, yes. The females always seemed more intelligent. The males were never deep thinkers. They were unsound tactically, and needed close supervision and guidance. We used that to our advantage time and again."

James nodded. "We've always known they breed for certain traits, General. Unlike the Shan caste system—which I have come to admire the more I learn of it by the way—the Merkiaari system is rigid with well-drawn boundaries. The fighting males and females are bred for strength and endurance. Their commanders are bred for speed and intelligence; that's why they're generally smaller."

"But you say things have changed?"

"They have, General, that they have. They have learned that strong but stupid soldiers are a liability when fighting people like us. Killing the leaders no longer confuses them. I've put this to the test many times, General. Kill a patrol leader, and before he hits the ground, another trooper will have taken his place and given new orders. Not only are they more intelligent, they're just as strong as they ever were. Worse, I've seen them heal from wounds that should have killed them."

"Regenerating you said," Flowers put in.

James nodded. "They keep fighting despite unbelievable wounds, and if they don't die immediately, they regenerate very quickly."

"Nanotech?" Burgton asked uneasily.

James shrugged. "Their version perhaps, or something we've never heard of. It doesn't matter."

Burgton pursed his lips. "No, I suppose not. We had considered sending two companies to Harmony, but I think all four will be needed here."

"I think you're right, General, but what of the people living on Harmony?"

"I'm afraid there aren't many left—at least not out in the open. The Keeps are shielded from our sensors, so we can't know how many may be inside, but I'm sure there must be a great many survivors. "

"But you can't be sure," James said, feeling sick.

"No I can't, but I can tell you there are roughly twenty divisions of Merkiaari left on Harmony—in the region of two hundred thousand troopers, and they're scattered all over the planet. They'll not be easy to track and remove."

"Can it be done?"

Burgton nodded. "Eventually yes, but not just yet. It seems they hit Harmony first, and then moved here taking the greater portion of their forces with them. The damage is already done. We can do little to change that, so I propose to concentrate on matters here while there is still something to save."

James frowned. "I know we have no more than a single division here in Zuleika." That was an estimate based on enemy landings. He knew how many troopers were customarily transported aboard their landers. He had based his figures on that, possibly out of date, knowledge. "I only know what our couriers have managed to sneak out as far as the other cities are concerned."

Flowers nodded. "Child of Harmony has the equivalent of *thirty divisions*. That works out to roughly three hundred fists."

"*Three hundred*," James gasped. There were a thousand troopers to a Fist. That meant there was close to three hundred thousand Merkiaari on the ground.

Burgton smiled at his shock. "A planet is a big place, Professor. Three hundred fists is nothing on that scale, but it does pose us some problems."

"Problems... I should think it does!"

"Not what you're thinking, I assure you. Three hundred fists split over two main continents, the small island chains are so far untouched by the way, gives us plenty of opportunities to hurt them. We have air superiority including full satellite surveillance. We have the ability to move our forces quickly and with impunity. We have complete control of the system, and resupply from orbit is not a concern. Fifth Fleet has been alerted, and will be here in a matter of months, but in that time we should have the situation here dealt with."

James shook his head gently. "I admire your confidence, General, but I can't agree with an estimation based on old intelligence. Your information was gained two hundred years ago. Until I see Zuleika cleared, I have to doubt that you can do what you say. I'm sorry."

"Don't be sorry, Professor," Burgton said. "It could be as you say, but I choose to believe otherwise. Either way, we need to clean out the enemy from Zuleika as soon as possible. This port is mine. I'll not let them have it back. It's too important."

James nodded. "I agree."

They needed the port for the fighters to rearm and refuel. Supplies would be delivered here from orbit, and troops would embark transports here on their way to battle Merkiaari in cities thousands of kilometres away. It was the only intact port left on the planet.

"With all this in mind," Burgton went on, "I have ordered Charlie and Delta Companies down from *Grafton*. We will commence full scale operations to remove the Merki infestation of Child of Harmony at sunrise tomorrow..."

*Infestation?*

Burgton sounded like a Merki discussing the vermin they were about to exterminate. They were the enemy, true, but they weren't animals. They were thinking breathing beings, not some kind of insect to be crushed. James hoped he never viewed them in such a light.

"...and the fighters have already begun softening up the bases and outposts uncovered so far. They will continue their efforts. *Sutherland's* fighters will be on standby, and available to support us as and when necessary." Burgton glanced at the Shan and then back at James. "Ask them if they realise their city will be badly damaged."

"They won't care," James said.

"Ask them any way," Flowers said for his General.

James shrugged and turned to Shima. "Tei'Burgton wishes me to tell you that Zuleika will be badly damaged when they attack tomorrow. He wants me to ask if you realise this."

"The city is nothing," Shima said in surprise. "You should know this by now, James. The Great Harmony isn't buildings or cities; it's a way of life. As long as some of my people survive, Harmony will endure. Destroy the city, James, if that is what it takes to save my people—destroy them all."

James smiled grimly. "I do know it my friend, but these other Humans do not. I can tell you now that they will not hit the cities from orbit. It's forbidden by the Accords."

"Even when the Murderers are the only ones living there?"

"It makes no difference who the target is, Shima. When the Merki War was at its height and things became desperate, nuclear weapons were used not just in space but on captured cities as well. It doesn't matter now who began that policy, only the aftermath matters. A beautiful planet called Kushiel was invaded and its cities taken. Our forces were spread too thin. The Fleet couldn't help without risking other worlds nearby. It was decided by the people living on Kushiel, that if they couldn't win, they wouldn't let the Merkiaari win either. Mutual annihilation... you understand the concept?"

Shima's ears were tight against her skull. "I understand the words, but..."

James nodded. "I know. It's a terrible thing, but they were desperate. They thought the Merkiaari would give up and leave if they proved to them they were willing to destroy the cities themselves. They were wrong. After the first two cities were destroyed, the Merkiaari did withdraw their forces to orbit, but then they rained destruction on the planet in a nuclear bombardment that lasted many days.

"You see, Shima, they understood the concept better than we did. They destroyed every living thing on the planet in retaliation. Its atmosphere, what's left of it, is still poisonous to this day. The planet will never recover. Shortly after what happened on Kushiel became widely known, both sides stopped all use of nuclear weapons in planetary environments. In the Alliance, all members were required to sign the Accords. We don't know what the Merkiaari chose to do, but the result was the same. The Accords state that the Fleet will visit any nation or planet, making war on another in such a fashion. Its cities would be destroyed, and its population eradicated by nuclear bombardment. It has never been put to the test."

Shima's ears struggled to rise, but then flattened again. She drew in a sharp breath. "A hard thing, this Accord. Humans are a strange people, James. Your ships could devastate every city on Child of Harmony without loss, but instead you choose to fight on the ground, and will perhaps die for us."

"It's our way," James said with an apologetic smile.

"What did she say, Professor?" Burgton asked.

James had a feeling that Burgton already knew, but he played along. "She said what I expected she would say. Asking any Shan that question would receive the same response. Her answer is, and I quote: destroy every city if that is what it takes to save my people."

There was a profound silence among Burgton's men. The only sound was Shima discussing the situation quietly with the others.

"I see," Burgton said finally. "You told her about the Accords."

"I did, and she understands the reasons behind them. For my part, I believe the Accords must stand in their present form. Any weakening of the Alliance's resolve regarding orbital bombardment will lead us all to disaster."

Burgton studied James and his friends in silence, but then he said, "There will be no orbital bombardment."

There were sighs from the other officers in the room, as if the decision had been in doubt. James glanced at Flowers, but received nothing but a blank-faced stare in return.

Burgton began laying out his plans. "First Battalion will clear Zuleika, thereby safeguarding my spaceport. We will then begin the work of liberating the rest of the planet. You and your people may assist us or not as you choose, Professor, but I take no responsibility for their safety. I will not endanger my people needlessly by tasking them with your protection. I strongly suggest you leave this fight to us."

"No," James said simply.

"Fine," Burgton said, sounding not in the least surprised. "Colonel Flowers will issue you and your people with body armour and weapons that you may use. As I'm sure you're aware, viper weaponry and equipment is somewhat different to the standard

Alliance gear. We don't have much you can use, but what we have you're welcome to."

"The armour is welcome, General... if it can be modified to fit my men that is, but what we really need are power cells or the means to recharge those we have."

"We have nothing to fit those pistols of yours, Professor, but Colonel Flowers will arrange for a charging station to be modified to suit your needs. Give him the specs after this meeting."

"I will, sir, and thank you."

"Don't thank me," Burgton said without so much as a flicker of emotion. "You will likely die of my generosity."

"But still I thank you," James said, this time more solemnly.

"Two fighter wings will overfly the city at dawn tomorrow, and bomb the main concentrations of the enemy detected yesterday by satellite. That will be followed by an artillery and rocket barrage set up near the old Merki fortifications that Captain Richmond secured for us. The launchers and artillery pieces are being off loaded for that as we speak. Alpha and Bravo will attack from the north simultaneously, while Charlie and Delta will swing wide and come in from the west and east respectively." Burgton eyed James thoughtfully. "The... *resistance* will tag along with Alpha and Bravo, which will carry the brunt of the attack until Charlie and Delta can flank the Merkiaari. If all goes well, tomorrow evening should see us mopping-up stragglers. Questions?"

"Yes, sir," Captain Richmond said. "Are you averse to my use of the APCs?"

"Not specifically, but they have yet to be dropped to us and may not be down for the attack."

"What about a couple of platoons using mechs?"

Burgton frowned. "To blunt their initial response?"

"Exactly, sir. I would issue one platoon from Alpha and one from Bravo with mech armour to act as a forward recon. They may even be able to direct a fire mission or two."

"Spotters eh?" Burgton nodded thoughtfully. "Very well, Captain. Two platoons deployed forward it is. Dan, contact *Grafton* and arrange an extra drop."

"Yes, sir," Flowers said and made a note on his compad.

"Anything else?"

"Yes, sir," Captain Greenwood of Charlie Company said. "Who are you planning to use to service the guns?"

"One squad from each company will do it. I had planned to leave the choice to the company commanders. Have you a preference?"

Greenwood shook his head. "No, sir, one squad from each

company is fine."

"Good. Anything else?" Burgton said, looking around the table.

There were no more questions, and the meeting adjourned. James left the room with Shima and the others, and went to inform the rest of his people about the meeting. The Colonel came in a short while later to ask for a sample power cell for the new charging station.

"Here," James said, removing a nearly spent cell from his pistol. "All Shan beamers use these."

"Fine," Flowers said. "I'll get a hurry up put on the charger."

"Can you get them to run up a couple of hundred spare cells as well?"

"Can't see why not," Flowers said, bouncing the cell on his palm. "They might not be ready soon enough though."

"The charger will do for tomorrow, but I'm sure we'll need replacement cells sometime in the next few weeks. They don't recharge forever."

"Good idea. I like forward thinking."

Flowers left and James holstered his empty beamer. "If anyone is hungry, food is being served down the hall." No one was interested. "We have a new charger on the way, and power cells to go with it. Armour will be supplied. We attack at sunrise tomorrow. The city will be ours again when it sets. My people will fight by your side to make it happen."

That got a reaction. James smiled at the howls and yips coming from his men. They were more than ready to see the murderers of their people dead.

* * *

# 26 ~ The Markan'deya

WHUMP! WHUMP! WHUMP! WHUMP! WHUMP!

Colonel Flowers watched the city erupt for the second time as more fighters flew over. The sun was just coming up, and light amplification was no longer necessary. He deselected it and viewed the city at X4. There was fire; it was to be expected, there were falling buildings, also as expected. What wasn't expected was the complete lack of return from the Merkiaari. Surely they had something to hit the fighters with? If they did there was no sign of it.

"It's time," Flowers said, and nodded to Stone.

"*Open fire!*" Stone roared at the top of his enhanced voice.

Twenty artillery pieces spoke as one on the instant, then again and again with a mere half second between firings. Rocket launchers began flushing their racks and scores of hellfire rockets flew skyward. Flowers tracked them by their vapour trails as they headed for targets in the city. More buildings were smashed. Clouds of smoke and dust billowed up and darkened the sky. The city was plunged into night by the black and stinking smoke.

"*Reload!*" Stone roared again.

Each of the self-propelled guns had a three unit team servicing it. The drivers had the least to do, but it was essential they be ready to drive in case the enemy targeted the battery. They only had so many of the guns with them, and any losses could prove devastating. The two remaining units worked the weapon itself. One man worked the controls to elevate the hot barrel a couple of degrees, while the other rushed to re-stock the gun's autoloader with three 155mm HE contact fused rounds.

"*Fire!*"

Flowers ignored the thunder of his guns, and concentrated on evaluating their effectiveness. After each firing of three rounds the guns were elevated and fired again before repeating the cycle. He watched the line of explosions advancing into the city and was pleased. His men had learned their gunnery lessons well; everything was proceeding as planned.

"*Fire!*" Stone said with metronomic precision.

Dozens, and then hundreds of buildings were smashed. There was no help for it. When this day was over the city would need extensive work, but as Wilder's people had already reminded them, killing the enemy was all that really mattered. Buildings could be replaced; lives could not.

"*Reload!*"

Flowers split his attention between his guns and TacNet. Alpha and Bravo were advancing behind the curtain of his artillery fire, and were fast approaching the cut off point. They reached it not two minutes later, and he nodded to Stone.

"*Cease firing!*"

"Now we wait," Flowers said, and Stone nodded.

\* \* \*

### The streets of Zuleika, Child of Harmony

Cragg ducked as the artillery popped three rounds into a building just ahead. He waited a few seconds in case another three were on their way, but after a moment of relative silence, he decided he was in the clear. Whoever had called in the fire mission was apparently satisfied with the results.

"Clear," he called to Hiller and dashed across the street into the building opposite.

He fired at the enemy troop in the doorway and it staggered back, but the wounds only seemed to make it mad. Cragg selected semi automatic despite the energy expenditure, and dove for the floor keeping his rifle on target. As he hit the ground, his fire finally had an effect. The trooper went to his knees snarling at the pain. In frustration, Cragg jacked his grenade launcher and fired from where he lay prone.

*WHUMP!*

He sat up amid the smoking debris, and saw a pair of legs twitching nearby. Of the rest of the enemy troop, there was no sign.

"Ground floor secure," Cragg reported over his comm, and stood to cover the ramp as the rest of First Squad burst in to join him. "I have two hostiles on the third floor, no others on sensors," he said when Hiller looked the question at him.

"These bastards are hard to kill," Gordon said kicking the severed legs. "The way we're going we'll need resupply soon."

Hiller nodded. "I've already put in a request for more grenades along with the rest of the ammo and power cells."

"Wouldn't mind a couple more railguns, Sarge," Cragg said. "They're the only things these bastards don't sneer at."

"Yeah I know. We do what we can." Hiller detailed two groups of three to take out the troopers hiding on the third floor and search the rest of the building.

Cragg stood guard at the ground floor entrance while the others cleared the upper floors. The battle was going quite well, albeit slowly, but then it should; they had all the advantages. With the navy's hotshot pilots overhead, and the Colonel's artillery ready whenever anyone called, they couldn't lose... so long as their ammunition didn't run out.

Zuleika was different to anything he had ever seen before. Unlike the Alliance, the Shan didn't like building vertically. Most of the buildings were three stories or less, and tended to sprawl over a wide area. They didn't cram them together either. Most of the building's interior spaces were below ground. Zuleika was a huge city in terms of the area it covered, but he bet it had housed less than a quarter of the population that an Alliance city of similar size would have. It must be a psychological thing, or maybe a cultural one. The natives were different in a lot of ways, not just physically. For one thing, they seemed far happier living underground than a Human would be.

Cragg checked his sensors again. Alpha Company's four platoons, with Bravo's four in support, were herding the Merkiaari to a position where they could be killed en masse. The little beggars had scattered after the flyboys bombed their positions, and were making life difficult. House to house fighting was awkward and could be costly in a city this large, but so far, his squad had suffered no casualties or injuries of note.

"Building secure," Hiller announced over the comm.

Cragg prepared to go out the door by performing a sensor sweep. He found a splash of red on his sensors as he scanned in the direction of the push, but as he called up the city map to plot the best route, another red icon caught his attention.

"Jesus," he hissed dropping to the floor, and hastily swinging his rifle back the way they had come. "Alpha One-Three, Alpha One-

One. I have Merkiaari in the street and coming this way. I would appreciate it if you would come down and join the party."

"How many?" Hiller said intently.

"A full squad and heavily armed. They must have circled around Second Squad."

"We're on the way. If you get a chance, contact Arty and call in a strike."

"Copy." With Hiller's idea fresh in his mind, he called a satellite view of the city and noted the street's location. "Alpha One-Three, fire mission."

"Alpha One-Three, Artillery Control. Say coordinates," Colonel Flowers said instantly.

"Grid G-six sub-grid Gamma-eight."

"On the way."

Cragg waited a few seconds, and then ducked as explosions dotted the street. "Artillery Control, Alpha One-Three. Right on the money, sir. Pour it on."

"Artillery Control copies."

With those simple words, the street turned into a hell of flying concrete and crashing buildings. Round after round came in and wiped the Merki squad out.

"Artillery Control, Alpha One-Three. Target destroyed."

"Copy."

A last wave of explosions erupted, adding to the destruction before relative silence fell. There were still explosions going on, indicating a firefight somewhere, but his sector was quiet and free of hostiles. As Cragg rose to his feet and began scouting the way for his squad, he absently wondered what had happened to Second Squad.

* * *

"That should damn well never have happened," Gina snarled angrily.

"Sorry, ma'am," Wevers said shamefaced. "They must have stayed low while we cleared the others out."

Gina relented a little; she always found it hard to remain angry with her people. She was too concerned with their welfare to go beyond a simple chewing out.

"We have sensors, Gwen. Use them!"

"Yes, ma'am," Wevers said, blushing in humiliation.

"On your way."

Gina watched Gwen rejoin her squad and turned back to James. He had done well so far. The resistance couldn't keep up with a viper at full speed of course, but when weight of fire came into its own,

James and his people helped supply it. He was a strange man. She watched him chatting and laughing with a Shan female in her own language, and wondered where a professor of palaeontology got the guts to face down Merkiaari. She had watched him stand with her people as the building they were in came apart around them, and fire both his beamers into the advancing troopers. Perhaps it was his knowledge of the last Merki War. He was an historian as well as a palaeontologist. Maybe he saw history repeating and wanted to help stop it. Whatever the reason, he would have made a good LT—was in fact one already, though no lieutenant she had heard of had ever commanded three hundred aliens.

"She looks embarrassed," James said, as Gina approached him.

"She should be." Gina's mood suddenly plummeted. "Merki are damn dangerous—even more so now than before. That group could have killed Hiller's entire squad."

"But they didn't," James reminded her. "Hiller saw them coming."

"Yeah. You're right. At least Hiller had someone watching the street."

"I'm sure Ms Wevers has learned her lesson."

"*Sergeant* Wevers better had. We should have the Merkiaari where we want them pretty soon."

"And where precisely is that?"

"A large structure at the centre of the city."

James nodded. "The Markan'deya. It's where Shan teach their children of the Great Harmony—like a museum."

Gina wished he hadn't told her that. The museum was unlikely to be still standing in a few hours. "The museum is central…"

"That's right. They built it at the centre of their city, as harmony is at the centre of what it is to be Shan, or rather what it *was* to be Shan."

"Professor," she said warningly. "I'm not one of your students, please don't lecture me… and don't interrupt."

James aborted what he was going to say and grinned. "Sorry."

"We're pushing them from all sides now," Gina went on, ignoring the twinkle in his eyes. "They will have no choice but to make a stand. When they do, we call in the flyboys and finish them." James remained silent and she sighed. "What do you think?"

"I think the sooner the better. The Markan'deya can be rebuilt, Gina. The city is a mess anyway. Get the damn Merkiaari off the planet so my friends can get back to living."

"I plan to," Gina said, and turned back to the war.

* * *

## The Markan'deya, Zuleika, Child of Harmony.

The Markan'deya was a huge domed building with many entrances and windows. Its natural stone facade sparkled golden in the sunlight like all the buildings, due to the heavy concentration of pyrite in the local stone, but for all of that, it was designed quite unlike any other structure in Zuleika. It was perfectly round with tall intricately carved pillars standing like sentinels either side of the entrances. The windows were tall narrow things, perhaps designed to let lots of natural sunlight into the interior. Kate liked the building's design, but the Merkiaari, damn their furry hides, were making good use of it. It was extremely hard to target them when they kept ducking out of sight. Being so narrow, the windows reduced the angle she could use to almost nothing.

Taking careful aim at a shadowy figure in a window, she fired a quick burst and watched the enemy troop stagger back. He wasn't dead worse luck. There was no way to get a good shot off, but her fire did have the effect of keeping heads down. While they were ducking fire from all sides, they couldn't be thinking about breaking out.

Kate decided it was time to find out what was causing the delay. "Gold One, Alpha Leader."

"Alpha Leader, Gold One, go," Burgton said.

"I have them bottled up in the museum, sir, but they're fighting back hard. My men are running low on power and ammo. I'm conserving what little we have left, but without re-supply we can't hold. How long before the strike?"

"Charlie Company is under heavy pressure..." Burgton began.

*Aren't we all.*

Kate ducked as a rocket flew from the window she had just fired at. The explosion shook the ground to her right, and another wall collapsed. She looked worriedly through the rising dust. Gina's platoon was in that building.

"...five minutes?" Burgton asked.

"I don't think so, sir," Kate said, as more rockets and grenades began coming out of the museum. "They've realised what we're doing. They're pushing me harder now. I don't think—"

*WHUMP! WHUMP!*

The explosions were so close that Kate was lifted from where she lay prone, and was thrown ten metres along the street. She was dazed and in pain with blood running from her nose and ears. The noise of the battle seemed far away, but at least she was alive. A diagnostic showed yellow almost everywhere, but the damage to her head was a worry. The indicator was flashing orange around her head. After querying her processor, Kate realised it was indicating a fractured skull. She tried to regain her feet, but fell almost immediately with everything spinning sickeningly around her.

She tried again, but fell over before taking two steps. Only one eye was working. All she was receiving from the right one was a rolling targeting display that gradually grew worse until it winked out. Luckily, her left eye was functioning normally. She rolled onto her belly and regained her feet with slugs from a gauss rifle kicking up the debris around her, only to fall over her own feet. It was very embarrassing. She hoped no one could see her. She dragged herself to the top of the crater, rubble rolling by as she struggled to the top. She was intending to dash back to her people, when something hit her solidly in the belly. Air blasted out of her, and she folded like a puppet with its strings cut.

Darkness washed over her, and she knew no more.

INITIALISE REBOOT SEQUENCE...
DIAGNOSTICS: UNIT UNFIT FOR DUTY.
INITIATE HIBERNATION... DONE.
ACTIVATE BEACON FOR PICKUP... DONE.
BEACON TRANSMITTING.
WARNING: HOSTILES DETECTED.
ACTIVATE COMBAT MODE... DONE.
INITIATE EMERGENCY REPAIRS... FAILED.
WARNING: IMS FAILURE. REPORT TO MEDICAL FOR FULL SYSTEM ANALYSIS.
FAULT LOGGED. CONTINUE REBOOT SEQUENCE...
TRS... DONE.
SENSORS... DONE.
TARGETING... DONE.
COMMUNICATIONS... FAILED TO INITIALISE.
RETRY/ABORT? >_
RETRY/ABORT? >_
RETRY/ABORT? >_
FAULT LOGGED. CONTINUE REBOOT SEQUENCE...
INFONET... SERVICE NOT AVAILABLE.
TACNET... FAILED TO INITIALISE.
RETRY/ABORT? >_
RETRY/ABORT? >_
RETRY/ABORT? >_
FAULT LOGGED. CONTINUE REBOOT SEQUENCE...
INITIATE EMERGENCY REACTIVATION...

Kate regained consciousness face down in the still smoking crater. She lay still and listened to the General trying to tell her something, but she couldn't understand what he wanted. His words faded in and out, and she couldn't associate them with any action needed by her. She listened and tried to understand.

*"...Leader is down! Repeat Alpha Leader is down!"* a voice cried over TacNet.

Who was Alpha Leader again? "Oh yes, that's me," she mumbled coughing up what seemed like a gallon of blood.

The pain made Kate's eyes bug, and she clutched at her belly. She felt broken armour under her fingers, and something soft and squishy pushing through it. She rolled onto her back and craned her neck trying to see what it was.

*"I'll get her,"* Fuentez said.

"No stay there," Kate hissed angrily, and tried to access the net. Her helmet was MIA with its comm, and her internal comm was out of commission too, but she still had TacNet. "Alpha Leader..." what was she going to say? "Alpha Leader to... anyone, stay away," she said, but no one heard her. She had too much damage.

*"...will follow orders. Katherine is one person, you have an entire Company to see to."*

*"But, sir!"* Fuentez said. *"I can see where she must be."*

*"You have your orders. You have command of Alpha Company for the duration. In exactly three minutes the navy is going to flatten the entire area."*

*"Yes, sir,"* Fuentez said stiffly.

Kate blinked rapidly, trying to make sense of her situation. Flatten the area... that didn't sound very good, did it?

\* \* \*

Stone listened intently, and hissed with rage when he heard the news about Richmond. He looked at the Colonel appealingly, and received a slight nod. That was all he needed.

He sprinted at max toward the burning and broken city.

Leaping rubble and craters alike, he stretched his awareness out ahead of him. He had his rifle ready in case the opportunity arose to increase his score, but Richmond was thorough. He found no sign of the enemy as he made his way through the smashed streets.

*"You have your orders,"* Burgton said. *"You have command of Alpha Company for the duration. In exactly three minutes the navy is going to flatten the entire area."*

Stone accelerated and flew over the rubble barely touching the ground. Three minutes wasn't long enough. He felt like howling in frustration, but instead he accessed a satellite in an attempt to find a quicker route.

He found one.

"*Yes, sir,*" Fuentez acknowledge the order stiffly.

Stone dashed through a building, and fired his rifle at full power into the wall before he slammed through it. His display flashed yellow on both arms, but he ignored the pain. He'd had worse. Besides, a viper could take a lot more than hitting a wall at speed. The new street was clear of obstructions, and he made up some time, but before long, it ended in another wall. He raced toward it and leapt—

—And smashed down onto the roof of a low building. He had no idea what it was for, and cared not at all. He ran and leapt onto higher roof, and then onto another using each like a set of stairs until he was close to his target. He looked down at the firefight far below and tensed. This was going to hurt big time.

Stone jumped.

* * *

Kate flinched as something smashed to the ground nearby. She thought at first that one of the flyboys had dropped a Titan on her, but there was no explosion. Instead, she heard a lot of groaning and cursing in retro. She couldn't stop herself from laughing between bouts of coughing.

"What are you doing here?" she said, as Stone dragged himself over the lip of her crater.

"I thought I'd drop in to say hello."

"Your leg…" Kate winced in sympathy. His right knee was smashed to splinters.

"It's nothing," he said, sweating as the pain threatened to break from his control. "How bad you hit?"

"Don't know. A diagnostic says I'm screwed one minute, but then it says I'm a hundred percent combat capable the next. My wristcomp is out too. I can't see out of my right eye, and when I stand up I fall over. My—" Kate hissed as the pain slammed through her again. "My belly hurts."

"Not surprised," Stone said doing something to her down below. "Half your guts are hanging out. You hit by a tank or what?"

"Gauss slug I think." Stone probed her belly with his fingers. "What you doing?" She hissed as agony blossomed. "*Fuck!* Leave it will you!"

"I've got to push it back in or I can't get you out of here, bitch-girl. Stop your whining."

"Sorry," Kate said, and panted as the pain stuttered along outraged nerves. "How are you going to do it with your leg hanging off?"

Stone grimaced. "It's not that bad."

It was, but Kate said nothing as Stone dragged her upright. She took the weight off his smashed leg so that they could move, and he held a hand over her belly to stop her insides slopping out. Kate's world became one of excruciating pain as he half dragged half carried her over the rubble-strewn streets. Splinters of concrete and brick pelted them as ricocheting slugs kicked up the debris around them. She felt like the world around her was spinning out of control, and it made her dizzy and sick. She heaved wanting to throw up her last meal pack, but all that came up was more blood. Her armour and uniform was covered in it. She fumbled at her face with a shaking hand trying to wipe her mouth, but only succeeded in smearing the disgusting stuff over her chin. Her face felt numb. She stared at her hand, and found it slick with more blood. Shouldn't her bots be taking care of that little thing?

Kate blinked dazedly around, hoping to see Gina and the others, but they must have pulled back already. That meant the strike was imminent. They would not have pulled out otherwise. She ordered her sensors to find her friends, but nothing happened. The data on her display kept insisting she was falling. She watched her altimeter spiralling down, and winced when it hit zero, but nothing happened of course. It was just her processor having a whigout.

"Where are we going?" she said, slurring the words. Her lips weren't working right. Hell, what was these days?

"God knows," Stone said as the bombers came in to drop their loads on the museum.

*WHUMP! WHUMP! WHUMP! WHUMP! WHUMP! WHUMP!*

\* \* \*

# 27 ~ Trouble at Masaru

Flight lieutenant Gary Newlove, otherwise known as Scorpion Leader, paced slowly around his ship's forward intakes, open now that she had an atmosphere to breathe again, and along the fuselage passing the one-step ladder waiting for his foot. He ducked under her starboard wing, and paused to check that her pylons were all secure. The SPAF-18 Nighthawk had four pylons, two under each wing, which could take a variety of munitions in any configuration a mission required. The Nighthawk was a very versatile craft. Fast and manoeuvrable enough to ensure air superiority against other fighters, while retaining enough spare payload to make it a very respectable bomber in its own right. His ship was currently configured for ground attack. The white tipped Hornet AG missiles were a dark menacing shadow within their launcher hanging from her inner pylon, while the fat and happy bulk of an Atlas bunker buster bomb took her outer pylon. All her munitions had the white tips indicating war shots. Red tips would have indicated this was a training mission, and incidentally would have had him screaming bloody murder, but all was fine.

Before leaving to check her portside, he grabbed the Atlas and shook it roughly. It barely moved, as it should be. If the movement had been excessive, his baby would have been down checked. The inner pylons, which were designated one and two on his weapon's consol, held the twelve shot box launchers rarely seen by anyone these days. Not counting missions here on Child of Harmony, he had used them only twice before, both times during his academy days. All cadets were expected to make at least one run over the range with them.

Pylons Three and Four were encumbered with the two Atlas bunker busters he was carrying. The Atlas was a 250kg bomb designed to penetrate hardened targets such as missile silos or reinforced bunkers. It had a destructive capability out of proportion to its seemingly small size, almost bordering on a mini-nuke in the results it could produce. He had great confidence in its ability to do the job, and in his ability to deliver it on target. He had never dropped anything bigger, though *Sutherland* did carry them among other nastier things. Nukes were never used on planetary targets of course, but again *Sutherland* did carry them.

He had heard through the grapevine that a Shan delegation in the east wing had asked that the cities be nuked, and the Merkiaari with them. That was fine by him, but Burgton had vetoed it saying it was too close to breaking the Accords. To his mind, that was a specious argument, but there were other reasons not to nuke the cities. Fallout for one thing and where would the natives live afterwards? No, on the whole he was happy with his part in the campaign.

Newlove checked his portside pylons and found all well. He walked into the open and found that his people were already climbing up into their cockpits. He was running late.

He trotted up to his bird, automatically thumping the second step cover, before climbing up and into the cockpit. He flicked the master power switch to on, and his instruments activated and calibrated themselves. His helmet went on his head, and he plugged his flight suit into the life support consol. He grunted as the suit pressurised. It squeezed as if his ship had just gone to max thrust. It lasted a moment only, and the computer beeped, indicating he had a good seal. His harness was next, and then he flicked more switches to activate the fuel pumps.

Newlove keyed his mic live. "Scorpion Leader to all Scorpions. Ready to roll?"

"Scorpion Two, all systems nominal."

"…Three ready to roll."

"…Four, affirmative, Scorpion Leader."

Newlove listened as the twelve ships of his wing reported in, but kept his eyes glued to his pressure gauge until it reached the green zone. Depressing the engine preheat button, he counted to ten under his breath, and then pressed engine start. The explosive roar of his burners punctuated the familiar whine of his two Megabyne Dynamics engines as their revs built. He watched his instruments, but all was in the green.

"Zuleika Tower, Scorpion Leader," Newlove said over the comm.

"Ready to roll."

"Roger, Scorpion Leader. You are number two for takeoff. Repeat number two."

"Roger tower, Scorpion Leader copies number two."

Hanna led the twelve ships of Jaguar wing onto the runway. They could have taken off vertically of course, but that was slower and used more fuel. There was no need for it here. One after another, the fighters accelerated hard down the runway, and leapt into the sky. Newlove watched with pleasure as they pulled into a steep climb to clear his sky. Even after all these years, it was still a thrilling sight watching the twin burners shoving a Nighthawk through six gees.

"Zuleika Tower, Scorpion Leader, rolling."

"Roger, Scorpion Leader. Good luck."

Newlove taxied onto the runway and stopped. Setting his brakes he throttled up until his baby was straining at the leash. He let her go. She mashed him into his acceleration couch as she raced down the runway, and leapt into the sky. His vision greyed as his flight suit squeezed his extremities, but that was normal. He endured, and pulled up violently into a vertical climb to two thousand metres. He levelled off, and led his wing to join Hanna's people.

"Scorpion Leader, Jaguar Leader."

"Scorpion Leader. How do you want to play this one?"

"Me first?"

"Fine by me," Newlove said. He had led the attack the last couple of times over the cities. "I'll circle around until you drop your loads, and then you do the same for me. Okay?"

"Copy that. We hit them with the hornets together from the south."

Newlove nodded; it was the best way. "Copy Jaguar Leader, you have the lead. Scorpion Leader out."

He contacted his wing and gave his orders.

Jaguar and Scorpion wings climbed to forty thousand feet where their pilots set their computers to supercruise. In supercruise mode, the pilots had little to do but monitor their instruments. Their ship's flew themselves, but after the warm welcome the Merkiaari had laid on for them on their first night on Child of Harmony, they weren't willing to relax their guard. Merki interceptors had the advantage over them. They were faster and more manoeuvrable, as some had found to their cost when they were shot down over Zuleika. The survivors didn't want a repeat performance, nor did they wish to join those who hadn't been lucky enough to eject in time. Paranoia was a hobby that veteran pilots cultivated diligently.

Flight time to the city of Masaru was a little over two hours.

The mission went according to plan. Hanna led the attack, and then played high guard while Newlove's Scorpions dropped their bomb loads on the selected targets. Flashes lit the darkened city, and buildings crashed down upon already deserted and rubble-strewn streets. Fires raged out of control and unopposed, while both wings roared away only to turn back a minute or so later to engage secondary targets with their Hornet AG missiles.

Unbeknown to Newlove and his superiors, who were even now evaluating the results of the attack real time via satellite, the Merkiaari ground forces occupying Masaru had already left the area under cover of darkness. They were many kilometres distant by the time the attack commenced.

The mission was a complete and utter failure.

"Bandits, *bandits!*" someone screamed, and Newlove's heart skipped a beat. "Many bandits bearing one-two-zero degrees, angels three-niner thousand."

"Roger. Bandits incoming one-two-zero. Scorpions break, break." Newlove pulled up hard and to the right. His vision greyed as the gee-stress built, but he was concentrating hard upon his instruments and ignored the discomfort. "Take them two against one."

They had learned not to try attacking one on one. SPAF-18s simply couldn't compete with Merki interceptors, and neither could its pilot compete with the Merkiaari pilots. It was an unpalatable truth, but they were simply better suited to withstand g-stress. They had evolved in a heavy grav environment, and could withstand faster and tighter turns. All was not lost however. Newlove's people were highly trained professionals, and had fought successfully against the Merkiaari at Zuleika and other cities over the last few weeks. The new doctrine hammered out using those experiences, paid good dividends in the opening seconds of the dogfight.

Two of the interceptors went down almost immediately under intense cannon fire, but a minute or two into this new battle, the tide turned against the Alliance. They were outnumbered three to two, but worst of all, both wings of fighters were configured for ground attack. The only weapons they had after bombing Masaru were a pair of twin barrelled railguns one on each wing. These cannons, though effective when on target, were not self-seek weapons. They relied upon the pilot's dog fighting and gunnery skills. Against so many interceptors fully armed for air-to-air combat, they had no chance.

Heat-seeking missiles criss-crossed the sky in appalling numbers. Missiles designed to memorise an enemy's radar footprint, and hunt that enemy down, locked on. Missiles that did nothing but sow the sky with electronic interference hashed the fighter's sensors. Missiles everywhere. Fighters dove and jinked trying to shake them off, but a pilot lucky enough to do so once, might immediately stray into the path of two more a moment later. Should he successfully avoid those, he might then be shot down by pulser fire from the interceptors that had managed to get behind him while he was preoccupied shaking off the missiles. Explosions pocked the sky. Engines howled, cannon fire roared, and men screamed as their ships came apart around them.

"Mayday, mayday... Scorpion Six going down," Briggs began, but a moment later his ship disintegrated, and rained burning debris down onto the trees below.

"I'm hit! Ejecting..."

"Behind you, Lou, behind you!"

"Get him off me, get him off me!"

"Eject, eject, eject... noooo!"

Newlove tried to watch for threats both to his right and his left. He tried to watch his instruments for missiles locking on. He tried to chase down an interceptor while avoiding the others of his wing engaged in their own battles. He tried to get good position and fire while glancing back over his shoulder for the reassuring sight of his wingman. Mike wasn't there. Then he was, and then he wasn't again. Mike had a missile on his tail, and he was jinking to lose it. He succeeded, but then another Nighthawk, one of Hanna's people, roared through his airspace with an interceptor on its tail, and all three collided in an eye-searing ball of light.

"Noooo," Newlove howled, as Mike's ship flipped over minus its right wing. The fighter burned spiralling out of control toward the ground. He willed his friend to eject but he was either dead or unconscious from the collision. The broken ship struck the ground in a ball of fire. "*Mike!*"

Half of the fighters sent to attack Masaru were shot down in the first three minutes of battle. Five of those twelve brave pilots ejected safely, while their comrades fought for their lives above them.

On his own now, Newlove seemed to enter another state of consciousness. His vision tunnelled, populated only by his HUD and the interceptor swooping crazily left and right up and down trying to evade him. His breathing was loud in his ears, yet he couldn't hear his ship's engines as they howled in protest. He didn't even notice the warning light that denoted an overheating engine. His fear had pushed him as far as it was possible to go. His unblinking eyes were fixed only ahead of him. They only had time for the enemy now. What was behind him was of no interest. What was to right and left was irrelevant. All that mattered was killing the enemy, even if that meant his own death.

The chase he was involved in turned to a game of cat and mouse as the interceptor dove for the deck in an effort to evade him. He followed at tree top level along a valley that ran north to south for kilometres. He had no idea where he was, and cared not at all. All that mattered was the interceptor in his gun sights. He fired and missed. Fired again. The interceptor clawed for a little altitude, and swept around in a tight turn. He fired a burst, and hit his target, but before he could fire again, the Merki pulled up into a vertical climb.

Newlove tried to follow as the interceptor pulled into an unbelievably fast and steep climb. His flight suit squeezed his legs so hard he felt in danger of being crushed. His vision greyed and dimmed. He fired as his target crossed in front of him, but he was too late. The Merki dove managing to evade his fire. He gave chase recklessly, and almost collided with the Interceptor when it decelerated hard in an attempt to get behind him. He poured fire into it, and this time the job got done. The Interceptor disintegrated into a ball of fire and debris.

"Splash one," Newlove said, and pulled up steeply looking for another target.

*Pe-peep... pe-peep... pe-peep, peep, peep, peep, peep!*

The target lock warning went frantic. Newlove went to max thrust in an effort to outrun the missile that had dropped onto his tail. Where the hell had it come from? He didn't have time to ponder. He jinked and dove, and then pushed the throttles through the stops. He couldn't shake it loose! He dove hard, and pulled into a five-gee positive turn to starboard, but the missile had him locked solid into its tiny little brain. Decoys automatically popped free from their bays in the tail of his ship in an effort to suck the missile off target, but it wasn't interested in being decoyed. Flares lit the sky, but they also failed. The missile wasn't letting go. He continued the turn, and pulled up hard. His vision greyed as the g-stress built.

*Booom!*

"I'm hit," Newlove gasped as his ship shuddered from the impact.

His ship bucked and fought him as he tried to maintain control. His display was awash with warning lights, and the air was filled with warning sirens. Number two, his starboard engine, was on fire. He used the extinguisher, but already he could feel the loss in power.

*Pe-peep... pe-peep... pe-peep, peep, peep, peep, peep!*

Newlove gaped in disbelief as another missile locked on and began homing. Where the hell were they coming from? He dove away from the new threat trying to gain time to assess the damage to his ship. He was losing power in number two, and fuel pressure was dropping. He glanced quickly over his shoulder and realised his starboard wing had been shredded.

*Booom!*

His ship shuddered again, and this time he knew it was all over.

*Beep, beep, beep...*

Flame out on number two. Newlove pulled up, desperately needing the altitude. He would surely die if he ejected so close to the ground. His ship clawed for height shaking so badly he feared it would shake itself apart.

"Mayday, mayday... Scorpion Leader going down. Position..." the stick went dead, and so did most of his displays. His ship began to roll starboard and down. "Position unknown... ejecting."

Newlove yanked the black and yellow handle between his legs. The canopy above his head blew clear, and his acceleration couch rocketed out of the cockpit. The force of his ejection must have knocked him out because when he awoke, his chute was already deployed. He drifted sedately toward the ground. The sky was utterly black. His comm was dead... of course it was dead. His ship was gone. All he heard was the whistle of the wind.

Fires raged upon the ground below. An explosion to Newlove's right had him spinning that way in an effort to see. He needed to get his bearings. He couldn't tell what had caused the eruption of flame. Maybe it was his own ship. The ball of fire had leapt skyward, but it was gone a moment later leaving nothing in its wake. A building would still be burning, but a fighter's tanks would explode exactly like that. He had seen it before.

Newlove tensed as he dipped below a hundred metres, and winced at the impact of his seat hitting the ground. He thumped his chest to release his harness, and sprinted away from the area and into dense trees. He ran blindly at first, he had no choice. It was pitch dark and he had no point of reference to get his bearings, but he had to clear the area before the Merkiaari came to investigate. His compass would put him on the right course, but should he head south now or wait where he was for rescue? With so many of the enemy in the area, all he wanted to do was hide, but that was no guarantee of safety.

He chose to head south along the valley.

\* \* \*

## APPROACHING CAMP CHARLIE EPSILON, CHILD OF HARMONY

Gina stepped off the trail to watch her people wearily trudging by in the rain. "I can't promise you hot showers," she said in halting Shan. "But there will be hot food at least."

The tired and bedraggled looking warriors raised a ragged cheer at that, but it was half-hearted at best. They were completely done in, and were marching for pride alone.

Gina felt fit to drop herself. Mud caked her legs up to her thighs, and her feet squished in her waterlogged boots. Her armour, that had looked like new a few short weeks earlier, was now scorched and battle scarred. She was soaked to the skin and chilled to the bone. Her rain cape did little to help the situation. She could only imagine what the unenhanced Shan felt like. She wasn't sure if they realised how remarkable their effort to keep up was. Did they really understand what the black battle dress uniform meant? James said they did, but she had her doubts. No unenhanced Human soldier could have kept up in such conditions, and knowing their limitations, they wouldn't have tried. Not so the Shan. After working with them the last few weeks, Gina had come to know and admire them for their courage and resilience. They didn't know what the word limitation meant.

Gina took off her helmet and raised her face skyward. The rain fell like there was no tomorrow, and the clouds looked set to stay. She swept her hair back, and let the rain wash her face. It refreshed her a little. While she stood there, the warriors continued on their weary way, following the trail blazed by Cragg and Takeri. Gina was lucky to have them. They were all that remained of Hiller's squad. Hiller himself had only recently returned to duty after a prolonged stay in sickbay aboard *Grafton*. He had been leading a patrol much like this one—though without the large number of natives that she commanded here it had been of much smaller size—when he was hit. It had been touch and go there for a while. He had been hit in the throat, and only Zack Gordon's quick thinking had saved his life.

Alpha Company was in a sorry state these days with, in some cases, squads containing only three units attached to squads containing five or six. Gina had to patch and rearranged things as best she could. Sergeant Hiller wasn't the only one who found himself assigned to another squad. Of the one hundred and sixty viper units assigned to her company at the beginning of the operation, only ninety-six remained. Thirty-six units were either dead or out of commission for the duration of the mission. Twenty-eight had been temporarily reassigned to Charlie Company as reinforcements to help replace the losses incurred at the battle of Kachina Eight. Bravo and Delta had also donated men and equipment.

The fighting within the Keep had been brutal, resulting in the worst casualties so far inflicted on the regiment. Charlie Company had been smashed with most of its officers dead or wounded together with many of its NCOs. The Colonel himself was now in direct command,

and would remain so until they left for home. The losses among the people sheltering in the Keep, had been simply catastrophic. On the plus side, the loss of Kachina Eight and its inhabitants, and the later attacks on Kachina Six and Seven had galvanised the Shan as nothing else could have. Knowing that even the Keeps were no longer safe, people numbering in the hundreds of thousands had decided to take their chances against the enemy under the open sky rather than in holes in the ground. They had boiled out of the Keeps seeking to link up with the dwindling Shan military. Alpha Company, and the other Human units on Child of Harmony, had benefited enormously when many of them decided to fight alongside Humans instead of their own people.

Gina pulled her helmet back on and watched the last of the natives trudge by followed by the rear guard. The rear guard consisted exclusively of Marines in mechanised armour. Of all those here with her, they were in the best shape. Cocooned in their mechs, they were shielded from the bad weather, and their mechanical 'muscles' took much of the strain of the long march off the Marines themselves. She had ordered them to cover her Shan warriors from the rear while her vipers did the same from the front. In that way, the weakest members of her now greatly augmented company (at least in sheer numbers) were sandwiched between professionals with high tech detection systems.

Gina watched the mechs striding by, and decided it was high time to re-take her place at the front of the march again. With her rifle angled down and safely under her rain cape, she pushed herself into a run and overtook first the Marines and then the Shan. A minute or two later, she was splashing by waterlogged vipers.

"Anything?" Gina said, slowing to march beside Sergeant Hiller.

"Cragg says all clear."

"Good. I like killing Merkiaari, but I prefer it when the sun is shining."

Hiller grinned. "Me too."

Camp Charlie Epsilon was the forward-most camp in the front line. It had been set up after the enemy declined to engage and retreated into a complex of hills and valleys where they had thus far managed to remain concealed from surveillance. Gina's patrol was one of many sent into the area looking for them.

Gina signalled the closest observation post about her intention to approach the camp, and then led her people through the fixed defences surrounding it. The bulky shapes of APCs, Shan field artillery, viper self-propelled howitzers, sentry guns, mortars, and rocket launchers came and went as they moved deeper into camp.

Gina dismissed her men to find something to eat and a long deserved rest. It would be a little while yet before she could do the same. She had to make her report first. The General's CP (command post) was basically a hole in the ground roofed over with heavy logs and sod. A lot of the camp was like that. It was hastily constructed of local materials, and wouldn't survive a direct attack by arty or aircraft, but that was why the General had the navy flying round the clock air patrols. The interdiction zone around Charlie Epsilon kept them safe from air attack, and regular patrols kept the Merkiaari at a distance on the ground. At least that was the theory.

Gina found the General in the CP standing with Commander Heinemann, Colonel Flowers, and Major Faggini, listening to a report relayed to them from orbit. They looked very grim, and Gina was unwilling to disturb them. She looked around the dim interior of the bunker for someone else to report to. She found Captain Penleigh of Delta Company and Captain Elliot of Bravo. They were standing together next to the map table that had been set up on one side of the bunker. Its glowing multi-coloured surface threw both men's features into shadow; she could not tell what they thought of the General's demeanour.

She went to join them carefully stepping over the naked power leads leading to the comm station and map table. "What's going on?"

"Trouble at Masaru," Captain Elliot said, and nodded at Heinemann where he spoke with someone on the comm.

Penleigh nodded. "Heinemann is trying to get a sitrep from *Sutherland* now, but it doesn't look good. We lost contact with all our fly boys shortly after their bomb run."

"All of them?"

Elliot nodded.

Penleigh manipulated a control on the map table, and the current view changed to the countryside surrounding Masaru. "You can see why the Merki's First Claw chose the city for his base when he pulled back from our advance. The natives stopped him cold when he tried to break west, and the mountains to the north are impassable on foot. Gravsleds don't operate well at high altitudes, and often have trouble on broken ground; especially when the slope is greater than forty or forty-five degrees."

Gina nodded remembering similar problems she and Major Stein had on manoeuvres. "The Marine's ground effect vehicles are no better."

"Agreed," Penleigh said. "That's why the regiment uses wheeled or tracked vehicles exclusively. Remember that time on Faragut?"

"God yes, what a nightmare," Elliot said, but then realised Gina didn't know the story and explained. "This happened a couple of years after the war remember. Things were still tight for a lot of people. Industries and cities had been smashed, and entire planetary populations were still on the move. On many planets, the cities were abandoned in favour of the countryside where, if you were tough and clever enough, you could survive by farming or hunting. These people had no idea how to survive cut off from the mall and their autochefs, but the only alternative was starvation. The Fleet struggled to cope. They had too few ships, too few resources to fulfil their obligations. I'm afraid the Border Worlds were left to fend for themselves for a long time. They do have some justification for their current resentment you see?

"Anyway," Elliot went on. "Fleet shipped in supplies where it could. They saved a lot of lives, but for many they were too slow. Those abandoned people had to take matters into their own hands if they were to survive. On Faragut, that meant hijacking a supply ship, which they did almost too easily. The Fleet was stretched thin, and they hadn't expected an attack by their own people. They lost not only the supply ship, but also its entire escort. We were sent in to rescue the crews of the ships, which for the most part were unharmed but imprisoned. We did that all right, but the only place not in rebel hands was a city clear across the continent through a mountain pass. We chose to load up on a bunch of hover trucks and drive there. It was a bloody disaster. We could have walked faster than those damn trucks would go over the pass."

"We did walk in the end," Penleigh said. "I spent most of my time hauling on a rope trying to stop the trucks sliding down the slope."

Elliot nodded. "I felt like a mule or something. Gawd, my back still hurts thinking about it."

Gina smiled.

Penleigh laid a hand on the glowing map table. "This is us at Charlie Epsilon." He moved his hand to another location. "This is Masaru, and *this*," he circled an area south of the city, "is where our fly boys were jumped. All twenty-four birds were shot down. We think there might be as many as ten or twelve downed pilots still alive. It's just a guess, but we heard at least that many eject. They might make it for a while."

Gina frowned at the map. "What are we going to do about it do you know?"

Penleigh shrugged. "Maybe nothing, it depends on what George decides."

"Or on what the Admiral thinks about it," Elliot added. "The thing is, the terrain is bad. You can see it on the map. There are hundreds of valleys, any one of which could be full of Merkiaari. We have no idea where the pilots are. They might be scattered over any of a dozen hills and valleys in the target area."

Gina nodded. "What about their transponders?"

"We picked them up for a few seconds after they landed, but then one by one they went off the air. Dan thinks that means they're dead, but it might simply be caution on the part of the pilots. We just don't know."

Gina pursed her lips thoughtfully, and reached for the map controls. She scrolled the map, and pointed out the valley that her patrol had just finished investigating.

"We found zip. According to this, the valley opens out a couple of klicks further on, and links up with another running north south. If we got into *that* one undetected, we could follow it almost all the way to Masaru. We would have good cover all the way."

"So would the enemy," Penleigh warned.

"Well, yes, but I'm pretty sure a small group could get in there undetected. Give me a squad of our people, and one or two of James' best scouts, and I could do it. I did something just like this a couple of years ago—an op against smugglers."

Unbeknown to her, the General had come up behind Gina while she was making her pitch. "Who would you take?"

Gina stiffened and turned to salute.

"At ease, Captain," Burgton said. "Who would you take?"

"Any one of my people could handle it, sir, but if I was given the mission, there are a few exceptional people I would take along. I would want Hiller, Cragg, and Takeri with me for certain. I would like Zack Gordon too, if Colonel Flowers could lend him back to me. Ricky Strong and Sue Lyons of Bravo Company are really good—"

"Damn, Gina!" Captain Elliot said in outrage. "They're two of my best."

"I know, that's why I want them," Gina said with a brief grin. "I want at least two of our Shan scouts. None of mine are fit to go out again so soon, but there is one I particularly remember from the fight at Zuleika."

"Oh?" Burgton said. "His name?"

"Her name was Shima, sir. She was one of Professor Wilder's team leaders."

Burgton nodded. "I remember her. She's the one with the visor."

"That's her. She has something wrong with her eyes, but it doesn't affect her work. She's a damn good fighter, and a hell of a tracker. I would take her and another tracker along. She can suggest someone."

"That's only nine."

"Sir?"

"You can have all those you named, but that's only nine including yourself." Burgton glanced at the worried looking Heinemann, and then at Colonel Flowers. "Rutledge?"

"I've got him overseeing the supply drops," Flowers said. "I think we can spare him. It would be good to have one of the veterans along."

"All our people are veterans now, but I would like David along. See to it."

Flowers nodded and went to contact Rutledge about the mission.

Burgton turned back to Gina. "Get some food and rest, Captain. It will take a few hours to assemble your team. I'll expect you back here for a briefing at… let's say fourteen-hundred."

"Thank you, sir," Gina said, and hurried outside.

\* \* \*

# 28 ~ Sacrifice

Newlove had never been more frightened than he was right now. He had thought the dogfight over Masaru was the most frightening thing ever to happen to him, but since then, he had discovered that fighting Merkiaari in the air was much preferable to fighting them on the ground. At least in the air he could see them coming. That was a hell of a lot better than the situation he was faced with now.

He was roughly a hundred metres up slope from the stream, hidden among dense trees and undergrowth. Until now he had been heading steadily south toward his own lines using the terrain to keep hidden. There had been no sign of the others sent north with him, and considering the terrain, he doubted he would find them. He could only hope they had been picked up.

Newlove kept his breathing low, and peered through the underbrush at the enemy in the valley below. He badly wanted to run away, but he couldn't. They were up to something. He wished he didn't know that, but he did. That meant it was his duty to find out what they were doing. He watched those huge monsters in their camp and loathed them. This was all their fault. If they hadn't stopped right there where he could see them, he might have been kilometres to the south by now.

With his pistol in one hand, and a ration bar from his emergency survival pack in the other, he watched them going about their business. He was fascinated when one of the monsters said something to his companions and they all laughed. Merkiaari laughing? He wondered what they found amusing. Their language was a mystery, but laughter was universal. Merki humour, the mind boggled.

The patrol eventually moved out again.

Newlove watched them until they were hard to see clearly before he dared follow. He was no match for even one of these troopers on the ground, let alone a score of them. He kept his distance. He was satisfied with catching glimpses of them moving through the trees. Had he known where he was going, he might well have discarded his plan as foolhardy and scurried over the ridge into the next valley, but he didn't know. He didn't know the Merkiaari were on the return leg of their patrol, he didn't know they were in contact with their First Claw. He hadn't thought that far ahead.

All the rest of that day, he followed them up the valley as they performed their sweep. He had a vague notion of using his transponder to lead the cavalry right to them, but first he wanted to know the location of their camp. It couldn't be too far, he reasoned. As he tried to negotiate the slippery slope, he stumbled and fell. He tumbled down the hillside, and fetched up hard against a tree. Cursing under his breath, he quickly scrambled back under cover. He was sweating and panting fearfully when he finally had time to look for the enemy. He peered ahead then moved to a better vantage.

"What the...?"

They were gone. Newlove hurried forward in a panic cursing his stupidity all the while. He had let them get too far ahead, and now he was risking detection to catch up. Fool, fool, fool! He reached the last place he had seen them, and hunkered down trying to think. They weren't in sight, and there was nowhere for them to hide. The valley was quite open along the river. They couldn't have gotten that far ahead, certainly not far enough to lose him like this. What did that leave?

Upslope?

He turned and surveyed the ground looking for signs they had gone that way. At first he despaired of finding anything, but then he remembered how big they were. He scurried upslope checking out the trees, and sighed in relief. Above his head, he could make out fresh claw marks on the bark of a tree. He could easily visualise one of the troopers slipping and grabbing the tree for balance. He had done the same hundreds of times on this journey. Checking the ground for tracks, he confirmed they had taken to the heights, but why? There was only one way to find out.

He began climbing.

Newlove hugged the dirt when he reached the crest of the ridge. He didn't want to be silhouetted against the sky for all to see. The troopers were making their way down the far side of the ridge moving rapidly and no longer interested in a stealthy patrol of the area. That said to him they were confident of their safety. They must be close to support from their own side. The problem was, he couldn't see any evidence to support that. The valley below his hiding place was a mystery to him. It was filled with so many trees that the canopy became one solid shroud hiding everything below. He watched them for a few more minutes then carefully followed them under that green blanket.

As before, he kept low moving from one patch of good cover to another, always keeping his quarry in sight. In this way he was witness to something that chilled him.

He eased himself flat to the ground, and crawled down slope until he was in danger of losing his cover. The patrol disbanded as he watched, and lost themselves among their fellows, but he didn't care about that. He had other things on his mind. For as far as he could see the valley ahead of him was filled with Merkiaari and their equipment. He counted hundreds of gravsleds sporting the ominous silhouettes of twin-barrelled pulsers, and knew there must be hundreds more further on that he wasn't close enough to see. There were thousands upon thousands of enemy troops in the camp. It was more like a full-blown base than a camp.

Amid smashed and fallen trees, he could make out a pair of huge troop ships. They were covered in tree branches and camouflage netting little different from that used by grunts throughout the Alliance. In fact, the entire base was concealed by the forest canopy and the cunning application of netting strung between the trees. Done properly it was very effective in shielding ground targets from air attack, and he should know. He'd lost count of the number of times he had attacked such targets aided by spotters on the ground.

Those ships... he couldn't understand how anyone could have landed such a monster in a congested valley like this one undetected, let alone two of them. Not while the task force kept watch from orbit. There was no way... understanding dawned like an explosion in his head. They had landed *before* the task force arrived not after, or rather they had *crashed* before the task force arrived. The Shan military had opposed the Merki landings with salvos of missiles launched from surface and underground installations after the fortresses in orbit failed to stop them. The landers here must have been damaged, and forced down on their way to Masaru. By the looks of them, they would never fly again, but that was unimportant. What mattered was that he had found Merkiaari reinforcements and the Admiral was unaware of it.

He had to give warning.

Newlove fumbled for his transponder, and was about to activate it when he realised he was being watched. He looked fearfully around, trying to find the source of his sudden unease… there! A pair of eyes were watching him from the undergrowth. They blinked and seemed to disappear for a second, but then they were back still watching. He pulled his pistol and—

"I wouldn't do that were I you."

He gasped in shock, and nearly pulled the trigger.

* * *

"I wouldn't do that were I you," Gina said, from directly behind the pilot.

Newlove started, turning to look back. "How… where did you come from?"

"No time for that now, Flight Lieutenant," she said, and gently moved his pistol aside so that it was no longer pointed at Varya. "He's with me."

Gina signalled to Varya, and the tracker slinked out of the shadows on all fours. She shivered a little, seeing the way he moved. He came out of cover like some great cat, like a predator with his head close to the ground between muscular shoulders and stalking his prey. It was only his harness, studded with spare ammo and power cells, that clashed with the image of a wild cat intent on dinner.

"Varya, this is Flight Lieutenant Newlove. You should call him Gary."

"Honoured." Varya's whiskers and nose twitched as he gathered the scent of this new Human. "Why should I call you Gary?"

"Because it's my name," Newlove said.

Varya blinked. "Ah yes, I keep forgetting. Humans have so many names, Gary Newlove. I am simply Varya."

"Honoured to meet you. Were you looking for me?"

"You and your friends, yes. You are the first still alive we have found."

Gina studied the camp while Newlove got to know Varya. Her team was already circling it in pairs so that they might make the fullest report they could to the General. Shima and Varya had been a godsend. Shan were unbelievably good at tracking. Viper sensors were good, better than any she had ever used, but even they had limitations. They couldn't find something that was not in range. Shima not only could find someone out of sensor range, she had done it with apparent ease. She tracked Newlove down with nothing but her nose and hunting skills. Varya said there were very few people the equal of Shima despite her eyes. When all Shan were born hunters, it was very high praise indeed.

Gina wished she dared go active on her sensors, but it was too risky. Although it was hard to do, even viper sensors could be backtracked. She didn't dare take the chance that her emissions would give her team away. The General needed to know exactly what he was facing. Being discovered before then was unacceptable. With that in mind, she had ordered her people to keep constantly updating TacNet as they went along. In that way, the General would get at least some information should they fail.

"May I?" Gina held out her hand for the transponder. Newlove surrendered it, and she opened the case. "Hmmm. I think I have a use for this... if the General agrees."

"Yes?" Newlove said.

"What would the Admiral say if I asked her to nuke this valley from orbit?"

"Hell no I should think. Why, is that what you plan to do?"

Gina shrugged. "No point. She would say no. So we go with Plan B."

"What's Plan B?"

Gina smiled crookedly. "I set the transponder to tight beam a signal, *Sutherland* launches all your friends to home on it, and they blow the crap out of this valley."

Newlove grinned. "Good idea."

Varya handed Gina the cleaning kit he used for his blaster. The little toolkit was basic, but adequate for her needs. Transponders were omni-directional long-range beacons. With a few adjustments they could be made to transmit a tightly focused signal less likely to be intercepted, which would defeat the purpose of a beacon designed to lead rescuers to a downed pilot, but would suit Gina's purpose perfectly. With luck it wouldn't be detected by the enemy. She finished tinkering, and replaced the back cover. Varya put away his tools and the three of them waited.

Not long after they settled down to wait, Cragg arrived slithering through the underbrush on his belly. "We have a problem."

"No shit, Cragg," Rutledge growled, joining them from the opposite direction. "You have a flair for stating the obvious."

Cragg brightened. "Hey thanks, Sarge."

Rutledge scowled at the mockery. "They're getting set to move out."

Gina frowned at the transponder in her hand. "Any idea of time scale?"

Cragg shrugged then shook his head. "Sarge?"

Rutledge pursed his lips and peered at the encampment. "Could be any time. No way to know for sure, but it won't be long. My guess is a couple of hours. What have you got in mind?"

"I've been tinkering with this thing," Gina said, and showed Rutledge the transponder. "I've set it to transmit a tightly focused homing signal."

Rutledge's interest quickened. "Nice, very nice."

"We have to deliver it before they move out."

"But if they move…" Newlove began, but then his eyes widened. "You can't mean it."

The three vipers just looked at him silently.

"That's crazy," Newlove hissed. "You'll never make it!"

Gina shrugged. "It's the only way. We have to put this where it will do the most good. Inside one of their vehicles would be best. Somewhere out of sight. We can't just leave it here in the valley. They might move out before the strike can be laid on. We'll have lost a great chance to hurt them."

Newlove was still in shock at the sheer audacity of the plan. "Yeah I know, but who's gonna go in?"

Gina frowned at him. "I will of course." She noticed Rutledge watching her. "What?"

Rutledge shrugged. "Two of us would be better."

"Good idea," Cragg said quickly. "I'll watch your back, Gina."

"I meant me," Rutledge growled testily.

"You're both *crazy*," Newlove hissed.

Varya's ears flicked, and his jaw dropped in amusement. "To me they sound very sane, but it should be me that goes. I'm quicker and… how do you say… hard to see?"

"Stealthy?" Cragg offered. "It means sneaky or hard to catch."

"Yes, that is me. I can be very stealthy. Especially at night."

Gina shook her head. "I've made my decision."

"Fuentez…" Rutledge began. "Captain, you're not thinking this through. You have two of the best trackers alive right here, and both of them are Shan. You know how well they blend in, but have you seen how fast they can run on all fours? I have. Shima and Varya have the best chance of getting the job done, and getting out in one piece."

Gina hesitated. "A compromise then. Shima and I will do it, and the decision is not open to debate."

Rutledge snapped his mouth shut.

"Gina—"

"No, Martin. I'm in command and the decision has been made. I won't risk sending both of our trackers in there. We can't afford to lose both. When the others get back to us, Varya will lead you all out of here. We still have three missing pilots to find."

"Three?" Newlove said sickly. "Only three?"

"Sorry. The others are dead. You're the first we've found that the Merkiaari didn't get."

"Oh God... they were my friends. I led them here to die."

Gina knew exactly how he felt. "Sergeant Rutledge?"

"Captain?"

"Inform the General of what I intend, and make sure he's aware of what's coming his way."

Rutledge nodded. A moment later his eyes went vacant as he contacted General Burgton using TacNet. His comm might be tracked, but TacNet was secure.

Hours later, Rutledge led the team over the ridge to wait. It hadn't been said, but everyone was thinking that Gina's self imposed mission was suicide. She thought they might be right. As soon as they were gone, she went into action. Crawling through the underbrush, she found an ideal position to watch while Shima took the transponder into the Merki camp. She would have been invisible if not for Gina's knowledge of her position, and her low light amplification. Shima's pelt blended so well with the shadows, it was like watching the night itself slink toward the camp.

Gina had her rifle panning across the camp looking for threats to her friend, but Shima had made her promise not to fire unless she was absolutely certain she couldn't deal with the threat. They both knew that the mission would be over the moment Gina fired. She was determined to give her friend every chance to deliver the package.

She watched the Shan scientist turned warrior moving around the edges of the camp. Shima needed a way in that gave her maximum cover, and the chance to move undetected. They had discussed the placement of the transponder before Shima set off to deliver it, and had decided the best place would be one of the larger transporters. The combat gravsleds were out. The crew might notice if she put the transponder in the cockpit or gunner's position. The transporters were another matter. No one would stumble upon it if Shima could secrete it amongst all the supplies in the cargo area. The problem was, she would have to penetrate the camp deeper than if she simply chose the closest gravsled. The sleds had been placed near the perimeter where they could be used in place of fixed defences in case of emergency. Worst of all, was the state of the Merki's preparedness to move. They were getting ready to advance on Charlie Epsilon and points south. That meant instead of a camp that was settling down for the night, Shima had to contend with one that was a hive of activity.

Shima froze as the huge form of a Merki trooper walked by within touching distance. Gina had her rifle up and targeted on the Merki's head, but she didn't fire. He hadn't seen Shima who was on her belly watching him intently. A few seconds went by before Shima moved out again. When she did it was awesome. Gina gasped when her friend went into a sprint from a standing start. One moment she was on her belly watching the retreating figure, the next she was streaking across the open space ahead. Shima was just a blur of speed.

Gina lost her the moment she moved, and then found her again just in time to lose her as she hid behind a pile of crates—munitions if she was right. She watched the pile for a few seconds, and only realised Shima had gone when she noticed movement further on. She quickly panned to the new location and zoomed in. She caught another glimpse of Shima, but then she was gone again.

Gina shook her head in admiration. What a viper Shima would make. She switched to thermal imaging, and found Shima just as she went to ground. There were troopers all over the place. They were easy to see using thermal imaging. Shima stayed still for the longest time yet. Gina was beginning to wonder if her friend had lost her nerve, but no, she was stronger than that. Like all Shan, she hated the Merkiaari with a passion. Her father had died early during the current incursion, and there wasn't a day that went by that Shima didn't remember him. She often told stories about him. Tahar sounded like an amazing man. Gina wished she could have known him.

Shima was close to her goal, but things were happening in camp. Gina watched as a section of gravsleds on the perimeter fired up, and began moving off to the south. Following them were hundreds of troopers just then falling in for the march, while others boarded the Merkiaari equivalent of APCs. Shima was aware her time was running out. She took one hell of a risk by moving into the open.

Gina cursed as her friend almost ran straight into the back of a sentry. Shima rose to her hind legs, and pulled her beamer. Gina targeted the sentry but waited for Shima to fire first, but she was hesitating. Shima holstered her weapon, and eased back from her enemy. Two paces back, she went to her belly and crawled under the armoured flange of a parked gravsled. She was taking a hell of a risk. If someone fired up the gravsled's systems while she was underneath... Gina shuddered preferring not to think about it.

A minute went by, and Shima crawled out on the far side of the sled. The transporter she chose was the closest one to her position. It wasn't the best one by any stretch of the imagination, it was still being loaded, but Shima was running out of time and she knew it. She waited for the troopers to descend the loading ramp on their way for more cargo before moving.

Gina panned her weapon around the transporter watching for guards. There was a brief lull in activity, and Shima took full advantage. She sprinted up the ramp and into the cargo hold. Gina counted under her breath imagining herself in the Shan woman's place. She had to scout out a good place among the crates to hide the transponder. She gave Shima a count of ten for that. Another count of five to activate it, and a further five to get back to the ramp.

Twenty seconds after her dash up the ramp should have seen Shima ready to get out, but luck turned against her. Gina tensed as the Merkiaari returned with more cargo, and climbed the ramp to stow it in the hold. She watched with fading hope as more and more cargo went into the hold, but there was no outcry or the shattering sound of blaster fire. Gina watched in disbelieving silence as the Merki reappeared and descended the ramp. The ramp retracted and the transporter powered up. Gina zoomed in and caught a glimpse of Shima's frightened face before she ducked back into the shadows within the hold.

"Oh no," Gina breathed. "Oh Shima, I'm sorry."

Gina watched as the transporter moved away to join the others in the supply convoy. There was nothing she could do. Shima was on her own. Gina eased back, and put some distance between herself and the camp. As soon as she could, she began climbing straight up the ridge in an effort to get back to Rutledge in the next valley over.

She made it to the crest of the ridge unseen.

As soon as Gina had put the bulk of the ridge between herself and the Merki camp, she went active on her sensors. It didn't take long for her to find Varya who was a friendly blue icon on her display waiting for her on the edge of sensor range. Gina quickly made her way along the ridge toward him. She could not see him, not even when her sensors assured her that she was within a few metres of him.

"Shima?" Varya said easing out of his cover.

Gina shook her head. "She did her job but…"

"Dead?"

"She couldn't get out without being seen. She stayed behind."

Varya's ears lay back and then struggled half erect. "May her ancestors welcome her," he said softly, and shook himself like a dog shakes off the rain. "Come Tei'Gina, we have new orders."

She hurried to follow. "We do?"

"Rutledge and the others have gone ahead. The Murderers have attacked our line and broken through. To my eternal shame, it was my people who failed to hold the Murderers at bay. Your metal men fought and killed many, but they too have been overrun. Our camp is in danger of being surrounded."

Gina gritted her teeth in anger. They had to get the General out of there! Metal men were what the natives called Marines in their mechs. For the Marines to have been overrun meant the enemy was mounting a major offensive. The timing of such an offensive was ominous when combined with the movement she had just witnessed.

"Let's try and catch Rutledge," Gina said, and pushed her jog into a run. Varya dropped to all fours to keep up.

\* \* \*

# 29 ~ Charlie Epsilon

Admiral Alice Meyers, commanding officer of *TF19*, paced anxiously. The holotank was the centre of attention, with most of her officers almost fascinated by the current view being displayed. She was more interested in what was happening on *Sutherland*. She stopped her pacing for a moment, and reached over the shoulder of a young ensign to bring up another view on his main monitor. He glared up at her in irritation for a moment before realising who was interfering with his station. Meyers ignored his whispered apology, and selected another view. This one was a simple list of assets in theatre, and was being constantly updated by CIC aboard *Sutherland,* and other ships within *TF19*. The satellite networks in orbit of Child of Harmony and Harmony were also linked in to *Victorious'* CIC, giving her almost godlike control over information flow. It didn't make her feel any better about the current situation.

Despite almost four weeks of constant battle, the Merkiaari ground forces had been reduced by barely a third. In that same time however, Burgton had lost almost eighteen percent of his vipers, and close to forty percent of his Marine contingent, most of which had died not two hours ago when their lines were overrun. The unpalatable truth was that the Marines had been caught with their pants down. Until now, the bulk of the Merki forces had been steadily retreating and that more than anything had fooled Major Papandreou of the 7th Marines into letting his guard down. Burgton on the other hand, had not been fooled. His lost men had all fallen in offensive operations in which he had inflicted awesome casualties upon the enemy. All his battles were victories, but he was so outnumbered that the losses he had sustained, though almost minuscule in comparison to those sustained by the Merkiaari, did in fact weaken him much more than they were weakened.

The long and the short of it was that although the Shan were now actively engaged in the fighting, they were in fact losing the war on the ground for Child of Harmony. It was just as Burgton said at their first meeting. They were fighting a delaying action, and trying to prolong things long enough to ensure that when Fifth Fleet finally arrived, there would be people alive to greet them. That was all very well, but watching the battles from orbit was harder than Meyers had imagined it would be. The strain of watching people she was responsible for die while she remained safe, was beginning to tell. She was getting snappish and short tempered. She tried to curb it, but lack of sleep and constant worry made that almost impossible.

"How long before *Sutherland* can launch again?" Meyers said.

"They estimate another twenty minutes, Admiral," Joshua said, from behind her. "I think that's optimistic. I would guess thirty five to forty minutes."

"Why so long?"

"Her launch bays are still taking aboard our bombers from the last wave of strikes."

"Damn." *Sutherland's* bays would be a chaos of landing, taxiing, and rearming spacecraft. It would take time to reconfigure the bays from landing to launch operations.

"Has the General made another request for air cover, ma'am?"

Meyers shook her head. "No. Commander Heinemann's last report was routine. When is the next launch scheduled, and what's the target?"

Joshua sat at an empty station to call up the data. "We have... hmmm. We have two launches scheduled for eighteen-hundred. *Sutherland's* launch rails will be fully committed. The target is Intari— another bomb run. Commander Heinemann requested fighter cover for the bombers after what happened over Masaru. Captain Alston concurred with him. She ordered the bombers be accompanied by a second wing configured for air to air combat." Joshua checked the time. "*Sutherland* reports on schedule for that double launch, Admiral."

Meyers turned and regarded the holotank. It was still somewhat jarring seeing a battlespace consisting of a map of green hills and valleys, and not the more usual blackness of space populated with coloured icons representing ships and battle groups. The three dimensional map was perfect in its details. It could be zoomed in to show a single APC racing over the ground, or out to show the entire continent as seen from orbit. It was currently centred over a complex of valleys to the south of a city called Masaru. Masaru was shown at the top left corner of the tank while Charlie Epsilon, Burgton's camp, was two thirds of the way down. Between the two, a blip crawled southward along one of the valleys. It was that innocent seeming blip that was worrying her.

"Show me the breakout please," she said.

An ensign sitting at the holotank controls made a few adjustments and the battlespace reformed.

Meyers leaned on the control panel to study what the tank was showing her. The enemy had broken through in three places. The central column was pushing forward and heading directly for Charlie Epsilon, while another two had turned aside to roll up the natives where they were struggling to reform the line and oppose the movement. It was obvious they were outgunned. Even without the evidence before her, she would have known that. Most of them were civs—if any Shan could be termed such. They only had their hand blasters to fight with.

The remnants of the Shan military had been placed at the far ends of the front line, in an attempt to anchor it. It was there that they were at their strongest. Burgton had placed some of their artillery in the centre with his own guns at Charlie Epsilon, and a good thing he had. He was now facing a battle that he had done everything in his power to avoid—a battle against a superior force from poor but fixed positions. Such a situation negated his viper's speed and manoeuvrability, which was why he had been avoiding it. If he pulled out, he would be giving the Merkiaari free and open access to the south, and leaving almost half a million people to die. Perhaps worse than that from Meyers' point of view, he would be giving them an open road back to Zuleika and the spaceport.

Things were coming to a head down there. She could feel it. The battle about to take place at Charlie Epsilon would be a turning point. She had to ensure it turned her way.

"Show me Charlie Epsilon."

The battlespace reformed once again. Burgton obviously had no plans to pull out. His men were digging in. She keyed a control and a window seemingly hovering over the camp opened full of text. She scrolled down the list noting the number of defenders and their weapons.

"Any chance of getting another supply drop to them before they're hit?" she said not liking what she found.

Joshua shook his head. "The General has been receiving drops from *Grafton* almost constantly since he learned of the break out, but he only has the two *Wolfcubs*. They're on their way back to *Grafton* from their last run now. They won't have time for another."

Meyers nodded and closed the text window. "Give me a real time view over the camp."

The map was replaced with satellite imagery showing Burgton's vipers digging like demons at the wet soil. Still more were using their weapons to blast down trees while hundreds of Shan hitched themselves to ropes and pulled the logs back to camp. She ignored the murmurs of awe as a pair of vipers hefted a tree between them and trotted back to their dugout. They dropped the thing in front of it and ran back for another. AARs were raving at the trees and blasting them into tooth picks. She assumed the idea was to deny the enemy cover. Already a huge cone was taking shape with its narrow end pointed at Charlie Epsilon. Suddenly she realised what it was meant to be. It was a funnel. Burgton was offering the enemy an easy path to follow. Zooming in she found the now expected Marines burying mines and other explosives in a frenzy, while vipers dashed about adding their own nasty surprises. The Shan field guns, together with Burton's howitzers, had been moved back from the perimeter and sighted upon the cone to add their destructiveness. In many places, pits had been dug with one sloping side facing the cleared zone. Burgton's rocket launchers had been driven down the ramps. Only the launch racks were showing above ground.

"This is going to be ugly," Joshua whispered.

"You're not helping!" Meyers bit her lip and rubbed her forehead trying to think. She had to do something about this god-damned mess before it was too late. "Get me Captain Alston."

"Captain Alston… not Captain Fernandez, ma'am?"

"Yes… no." She took a breath. It wasn't good procedure for her to contact Alston directly. It could be seen as a snub to her flag captain. "Get me Tomas first please, Joshua. Sorry for my bad temper."

Joshua smiled briefly. "Part of my job, ma'am," he said while he called the bridge.

She snorted feeling her mood lighten. "That's as maybe, Joshua, but it's still bad manners on my part.

"I have Captain Fernandez for you, Admiral."

She took her aide's place before the consol. "We have a situation at Charlie Epsilon, Tomas."

"I've been keeping an eye on it, ma'am."

"I knew you would be. I have something in mind that might help the situation, but there could be consequences… no scratch that.

There will be consequences. A board of inquiry at the least."

"I'll back you on whatever you decide…"

She raised a hand. "I know you would, Tomas. But this decision is mine, and mine alone to justify. I will be contacting Liz shortly. I just wanted you to know what I'm doing, and that I'm not going behind your back because of a lack of confidence in you."

"Thank you, Admiral." Fernandez smiled briefly. "But that wasn't necessary."

"Indulge me. It makes me feel better."

Fernandez nodded. "Good luck."

She broke the connection. "Get me Captain Alston. A secure channel please, Joshua."

Joshua nodded and contacted *Sutherland*. The monitor flickered and Captain Alston appeared.

"Good afternoon, Admiral."

"Liz. Are you alone?"

Alston blinked. "I'm in my quarters… alone, yes Admiral. Is something wrong?"

"I want an immediate block on all further launches. I have a special op for your people. It will take all of them."

"All of them?"

"Yes, all. I'll wait while you pass on the order, Liz. I don't want a single ship in the air until I say."

"Yes, sir, Admiral." Alston turned away to give the order. A few moments later she turned back. "Done."

"Good. I'm going to ask you to begin recording this in a minute, Liz, but first I want to discuss the operation. General Burgton is digging in at Charlie Epsilon. He's not pulling back."

"He can't," Alston said.

"He could actually. Unless you've seen it, you can't imagine how fast a viper can move, but Burgton won't pull out and leave them to die. We've just about gotten to the point where joint operations between us are paying off. We can't let them scurry back into their holes, Liz. We haven't the numbers to fight them alone… not if we want some of the natives alive when Fifth Fleet arrives."

Alston nodded grimly. "Agreed. Harmony is a charnel house."

Meyers nodded. She was still having nightmares about what was happening down there. That was another reason for her decision. Decisions based upon emotion were suspect but not necessarily wrong. She would stand by this one.

"I want you to pick two pilots, Liz. I want your most reliable. I don't care if they're from the same formation. I want your best… clear?"

"So far," Alston said.

"When the time comes, I want you to put them in direct contact with me. I'll brief them personally. They will launch with the rest of your ships, and be protected by the fighters until they're in position, but they'll have their own special target to deal with. The main operation is primarily going to be a bomb run. There are two columns currently attacking Point Zero. I want them smashed."

"Could be messy, Admiral," Alston warned. "They're fighting at almost hand to hand ranges now."

"I know. Blue on blue is always a nightmare, but doing nothing would be worse. All we can do is limit the damage as best we can." Blue on blue was a term given to casualties caused by friendly fire. Not that any fire was ever friendly.

Alston nodded. "I'll get on it right away. With so many Interceptors unaccounted for, together with what happened to us at Masaru, I'll want extensive fighter cover for my bombers."

"Agreed. You run this however you think best. The two pilots I mentioned… I want them armed with Zeus III missiles."

Alston's jaw dropped. "But… are you sure?"

Meyers nodded solemnly. "The target is the Merkiaari reinforcements we've been tracking. You know about that?"

"We've been tracking the transponder."

"Good. We can't see them, but we know they're there. We can't hit them with anything like precision with conventional warheads. That's why we're using Zeus."

"But the Accords specifically prohibit nuclear detonations in atmosphere. The Council will crucify you. You can't…"

She raised a hand to silence the protests. "I have the authority, Liz. I alone will pay the penalty."

Alston's jaw clenched. "That isn't what I meant. Of course I'll back whatever you decide, but that doesn't mean it's worth the price you'll pay. You're throwing your career away… and maybe your life too. You know the penalty if a court decides against you."

"I know, and I'll pay it if it comes to that. I don't think it will."

"How can it not? The Accords are clear. There's no wriggle room, Admiral. They were written that way on purpose."

Wriggle room? She grinned. "There is only one possible justification for what I'm about to do, Liz, and that's preventing the extinction of an entire race. Put that together with the loss of Burgton and his vipers, and the probable loss of our alliance with the Shan if we do nothing…" she shrugged. "I'll be fine."

Alston didn't look convinced. Her eyes narrowed. "How do you feel about stacking the deck a little more in your favour, Admiral?"

"Go on."

"Contact the Elders and ask them to make it an official request... or at least inform them what you plan, and ask they back your decision. What can it hurt?"

It could hurt a lot if the Elders said no, but she didn't think Kajetan would allow that. She was one hard lady.

"I'll contact them, but in the meantime, I want you to set up for the operation. I'll brief the two pilots you choose after I've spoken with Kajetan."

"I understand, Admiral."

"Begin recording now, Liz."

Alston nodded. "Go ahead, Admiral."

Meyers took a deep breath, determined to give an order that might see her out of the service in a firm voice. "Captain Alston, in my opinion the situation on Child of Harmony represents a clear and present danger to the Alliance. General Burgton and his men are severely outnumbered. They're in danger of being wiped out as are our Shan allies. Losing such a resource would be a devastating loss to the Alliance, and one I cannot in good conscience allow. I am hereby authorising your use of the Zeus III tactical nuclear missile, in whatever numbers you deem necessary, in the furtherance of the mission previously discussed."

"I must ask for the codes granting you nuclear release authority."

"Of course," she murmured. "Keyboard entry."

"Preparing to copy, Admiral."

Meyers quickly typed a string of text and transmitted it. She knew the codes were correct and active. As always, the codes for this and other contingencies had been given to her upon taking command of the task force. She waited while Liz carefully checked and matched the relevant portions of the code to her own command codes.

"Authorisation is accepted, Admiral. I estimate the operation will commence at nineteen-hundred. I will contact you with an update when I know more."

"Get it done, Liz."

Captain Alston nodded. "*Sutherland* out."

\* \* \*

## Camp Charlie Epsilon

"They're making their run now," Commander Heinemann said, one hand cupping his ear and listening to his comm intently. He had a direct link to *Sutherland,* and through her to the fighters making the attack on the Merkiaari approaching Charlie Epsilon.

Burgton nodded. They were too far away to see the results of the attack except via satellite, but he had little doubt it would succeed. Zeus was hardly what one would call a subtle weapon system. Meyers had surprised him with her willingness to deploy it—surprised and pleased. Very few naval officers would have the guts to deploy even micro nukes like Zeus within a planetary atmosphere, even when the situation so obviously warranted it, for fear of retribution from their superiors. Meyers would have her judgement closely questioned when all this was over. If he had anything to do with it, she would come through unscathed.

"I have Major Papandreou on the line," Flowers said raising a hand from out of the shadows to attract attention. "He has disengaged and is on the way."

Burgton nodded. "Good. ETA?"

"It's going to be tight, George. He estimates over an hour for his Marines—even longer for the natives."

That didn't surprise him. "Tell him to expedite, but to keep his Shan forces consolidated with his mechs. They won't do us any good arriving in penny packets."

The Marines were all equipped with mechs to give them a chance against the Merkiaari, but mechs were clumsy things and nowhere near as fast as a viper. It would take Papandreou an hour or more to cover a distance that a viper could cover in a tenth the time. Shan were quick, but they couldn't hope to maintain a run for the entire distance—not and still fight when they got here. They would hold Papandreou back, but their presence would multiply the Marines' strength a thousand fold.

He crossed the bunker to the map table and began making plans for a second line of defence. If things went as he expected, they would need it. He called Flowers over to explain what he had in mind.

"Let's look at splitting Alpha and Bravo, Dan, we can—"

He didn't have time to finish his plans. The last thing he saw before his processor took over and shunted him into oblivion, was the huge tree trunks of the bunker roof caving in on top of him.

* * *

The ground erupted showering Gina with dirt. Another explosion followed and another, cutting Shan warriors down left and right. Everyone was screaming, even the Merkiaari. A huge trooper jumped down into her trench, which was chin high on her, but on him it barely reached his chest. She fired into his belly, reversed her rifle to smash his jaw as he crumpled forward, reversed it again and blew his brains out. Before he toppled dead to the ground, she was climbing over him trying to reach Gordon.

"Hail Mary full of grace, hail Mary full of grace," Gordon chanted with a grin of fear and pain on his face as he fired on full auto into the uncountable Merki troopers.

Racks of missiles erupted into the air and rained upon the gravsleds where they ducked and dived with their pulsers raving. Her people scrambled to reload the artillery, and fire on the Merki troops running and dying amid the minefields. Hundreds of AARs were firing constantly from all over the camp. Tracers zipping through the air scythed the enemy down literally cutting them in half. Automatic grenade launchers were firing so fast that their ammunition hoppers were in danger of running dry before they could be reloaded. The barrels of sentry guns, set to kill anything in front of them, were glowing red hot and threatening to melt as they swung back and forth killing Merki troopers by the score. There were Shan cowering, screaming, frothing at the mouth. Shan warriors dying upon the ground half buried in mud and bodies. Warriors grappling with Merkiaari still biting and clawing as they took their enemies down into death with them. There were lines of Shan standing side by side with vipers or Marines as they were overrun. Blood ran like a river along the bottom of the trenches. Bodies and pieces of bodies rained from the sky. Bodies buried by explosions and trampling feet, were launched skyward again when another round of explosions dotted the camp.

"Zack!" Gina screamed over the noise but he didn't hear her. He didn't seem to know that he was dying.

She fired another burst over the top of the trench. She jacked a grenade and fired it. Then again and again until the launcher locked open on an empty chamber. She didn't have time to reload. She reached Gordon and grabbed him. In a blur of speed, he rounded on her still chanting his prayer, and pulled the trigger. She froze. The barrel of his weapon looked like a howitzer in that moment. Gordon fired again and she realised she was still alive. Unbelievably, he was out of ammo.

She struck the rifle aside and grabbed him. "*You crazy fuck, it's me!*" She threw him onto his back.

"What... what...?" Gordon panted. He was still in melee mode (boosted to the max) and didn't seem to know where he was. He reached for his pistol, but a crunching punch to the jaw woke him up a little. "Ow! Christ Gina, what the hell did you do that for?"

"That was for scaring the shit out of me, now let me fix this."

She ripped open his pants and clamped a hand over the arterial bleed in his thigh. His bots needed a little help to deal with this. They could heal anything given time, but long before they got a handle on the wound, Gordon would have dropped into hibernation. If he had been paying attention, he could have ordered his processor out of melee mode back into combat or even maintenance mode, long enough to seal off the vessel until it could be fixed, but no, he was too busy killing Merkiaari!

A viper's natural inclination to heal damage was suppressed in melee mode, its resources shunted away from maintenance in favour of combat. That's why monitoring diagnostics was so important. Being forced into hibernation for essential repairs in the middle of a battle would be a death sentence. That was one reason she didn't like using it. Melee mode felt almost godlike, and it skewed her reasoning. It was too easy to ignore natural caution while boosted to that degree. She preferred combat mode and allowed her processor to repair damage on the fly. Sergeant Rutledge had taught them that most vipers felt that way, and only ever used melee mode as a last resort. If she hadn't been checking on her people's stats and noticed that Gordon wasn't dealing with the problem... but she had been checking.

She grabbed one of the aerosols out of her medikit and sealed the wound in plastic. She watched as his blood pressure formed a bubble in the plastic, but it held. There were no leaks. She grabbed the nano-injector.

"How many times have I told you to watch your god-damned diagnostics?" she grumbled as she pumped the bots into him directly over the wound as Lieutenant Hymas had taught them. "If I've told you once, I've told you a dozen times. You have got to watch your diagnostics."

Gordon looked sick. "I didn't even notice."

"Keep an eye on it," she said packing her kit and stowing it back in its place on her webbing. "I mean it, Zack. If you puncture the seal before the artery is fixed, I'll kill you."

Gordon grinned weakly but a second later his eyes popped wide in alarm, "Behind—"

Gina spun snatching her knife free as she turned and plunged it into the Merki female's belly. She sawed upward probing for the monster's heart then pulled it out in a gout of blood that covered her from head to foot. The female toppled, dead before she hit the ground.

"—you," Gordon finished shouting.

"It's bloody dangerous around here," she muttered wiping her knife clean on her thigh. She grabbed her rifle. Gordon was already reloading his. She took a moment to load her grenade launcher. "You okay here on your own?"

"No," he muttered as he popped up to fire at a gravsled.

Gina didn't hear him as she jogged away.

It was a miracle they had managed to hold out so long, she mused as she ran in a crouch along the zigzagging trench connecting the dugouts for the sentry guns with the fighting pits. Her people were too busy to notice her passing behind them. The enemy had been repulsed no less than three times already with massive casualties. Their gravsleds no longer attempted to draw near the camp. They didn't dare. The evidence they were no match for viper gunnery lay smashed and broken all over the landscape. The remaining sleds were reduced to sniping at the camp's defenders from a distance. Not that distance meant safety, far from it, but it was at least a little safer for them. The sentry guns were set to kill anything in front of them within a certain radius of their positions. The same with the grenade launchers and mortars. They were set to provide area denial to the Merki ground troops, but they would still attempt to knock down a gravsled if it came within their area of responsibility. Such kills were rare now, but they hadn't been at the start of the action, as evidenced by the still burning wreckage of so many vehicles.

As the battle progressed, she had felt the need to reassure herself with direct observations of what her sensors and TacNet were telling her. It wasn't logical, she knew that, but that was how she felt. She justified her need with the knowledge that is was good for the morale of her troops having her appear to fight with them. Maybe it was a holdover from her time in the Corps. Whatever the reason, she was still most comfortable fighting side by side with her troops. Being a captain, even one temporarily raised to the position, didn't change that. With a viper's abilities, she could indulge herself without guilt. With instant access to comm, TacNet, and sensors, she didn't have to remain at a fixed CP to give her orders. Anywhere would do. From the front line trench was her preference.

"How goes it, James?" she said slipping into position beside him. She tried to ignore the number of dead Shan warriors and enemy corpses heaped around him, and added her fire to his. The Merkiaari just kept coming. "James?"

James glanced at her then back to what he was doing. The lost and empty look in his eyes sent a shiver down her spine. He was looking more and more like those he led. The warriors fighting with him had lost everything and everyone they loved. They had seen so much death that it almost seemed to fill them up until there was no room for anything but killing. No hope left, just the grim determination to make the enemy pay dearly for their deaths.

James popped up and fired both his beamers repeatedly. "I heard our fighters heading north a little while ago," he said without inflection. "The Merkiaari didn't knock them all down. Maybe we should tell the Admiral to bomb the camp now."

"It's not time for that yet," she said emptying her grenade launcher at the enemy lines. Bombing the camp would kill a lot of the enemy, but it would kill all of the defenders too. "We're not that desperate yet."

Gina sank down behind the cover afforded her by the trench to reload. There were empty munitions boxes scattered all over the place, but she found one that still had a few grenades left in it buried beneath the others. While she hurriedly reloaded her rifle, she sent an urgent message over TacNet requesting fresh supplies be sent to James' sector. The acknowledgement flashed upon her display a moment later.

She stood to rejoin James, and picked off a few troopers that were getting a little close. Some of the sentry guns had fallen silent now, either destroyed by enemy fire or out of ammunition. The Merkiaari were too close to overrunning them to risk sending a squad to reload those guns. That meant there was a gaping hole in the defence of James' sector with nothing to plug it with but bodies. She quickly accessed her comm and reinforced the line with vipers taken from other areas. Changing channels, she informed the General that she expected a major Merkiaari push here very soon.

There was no acknowledgement.

She ducked as a gravsled opened up on her but too late. "AEiii," she screamed as something buzsawed through her shoulder and her right cheek.

Her mouth filled with blood and diagnostics flashed a warning to her display, but the damage was not too bad. It was bloody and it hurt, but she wouldn't die or anything close. Her processor automatically began repairing the damage. A warrior next to James wasn't so lucky. He was blasted back to fall amid the corpses of his people, dead before he landed. James blinked at the alien blood running down his face and continued firing. Gina spat blood and dirt, raised her rifle to her injured shoulder and squeezed the trigger.

* * *

## Approaching Charlie Epsilon

Major Papandreou of the 7th Marines cursed the bad luck that had dogged his heels on this march. He had just been informed that yet another mech was out of commission. The road to Charlie Epsilon was littered with equipment and broken mechs. Marines numbering in excess of two platoons were already dismounted due to mechanical failure, and they had a way to go yet.

Something streaked by him and into the underbrush. He muttered under his breath and lowered his AAR. With thousands of Shan along on this march, it was little wonder the local wildlife was running scared. He had been informed that this entire area was some kind of nature preserve. They were called Sanctuaries, but there was nothing safe about this one now.

Charlie Epsilon was maybe ten klicks ahead as the crow flies. Even surrounded by hills and trees, he could tell Burgton was already engaged. The air was leaden and smoke hung thickly just beyond a line of hills ahead. He couldn't see much—the occasional rocket contrail was about it.

"Dragon this is Sword, come in Dragon."

"Dragon copies," he replied. Sword was the call sign given to his forward-most element. His recon platoon.

"I have the objective in sight, sir, but I think we're too late. I can make out Merkiaari already within the perimeter."

Dammit! "Can you estimate numbers?"

"Too many to count, sir... maybe a couple of hundred in the camp? I dunno for sure. I can still see some fighting. The defenders have pulled back to make a stand at the CP. I don't think we can get there in time... *oh shit!*"

He listened to the open comm line. "Sword? Answer dammit!"

"Wait one."

Papandreou fumed for a few seconds then turned his thoughts to the coming battle. If Burgton and his people were already dead, he would be a fool to lead his men into the trap that Charlie Epsilon had become. On the other hand, vipers were tough bastards. If anyone could survive being overrun by Merkiaari, Burgton was that one. He throttled his mech into a lumbering run. He needed to see the situation with his own eyes before making a decision.

"Dragon this is Sword. I have a situation here. The goddamn Shan are advancing independently. They're charging straight in. I can't hold 'em!"

Papandreou checked his sensors. It was worse than Sword had reported. "Hold your position. Repeat, hold your position."

"Copy."

He checked his sensors again. Shan warriors were pulling ahead of his mechs. Not just those accompanying Sword, but *all* of them. All over the map, thousands upon thousands of them dropped to all fours and streaked away. He stared at his display in disbelieving silence. They were advancing upon Charlie Epsilon at a flat out run.

They would engage the enemy scattered and unsupported. He could feel a disaster looming. He had only two options. Advance at flank speed in foolhardy support of the crazy bastards, or retreat and leave them to die.

"Oh shit..." Papandreou whispered, making his decision. He opened a channel. "Throttle up Marines!"

Papandreou and his Marines charged into battle.

\* \* \*

### Camp Charlie Epsilon

> REPAIRS COMPLETE.
> DIAGNOSTICS: UNIT FIT FOR DUTY.
> DEACTIVATE BEACON... DONE.
> INITIATE REACTIVATION SEQUENCE...

Gina awoke covered in soil and debris not sure where she was or what had happened. Her chest hurt... no it didn't. It was just the memory of pain. Her hand wandered over her armour and paused at the hole it discovered. She probed through it and felt smooth skin. Her uniform ended in a burnt and tattered hole that matched her armour in its shape, but her body was whole. Healed? Her chrono said that she had lost time. How much time? Hours at least. She lay quiet looking up at the sky and listening to the silence. Why was it so quiet, was she deaf? Not according to her diagnostics. According to her processor, she was one hundred percent operational.

She frowned and tried to remember what she was doing. She had fought beside James and his people for a time but had moved on to Cragg... was that right? She didn't have time to consult her log, but she thought that was right. The time legend on her display was telling her hours had gone by since then. Long enough for reinforcements to join them? Possibly, but where the hell were they?

She staggered erect pulling her rifle free of the mud as she did. For as far as she could easily see, there were Merki corpses lying in heaps. It was as if a bunch of hills had reared up out of the ground. The landscape was utterly different to what it had been. Craters dotted the ground. Trees and smashed vehicles still burned and smoke hung thickly upon the leaden air.

Gina turned in a circle trying to get her bearings. Everything looked different. She stooped to drag a half buried and broken rifle out of the bloody soup the soil at the bottom of her trench had become. She ejected her empty magazine and replaced it with the half spent one from the broken rifle. She didn't know who it had belonged to. She didn't want to know. He was most likely dead. That was the only way to separate a viper from his or her weapon.

She dropped the useless thing, and dragged herself out of the trench only to throw herself flat at the sound of gunfire. Her rifle was up and ready, but the noise died away again. It was simply someone finishing off a wounded Merki. She struggled tiredly to her knees, and then back to her feet trying to orientate herself. There were a number of craters with the mangled remains of Shan field guns still jutting into the air just ahead of her.

"If that crater is... was Battery 201, and for some reason I think it was, then that means..." she muttered to herself trying to match what she was seeing with the map glowing in front of her eyes. "That must be the CP then."

She made her way toward the greatest concentration of people and smoke.

As she walked, more and more people began struggling out of their dugouts some of which had collapsed in upon them. Many of the trenches were full to the brim with corpses. She had no idea how many vipers lay among them. During the battle, communications had become fragmented as more and more squad leaders fell off the net leaving individual vipers to fight on alone. She hoped time would prove that many of those now silent units were only wounded. With their squad and platoon leaders out of contact, individual vipers had fought and died holding whatever line they could. She had done her best to keep everyone fighting as a unit by assigning at least one viper to each battalion to relay her orders, but it was only partially successful. Sometimes it seemed that almost as soon as she put a unit in charge of a position, he would go offline and she had to begin again.

According to her sensors there were still Merkiaari alive both within and without the camp's perimeter. None of them were fit to fight, and slowly the red icons inside the perimeter disappeared as the surviving warriors sniffed them out and killed them. She couldn't care less about the Merkiaari. She was more concerned with the blue viper icons that her sensors had picked out and were displaying. Most of them were blinking on and off denoting a unit either dead or in hibernation awaiting recovery. She was willing to bet that she had been one of them not long ago.

If they were dead... she refused to believe so many could be dead, but if they were dead, then the battalion had been reduced to a single company of effectives, and her company to almost zero. She refused to believe that—categorically refused.

Gina wanted to know where the General was. She wanted to know if he was all right. She wanted to know if Eric was alive and all her friends. Was James dead, was Rutledge? What about Gordon and… she took a deep breath and stopped where she was. She had just survived one hell of a battle. She wasn't going to pieces now.

She watched the survivors picking through the debris and tried to formulate a plan. There were Shan frantically digging among the wrecked dugouts and pieces of equipment. As she watched, they pulled out those lucky enough to be alive and hurried them to the field hospital for medical attention. Marines in mech armour dragged themselves out of craters and began assembling. So, the Marines had made it after all. This couldn't be all of them. She turned to the north in speculation. It was the logical place for them to be.

If Major Papandreou had arrived to push the enemy back, there would be fighting to the north. She couldn't see any sign even with her sensors at max range, but that didn't mean much. He might have pushed them all the way back to Masaru by this time. It wasn't impossible. She would check the satellite feeds, but later. She sighed in relief when she began seeing vipers wandering around the camp.

"Alpha Leader to any active unit," she said over her comm and watched as every viper she could see paused to listen. "Has anyone seen the General?"

No one spoke up.

"Okay. Rendezvous with me at the CP. We need to organise ourselves and figure out who we have left. I'm going to call *Grafton* and evac the wounded."

She ignored the acknowledgements to contact *Grafton*. With the *Wolfcubs* on the way, she was about to join the others when a familiar voice startled her.

"Gina?"

She spun back toward the trees in disbelief. "Shima?" she whispered in shock as her friend wandered out from among the trees. She was on all fours and in a pitiful state. "Shima!"

Gina ran to her friend and threw herself to her knees before her. Blood and dirt was matted in Shima's fur and her visor was missing. She still had one of her beamers in its holster but the other was gone.

Shima hung her head wearily. "I wasn't sure it was you, Gina. Your scent among so many Merkiaari… I wasn't sure I could find my way back. I… I'm blind. Ancestors help me, I'm blind!"

"Shush, it's okay, Shima. We'll find you another visor. Hell, we'll make you one."

"It's not that. I threw the cursed thing away after it happened."

"After what happened? I don't understand."

"When you left, I had to hide until I could get away without being seen. I jumped off the transporter as soon as I could and went to ground. I didn't dare climb the ridge to follow you… not while the Murderers remained so near."

"I understand. You did the right thing."

"It was all I *could* do," Shima said bitterly. "I waited in hiding until your people attacked the Murderers from the air like we planned. I've never seen anything like it." Her jaw dropped in amusement at that. "I'll certainly never see such again. The explosion was like the end of the world. The ground leapt beneath me it was so big. There was a really bright light. It was so bright… and that's the last thing I saw. There was a wind and I heard trees crashing all around me. One knocked me down, but only the branches caught me. When I crawled out, I started to climb up the hillside and into the next valley. I was lucky "I found your scent and followed you here."

Gina knew what had happened. Shima had been flash blinded by the blast unleashed upon the Merki reinforcements by Admiral Meyers. Her heart went out to her friend. She knew how much Shima had feared her encroaching blindness.

"Well, you're among friends again now, Shima. My people can grow you a new pair of eyes as good as your old ones… no, *better* than your old ones."

Shima's ears struggled fully erect. "Truly? Your people can do that?"

"They can do it for Humans. I can't see why they can't do it for you. Even if they can't, you can have a pair like mine. I promise, Shima. *I promise.*"

Shima reached out to clutch Gina desperately. "Thank you, oh by the harmonies, thank you."

* * *

# 30 ~ Aftermath

Gina stepped tiredly off the ramp of the shuttle into *Grafton's* boat bay. She snapped to attention and saluted when she recognised the General approaching her.

"At ease, Captain."

She relaxed slightly.

"I just wanted to say you did a hell of a job at Masaru."

"Thank you, sir, but Cragg deserves a lot of credit."

Burgton smiled. "Yes, he's performing well."

Gina nodded. Cragg had temporarily taken her place as Lt for Alpha Company's First Platoon, just as she had taken Hames' slot from Richmond. "Have you new orders for me, sir?"

"They can wait, Gina. I know you want to see how Katherine is getting along. I won't keep you. There's a briefing at twenty-two hundred at the port."

"I'll be there, sir," she said and saluted.

Burgton returned her salute then mounted the ramp to board the shuttle.

Gina found her friend in the infirmary chatting with Zack Gordon. Richmond was sitting up in bed when she came in. Gordon was sitting nearby with his leg propped up gesturing at the wall screen. Gina glanced at it and found a live feed of Masaru. She paused to assure herself that her people had everything under control.

Red icons still outnumbered blue by a significant amount, but the green of Shan forces outnumbered both by far. Blue icons were leapfrogging forward in a planned manoeuvre intended to take out the enemy as quickly as possible while also giving the units involved maximum cover and support. Green icons ringed the area slowly closing in and compacting the enemy into a smaller and smaller area where they could be taken down en masse.

Gina clenched a fist as the leading viper units suddenly stopped, and their icons flashed the yellow of light to moderate damage. She waited with baited breath, but released it in a whoosh as each unit's processor reported in. She read the light codes flashing beside each icon and relaxed.

The damage was not too bad.

"...some company up here," Gordon was saying.

"I could wish for less of that kind," Richmond said slurring the words. She turned to Gina. "Good to see you, *Captain*."

"Likewise, *Captain*. How are you feeling?"

Richmond shrugged. "Decidedly unenhanced."

She snorted. Richmond's processor was too badly damaged for a quick fix. She had taken a lot of punishment at Zuleika and it had been touch and go whether she would live. The left side of her face was paralysed, and it often caused her to slur her words. Her left eye was gone as well. The empty socket stared at Gina amidst the wreckage of a once handsome face. Richmond was no longer pretty. The thick heavy scarring pulled her wry smile off centre almost turning it into a sneer. She wouldn't be her old self for quite a while. The equipment necessary to replace her damaged processor was only to be found on Snakeholme. Richmond needed major reconstructive surgery.

Gina glanced at Gordon. "How's it going, Zack?"

He patted his new leg. "I'm outa here tomorrow. Have you left me some?"

"That's the last big concentration on Child of Harmony," she said nodding at the screen. "We have a few mopping-up operations to do; the Marines are taking care of that mostly, but the General did promise Papandreou we would back him up on the tricky ones."

Major Papandreou had what amounted to an under strength battalion of Marines on planet. His command had been created by culling the detachments assigned to each of the ships in the task force, and consolidating them. He was the senior Marine officer in-system, officially attached to *Victorious*, and was leading the mopping-up operations on Child of Harmony with a great deal of help from the Shan. From reports she had read, the Marines were doing well. That hadn't surprised her of course.

Gina sat on the edge of Richmond's rack. "The General is briefing us tonight on the next round."

"Damn," Gordon said. "Wouldn't you know it, I missed the ending."

Richmond laughed at Gordon's put upon sigh. "Don't pout, Zack. Now that Fifth Fleet is here, you can go down to Harmony. If I know the General, that's what the briefing will be about."

Gordon brightened. "Hey yeah, you're right."

Gina nodded. It was the next logical step. Months of fighting had taken its toll, but everyone was hoping that the Keeps were full to bursting point. They certainly had been on Child of Harmony before they came out to join the fight, but no one knew for sure what they would find on Harmony. Communications with the surface were fragmentary and sporadic; the Merki jamming was complicating things no end. They knew that some of the Keeps had been penetrated. Satellite surveillance showed those gaping and radioactive craters clearly, but it was assumed that most of the Keeps were still intact. Harmony had fewer Merkiaari to kill than Child of Harmony used to have, but the General wouldn't stop until the entire system was clear. That was certain.

"I've a present for you," Gina said, remembering the reason for her visit.

"A pressy?" Richmond said eagerly. "A pressy for me? What is it? A new grenade launcher... no, I know, a rocket launcher with extended range capacity. You shouldn't have."

"I didn't," she said laughing and passing her friend the gift-wrapped box.

Richmond grinned and destroyed the wrapping in milliseconds. "It's a... it's a..." she frowned. "What is it?" She dangled the thing between thumb and forefinger.

Gordon looked puzzled as well.

"It's an eye patch. James told me about it."

"An eye patch?"

"Yeah, you wear it over... you know," Gina flicked a hand at Richmond's damage. "James said people wore them before cybernetics and prosthetics were available."

"I like the decoration," Richmond said with a lopsided grin.

"That was Cragg's idea."

Cragg had wanted to liven it up a little. The result was a black eye patch with the viper emblem worked into it in silver thread. It was quite fetching.

"Here, gimme," Gina said and took the patch. A minute later it was in place

Richmond viewed herself in Gordon's hastily found mirror.

"Hey, hey, hey! Looking good," Gordon crowed.

"Cool… that means I like it," Richmond said quickly explaining her brief foray into retro.

"If you don't quit that, I'm going to need a download to understand you," Gina said with a snort of laughter. "I thought only Stone talked that way."

Richmond had that 'I have a secret' look in her eye. "Stone talks retro 'coz he grew up surrounded by it. I use it 'coz I like it."

"It's different anyway. Talking of Stone, where is he?"

"Back dirtside," Gordon said. "He keeps getting banged up but he's always ready for more."

"Yeah," Richmond said nodding in approval. "His bots fixed him up in a in a jiffy this time. He said he wanted to add a few more Merkiaari to his score."

"Gotcha. So then, your war is over."

"Yeah, worse luck. At least I'm alive. Others aren't so lucky."

Gina nodded sadly, remembering their fallen friends. Chrissie Roberts was only the first of many to fall. The regiment had lost three hundred and sixteen units so far. Not quite half the force they had brought here was dead, and the war wasn't yet won.

"There's nothing they can do about your processor?"

Richmond shook her head. "Not here, but other than that and my eye, I'm fine. Major Faggini said I can help out on the bridge. I can still use the satellite feeds the old fashioned way. How are you getting along with Wilder and his resistance people?"

"Surprisingly well. He does what I tell him when I tell him to do it. For a civ he has discipline. He knows stuff."

"Yeah? Like what?"

Gina shrugged. "Like all about the Merki War."

Richmond snorted. "Everyone knows about that."

"Not like James. He knows *everything* about it—and I do mean *everything*. He teaches history at Oxford you know. He's no slouch as a leader either. The Shan resistance insist he's their Tei, and they do whatever he says."

"You like him. Jumped his bones yet?"

She didn't need a translation; she got the message. "He has someone aboard *Victorious*."

"Shame."

Gina did like James, but not in that way. She was a soldier and he a civ. The two didn't mix easily in her experience. Besides, she was a viper. She seriously doubted that any viper would find a relationship outside of the regiment. They were too different now, and what about the longevity issue? No one spoke of it, but they were all very aware that they would outlive their friends and family. The regiment and their squadmates were all their family now.

She chatted with her friends for another half hour or so, but then the infirmary started filling up. Casualties from Masaru were arriving—nothing life threatening this time thank God, but all the hustle and bustle did cut short her visit.

"I better get down there," she said.

Richmond nodded.

She patted her friend's knee as she stood. "Take care of yourself."

"Make sure you do the same. I like your visits, but I don't want you up here as a patient."

"I don't want me as a patient either," Gina said with a laugh and hurried away.

\* \* \*

# 31 ~ Epilogue

James glanced at his silent companion and then back at the view. Thousands of lights winked at him from the inky blackness of space—running lights pinpointing the locations of hundreds of warships. The ships themselves seemed like toys at this distance, but that was very far from the reality. *TF19* was a mere sideshow compared with the firepower Fifth Fleet had brought here.

Behind him, the quiet murmur of *Victorious'* officers and crew continued with ship's operations as if unaware of the momentous events about to take place. They weren't of course. He could feel the surging emotions just below the surface. The Alliance had taken an irrevocable step in welcoming the Shan as an allied power. No one knew where it would all lead, but everyone was agreed that this moment was pivotal in the Alliance's future dealings with other races.

"There," Tei'Varyk said pointing. "It has begun."

They watched as wave after wave of transports erupted into space escorted by hundreds of fighters. Their targets? The Merkiaari sniffed out and hunted by Burgton's vipers. Tei'Varyk lingered a moment longer and then turned to leave.

"A storm has come," James whispered. "A storm to cleanse the world."

He turned away and silently followed his friend.

\* \* \*

# Also available from Impulse

If these books are not available from your local bookshop, send this coupon together with your check made payable to:

**Impulse Books UK**
At the following address:

**Impulse Books UK**
18, Lampits Hill Avenue,
Corringham
Essex SS177NY
United Kingdom

Please send the following great titles from Impulse Books UK

Tick as approrriate:

**The God Decrees**  (Pb)
ISBN: 978-1-905380-45-9  £10.99 _____ ☐

**The Power That Binds** (Pb)
ISBN: 978-1-905380-46-6  £10.99 _____ ☐

**The Warrior Within** (Pb)
ISBN: 978-1-905380-47-3 £10.99 _____ ☐

**Dragon Dawn** (Pb)
ISBN: 978-1-905380-48-0 £11.99 _____ ☐

**Wolf's Revenge** (Pb)
ISBN: 978-1-905380-43-5 £11.99 _____ ☐

NAME _____

ADDRESS _____

_____

_____

I have enclosed a check for the sum of  £ _____

Please be sure to add £2.25 to your order to cover shipping and handling charges.

# Also available from Impulse

If these books are not available from your local bookshop, send this coupon together with your check made payable to:

**Impulse Books UK**
At the following address:

**Impulse Books UK**
18, Lampits Hill Avenue,
Corringham
Essex SS177NY
United Kingdom

Please send the following great titles from Impulse Books UK

Tick as approrriate:

**Hard Duty** (Pb)
ISBN: 978-0-9545122-3-1  £10.99 _____ ☐

**What Price Honour** (Pb)
ISBN: 978-1-905380-44-2  £10.99 _____ ☐

**Operation Oracle** (Pb)
ISBN: 978-1-905380-52-7  £10.99 _____ ☐

**Operation Breakout** (Pb)
ISBN: 978-1-905380-57-2  £10.99 _____ ☐

NAME _____

ADDRESS _____
_____
_____

I have enclosed a check for the sum of £ ____

Please be sure to add £2.25 to your order to cover shipping and handling charges.